FEAR

IN THE 41ST millennium, mankind has extended its reach across the universe and forged the mighty Imperium. Led by the power of the Space Marines and the devotion of the Imperial Guard, planet after planet thrives beneath the Emperor's gaze. But there are other forces at large amidst the stars, forces far more ancient than man can imagine, creatures of pure malevolence that live only to conquer. The threat from the xenos is ever-present, from the bestial greenskins to the cruel dark eldar and the waves of pure destruction known as the tyranid. Mankind may dominate the universe, but they will always fear the alien...

Fear the Alien collects short stories from Dan Abnett, Aaron Dembski-Bowden, Nick Kyme, C. L. Werner and many more in an essential Warhammer 40,000 anthology.

Also available from the Black Library

· ULTRAMARINES SERIES ·

THE ULTRAMARINES OMNIBUS
(Contains books 1-3 in the series: *Nightbringer*, *Warriors of Ultramar* and *Dead Sky Black Sun*)
Graham McNeill

Book 4 – THE KILLING GROUND
by Graham McNeill

Book 5 – COURAGE & HONOUR
by Graham McNeill

Book 6 – THE CHAPTER'S DUE
by Graham McNeill

STORM OF IRON
by Graham McNeill

· BLOOD ANGELS ·

THE BLOOD ANGELS OMNIBUS
(Contains books 1 and 2 in the series: *Deus Encarmine* and *Deus Sanguinius*)
James Swallow

Book 3 – RED FURY
James Swallow

Book 4 – BLACK TIDE
James Swallow

· OTHER SPACE MARINE NOVELS ·

THE SOUL DRINKERS OMNIBUS
(Contains the novels *Soul Drinker*, *The Bleeding Chalice* and *Crimson Tears*)
Ben Counter

BROTHERS OF THE SNAKE
by Dan Abnett

ASSAULT ON BLACK REACH: THE NOVEL
Nick Kyme

WARHAMMER 40,000 STORIES

FEAR THE ALIEN

Edited by
Christian Dunn

BLACK LIBRARY

A BLACK LIBRARY PUBLICATION

First published in Great Britain in 2010 by
The Black Library,
Games Workshop Ltd.,
Willow Road, Nottingham,
NG7 2WS, UK.

10 9 8 7 6 5 4 3 2 1

Cover illustration by Clint Langley.

© Games Workshop Limited 2010. All rights reserved.

The Black Library, the Black Library logo, Games Workshop, the Games Workshop logo and all associated marks, names, characters, illustrations and images from the Warhammer 40,000 universe are either ®, TM and/or © Games Workshop Ltd 2000-2010, variably registered in the UK and other countries around the world. All rights reserved.

A CIP record for this book is available from the British Library.

UK ISBN: 978 1 84416 894 1
US ISBN: 978 1 84416 895 8

No part of this publication may be reproduced, stored in a retrieval system, or transmitted in any form or by any means, electronic, mechanical, photocopying, recording or otherwise, without the prior permission of the publishers.

This is a work of fiction. All the characters and events portrayed in this book are fictional, and any resemblance to real people or incidents is purely coincidental.

See the Black Library on the internet at
www.blacklibrary.com

Find out more about Games Workshop
and the world of Warhammer 40,000 at
www.games-workshop.com

Printed and bound in the UK.

IT IS THE 41st millennium. For more than a hundred centuries the Emperor has sat immobile on the Golden Throne of Earth. He is the master of mankind by the will of the gods, and master of a million worlds by the might of his inexhaustible armies. He is a rotting carcass writhing invisibly with power from the Dark Age of Technology. He is the Carrion Lord of the Imperium for whom a thousand souls are sacrificed every day, so that he may never truly die.

YET EVEN IN his deathless state, the Emperor continues his eternal vigilance. Mighty battlefleets cross the daemon-infested miasma of the warp, the only route between distant stars, their way lit by the Astronomican, the psychic manifestation of the Emperor's will. Vast armies give battle in His name on uncounted worlds. Greatest amongst his soldiers are the Adeptus Astartes, the Space Marines, bio-engineered super-warriors. Their comrades in arms are legion: the Imperial Guard and countless Planetary Defence Forces, the ever-vigilant Inquisition and the tech-priests of the Adeptus Mechanicus to name only a few. But for all their multitudes, they are barely enough to hold off the ever-present threat from aliens, heretics, mutants – and worse.

TO BE A man in such times is to be one amongst untold billions. It is to live in the cruellest and most bloody regime imaginable. These are the tales of those times. Forget the power of technology and science, for so much has been forgotten, never to be re-learned. Forget the promise of progress and understanding, for in the grim dark future there is only war. There is no peace amongst the stars, only an eternity of carnage and slaughter, and the laughter of thirsting gods.

CONTENTS

Gardens of Tycho by *Dan Abnett* — 9

Fear Itself by *Juliet E. McKenna* — 51

Prometheus Requiem by *Nick Kyme* — 95

Mistress Baeda's Gift — 157
by Braden Campbell

Iron Inferno by *C. L. Werner* — 189

Sanctified by *Mark Clapham* — 213

Faces by *Matthew Farrer* — 243

Unity by *James Gilmer* — 293

The Core by *Aaron Dembski-Bowden* — 323

Ambition Knows No Bounds — 373
by Andy Hoare

GARDENS OF TYCHO
Dan Abnett
A Magos Drusher story

THE NATURE OF Master Dellac's line of business had never come up in conversation, and Valentin Drusher was in no position to ask impertinent questions. Certainly, Master Dellac was a successful man, one of the most conspicuously wealthy citizens on that dusty stretch of the Bone Coast. Drusher had an idea or two, but decided it was probably safer not to know. He just did what he was told. Two visits a week, after hours, to Master Dellac's mansion up in the hills, providing his specialist services on a private basis, in return for an agreed wage. And no questions asked, either way.

Sometimes, Master Dellac would supplement Drusher's payment with a gift: a smoked ham, a packet of expensive, dainty biscuits, perhaps even a bottle of imported wine. Drusher knew he could get good prices selling these items on later, but he always kept them for himself. It wasn't that he was greedy, or some kind of epicure (although, Throne knows, it had been a long, long time since Valentin Drusher had known any luxury in his life). It was simply because there was a line Drusher wasn't prepared to cross. So many aspects of his life, his respectability, and his good character, had been eroded over the years, he held on tight to those he still had.

Besides, he was a meek man, and he was too afraid of getting caught.

Late one Lauday evening, Drusher was making the return journey from Dellac's house to Kaloster. Drusher went to and from the mansion on foot, a solid journey of an hour each way. Dellac never offered him transport, even though he had a driver. Drusher tried to consider the bi-weekly trips the sort of decent exercise a man of his age ought to be getting, but by the time he returned to his habitat on Amon Street, he was always weary.

The sun had gone, leaving the sky over the small coastal town stained like pink marble. A night wind was picking up, sifting white dust from the dunes across the town road, and Kaloster itself seemed shuttered and dark.

There was no nightlife, no remission from the frugal, small-town quiet. But in addition to the payment in his coat pocket, Drusher carried a piece of good brisket in his satchel. He would eat well for the next few nights at least.

Amon Street was a tenement slope running down from Aquila Square to the rusty wharfs and the condemned fishworks. The buildings were drab brown with age and neglect, and their roofs were in need of repair. The air in the street stank because of the lime burners just across the way. Drusher rented rooms on the fourth floor of number seventy.

A large black transporter with big chrome headlamps was parked just down the street. Drusher noticed it as he was fumbling for his key, but paid it little heed. He went up the narrow wooden staircase to his door.

It was only when he stepped into his little room, that he realised someone was already there.

The man was robust and rather ugly. Heavy-browed with a shock of thick, dark hair and a shapeless, asymmetric face, he wore a thick, high-buttoned suit of black serge and a heavy leather stormcoat, also black. He was seated, casually, on the wooden pole-back chair behind the door, waiting.

'What are you–' Drusher began, his voice coming out thin and reedy.

'You Drusher?' the man asked.

'Yes. Why? What are you doing here? This is my–'

'Valentin Drusher?' the man pressed, glancing at a small data-slate in his left hand. 'Magos biologis? Says here you're forty-seven. Is that right? You look older.'

'I am Valentin Drusher,' Drusher replied, too scared to be offended. 'What is this about? Who are you?'

'Sit down, magos. Over there, please. Put your satchel on the table.'

Drusher did as he was told. His pulse was thumping, and his skin had become clammy. He had an awful feeling he knew what this was about.

'I'm Falken,' the man said, and briefly flashed an identity warrant at him. Drusher swallowed as he glimpsed the silver seal of the Magistratum, attached to which was a small orange ribbon that denoted the Martial Order Division. 'How long have you been here on Gershom?'

'Ah, fourteen years. Fourteen years this winter.'

'And here in Kaloster?'

'Just eighteen months.'

The man looked at his data-slate again. 'According to Central Records, you are employed by the Administratum to teach Natural History at the local scholam.'

'That's correct. My papers are in order.'

'But you're a magos biologis, not a teacher.'

'Employment prospects on this world are not great for a man of my calling. I take what work I can. The teaching stipend offered by the Administratum keeps a roof over my head.'

The man pursed his lips. 'If the employment prospects for your kind are thin on the ground, magos, it begs the question why you came to Gershom in the first place. Let alone why you chose to stay here for fourteen years.'

Despite his fear, Drusher felt piqued. This was the old injustice again, back to haunt him. 'When I came to this world, sir, I was gainfully employed. The Lord Governor himself was my patron. He commissioned me to produce a complete taxonomy of the planet's fauna. The work took seven years, but at the end of it, complications arose—'

'Complications?'

'A legal matter. I was forced to stay on for another two years, as a witness. All the money I had earned from the commission ran out. By the time the case was settled, I could no longer afford passage to another world. I have been here ever since, making a living as best I can.'

The man, Falken, didn't seem very interested. In Drusher's experience, no one ever was. On a downtrodden outworld like Gershom, everyone had their own sob story.

'You keep glancing at your satchel, magos,' Falken remarked suddenly. 'Why is that?'

Drusher swallowed hard again. He had never been any good at lying. 'Sir,' he said quietly, 'could you tell me... I mean, would things go better for me if I made a full confession now?'

Falken blinked, as if surprised, then smiled. 'That's a good idea,' he said, sitting down to face Drusher across the low table where the satchel sat. 'Why don't you do just that?'

'I'm not proud of this,' said Drusher. 'I mean, it was stupid. I knew the mMagistratum would find out eventually. It's just... things have been so tight.'

'Go on.'

'The Administratum pays me a stipend for my services, along with certain ration benefits as per the Martial Order. This is of course contingent on me not... on me not supplementing my earnings.'

'Naturally,' nodded Falken. 'If you break the terms, there is a penalty. It can be severe.'

Drusher sighed, and showed Falken the contents of his satchel. 'There is a man, a local businessman, who employs me, two evenings a week. It is a private arrangement. He pays me in cash, no questions asked.'

'How much?'

'Two crowns per evening. He has a daughter. For her, he retains my services…'

Falken looked at the things Drusher was showing him.

'You do this with his daughter?'

'Yes. Sometimes he watches.'

Falken got up. 'I see. This is a pretty picture, isn't it?' For some reason, Falken seemed to be stifling a smile, as if something amused him terribly.

'Am I in serious trouble?' Drusher asked.

'You'll have to come with me,' Falken said. 'To Tycho.'

'To Tycho?'

'The Marshal wants to speak with you.'

'Oh, Throne!' Drusher gasped. 'I thought perhaps a fine…'

'Pack your things, magos. All of them. I'll give you five minutes.'

Drusher had very few belongings. They fitted into two small bags. Falken didn't offer to carry either of them down to the transporter.

It was dark now, fully night. When the transporter's engine turned over, the glare of the headlights filled the depths of Amon Street.

Drusher sat up front, beside the Magistratum officer. They drove up through the town, onto the coast highway, and turned south.

* * *

THE CITIES OF the Southern Peninsula, Tycho amongst them, had been the arena of a savage civil war that had raged for over ten years. The popular separatist movement had finally been defeated by government forces two years earlier, but by then the war had critically weakened Gershom's already-ailing economy. Strict, Imperial martial order had been imposed throughout the Peninsula and right up through the Bone Coast into the Eastern Provinces.

The civil war had stained the air with smoke, and poisoned the coastal waters, killing off the fishing industry. The cities of the Peninsula were urban ruins where the Martial Order Division worked to re-establish Imperium law and support the impoverished civilian population.

Falken drove for two hours without speaking. The vox-set under his dashboard, turned down, crackled with Magistratum traffic as if it was talking in its sleep. Drusher stared out of the window at the darkness and the occasional black ruin that loomed out of it. This was it, he felt. Gershom was his nemesis. It had lured him in, a bright young man with an equally bright future before him, and it had trapped him like a fettle fly in amber. It had drained him dry, throttled his spirit, made him destitute.

And now this, after all his efforts to earn a crust to live, let alone a ticket off-world, was going to destroy him. Disgrace. Shame. Perhaps a custodial sentence.

'I don't deserve this,' he murmured.

'What's that?' asked Falken at the wheel.

'Nothing.'

They began to pass through armoured roadblocks where Magistratum troopers wearing the orange ribbon of the Martial Order Division waved Falken through. They were entering the Peninsula proper now, the real war-zone. Ghost cities, tumbled and forlorn, drifted past, lit by searchlights and military beacons. The dark landscape outside the transporter became a phosphorescent waste of fragile walls and empty habs.

Tycho was the principal city of the Peninsula region, and when they drove in through its empty streets, four hours after leaving Kaloster, Drusher saw a miserable calamity of twisted girders, piled rubble and smoke-blackened buildings. His face, half-lit by the luminous dials of the dashboard, reflected back to him off the window, superimposed on the ruins. Pale, thin, bespectacled, the hair thin and grey. Drusher wasn't sure if he resembled the wastes of Tycho, or if they resembled him.

They pulled up outside a mouldering ouslite monolith in the city centre.

'Leave your bags,' Falken said, getting out. 'I'll have them brought in.'

Drusher followed him in through the towering entrance. Magistratum officers hurried to and fro in the echoing atrium, and limp Imperium flags hung from the roof. There was a smell of antiseptic.

'This way,' Falken said.

He led Drusher to a room on the fifth floor. The elevators were out and they had to use the stairs. Falken made him wait outside the heavy double doors.

The hallway was cold, and night air seeped in through the cracked windowpanes at the far end. Drusher paced up and down. He could hear the rattle and clack of cogitators in nearby rooms, and an occasional shout from down below. Then he heard laughter from behind the double doors.

Falken emerged. He was still chuckling. 'You can go in now,' he said.

Drusher walked in, the doors closing behind him. The office was large and grim, a single metal desk planted on a threadbare rug. Half a dozen wire-basket carts heavily laden with dog-eared dossiers and files. A cogitator, whirring to itself. Faded spaces on the walls where pictures had once hung.

'Throne. I wouldn't have recognised you, magos,' said a voice.

She was standing by the deep windows, silhouetted against the night-time city outside. He knew the voice at once.

'Macks?'

Germaine Macks stepped forward to meet him, a smile on her lips. Her hair was still short, her face still lean, the old, tiny zigzag scar above the left-hand side of her mouth still visible. The other, newer scar on her forehead was half hidden under her fringe.

'Hello, Valentin,' she said. 'What's it been now? Five years?'

He nodded. 'Deputy Macks...'

She shook her head. 'It's Magistratum Marshal Macks now. Chief of Martial Order, Tycho city.'

He stiffened. 'Mamzel, I can explain everything. I hope the fact that you know me of old might mitigate the–'

'Falken was playing with you, magos.'

'Excuse me, what?'

Macks sat down behind her desk. 'I sent Falken up the coast to get you. Throne knows why you started confessing things to him. Guilty conscience, Valentin?'

'I...' Drusher stammered.

'Falken was beside himself. He told me he didn't think he could keep a straight face on the journey down here. Did you think you were in trouble?'

'He... that is... I...'

'Teaching the daughter of some small-time racketeer the art of watercolour painting? To supplement the pittance Admin pays you? Come on, Valentin! I'd hardly spare a chief investigator to go all that way to bring you in. You criminal mastermind, you.'

Drusher felt a little giddy. 'May I sit down?' he asked.

She nodded, still chuckling, and reached into a desk drawer for a bottle of amasec and two shot glasses.

'Get this inside you, you filthy recidivist,' she grinned, handing one glass to him.

'I really don't understand what's going on...' Drusher said.

'Neither do I,' she said. 'That's why I want some help. Some expert help. I said you weren't in trouble, and I was lying. You're not in personal trouble, but there is trouble here. And I'm about to drop you right in it.'

'Oh,' he said.

'Drink up,' Macks said. 'You'll need it where we're going.'

'IN YOUR EXPERT opinion,' she said, 'what did that?'

Drusher took a long, slow look, then excused himself. Coming up, the amasec was a lot hotter and more acid than it had felt going down.

'All right?' she said.

He wiped his mouth, and nodded reluctantly. Macks took a little pot out of her uniform pocket and smeared what looked like grease under her nose. She reached out and did the same to Drusher. The fierce camphor smell of osscil filled his sinuses.

'Should have done that before I took you in,' Macks apologised. 'Old medicae mortus trick. It masks the stench of decay.'

She led him back into the morgue. The place was chilly, and tiled with mauve enamel squares. There were brass plugholes every few metres across the floor, and in the distance, Drusher could hear water pattering from a leaky scrub-hose. High-gain glow-strips, sharp and white, filled the chamber with a light like frost.

The cadaver lay on a steel gurney beside an autopsy unit. Other shapes, tagged and covered in red sheets, lurked nearby on other trolleys.

'All right to take another look?' Macks asked.

Drusher nodded.

She folded the red shroud back.

The man was naked, his body as white and swollen as cooked seafood. His hands, feet and genitals seemed shrivelled with cold, and the fingernails stood proud and dark. The hairs on his chest and pubis were black and looked like insect legs.

He must have been about one-eighty in life, Drusher figured, fighting back another wave of nausea. Heavy-set. Bruises of lividity marked his lumbar region, and there were other darker blue bruises around his ribs.

The front of his face, and most of his throat, had been bitten away. Parts of the skull structure had gone along with the soft tissue. Cleanly severed, like industrial shears had…

Drusher gagged, and looked aside.

'Animal, right?' Macks said.

Drusher mumbled something.

'Was that a yes?'

'It would appear to be a bite,' Drusher said, his voice very tiny. 'Very deep and strong. And then… the suggestion of some feeding. Around the face and neck.'

'Animal, right?' she repeated.

'I suppose. Nothing human could have… bitten like that.'

'I measured the bite radius. Just like you taught me. Remember, in Outer Udar? I measured it.'

'That's good.'

'Twenty centimetres. And I checked too. No tooth fragments. This was clean. I mean, it just bit his face right off.'

Drusher turned slowly. 'Macks? What am I doing here?'

'Helping my investigation,' she said. 'I thought we'd covered that. I'm in charge down here in this neck of the woods, with plenty enough problems to contend with, I can tell you… and then this crap happens. I look for an expert, and lo and behold I find Magos Biologis Valentin Drusher, my old pal, working as a teacher in Kaloster. So I thought, Macks, that's perfect. We worked together so well before, and this clearly needs a biologis expert.'

'That's great…'

'Valentin, cheer up. There's money in this. I'll bill your hours out to the Magistratum, and you'll get three times what the Administratum was paying you. Expert witness and all.'

'You're running the Martial Order programme here in Tycho and you pull strings like that to get me to consider one case?'

'No,' said Macks. 'I should have explained that too, I guess. This isn't the only victim.'

'How many others?' he asked.

Macks made a vague gesture that encompassed all the other gurneys in the chamber. Twenty-five, thirty, maybe more.

'You're joking?'

'I wish I was. Something is chomping its way through the population.'

Drusher steeled himself and turned back to the exposed corpse, switching his standard glasses for his reading pair. 'A fluorescing lamp, please. And a close glass.'

She handed him the glass from the autopsy cart and held the lamp up, bathing the dead man's devastated skull with blue light.

Drusher picked up a steel probe and gently excised the lip of one of the revealed bone edges. He fought to keep his gorge down.

'No tooth fragments.'

'I told you.'

'I mean nothing,' he said. 'Not even the bacillus residue one would expect from the wound mark of a predator. This wasn't an animal. It's not a bite.'

'What?'

'It's too clean. I'd say you were looking for a man with a chainsword.'

Macks shook her head. 'No.'

'Why no?'

'Because if there was a maniac with a chainsword running around downtown Tycho, I'd know about it. This is animal, Valentin.'

'How can you be so sure?' he asked.

'Come on,' she said. 'I'll show you.'

THE HEADLAMPS OF her transporter picked out the sign over the wrought-iron gateway.

The Gardens of Tycho.

'Well-stocked before the civil war,' she said, pulling on the wheel. 'The biggest xenozoological exhibit on the planet. The local governor had a thing about exotic animals.'

'And?'

'And, Valentin, it was bombed during the war. Some animals were killed, but many more escaped. I think something from here is roaming the ruins of Tycho, hungry, neglected, killing people.'

'And that's why...' he began.

'That's why I need a magos biologis,' she finished.

They pulled up and got out. The gardens were dark and quiet. It was still two hours before dawn. There was an awful damp reek in the air, emanating from the empty cages and the dank rockcrete pens.

Macks had given Drusher a stablight, and carried one of her own. They walked together, their footsteps gritty and crisp on the ground, playing the beams around.

The Gardens of Tycho had not been a sophisticated collection. Drusher remembered the spectacular xeno-fauna halls of Thracian Primaris that he had visited as a young man. There, the pens and enclosures had been encoded to create perfect habitats for the precious specimens, often with their own atmospheres, their own gravities even.

Such expertise – and the money to realise it – had not been available on Tycho. These were simple cages and, in places, armoured holding tanks, where exotic creatures from the far-flung corners of the Imperium had lived out their days on Gershom in miserable confinement.

Drusher knew exactly how they felt.

'If it's been caged like this, Macks, it will perhaps have become psychotic,' he said.

'The animal?'

'The animal. It's common in poor conditions such as these. Animals held in crude cages often develop behavioural problems. They become unpredictable. Violent.'

'But if it's a predator anyway...' she began.

'Even predators have patterns. The need to hunt, to breed, to territorialise. Limit those things, and you break the pattern.'

'That's important why?' she asked.

'If this animal is a carnivore, and I would suspect as much, it isn't feeding on its kills. Well, only minimally. It is killing simply to kill.'

'Like the hill beast?' she murmured, thinking back to that haunted winter in Outer Udar.

'No,' he said. 'That beast was different. Killing was its behaviour. Here we have aberration.'

As they walked further, Drusher began to see the awful damage done in the course of the war. Bomb-shattered pens, mounds of rubble, plasteel cages shorn from their mounting blocks.

And bones.

There were corpses in the intact pens too. Limp sacks of dried flesh, scattered vertebrae, the lingering stench of dung and decay. A row of wire domes that had once held rare birds was now littered with bright feathers. Tufts of down caked the wire mesh, evidence of frantic, starving attempts to be free. They reminded Drusher of Baron Karne's poultry stoops.

'We thought everything had died,' Macks said. 'The stink when we first came down here. I mean, nothing had been fed or cleaned out in months. Everything in a sealed cage was dead, except some kind of emaciated dromedary horse, which had been living off its own fat deposits, and even that died a few days after we freed it. And everything in the bombed cages we figured was wiped out, although there are some finch-monkeys loose in the Lower Bowery, freaking little things, and Falken swears he saw a grazer on Lemand Street one night, though I say he was drunk.'

'So if something's loose, it came from the bomb-damaged cages?' Drusher said.

She shrugged. 'Unless some well-intentioned citizen came along during the war, and let something out and then locked the cage again. Some of them seem to be empty, though the collection's manifest doesn't say if they were just unstocked pens. It's years out of date.'

'You have a manifest?'

Macks nodded and produced a data-slate from her coat. 'I've highlighted any item that was caged in the bombed area, and also anything connected to an empty cage. Throne, Valentin, I haven't the first clue what half of them are. So glad to have an expert on board.'

He started to look at the list. 'So it could be anything highlighted, or anything at all, given the fact that the stock might have been changed or rotated after this list was made?'

She was about to reply when her vox-link chimed. The sharp little note made Drusher jump. Macks took the call.

'We have to go,' she said, turning to head back to the exit. 'I've been called in. Some drunken idiots brawling in a tavern after curfew.'

'Do I have to come?' he said.

She turned back and shone her stablight in his face. 'No. Why, would you like to stay here?'

Drusher glanced around.

'Not really,' he said.

THEY DROVE THROUGH streets that were deserted but for burned-out vehicles and the occasional Magistratum transport rushing off on a response. He sat in the passenger seat, studying the slate, rocked by the jolts of the uneven roadway. Relief was beginning to seep into him, relief that he wasn't bound for disgrace and a custodial sentence after all. A little part of him hated Falken for his trick, but a greater part despised himself for being so foolish. Gershom wasn't his nemesis. Valentin Drusher was his own worst enemy, and his ruined life was testament to the way he had studiously taken every wrong turn destiny had ever offered him.

'Your hair's gone grey,' Macks said, her eyes on the road.

He looked up. 'I stopped dyeing it.'

'You dyed your hair?' she asked.

He didn't reply.

'So you've matured out of that vanity, then, Valentin?' she smirked.

'No. I just couldn't afford the treatment any more.'

She laughed, but he was sure he detected some sympathy in her tone.

'I like it,' she said after a while. 'It's distinguished.'

'You haven't changed at all,' he said.

She pulled the vehicle to a halt outside a battered townhouse where Magistratum officers were attempting to restrain nine or ten brawling men. There was blood on the pavement, and the air was lit by the blinking lamps of the armoured patrol vehicles.

Macks got out. 'Stay here,' she said. She peered back at him through the open door. 'So, is that a good thing?'

'What?' he asked.

'The fact that I haven't changed?'

'I never thought you needed much improvement,' he replied, immediately appalled that he'd made such a bold remark out loud.

Macks laughed, then slammed the door.

In the sealed quiet of the transporter, Drusher watched for a while as she waded in with her riot baton and brought order to the scene. Then he turned his attention back to the data-slate.

Time passed.

The driver's door opened, and the transporter rocked on its springs as she clambered back in.

'I think we're looking for a carnodon,' he said.

'Yeah?' she said, gunning the engine and throwing the vehicle forwards in a rapid acceleration.

'Yes. I mean, working from the details here. I could be wrong if the specimens were changed after this list was made up, but it's a simple process of elimination.'

'Is it?' she asked, throwing them round a street corner so fast the tyres squealed.

'There were only four predators listed in the bombed-out pens. Discount the Mirepoix treecreeper because it's an injector, not a biter.'

'A what?'

'It injects its prey with a long proboscis and dissolves the internal organs, sucking them out.'

'Enough.'

'I mean, it doesn't have a mouth.'

'All right, all right.'

'So, no bite wounds.'

'Right.'

'Right, so the saurapt from Brontotaph is off the list as well.'

Macks changed down and raced them along another empty boulevard. 'Because?'

'Because it's the size of a hab block. Falken wouldn't have had to be drunk to spot it already.'

She grinned.

'And the pouncer here, from Lamsarotte, we can cross that off too. It's a felid, but far too slight to cause the wounds you showed me. Besides, I doubt it would have lasted long in this climate outside a heated pen.'

'So we're left with the, what did you call it?' she asked.

'Carnodon. From Gudrun. Throne, there shouldn't have been one in captivity here. They're virtually extinct, and listed on the Administratum's prohibition order. It's a felid too, but big, and from temperate habitats.'

'How big?'

'Five or six metres, maybe eight hundred kilos. Quite capable of biting off a man's face.'

'So, magos biologis, how do we catch a carnodon?' she asked, heaving on the wheel.

Drusher looked up. 'We're… we're going rather fast, Macks,' he said. 'Another call?'

'Yes,' she replied.

'Another breach of curfew?' he asked.

Macks shook her head. 'Question stands, Valentin. How do we catch a carnodon?'

THE HABS WERE clustered together at the northern extremity of the town, gathered in tight, conspiratorial knots. Acres of wasteland surrounded each stack, littered with the flotsam of war and poverty. Much of the intense fighting during the civil war had taken place in this shell-damaged suburb.

Macks slowed the transporter and guided it in between piles of shattered bricks. They were approaching one of the most ramshackle towers. Ahead, the lamps picked out a pair of Magistratum transporters, parked near the stack's loading dock. A heavy morgue carrier was pulled up beside them, its rear hatch gaping.

'Come on,' Macks said.

Drusher got out into the cold, pre-dawn air. The rectangular habs stood stark against a sky slowly paling into a gold sheen. He smelled the sweet rot of garbage, and the unpleasant odour of wet rockcrete.

'Bring your stablight,' she said, making off across the rough ground to the group of Magistratum officers waiting by the stack entrance. She spoke to a couple of them, then signalled Drusher to follow her.

They entered the wide doorway and began to climb the crude stairwell.

'They've held off so you can get the first look at the scene,' she said.

Drusher took a deep breath. They climbed to the fifth floor.

'Hurry up,' she called back to him.

'Hang on,' he said. Drusher stooped to examine the rough wall, touching a dark patch amongst the lichen with his fingertips, then sniffing them.

'You'll catch something,' Macks said, coming back down the stairs to join him.

'I thought that's why you hired me,' he said. 'Smell this. Ammonia, very strong. Other natural chemicals, pheromones. This is a territorial mark. The animal spranted here.'

'What?'

'It scent-marked the wall with urine.'

'And you wanted me to sniff it?'

Drusher looked up at her. 'It's textbook felid behaviour. The stain suggests quantity, so we're looking at something large.'

'Carnodon?'

'It fits.'

'See if this fits too,' she said.

THE DERELICT HAB stack had become home for vagrants, and it was rare for these dispossessed souls to have any contact with the Magistratum. But one of them had been scared enough to raise the alarm, having heard a commotion on the fifth floor.

The stack apartment was a four-room affair, a kitchen-diner, a bed vault, a lounge and a washroom cubicle. The place stank of mildew.

And another smell Drusher hadn't encountered since Outer Udar.

Blood.

The Magistratum crew had set up pole lamps to mark the scene, and it had been picted and recorded.

'Watch your step,' Macks said.

As they went in, the smell became more intense. The corpse was in the lounge area. Even Macks, hardened to the uglier aspects of life, had to turn aside for a moment.

The body was that of an older female. The legs, swathed in filthy hose and support stockings, were intact. The torso had been stripped down to the bones, and these had been broken open so that something feeding could get at the soft organs. There was no head, no arms.

'They tell me the head's in there,' Macks said, indicating the kitchen area.

Drusher peered in through the doorway, glimpsing a brown, cracked object that looked like a broken earthenware pot. Except that it still had a residue of grey hair.

'What's this?' Macks called. In the bedroom, her torch beam was illuminating a brown, fractured stick.

'Arm bone,' said Drusher. 'Broken open to get at the marrow.' He was remarkably composed. This was perhaps the most horrific sight that had ever greeted his eyes, but a professional detachment was masking his revulsion. The magos biologis in him was fascinated by the killing.

'I think she was already dead,' he said. 'This is scavenging. A decent post-mortem will be able to confirm it. The feeder was big, but it took its time. Leisurely feeding, reducing the cadaver piece by piece, going for the most nutritional areas first. There was no struggle, no kill, although the carnodon probably made quite a bit of noise as it rendered down the carcass.'

'Carnodon?' she said. 'You're sure?'

'I'd stake my professional credentials on it,' he replied. 'For what that's worth.'

'Okay.' Macks breathed heavily. 'Can we get them in to clear this?'

'Yes,' Drusher said.

'And can you work up something? I don't know – a library pict, maybe one of your dandy watercolour sketches, so we know what we're looking for?'

'Glad to,' he replied.

'Good,' Macks said.' You look like you need sleep.'

He shrugged. 'Where is the Magistratum putting me up?' he asked.

Macks replied, 'We'll find somewhere.'

SOMEWHERE TURNED OUT to be a torn couch in the empty room next door to Macks's office. It appeared from the stale bedclothes that someone else had been sleeping there on a regular basis. Drusher was too tired to complain. Besides, as far as his relationship with the planet Gershom went, this was pretty much par for the course.

He fell asleep within minutes of lying down.

He woke with a start and found he'd only been sleeping for a couple of hours. It was barely dawn. As was often the case, rest had freed up his mind, and there was now an idea buzzing around in it so busily it had woken him. He felt strangely energised. After years of tedious dead-end employment, he was finally calling on his primary area of expertise again, using old skills that he had begun to believe had long since atrophied. He almost felt like a magos biologis.

Drusher got up, tucked in his shirt and put on his shoes. The building was quiet and dead. He went into the hallway and tapped on the door of Macks's office. When he got no reply, he let himself in and started to rummage amongst the dossiers piled on the wire carts.

He heard a metallic click behind him and turned. Macks, her hair tousled, stood behind the desk. The sidearm she had aimed at him was slowly lowering.

'It's you,' she grunted, her eyes puffy with sleep.

'Throne!' he said. 'Where were you?'

Rubbing her face, she gestured at the floor behind the desk, where Drusher could now see a few seat cushions and a crumpled blanket.

'You were sleeping on the floor under your desk?' he said.

She cleared her throat and holstered the sidearm in her belt pouch. She looked pissed off and weary. 'Well, you got my bed, didn't you?' she snapped.

'Oh,' he said.

Macks picked up her boots and shuffled across to the office door. She leaned out and yelled 'Watch officer! Two caffeines before I shoot someone!' Then she sat down on the rug and started to pull on her footwear.

'What time is it?' she asked Drusher grumpily.

'Early yet. I'm sorry.'

'What were you doing?'

'I wanted to check the autopsy files. From the victims. There was something I wanted to look at.'

'That pile there,' Macks said. 'No, the other end.'

Drusher started to look through the files, wincing at some of the more grisly picts he encountered. Macks left the room, presumably to kill whoever it was that was being slow with the caffeine.

When she returned, he'd spread a dozen of the dossiers out on the rug, and was making notes with a slate and stylus he'd borrowed from her desk.

'Macks,' he began. 'There's something here that–'

'Get your jacket,' she said.

IN DAYLIGHT (THOUGH daylight was a loose term) Tycho didn't look any better. From the side window of the speeding transporter, Drusher could now starkly see what had been merely spectral ruins the night before. There had been a melancholy air to the place in the darkness. Now everything was blunt and crass: the scars of fire, the pitting of assault weapons, the water-filled cavities of craters, the shock-fractures on slabs of rockcrete. Weeds furred the city ruins, thick and unlovely, reclaiming the wasteground between tenements and stacks. The Gardens of Tycho were everywhere now, Drusher thought. The wild was reclaiming the city.

They drove in convoy with two other Magistratum vehicles, rattling down the empty thoroughfares.

'Fresh kill,' was all Macks would say. 'In the Commission of Works.'

Falken was already on site, with four armed troopers in tow. Drusher wouldn't have been able to tell that the building before him was the Commission of Works. Penetrator shells had caved in the facade and chewed curiously geometric shapes out of the roof. The rear of the building was a dark cave-system of intact rooms.

'In here,' said Falken, shouldering his riot-gun and leading them into the mangled ruins. 'Routine sweep picked it up about thirty minutes ago.'

They clambered over fallen beams, disturbing the thick white dust. The body lay in a nest of broken floorboards.

'Civilian volunteer,' Falken said. 'He was on a registered night watch here. He had a weapon, but it doesn't seem like he got the chance to use it.'

The man lay on his side, facing them as they approached with a face that was no longer there. Something had severed his skull laterally in a line from the point of the chin to the apex of the skull. It looked to Drusher like an anatomical crosscut pict from a surgery text manual.

Drusher knelt down beside the body. The linear precision of the bite was baffling.

'Did you sweep?' Macks was asking Falken.

'A brief look. Rimbaud thinks he heard something.'

Macks looked at the trooper. 'Really?'

'Up at back, ma'am,' Rimbaud said. 'There was definitely something moving around. I think it's still here.'

'Is that likely?' Macks asked Drusher.

He shrugged. 'If it was disturbed before it could feed... I suppose so.'

'Let's go,' she ordered. She and Falken moved ahead, weapons lowered. 'Valentin, you're up,' she called back. 'Stick with Edvin. The rest of you cover the front. Rimbaud, show us where.'

They moved into the dark, crumbling hulk of the ruin, every footstep kicking up dust. Falken, Rimbaud and Macks made their way up a staircase that was hanging off the remains of a supporting wall. Edging forwards with the trooper named Edvin,

Drusher could hear the others walking about on the floor above, creaking the distressed floor, sifting dust down at them in hourglass trickles. Drusher could also hear Edvin's vox, turned low.

'To your left now.' That was Falken.

'Don't get too far ahead,' Macks replied.

'Something! No, false alarm.'

Edvin glanced nervously at Drusher. 'Okay there, sir?' he asked.

Drusher nodded.

'Some kind of cat?' the trooper asked.

'Some kind,' Drusher replied. He was becoming very aware of the beat of his own heart.

When it happened, it happened with such ferocity and speed, Drusher barely had time to react. There was a fantastic, booming detonation – in hindsight, presumably Falken's riot-gun discharging – swiftly followed by a series of pistol shots on auto. At the same time, the vox went mad with strangulated calls. The floor above Drusher shook with a violent frenzy. There was an impact, a crash. A scream. Two more blasts from a riot-gun.

'What the Throne–' Edvin began, raising his weapon and looking up.

The floor above them caved in. Drusher and Edvin were knocked flat and almost buried in a cascade of broken joists, planks and falling bricks. Mortar dust filled the atmosphere like a fog, choking and stifling. Another gunshot.

Drusher struggled to his feet, pushing the broken floorboards off his legs. He could barely breathe. Edvin was on his face, unconscious. Something heavy had come straight down through the floor and landed on him, half-crushing him.

Drusher blinked. 'No!' he cried.

The something heavy was the body of a Magistratum trooper, faceless, blood jetting forcibly from severed arteries. The blood sprayed up the walls, gleaming like rubies in the dust.

'Macks!' he cried. 'Macks!'

He tried to reach her, though he knew it was far too late. Then something else came down through the hole in the floor. Something fast and dark and feral. It was the animal, the killer, trying to find an escape route.

It slammed Drusher over hard with one flailing limb and he crashed into a plasterboard wall that shattered like old marzipan icing.

For a moment, just a fleeting second before he passed out, he glimpsed it. The shape.

The shape.

HE CAME ROUND staring up at Falken's face. 'He's all right,' Falken spat and turned away, wiping dust off his face.

Drusher sat up fast, his head pounding. 'Macks? Macks?'

'What?' she asked.

Drusher saw her, crouched in the rubble in front of him. Falken was getting the dazed Edvin back on his feet.

'Macks?'

She was leaning over the body. Drusher got up, and could see now the mutilated corpse was Rimbaud.

'It got away,' Macks murmured. 'It got Rimbaud and then it got away.' Falken was shouting for the other troopers to sweep the rear of the building.

'What happened?' Drusher asked.

'I didn't see it,' Macks said. 'Falken saw something move and fired. Then it all went to hell.'

'It came down this way. After it had...' Drusher paused. 'It followed Rimbaud's body down.'

'You see it?'

'I didn't get a proper look,' Drusher said.

Macks cursed and walked away. Drusher crouched down beside the trooper's body and turned it slightly so he could look at the wound. The same clean, ghastly cut right across the face. But this time, a second one, abortive, made behind the line of the excising blow, as if the predator had been in a frenzy – alarmed, perhaps – and had made a first hasty strike before following it up. Even so the first strike, deep and into the side of the neck and head, would have killed Rimbaud outright.

But even in haste, so clean. So straight.

'A cat? A cat did that?' Drusher looked round. Edvin, blood dribbling from a cut above his left eye, was staring at his friend's body.

'That's what the experts say,' Drusher replied.

They drove back to the Magistratum HQ in silence. The sweep had picked up nothing. The killer had melted into the ruins beyond the Commission of Works as fast as frost in summertime.

'You thought it was me, didn't you?' Macks asked finally.

'What?'

'The body. I heard you cry out. You thought it had got me.'

Drusher nodded. He felt they might be about to have a moment, something honest that approximated intimacy. He was prepared to admit how much he would care if anything happened to her.

'If you can't tell the difference between me and a hairy-arsed male trooper,' she said, 'I'm not holding out much hope for your observational expertise.'

He looked over at her. 'Screw you too, Macks.'

SHE LEFT HIM alone in her office, and let him get on with sorting the dossiers. A staffer brought him a cup of something over-brewed and over-sweetened late in the afternoon. By then, he was pinning things to the walls, and had switched to paper to make his notes. He accessed Macks's cogitator, and called up some city-plan maps.

Macks came back just as it was getting dark outside.

'I'm glad you're here,' he said. 'There's something I need to show you.'

She seemed cheerful, upbeat. 'Something I have to show you first,' she said.

Macks led him down to the morgue. A crowd of officers and uniformed staffers had gathered and there was almost a party atmosphere. Falken was passing round bottles of contraband amasec so everyone could take a slug.

'Here he is!' Falken cried. 'Magos Biologis Dresher!'

There was some clapping.

'Drusher,' Drusher said.

'Whatever,' Falken said, putting his arm around Drusher's shoulders. 'Couldn't have done it without you, friend! Really, you were on the money! Eh? What do you think? Is this a… a…'

'Carnodon,' Drusher said, painfully aware of how big Falken was beside him, squeezing him in the hug.

The felid had been laid across four gurneys, heavy and limp in death. Its tusked snout seemed to grimace, as if it, like Drusher, wished it was somewhere else. Small, dark punctures in its belly showed where Falken had shot it.

'May I?' Drusher asked, and Falken let him go over and examine the beast. The crowd turned back to toasting and laughing.

It had once been a wonderful thing, master of its world, afraid of nothing. An apex predator. Drusher smiled sadly as he thought of the phrase. A big specimen too, maybe five and a half metres body length, nine hundred kilos healthy body weight. But at the time of its miserable, hunted death, it had been less than six hundred kilos, emaciated, its ribs poking out like tent braces. It was old too, post-mature. The coat was raddled by sarcoptic mange and laden with lice, fungus and parasites. Drusher ran his hand along its flank anyway. So knotted, gristly, starved. He peeled back the black lips and examined the dentition.

'Where did you get it?' he called out to Falken.

'In the cellars under the Lexicon,' Falken said, coming over. 'We got a heads-up. We'd circulated your picture, you see. Thanks for that. I went in, saw it, and boom-boom.'

Drusher nodded.

'Truth be told,' Falken said, dropping his voice, 'it didn't put up much of a fight. But I wasn't taking any chances.'

'I understand.'

Falken turned back to the crowd. 'For Onnie Rimbaud, poor bastard!' he cried. 'This one's for you, son!'

Falken offered the nearest bottle to Drusher. Drusher shook his head. 'Thanks for your help, Dresher,' Falken said.

'Drusher.'

Macks came over.

'I want to thank you on behalf of the division, Valentin,' she said. 'You got us our result. I'll bill the Administratum for a whole week, fair enough? Go get your things together. Someone will drive you home this evening.'

Drusher nodded.

'I HAVE A transporter waiting,' Macks said. Drusher's bags were in a neat stack beside the office door. He was just closing the last of the dossiers and sliding them back onto her carts.

'Right,' he said.

'Well, it's been good to have you on board. Thanks. Like old times, right?'

'Like Outer Udar, Macks? I get the distinct impression you remember that more fondly than I do.'

'Things'll work out, Valentin,' she said.

'Before I go,' he said, 'I'd like you to look at something.'

'What?'

'Let's put it this way. I'd hate to have you come all the way up the coast to get me again.'

Macks frowned. 'What are you on about now?'

'The killer wasn't – isn't – that cat.'

Macks wiped her hand across her lips as if encouraging patience. 'Go on.'

'I said from the start it wasn't an animal.'

'You also told me to look for a carnodon.'

'Let me show you something,' Drusher said. He held up a data-slate. The compact screen showed a display of the city, overlaid with rune symbols. 'I've done some collating. See here? I've mapped all the sites where the victims were found. Thirty-two bodies.'

'I did that myself, on an ongoing basis. I saw nothing. No pattern, no discernible spread.'

'I agree,' said Drusher. 'I mean, there's a certain concentration of kill-sites here, in this crescent, but most of the others are too wayward, too random.'

'So?'

'That first body you showed me, in the morgue. So cleanly, so particularly cut. Minimal signs of feeding, if any at all. Just like the body today in the Commission of Works. And Rimbaud.'

'Right. The face bitten off.'

Drusher nodded. 'Yes, except I don't think it was bitten. Remember how clean I said it was? I mean almost sterile. None of the bacterial traces one would expect from an animal bite. Especially not from an old, diseased predator with gums receding from vitamin deficiency. Macks, I could wiggle that poor cat's teeth out with my fingers.'

Her face had gone hard. 'Keep going, Valentin,' she said.

'The body in the stacks we went to look at. That was the work of the carnodon. It had mauled and eaten the corpse away. I checked the autopsy files. Nine of the cases were just like that. Gnawed. The victims were all either dead already or helpless. Old, infirm. The carnodon had escaped from the zoological gardens, but it was weak and long past its hunting prime. It roamed the city, not preying, but scavenging. That was all it could do any more.'

'What are you telling me?' Macks asked quietly.

'Look at the map again. Here.' Drusher flipped a switch. 'Now I've taken away the bodies I can attribute to the cat. Cleans it up a bit, doesn't it?'

'Yes,' she admitted.

'The old carnodon was hungry and opportunistic. It had no pattern. It just roamed and fed where it could. What we're left with is a much more precise zone. Almost territorial. The killings here were like poor Rimbaud – swift, savage, clean. No feeding.'

'But it's still an odd crescent-shaped spread. How can we triangulate from that?'

'Look at the map, Macks. Territory is determined not just by hunter but also by prey. The crescent-shaped dispersal covers an area east of the Commission of Works. There are none to the west because that's an area interdicted by the Martial Order Division. It doesn't kill there, Macks, because there's no one there to kill.'

'Oh, Throne…' she murmured.

'And this is the good bit,' Drusher smiled. 'Look what happens when I mirror the dispersal, projecting it as if there was quarry in all directions. The crescent becomes…?'

'A circle.'

'Right, a circle. There's your focus. There's your bloody pattern. That's its territory. Right there.'

MACKS WAS DRIVING faster than ever. In the back seat sat Edvin and a trooper called Roderin. Both were checking their riot-gun loads.

'You're sure about this?' Macks hissed.

'I've very little left to stake on it,' Drusher replied, 'my professional credentials being long since used up.'

'Don't get smart,' she warned. 'You two ready?' she called over her shoulder.

Edvin and Roderin both replied in the affirmative. Edvin leaned forwards. 'I thought we'd got this thing, sir,' he said. 'I mean, I thought Falken had plugged it.'

'He got the cat,' Drusher said. 'But the cat wasn't it.'

Macks began to slow down, and it was lucky she did. A second Magistratum transporter swung out in front of them from a side street and ploughed ahead.

'Falken,' Macks whispered.

THEY PULLED UP outside the Commission of Works. Falken had two troopers with him, Levy and Mantagne.

'What the hells is this about?' Falken asked belligerently. He was still half-drunk from the party in the morgue.

'We're onto a lead,' Macks said. 'Behave.'

Falken looked at Drusher. 'I got it, stone dead. Boom-boom. What is this crap now?'

'Something else,' Drusher said.

They spread out in a line, entering the weed-choked waste behind the Commission of Works.

'Macks?' Drusher called. She came over to him.

'I'd like a weapon.'

'In the old days, you—'

'I'd really like a weapon,' he repeated.

Macks nodded, and lowered her riot-gun in one hand as she pulled the handgun from her holster. She handed it to him.

'The safety's by—'

'I know how they work,' he snapped.

They pushed on.

'So, this is all about territory, right?' she said.

Drusher nodded. 'You saw the map. We're entering its territory now. Its hunting ground.'

'How can you be so sure?'

'Like I said, you saw the map. The thing is, we're not talking about animal instinct. Not territory as a predator would understand it. We're talking about orders.'

'What? Orders?'

'What is this place, Macks?'

'The Commission of Works.'

'And what's behind it?'

'Just rubble, Valentin.'

'Yeah, but what was it before it was rubble?'

'It was the main building of the Administratum here in Tycho. Before the tank shells levelled it.'

'Exactly. The Administratum centre. Dead centre of the spread pattern. During the civil war, something was ordered to guard that vital point, secure it, defend it.'

Macks glared at him. 'A man?'

Drusher shrugged. 'Something. Something that's still doing it. Macks, I glimpsed the killer in the Commission of Works, right after it killed Rimbaud. It was humanoid.'

Spread wide, the line of officers entered the ruins of the Administratum. Some parts of the ruin were two or three storeys tall, held up, crippled and crooked, by the ferrosteel bars stripped through the rockcrete.

There were weeds everywhere, flourishing. Tinselbarb and frondwort, cabbage speculus and the limp foliage of climbing tracedy. The air was pungent with root-rot, stagnant water, mould.

Drusher slowly circled round. Macks was nearby, riot-gun raised. He glanced left and saw Falken bending in under a broken doorway. To his right, Edvin was aiming his weapon at the overhung, plant-swathed walls.

Levy raised his clucking auspex box. 'Getting something, very weak. It's coming from the west.'

Falken nodded and disappeared. Macks hurried onwards. Mantagne covered her, glancing nervously up at the blooming foliage. Weapon clenched high, Roderin shuffled round through a ruined archway.

'Getting hot now, getting really hot,' Levy called, lifting up his auspex, which was burring like a cicada.

'Throne, it must be right on us!'

Falken's gun went off. Once. Twice. Then another one echoed it. Macks started forwards, running, and Drusher followed. Levy was right behind them. Mantagne rushed around to the other side of the wall.

There was a scream. Two more shots. Three.

Mantagne was dead. He had been sliced open from the scalp to the sternum. Blood was still spitting from his opened body, high into the air.

'Throne!' Macks cried, turning round. She heard Falken fire again, then Edvin. 'Where is it? Where is it?'

Levy almost crashed into her from behind, following his auspex blindly. 'Right there! There!'

Macks aimed and fired, once, twice, grinding back the slide each time. She put a huge hole in the facing wall.

Shots again, distant, from Falken and Edvin. Macks and Levy followed the sound. Pistol raised, Drusher turned the other way.

This predator was smart. Very smart and very able. It knew all about misdirection. It could out-think any regular human and then split him open. It understood military tactics because that is what it dealt in. It had been programmed. It had been given orders.

Breathing hard, Drusher edged round another shattered arch, his weapon braced. His pulse was racing, but this felt entirely odd. This wasn't about his trained skills any more. This wasn't about an animal, whose habits and behaviours he had been schooled to understand. This was the opposite.

So he did the opposite. Facing any hungry predator, the last thing a magos biologis would want to do is step into the open. But he did so, turning a full circle, his pistol aimed in both hands.

On the rubbled floor before him, he saw Roderin. Roderin was dead, just like the others.

Drusher circled again, weapon tight.

The killer flew at him.

Drusher pulled the trigger and kept it pulled. Eight, nine, ten rounds, the full clip boomed out of Macks's borrowed sidearm and hit the killer head-on.

It fell, burst open, broken, puffed pink intestines spilling from its punctured torso. A man, but not a man. A product of the civil war. Augmetically strengthened, augmetically wired, its eyes a black visor, wires stapled into its flesh, its palsied hands curled over to expose the whirring chainblades sewn into its wrists.

The chainblades whined as they came together. Despite the rounds he had put into it, it got back up. And leapt at Drusher's face.

His gun clicked, dry.

'Down, Valentin!'

From behind him, Macks fired her riot-gun and the killer's head burst like a tomato. The impact knocked it sideways. When it landed, its chainblades were still whirring involuntarily.

'ALL RIGHT?' SHE asked Drusher.

He nodded.

'You were right. As ever.'

'Glad to be of service.'

'Seriously,' she said, leading him out of the ruins as Falken and Edvin fired shot after shot into the killer to make sure it was dead. 'Seriously, Drusher, I owe you.'

'A week's pay, you said. I do what I do.'

He began to walk away, picking his path through the rubble.

'Valentin, I could put it down as two weeks, no one would know.'

He shrugged. He looked back at her. 'What about a ticket off this rock?' he said, with a thin, sad smile.

'Can't afford that,' she said. 'Sorry. Budgets and all.'

'I had to ask,' said Drusher. He sat down on a chunk of bricks.

'Look,' said Macks. 'You've seen how stretched things are down here. The Martial Order Division can barely keep up. We can use all the help we can get, particularly sharp, educated minds with a thing for details. What do you think?'

'How would that work?' Drusher asked.

Macks shrugged. 'Not sure. I could probably second your services on a temporary basis using the emergency powers. It's not much, I know, but...'

Drusher frowned. 'My teaching post isn't much, but at least it's safe.' He handed her back the pistol.

'You sure?' she asked.

'Whenever I spend any time with you, Macks, it ends up getting exciting,' he said. 'Rather too exciting for a man of my disposition.'

'Hey,' she replied, as if hurt, 'I haven't got you killed so far.'

Drusher smiled. 'So far.'

Macks nodded. 'All right,' she said. She kissed him briefly on the cheek and turned to walk back to the transporters.

Every wrong turn destiny had ever offered him...

And which was this? Drusher sighed.

'Macks?' he called out.

'Yes?'

'Would I get my own desk?'

Turning back, she smirked. 'Valentin, you'll even get your own couch.'

Drusher got to his feet, and wandered down the path after her.

FEAR ITSELF
Juliet E. McKenna

THE LIGHTS IN this basement where they'd set up their medicae station were too bright for sleep. Catmos dropped onto a spare mattress and closed his eyes all the same. He needed rest to do his duty by the next batch of wounded. Of course, the fluorestrips would be less intrusive if he rolled over to face the wall, but Catmos would no more leave his back exposed than he would unstrap his laspistol.

He crooked an arm to shade his eyes. If he couldn't sleep, he could escape the stifled moans, the dull reek of blood pierced by counterseptic. On Alnavik, he would look up at cold blue skies instead of stained rockcrete. To the north, the Marble Mountains held back the grinding glaciers stretching across the horizon. To the south, muted conifers cloaked the valleys running down to the coastal plain and the berg-strewn Broken Sea.

Catmos felt the weight of the modified long-barrelled bolter in his hands, the cold ring of its magnification scope just touching his eyelid. He scanned the outcrops above the broad scar of the quarry. Even in this frigid air a man worked up a sweat wrestling machines that sliced the white stone like a power claw through ork armour. Waking with the spring, marble bears were drawn by the scent. Twice as tall as a man and six times the weight, their white fur was threaded with grey, all the harder to see among the barren mountains. They were stealthy despite their size, driven by unstoppable hunger after their hibernation. Their long talons could disembowel a man, slashing through chainsheet work gear. Catmos was there to stop them.

His thoughts might return to the home he'd never see again but his ears were still attuned to the aid station. Soft footsteps hurried towards him. Not another attack. He'd have heard the emplacement's lascannons. Something else.

'Field surgeon!'

A wounded man murmured at the urgent whisper.

'This had better be good, squid-sucker, or I'll stamp on your tentacles,' growled Catmos.

Mathein stifled a chuckle. Catmos moved his arm, glad to see the young orderly was finally learning to take a joke.

'Commissar Thirzat has arrived with a squad of cadets.' As Mathein jerked his head towards the entrance stairs, the harsh light glinted on his bionic right eye. A muscle spasm rattled the augmented fingers of his replacement arm.

He was nervous. Hardly surprising. Catmos didn't recall this particular commissar but he knew the breed. He got to his feet, stripping off the stained med-itunic covering his mottled-grey uniform. 'I'll make sure everything's in order.'

He headed for the rear storeroom he had claimed for the medicae support squad. His two junior surgeons, Etrick and Tind, were snoring on the floor, exhausted. Etrick's orderly, Haux, was wearily opening a ration pack. Catmos retrieved his data-slate and quietly closed the door.

Turning, he saw a Guardsman in the room opposite, shoving lasgun powerpacks into the recharging rack. The man's hands were shaking. He dropped a pack and swore as he bent to retrieve it.

'Not that one.' Catmos stepped forwards to take it. 'The casing's cracked.'

The last thing they needed was men injured by their own weapons exploding.

The youthful Guardsman looked at him numbly before blinking as if he'd just woken. 'Sorry, sir.'

Catmos recognised him now. The medical support squad he commanded had been attached to Captain Slaithe's company before. 'It's Nyal, isn't it?'

'Yes, sir.' Nyal's face slackened with dread. 'What happens when the tyranids come back, sir?'

'We fight,' Catmos said steadily.

Hollow-eyed, Nyal grimaced. 'We killed hundreds today and they kept on coming.' He glanced at the charging lasgun packs. 'What if they cut the power? What happens when the heavy bolter and mortars run out of ammo? We can't recharge those. The Sentinels–'

'We're being reinforced,' Catmos reassured him. 'A commissar unit has arrived.'

'Oh.' Nyal didn't look entirely relieved.

Suddenly, the walls of the narrow corridor seemed to press in on Catmos. He couldn't face the breathless basement until he'd had some fresh air.

'You've more powerpacks to collect?' He nodded at empty slots in the rack.

'Yes, sir.' Nyal squared his shoulders.

'Come on then.' Catmos headed up the emplacement's rear stair. Their boots rang on the newly installed metal, the sound echoing off the older stone walls.

As Nyal hurried inside the circular tower's middle tier, Catmos went onto the railed balcony. Above his head, the lascannons hummed, alert. He gazed out over the courtyard of this six-pointed star-fort, relic of the planet's continental wars, a century before the victors sought the Imperium's advantages for Shertore.

Thirty metres or so away, heavy bolters were stationed on each bastion, their crews ready to spring into action. Down in the courtyard, Guardsmen were resting: Captain Slaithe's battered platoons and the ragged remnants of Captain Kelloe's company.

Catmos glanced down at his data-slate. Fifty-six dead and wounded in total. Slaithe's company had taken heavy casualties and they had been inside the fort. Kelloe's men had been caught outside, so more than half had fallen victim to tyranid teeth, claws and obscene bioweapons. Only Captain Slaithe's valiant charge had allowed the survivors' retreat to the gates.

The surgeon gazed over the outer wall, towards the sunset's afterglow beyond the bridge this fort had been built to defend. Those soldiers had never imagined a foe as fearsome as tyranids. He contemplated the silent, fallen Sentinels. They'd fought valiantly to cover Captain Kelloe's retreat, flamer and autocannon obliterating countless vermin. Until they had been overrun, their ammunition exhausted. Because the tyranids could spare a hundred spawn to kill a single Guardsman.

Only yesterday, Catmos had been enjoying this new world, enchanted by Shertore's scented forests. Captain Slaithe was expecting an easy deployment training the Planetary Defence Force. Before dawn orders to hold this river crossing had rushed them to the star-fort.

'Sir?' His orderly, Mathein, appeared on the stair.

'I'm coming.' Catmos headed down.

'Who's in charge?' A commissar stood in the centre of the basement, glaring around.

'Vox-sergeant Biniam, please let Lieutenant Jepthad know reinforcements have arrived,' Catmos said calmly.

The burly vox-sergeant nodded, his scarred face impassive. Shoving through the cadets crowding the stairs, he headed for the uppermost observation platform.

'Who are you?' Thirzat's accent was that of the shore, like Mathein. His sneer suggested the coaster's contempt for anyone who didn't brave lethal storms and bergs to wrest glitterfish from shipslayer whales and killer squid.

'Field Surgeon Catmos of the 19th Alba Marmorea.' Donning his own peaked cap, he smiled at the commissar.

The pristine folds of the man's greatcoat hinted he insisted on uniform regulations. Despite the balmy evening air, he wore the cape of marble-bear fur favoured by the general staff. On the other hand, enamelled studs on Thirzat's collar indicated active service in the regiment's most dangerous campaigns, including the bloodbath of Narthil III.

'Captain Slaithe?' Thirzat surveyed the wounded men.

'He died this afternoon. Borer beetles.'

The recollection nauseated Catmos; slicing open suppurating channels drilled by the beetles, trying to pierce them with his electroscalpel before they shredded some vital organ. He had been too slow. There had been too many.

'Borer beetles!' Commissar Thirzat rounded on the wide-eyed cadets. 'Flesh worms that burrow through your nerve-fibres to consume your brain. Deathspitter maggots melting your armour. Strangler seeds, growing thorns to rip a man to pieces before he takes two steps. You must not flinch! Not if that man's your lifelong friend, your brother. Not if he's saved your life ten times over. You let him fall without a second glance!

'You must not fail. This enemy won't: the 'gaunts, the raveners, the rippers, whatever vile perversion of flesh and bone these tyranids send. If this corruption gets a single toehold on this world, every living thing is doomed.' Thirzat's sweeping gesture encompassed Shertore, mild, verdant, fertile from pole to pole.

'The Hive Mind seeks the utter destruction of humanity!' the commissar roared at the cadets. 'Tyranids will slaughter every man, woman, child and animal, down to skippermice hiding in ditches. They are fearless, merciless, unrelenting. Their sucking weeds will wither every tree, every shrub, every blade of grass. They won't stop till every last scrap of biomass is rendered down in pools of living acid. If you fail, your death will be the ultimate treachery, nourishing the loathsome monstrosity that spawned them.'

Even under the harsh fluorescents, Catmos could see the cadets pale. Whatever they'd learned in their schola progenium lectorums, now they faced the murderous truth of battle.

'So we will not fail,' Thirzat growled. 'You will man this emplacement and shoot down tyranid spores before they spew their poisons in the air. You will destroy tyranid pods so no more perverted beasts pollute this planet. You will slaughter the vermin already here. We will secure this agri-world for the Imperium, to the eternal glory of the God-Emperor. You will count your life well spent if that's the cost of doing your duty!'

A wounded man lying on a sensor-blanket moaned. 'No!'

The commissar loomed over him, plasma pistol in hand. 'What did you say?'

'Not again.' The casualty tried to shield his face. Stinking pus oozed through the dressings on his arms as his fleshworm wounds broke open.

'You refuse to serve?' The plasma pistol whined in Thirzat's hand. 'You know the penalty for cowardice?'

'Only when facing the enemy. He's on an aid station mattress.' Catmos stepped so close that Thirzat was surprised into a pace backwards. 'Judge him by his actions. He was wounded fighting to save Captain Slaithe. Now that tyranid poisons infect his blood and brain, you cannot read cowardice in his ravings.'

'We'll see about that,' hissed Thirzat. 'Out of my way, surgeon!'

As the commissar gestured with his pistol, Catmos had no choice but to step aside.

Bending over the wounded man, Mathein looked up. 'I'm sorry, sir.' Soft-footed as ever, he had come up unseen behind Catmos. 'He's unconscious.'

'Who are you?' Thirzat demanded.

Not about to let his junior face the commissar's wrath, Catmos answered. 'Corporal Mathein. His service as a platoon medic was so distinguished that the Officio Medicae took a special interest in his recuperation after Narthil III.'

'I just did my duty, like the rest of my squad, Stone Bears, every man of us.' With a crooked smile of embarrassment, Mathein quoted the Alba Marmorea's motto. '*Never Found Wanting.*'

Catmos saw Thirzat's wolf-pale gaze take in the young man's augmetics and the Medallion Crimson stud on his collar. He only hoped the commissar didn't see the glistening hypo-needle still protruding from Mathein's mediplas thumb.

Thankfully, voices sounded on the stairs.

'Commissar? I'm Lieutenant Jepthad.' The young officer saluted crisply.

Catmos stepped backwards, gesturing to Mathein to do likewise. He made a mental note to adjust the patient's medication after the tranquillium the orderly had administered.

'Let me show you our dispositions, sir, and review the tyranids' last attack,' Jepthad said with a hint of entreaty.

Catmos busied himself redressing the casualty's wounds.

'Vox-sergeant, let Headquarters know we're here.' Thirzat was clearly unimpressed. 'I'll make my full report later.'

'At once, commissar,' Biniam said promptly.

On his way to the stairs, Thirzat paused to look at the heavy-set man. 'Your reputation goes before you, vox-sergeant.'

Biniam looked the commissar straight in the eye. 'Argene Prime, sir?'

Thirzat didn't blink. 'That and other things.' He held Biniam's gaze for a moment before turning to Lieutenant Jepthad. 'Show me your defence lasers' field of fire and the terrain.'

Kicking aside an acid-etched flak-armour breastplate, he strode towards the stairs. The lieutenant and the cadets all followed.

Catmos checked his patient was sleeping soundly. Biniam strolled over to join him rather than heading for the vox-caster in the corner.

'Do you think he considers himself a Stone Bear?' he mused.

'I don't imagine he's much for nicknames.' Catmos said, though he imagined the cadets had some choice names for Thirzat behind his back.

'You were at Argene Prime?' Mathein asked, awestruck.

'He only wears his Honorifica Imperialis stud when he's in trouble with regimental command.' Catmos checked the coloured telltales on the sensor-blanket's corner. The wounded man's heart rate, blood-oxygen and pressure were satisfactory.

'We were both there. Not much to tell,' Biniam said repressively.

Catmos could see Mathein was still desperate to ask. Thankfully he didn't. Catmos had no wish to relive that campaign against the orks. Not when he and Biniam were the only two survivors from their entire company. The Alba Marmorea always boasted Alnavik gave far more than it accepted from the Imperium. They certainly had in the Argene System.

'How's the lieutenant?' Catmos asked in low tones. Jepthad had been expecting to learn from Captain Slaithe, not to replace him within three days of planetfall.

But the universe isn't fair and doesn't care. Every Alnavik child knew that.

Biniam shrugged again. 'He's doing well enough, for a valley whelp.' Like Catmos, he'd been raised in the Marble Mountain quarries. 'As long as his nerve holds.' He looked searchingly at Catmos. 'What about these lads you're patching up and sending out?'

The field surgeon knew what he meant. They couldn't afford to lose men to battle shock, not here, not now. Never mind Commissar Thirzat executing men he accused of cowardice. To have any chance of withstanding the tyranids, every man must hold his ground or die trying, for the sake of all the rest. Thirzat had only spoken the brutal truth. But what good was the truth if it only dismayed already-dispirited men? Fear could be as contagious as blister-pox. If it took hold, it would destroy them as surely and swiftly as any tyranid swarm.

Catmos had been thinking about that. 'Bin, the engineers refitting this place dumped every vox, pict and data-slate they broke down here. Can you scrounge what you need to make a starchaser?'

'A starchaser?' Biniam cocked his head. 'Where's your helmet? What hit your head and how hard?'

Catmos smiled. 'Just do an old comrade a favour.'

Biniam pursed his lips. 'All right, I'll bite, just to see what you want it for. As soon as I've reported in.' He headed for the vox-set, light on his feet for a big man.

'A starchaser?' Mathein was bemused.

'I have an idea. It may not work, even if Biniam can make the thing,' Catmos said evasively. 'Now, let's see who can be holding a lasgun by morning.'

He didn't need to tell Mathein they would need every mattress for casualties from the next tyranid attack.

THE FIELD SURGEON was wrapping the last of the night's dead in his sleepsac when dawn light spilled down the stairs to the basement.

'Ailure?' Biniam tugged at the fold over the man's face. 'He promised his marble bear pelt to Tremarc.' The shoulders of Biniam's own uniform were striped with bear fur.

'Tremarc is over there.' Catmos nodded towards another shrouded corpse. 'Help me get them upstairs.'

'Can't those puking cadets do some work?' Biniam took the dead man's feet nonetheless.

Emerging into the Planetary Defence compound, Catmos blinked in the strengthening sunshine. 'Where to?'

'Over there.' Biniam nodded to a hastily dug trench, paving slabs stacked beside it. The dead were being dumped, stripped of their weapons and gear. A Guardsman sprayed promethium over the corpses and ignited it with a flamer burst.

Catmos's throat tightened, but it was the only way to stay free of insidious tyranid organisms. He looked at more pits covered with habitents pegged flat. 'This can't help morale.'

Biniam scowled. 'Would letting the lads watch their dead pals twitching, splitting open to spill poison-maggots into the soil?'

Catmos looked towards the outer wall. Those lightly wounded the day before, whom he and Mathein had discharged, were arming to rejoin their comrades. Guardsmen unscathed in the first assault stood ready on the rampart. Lieutenant Jepthad was consulting the sentries.

'Still no foe in sight?' Catmos wondered how long it would be.

Biniam nodded northwards. 'Vox-chatter says their main assault hit Yota City. Whatever stink tells them their hivemates are in trouble here is blowing out to sea.'

'How are the other emplacements faring?' This was one of eighteen forts ringing this continent's only city. Catmos didn't imagine the companies sent to hold them were laughing and passing round lho-sticks.

Biniam shook his head. 'Some have dropped off the vox-net–'

Shouts from the rampart interrupted him. Catmos saw Lieutenant Jepthad raise a hand to his ear, intent on his micro-bead.

'Here they come,' breathed the vox-sergeant.

Guardsmen on the walls clustered around their heavy bolters. The weapons' racking cough sent deadly explosive rounds ripping into the tyranids. Oxy-phosphor flares indicated at least one heavy bolter loaded with Inferno ammunition.

In the paved hollow of the compound, mortar squads deployed in unhurried routine. One man dropped a shell in the gaping weapon. The other yanked the firing lanyard and the stubby barrel spat explosives high over the wall. Catmos saw the crews swiftly adjusting azimuth and bearing as spotters on the ramparts relayed details of each detonation. Every round must extract the maximum death toll from the tyranid multitude. Guardsmen resupplying the ramparts with ammo dodged around the mortars.

Retreating to the top of the steps, Catmos was about to go back down to the basement. He changed his mind. His first duty in a battle was assessing the wounded who needed skills and time the medics couldn't spare. He could do that as well if not better up here.

Despite all the heavy-weapon crews' efforts, the first wave of tyranids reached the walls. They leaped into the gaps between the heavy bolters, propelled by powerful hind legs that were bent and angled like a dog's, ending in a bony excrescence that was part hoof, part claw. Talons on their middle limbs hooked securely onto the rampart. They heaved themselves up, hissing and spitting, their forelimbs brandishing bony scythes as long as a man's arm.

One skewered a Guardsman under the chin, his face disappearing in a wash of blood. The creature lifted him off his feet, shaking him to free its claw. Neck snapping, the man's body fell away, limp in death.

The creatures' carapaces were segmented like some giant, loathsome insect. Overlapping plates jutted upwards from their backs, the colour of old rust and dried blood. Beneath, their skeletal limbs and thorax were the sickly white of leprous skin. Grotesquely swollen, red chitin-plated heads roved from side to side. Slime dripped from thrusting jaws, myriad teeth like a needle-shark's. Catmos locked gazes with one of the repellent creatures. Its cat-slit eyes were fever-bright, intent only on mindless murder.

How could they possibly survive? His chest was an empty hollow. Bolter rounds were falling like winter hail and they still could not prevail. Their lasgun power packs would fail before this onslaught faltered. If they killed these vermin till the corpses were piled as high as the rampart, that only gave the tyranids an easier way into the compound.

Catmos's heart raced with panic but his limbs were frozen with fear. He couldn't run. He couldn't reach his laspistol. What was the point? Even the men on the walls were huddling behind their heavy bolters. Seductive despair beckoned, a black blanket to hide beneath.

The lascannons ringing the tower's upper levels burst into life. The alien exploded in a reeking shower of bony fragments and cauterised gobbets of flesh. The same laser blast blew apart the handful following the trailblazer. The air rang with deafening shrieks as beam after beam of brilliant death cut a swathe through the chittering hordes.

The close-packed Guardsmen on the battlements were firing their lasguns. Pinpoint beams severed limbs and gouged deep into those swollen heads. They blinded noxious eyes and slashed flickering tongues clean through. Lieutenant Jepthad stepped out of a heavy bolter's shadow and calmly focussed his fire on one murderously flailing tyranid after another.

Catmos drew a shuddering breath. He felt like some fool turning his back on a winter blizzard to huddle over a petrosene stove, not caring that blocking winter's draughts through his house was starving the heater of fresh air. Not knowing the glowing element would burn all the oxygen, condemning everyone to sleep-sick death. Now he felt as if someone had kicked open the door and dragged him out, letting the biting wind scour the toxins from his blood.

Squad medics were patching up wounded men and sending them back. No one expected different. Back on Alnavik, if a marble bear chased you, you climbed a razor pine and didn't complain about your cuts. You were alive, weren't you? Catmos ripped his laspistol from its holster, ready to offer covering fire to a pair of medics carrying a casualty down from the rampart. The man clutched at his broken breastplate, blood oozing over his fingers.

'The gates! The gates!'

Men on the walls were yelling. Lieutenant Jepthad slid down a ladder and raced across the compound. Something hit the outer face of the gates, fifteen metres in front of the tower. The impact was deafening. The layered plasteel buckled but didn't break. Catmos's relief was short-lived. As the gates twisted, a narrow gap opened by one hinge. A massive barbed claw carefully explored the weakness.

There was a second explosion; something detonated right against the entrance. The plasteel held but gaps were opening all around the gates. Bubbling black acid oozed, weakening the ceramite plating.

The lascannons on the tower would defend the entrance if the gates gave way. Catmos looked around, shielding his eyes from the blinding beams. But the lascannons were aiming higher, not lower.

Bat-like shadows blighted the sunshine. These tyranids flew on leathery wings, membranes spread between the splayed bones of their mutated middle limbs. Their evil gaze searched for targets, their forelimbs clutching weapon-symbiotes. Catmos tensed as the monstrosities flew high above the ramparts, their viciously barbed tails lashing between their atrophied hind legs. Would they hover and fire or stoop like a hawk for the kill? Either way, the Guardsmen on the walls couldn't take their eyes off the tyranid ground assault, not if they wished to live.

Lascannons burned through the warm air. The flying tyranids caught in their crosshairs disintegrated. Any of the vermin too close to those initial casualties fell too, wings shredded by razor shards of shattered chitin. But as they tumbled from the sky, their weapon-symbiotes still spat borer worms at the mortar crews. Crashing onto the paving, their twisting tails cut Guardsmen's legs from under them. Contorted spines embedded in men's thighs as the flying tyranids flailed in their death throes.

Those monstrosities still aloft vomited lurid gobs of bio-plasma. Catmos saw one spatter a grey-haired Guardsman. Clinging green fire ignited his flak-armour, his hair. Snarling with agony and hatred, the man kept firing, bringing down the alien who killed him. The merciful ignition of his lasgun's powerpack freed him from his torment, an instant before Catmos's finger tightened on his laspistol trigger.

The twisted gate screeched. Massive russet claws slid through the foaming black acid. Barbs dug deep as whatever was outside pulled harder, inexorably widening the gap. Ceramite began to rupture.

'With me!'

Commissar Thirzat charged out of the central tower, flak-armour over his tunic, his plasma pistol in one hand, a power sword in the other. Cadets followed carrying flakboard. Others hauled rockcrete beams. Rallying to Lieutenant Jepthad, the Guardsmen in the compound began forcing a path to the entrance, despatching wounded tyranids fallen from the sky, stamping on ravenous borer beetles scuttling round their boots. Mortar crews dragged their weapons aside, sacrificing range and aim. Undeterred, they resumed firing blindly.

Catmos and every soldier on the tower's platforms concentrated their fire on the scything tyranids still scrambling over the wall. Up on the ramparts, men fought and bled. If those vermin attacked the Guardsmen and cadets, their attempt to reinforce the entrance was doomed.

Guardsmen and cadets formed a solid wedge, Thirzat at its tip. Step by dogged step, the commissar led them forwards. Catmos could see the shimmer of heat from weapons rising above the cadets in the centre, still grimly dragging forwards materials to repair the breach. Lieutenant Jepthad was walking backwards, resolute in command of the rear.

Too late. With a mighty heave, those monstrous claws ripped the left-hand gate in half. Unlike the creatures scuttling over the compound paving, this creature stood upright: a repellent parody of a man with its fingered hands clutching a weapon-symbiote. It was twice the size of the tallest Alba Marmorean, even standing on its bent legs. Its massive carapace and the chitinous plates jutting from its head were the putrid brown of rotten fruit. Its uppermost pallid limbs bore massive talons brandished high above its broad shoulders.

Catmos recalled an Officio Medicae briefing, longer ago than he could guess. This was a tyranid warrior. One of the most deadly creatures the Hive

Mind spawned, dominating lesser progeny and driving them to do its will.

Smaller tyranids were fighting to get through the gap behind it. Scurrying across the compound paving, they reared up on mid- and hind-claws, forelimbs clutching fleshborers and devourers.

For an instant that seemed half a lifetime, the tyranid warrior surveyed the carnage. As the closest Guardsman levelled his lasgun, a new horror sprang out from behind it, so fast Catmos took a moment to realise what had happened.

This was a different monster, more slightly built with twice-jointed uppermost limbs studded with fang-like claws to pierce and crush. It wasn't using those, flinging out its clawed hand instead. For an instant, Catmos allowed himself to hope. It had no hope of reaching the Guardsman. Then he saw that didn't matter. Bony hooks shot out from the tyranid's skeletal flanks, embedding in the Guardsman's arms and face. The creature raised its clawed limbs again. Sinews linking the hooks to its narrow body contracted. Despite his frantic struggles, the hapless Guardsman was drawn into the tyranid's grotesque embrace.

The hooks were already tearing him to pieces. Dripping tentacles hanging from the alien's maw caressed his head. Their tips slithered into his ears, his mouth. As the man writhed, the creature's grip tightened. Now the tendrils thrust into his eyes, his nostrils. Blood and mucus gushed as spasms wracked the dying man.

The vile tyranid shivered with obscene satisfaction, throwing its victim aside. Its gory tentacles gently licked each other clean of brain tissue. Jaundiced gold, its luminous eyes fastened on a new target. Another abrupt gesture flung its flesh hooks to snare the soldier.

Commissar Thirzat was charging towards it. His power sword cut through the sinews. A plasma pistol shot took it straight in the face and its seared tentacles shrivelled. The monster staggered backwards to collapse in a thrashing heap.

The massive tyranid warrior rounded on Thirzat with a roar, as soldiers, mortar crews and medicae were all turning their lasguns on the tyranids in the compound. The alien vermin shrieked and died as their armoured exoskeletons fractured under ceaseless las-fire. The heavy bolters on the ramparts were still mowing down the swarms attacking the outside of the walls.

No one could help Commissar Thirzat fighting the tyranid warrior. His plasma shots targeted its mouth, its eyes, the underside of its joints every time it swiped with a murderous claw. His power sword cut deep in its forelimbs as he ducked and weaved. Catmos hadn't ever seen a fighting man so quick on his feet.

With an ear-piercing shriek of fury, the monstrosity took an unexpected step back. The lesser tyranids behind it wavered. The warrior slipped on some fallen flyer's wing membrane, giving Thirzat the chance to break away. Jepthad and the rearguard fired a concentrated volley at it. Ichor glistening on its carapace, the massive creature retreated, lashing out indiscriminately at the milling cohorts outside the gate. As it vanished, the assault slackened, not much but just enough.

'Secure that breach!' Thirzat bellowed, near-breathless.

The cadets were already busy with their flakboard and rockcrete as Jepthad's men blasted the lesser spawn to bloody ruin. While the rest of the Guardsmen killed those tyranids trapped inside, Catmos assessed the most grievously wounded. A cut to the thigh, bright with arterial blood. He pressed a suction-dressing down hard. A hand half-cut, half-torn from its wrist. A styptic-bandage and some tranquillium and that could wait. A grey-faced Guardsman with bloody froth on his bluish lips. Priority Red: his first patient. Etrick and Tind were responsible for the wounded who could be returned to the battle. Catmos fought to save the worst injured for medevac.

Hurrying down to the basement, he found Mathein and the other two orderlies had shifted the recovering wounded to sit on rolled sleepsacs, leaning against the walls. On the mattresses, sensor blankets gleamed with fresh counterseptic, telltales blinking in readiness. Thermosealed trays of servoclamps and electroscalpels were stacked high. Etrick and Tind were ready at their operating tables and the blood recycler hummed. The resuscitrex diodes indicated it was fully charged.

'Let's get to work,' Catmos said grimly.

ONCE UPON A time, the field surgeon had kept a tally of the wounded he tended. When medics serving the Alba Marmorea were summoned by the Officio

Medicae, to be shown advances in battlefield surgery, orderlies compared notes. This many wounded, this many saved, so many restored with bionics, so many dead, the fallen toasted with shots of amasec.

Now Catmos simply concentrated on the patient bleeding beneath his electroscalpel, no thought for the body he'd just mended, for whoever the orderlies might bring next. His whole world was the life trickling through his fingers unless he could find the way to stop it.

He packed a wound with gauze. 'Next!'

Danger, hunger, weariness were all irrelevant until every wounded Guardsman was treated.

'That's all,' Mathein said wearily as he lifted the casualty away, his bionic arm making light work of it.

'Truly?' Catmos looked up, startled to see evening shadows clotting the stairwell. He had completely lost track of the passing day.

His meditunic was stiff with dried blood and discarded plastek gloves lay in drifts round his feet, along with a stray finger. It had been ripped from a Guardsman's hand, caught in his trigger guard when a tyranid smashed his weapon aside. A tattooed arm wrapped in mediplas was set to one side. The bone had been so mangled that amputation was the only option. The wreckage of an eyeball glistened in a steel dish, ruined by a boring bio-worm. At least cutting it out had saved that Guardsman's life. But a clotted tangle of entrails was testament to failure. The patient had bled out from a lacerated liver as Catmos fought frantically to kill all the borers wriggling through the man's abdomen.

Mathein would have an accurate tally. Catmos might not count them but someone had to. No, that could wait.

'Field surgeon?' Lieutenant Jepthad was coming down the steps.

'Sir.' Catmos saluted the young man, belatedly realising his arm was aching.

'How are the men?' Jepthad asked quietly.

Catmos considered his reply. 'Every man of Alnavik accepts life is lethal, whether he stays dirt-side or becomes a Stone Bear. So we stand firm when lesser regiments fail. But this enemy–' He shook his head. 'It's a sore trial.'

The lieutenant surveyed the wounded, on the mattresses and sitting by the walls. Unexpectedly, he smiled.

'It's said the tyranid are fearless,' he remarked. 'They're not. They're mindless. Did you see that today? There's no spark of independent thought in their eyes, and that's why we will prevail.'

Catmos covertly surveyed the Guardsmen's faces. They didn't look convinced, though plenty looked curious. At least that was better than exhausted dejection.

'Tyranids cannot think for themselves,' the young officer said scornfully. 'They're puppets doing the Hive Mind's will. We're men. We think for ourselves. Yes, we're scared.' Jepthad surprised everyone with that bold declaration. 'And we know why. Because those abominations somehow reflect the evils of the warp to cast this fearsome shadow over their foes.'

His voice was calm, reassuring. Valley-dwellers always prided themselves on their wisdom, Catmos reflected. Of all the descendants of Holy Terra hardy enough to colonise the ice-bound planet, they had the wit to claim Alnavik's sheltering dales. They didn't have to prove themselves quarrying the fine white marble that adorned Imperial temples across half the sector. They saw no merit in measuring themselves against the perils of the sea. Squid didn't care.

Jepthad walked round the room, entirely at ease. 'I could do without their psyker spite gnawing at my thoughts,' he said frankly. 'But we won't be found wanting. We have the intelligence to see that fear for a mindless lie. We know what we face. We know we can trust our weapons and our comrades. Best of all, we know help's coming.'

He gestured upwards. 'That's a single hive ship in orbit, some lost remnant of a splinter fleet that's been drifting through empty space since Hive Fleet Kraken was broken. I don't say it's no threat,' he allowed. 'Never underestimate tyranids. That's why the Praetors of Orpheus are on their way.'

Catmos was encouraged to see smiles of relief and hope. The Praetors of Orpheus had fought heroically on Narthil III. The Stone Bears recognised their debt to the awe-inspiring warriors.

After acknowledging the exultation that news prompted, Jepthad continued. 'So our task is to hold out against the tyranids till the Praetors of Orpheus attack them from space. Then the vermin will be crushed between us!'

'Then you'll be needing this, sir.' Biniam strode forwards from the stair. He held out a power claw. A bear's mask snarled above the three shimmering blades.

For the first time, Jepthad was shaken. 'That's Captain Slaithe's—'

'You've earned it,' Biniam insisted.

All the wounded shouted agreement. Several brandished the brass bear claws favoured by the rank and file: knuckledusters adorned with talons.

'It was damaged.' Reluctant, Jepthad accepted the fearsome plated gauntlet.

Biniam shrugged. 'I saw to that.'

Catmos reckoned the vox-sergeant could restart a stricken Imperial Navy cruiser with the wires from half a pict and some Sentinel datachips.

'I will wear it with pride.' Jepthad thrust his hand inside and flourished the weapon. 'To kill any tyranid that comes within reach, in Captain Slaithe's memory!'

'Stone Bears!' a man shouted.

'Hard enough to eat rocks and shit gravel!' yelled another.

The cheers and laughter broke off as a cadet hurried down the stairs.

'Commissar Thirzat's compliments.' He saluted Jepthad. 'Please compile your report for the vox-sergeant to transmit with his.'

Jepthad nodded. 'Sergeant?'

Biniam nodded at the resuscitrex. 'I just need to look at that.'

'Orderly.' Catmos glanced at Mathein. 'It's time the men were settled.'

As Jepthad headed for the stairs, Biniam came over to the operating table.

'To amuse yourself when you can't sleep?' Pretending to examine the resuscitrex, he passed Catmos some mongrel offspring of a pocket data-slate and a handheld pict.

'Drop by later and you'll see.' The field surgeon nodded to the storerooms by the rear stairwell. 'Just don't interrupt. And thanks for this.'

'What would you do without me?' Biniam sauntered after the hurrying lieutenant.

Seeing the junior surgeons making checks on the casualties, Catmos went to the storeroom where they'd dumped the junk from the rest of the basement. By the time he'd made space for two chairs Mathein appeared with the day's full report.

'Nine more dead, eighteen wounded.' The orderly looked expectantly at the curiously rigged data-slate, the screen barely the size of Catmos's hand. 'So what's that for?'

'Who's at worst risk of battle shock, among the men fit to fight tomorrow?'

Barely half were left unscathed now, of the comrades who'd been ordered to hold this emplacement. How many would freeze tomorrow, Catmos wondered, overwhelmed by fear, by recollection of the slaughter they'd already seen, by the sheer impossibility of their task? Until they were slaughtered by the tyranids or cut down by the commissar's pistol?

Mathein thought. 'Otharen.'

'Bring him here.' Catmos switched on the data-slate and smiled as coloured lights darted round the black screen. He quickly set the simple game's parameters.

As Mathein opened the storeroom door, he indicated a chair. 'Guardsman, please, sit.'

Otharen lowered himself down. His torso was swathed in bandages. 'Sir?'

'Report, Guardsman,' Catmos said briskly. 'Tell me exactly what happened to you today.'

'I crew a mortar,' Otharen said uncertainly.

Catmos took the other chair. 'You were close by when the gate was breached?'

Now he recognised the young man. He'd nearly been the second victim of the lanky tyranid the commissar had killed.

'Talwhit, he was my crewmate.' Rimmed with white, Otharen's eyes bored straight through Catmos, seeing only horrors. 'It ate– it ate–'

'Guardsman!' Catmos clapped his hands. 'Look at me.'

Otharen dragged himself back from the terrifying memory, though he was helpless to stop the shudders wracking him.

'Stand up.' Without asking Catmos, Mathein draped a sensor blanket over Otharen's chair. 'Now sit.'

As the Guardsman numbly obeyed, Catmos handed him the rigged data-slate.

'Otharen, I want you to tell me everything that happened, everything you feared and felt. But while you're doing that, you must play the starchaser.' He reached over and double-tapped the screen. 'Like when you were a cub.'

'Sir?' The Guardsman was utterly confused.

The starchaser beeped reprovingly. Otharen had failed to follow the pattern of lights with his finger.

'Just do it, soldier,' Catmos said sternly.

Ingrained habits of obedience set Otharen tapping the screen. Yellow top, blue left, green right, blue left catching out Otharen's finger anticipating the next light at the bottom. Red at the top, Otharen only just holding back in time. Red for danger, tap that and the game was over. The lights sped up, green, orange, purple, darting into the corners, each one needing a tap before the next one blinked into view. White, a double tap for that, the star itself.

'Tell me everything that happened,' Catmos repeated. 'No, don't stop. Keep chasing the stars.'

Otharen swallowed. 'Me and Talwhit were firing the mortar.'

This time he managed a few more sentences before the horror choked him.

The sensor blanket telltales were glowing red. Mathein stepped forwards but Catmos held him back with a raised hand.

The starchaser bleeped insistently. Otharen blinked and focussed on the screen. 'Sorry,' he mumbled.

'Reset the game,' Catmos insisted.

'We were firing the mortar.' Otharen doggedly obeyed, prodding the screen with a numb finger. 'Reynas was spotting for us, up on the walls.'

Catmos didn't know how many false starts and repetitions it took. But Otharen was finally able to endure reliving the terror of Talwhit's death. The sensor telltales still showed amber but his panicked brainwaves had subsided, the racing heartbeat and the sweating. The young man's voice was steady, his gaze fixed on the starchaser, his finger steadily following the flickering lights.

The device acknowledged his success with a sweet chime. Otharen looked up at Catmos and scrubbed tears from his stubbled cheeks with his other hand. 'Sir?'

'Very good, Guardsman.' Catmos smiled as he took the starchaser. 'Now get some sleep.'

Mathein was standing behind the chair, carefully watching the sensors. As he turned, he stiffened to attention. Thirzat was in the doorway.

'Orderly,' the commissar said curtly. 'See your patient to his mattress.'

Mathein looked uncertainly at Catmos.

'Go on.' The field surgeon nodded.

As Mathein escorted Otharen out, Thirzat entered the storeroom and closed the door. 'What was that?'

'A treatment for the mind, now we've tended his body.' Catmos spoke with more confidence than he necessarily felt. 'Like the lieutenant said, tyranids are mindless. We're not.'

'Some unsanctioned psyker trick? I'll break you if it is,' Thirzat warned, with more than the usual distaste for psykers.

'Check my records. I've no hint of psychic potential.' Catmos held up the starchaser. 'It's a variation on an old trick of my mother's.'

That prompted surprise in the commissar's cold eyes. 'Explain.'

Catmos gestured to the empty chair. 'My mother was a healer on Alnavik.'

'In the quarries?' Thirzat sat down, stiff-backed.

'Accidents are a fact of life, like ships going down in the ocean.' Catmos shrugged. 'She mended broken bones and amputated crushed limbs. Then there were the nightmares tormenting men and women who'd been digging out the dead and injured from under a rockfall, as well as crippling those who'd been trapped. The same as battle shock in the Guard.'

'Afflicting those lacking resolve.' Thirzat was wholly unsympathetic.

'You might think so,' Catmos said mildly, 'if you didn't know a person had been brave and steadfast before. My mother wouldn't abandon someone she knew to be true steel. She swore getting someone to talk through their trials enabled them to defeat their fear. When they could do that without flinching, they could face the terror again.'

Thirzat looked at him unsmiling. 'I'm waiting for your explanation.'

Catmos wondered briefly how the Commissariat surgically removed a sense of humour.

'Getting someone to talk through their fears is impossible if the fear's all they have to focus on,' he said crisply. 'Giving them something else to do with their hands, with their eyes, distracts them just enough to take the edge off the terror. I can't explain the whys and wherefores of it. I just know it works. My mother would give her patients a rhythm to tap out, one of the mountain songs everyone knows.' He held up the rigged data-slate. 'I don't know any music from the dales and the coast. But everyone plays starchaser.'

Thirzat looked at the field surgeon for a long moment. 'Will that boy hold his ground tomorrow?'

'I don't know,' Catmos said honestly. 'But the odds are better than they were before.'

'How many will you play this game with?' the commissar demanded.

'As many as I can. Why not?' Catmos challenged. 'If it does no good, can it do any harm?'

'Beyond depriving the wounded of sleep?' Thirzat grunted. 'We need every man standing.'

'We need every man holding his ground.' Catmos threw the commissar's own words back at him. 'And if that boy dies, I want him to die with honour, not condemned as a coward by your pistol. In the meantime,' he pointed at the sensor blanket's telltales, 'why don't I dress your wounds?'

'It's nothing.' A muscle flickering in his jaw, Thirzat rose to his feet.

'Commissar, don't be a fool,' Catmos said curtly. 'How will the men hold out without you?'

The first hint of a smile lightened the commissar's expression. 'Lieutenant Jepthad will do his duty.' But he shrugged off his greatcoat.

The commissar had removed his uniform tunic earlier. Despite Thirzat's skills and agility, Catmos saw the tyranid warrior's claws had sliced deep in a few places. 'Take off that undershirt.'

Mathein was waiting anxiously outside the door. 'Sir?'

'It's all right.' Catmos fetched counterseptic and suture-glue. 'Let me patch him up, then fetch another showing signs of battle shock.' He paused. 'Find a Guardsman called Nyal. See how he's faring.'

He went back and tended Thirzat's injuries. The wounds cut through old scars. It would be easier to dislike the commissar, Catmos reflected, without incontrovertible proof of his courage. Thirzat's back had no scars at all.

'So, can I continue?' Catmos scoured a red-rimmed gash, swollen with tyranid venom.

'If I thought we'd live to see the Praetors of Orpheus arrive, I'd forbid it, and report you to the Officio Medicae.' Now Thirzat's smile reminded Catmos of a death's head. 'Since I doubt I'll get the chance, you may as well carry on.'

'You don't think we will get out of here?' Catmos concentrated on matching the edges of the wound as he applied the suture-glue. 'We drove that monstrosity back, didn't we? A tyranid warrior, if I recall my training?'

'It didn't yield that ground,' Thirzat said through gritted teeth. 'The Hive Mind called it off once that other creature had learned what it needed. The one with the tentacles, that was a lictor.' He nodded with satisfaction when he saw Catmos's belated recognition. 'Not all tyranids are puppets, whatever the lieutenant says.'

The commissar rose and picked up his greatcoat. 'The bigger ones know what they're doing. That warrior will be back, or something worse, with a new plan to overwhelm us and ten times the vermin following.'

'What did they learn that could help it?' Catmos tried to hide his dismay.

'Doubtless we'll find out tomorrow.' Thirzat shrugged. 'Make sure your orderly knows what to do.'

'In case of the worst.' Catmos knew his duty. He swallowed hard. 'But I'll still hope for the best.'

'It's best not to hope. Then there's nothing left to fear.' Thirzat opened the door and strode through the basement, head high, shoulders back, exuding confidence.

While he was expecting everyone to die? Suddenly Catmos was furious. No. He wouldn't accept the commissar's dire prediction.

'What did *he* have to say?' Biniam approached from the shadowed back stairs.

Catmos was chilled by his friend's grim voice. 'What news on the vox?'

'HQ's astropath just died, screaming about shadows in the warp, bleeding from his eyes and nose,' Biniam muttered. 'No one knows where the Praetors of Orpheus are.'

'What about the other emplacements?' Catmos contemplated the wounded men.

'Six more dropped off the vox-net.' Biniam shook his head. 'No word from Yota City.'

'So we hold out 'til we're relieved or we're all dead.' Catmos beckoned to Mathein.

Which wouldn't be long, given they'd taken such devastating casualties in two days. But there was still work to do, to stop him succumbing to his own fear, if nothing else.

By dawn, Catmos was confident nineteen more men were safe from paralysing terrors, Nyal among them.

'Thank you, Mathein.' As the orderly escorted the patient out, he carefully closed the door. Then he hurled the starchaser at the storeroom wall. It shattered, useless fragments bouncing everywhere.

Those men might be safe from their fears but what could save them from being eaten by lictors? What use could twenty more lasguns be against numberless tyranids? Were his night's endeavours a waste of time? Was Commissar Thirzat right?

Catmos was too exhausted to decide. Still, there was nothing of the tyranids' insidious dread about his apprehension. He knew it for clear-eyed understanding of their mortal peril. But as his mother always said, if he understood his fear, he could fight it.

Leaving the storeroom, he saw Biniam hunched over the caster. The vox-sergeant looked up at Catmos and briefly shook his head.

The lascannon on the tower's upper tier opened fire. Everyone in the basement froze.

Catmos swiftly assessed the bedridden patients, counting those who could handle a weapon. He beckoned to a sergeant waiting with the men fit for the ramparts.

'Ask Lieutenant Jepthad for thirty lasguns or pistols down here,' he said briskly.

'Not sure if we have that many to spare, sir.' The sergeant's bleak face told Catmos how truly dire their situation now was.

'Field surgeon?' The skin around Mathein's augmetic eye was pale and taut, the other sunk in a bruise of weariness.

'Come with me.' Catmos went to the resuscitrex. He flicked switches and the machine hummed ominously.

Mathein looked at him with misgiving. 'What–'

'If the tyranids overrun the emplacement, give the most seriously wounded the Emperor's benediction,' Catmos ordered. 'A jolt stops a beating heart as surely as it restarts a dead one. Anyone capable of holding a weapon must save a shot for themselves.' Unlocking a panel in the resuscitrex, he removed two glass vials. Drawing the contents of one into a hypostick, he handed the other to Mathein. 'This is for you. Pruscyan. Quick and painless.'

'What are you going to do?' Mathein asked, alarmed.

Pocketing the lethal hypostick, Catmos walked towards the storeroom. 'If this is the last day I see, I'll die with a weapon in my hands.' He found his own kit, mismatched reminders of decades of travel and war. There were still a few things he'd brought from Alnavik.

'What's that?' Mathein looked wide-eyed at the unfamiliar weapon.

'A long rifle.' Catmos checked the ammunition before offering his hand. 'It's been an honour to serve with you.'

Mathein stepped back, shaking his head. 'I'll find a lasgun.'

'You will stay here and save our patients from the enemy,' Catmos said sternly.

The young orderly would be safer in the basement, if by some caprice of the uncaring universe, any of them lived through this day. Then there would be wounded to treat, Catmos reminded himself. He wasn't about to spend his life for no purpose, while that duty remained.

Mathein nodded, unable to speak.

Catmos hurried away up the back stairs though. He couldn't face walking through the wounded.

Heavy footsteps rang on the metal steps behind him. He turned, levelling the long rifle.

'Stone Bears!' Biniam held up his hands in mock surrender. 'Where are you going, scat-face?'

'I've done all I can for the wounded 'til this battle's over, one way or the other.' Catmos scowled. 'You should be on the vox.'

'Listening to dead air?' Biniam shook his head. 'I'll die with a gun in my hand.'

'Come on then.' Catmos turned and they headed upwards.

The warm sunlight on the topmost platform mocked their fatigue. This high above the reeking tyranid dead, fallen thick as autumn leaves as far as the eye could see, Catmos realised forest scents were sweetening the breeze. He took a deep, fragrant breath then looked down into the compound.

Not all the mortars were manned this time. Lacking ammunition or trained crews? Ammunition, Catmos guessed, seeing Otharen standing by one, lasgun in hand, ready to defend it or take over firing, depending on how the fight went. At least all the heavy bolters on the thrusting bastions were crewed. But how long before they emptied their remaining magazines? They couldn't hold these walls with valour alone.

'Here they come.' Biniam readied his lasgun.

Leaping, scything tyranids attacked from all sides. No matter how many the wall-mounted heavy bolters cut down, more followed. They flung their bony hooks, scrambling up the twisted sinews linking the living grapnels to their bodies. Once up on the ramparts to right and left of the gates, they hurled themselves at the bolters. For every five shot down by the Guardsmen desperately defending the weapons, ten more followed.

These were different beasts to the previous day's assailants. Their carapaces thicker, they clutched stubby symbiotes that spat seemingly insignificant glittering showers. The Guardsmen screamed in agony out of all proportion to their tiny wounds. Dropping their lasguns, they clawed at their faces and scraped their hands against the rockcrete, not caring as they spilled their own blood. Then racked by sudden convulsions, every man fell to lie rigid and helpless.

Some toppled from the ramparts, making no effort to save themselves. Catmos winced as skulls shattered on the paving. Others sprawled broken-legged, splinters of bone piercing their clothing. Those lying stiff on the ramparts were ripped to pieces by the tyranids. But the bolter crews on the neighbouring bastions swiftly turned their fire on the vermin, to deny those weapons to the enemy as well as avenge their comrades. The bolter to the left of the gate exploded, the remaining ammunition deliberately detonated in a Guardsman's dying defiance.

Biniam was cursing, repetitious, monotonous as he fired shot after shot with his lasgun. Catmos rested his long rifle on the platform's rail and carefully took aim at a sturdy tyranid with a blotched head. It disappeared from his reticule in a shower of slime.

Below, the lascannons on the tower swivelled on their mounts. Taking his eye from the scope, Catmos searched the sky. He couldn't see any of the flying vermin today. The defence lasers hummed and Catmos realised they were levelling at the ramparts on either side of the gate.

The lascannons opened fire, sweeping from one side to the other. Because no friends were holding those forward walls, any Guardsmen still alive was a helpless victim of the tyranids' paralysing, agonising poisons.

'With me! With me!'

Lieutenant Jepthad was down in the compound with a squad of veteran Guardsmen. They took a stand between the tyranids leaping down from the ramparts and the single-minded mortar crews still clustered in the centre, firing salvo after salvo aimed just outside the gates. Shoulder to shoulder, the Guardsmen didn't flinch, steadily pouring las-fire into the chittering, flailing beasts. The compound paving was littered with broken chitin and slick with ichor spewed by dying tyranids.

The gates abruptly disintegrated in a cloud of black dust. No explosion, it was a sigh of defeat. The deadly pall swept into the compound and Guardsmen caught up in it collapsed, choking, unable to even gasp a last curse.

As the dust settled, a new horror stood in the entrance. One clawed hand held a monstrous sword of blackened bone. The other brandished an obscene lash, whips of living muscle twisting around each other, tipped with razor talons.

Biniam swore.

Was it the same tyranid warrior as yesterday? Catmos couldn't tell and it really didn't matter. He found it with his scope and saw murderous purpose lighting the amber eyes beneath the fanned chitin plates protecting the creature's head.

He recalled the commissar's words. The big ones know what they're doing. Thirzat was shouting something else now but Catmos couldn't make it out over the din of battle.

The tyranid warrior brandished its sword and threw back its head, shrieking. Every creature in the compound answered with a cry of bloodlust. The sound went beyond simple hearing, lacerating every Guardsman's resolve. The tyranids resumed their attack, even more deadly than before.

Biniam's voice shook. 'Kill the big ones, the commissar's saying.'

He had the weapon to do that and crucially he had the skills. Catmos concentrated and drew a long breath. Exhaling till his lungs were empty, counting his pulse to fire between heartbeats, he gently squeezed the trigger. He missed. Of course. The breeze.

'How far off?' Biniam demanded.

'No idea,' Catmos spat. Pain in his shoulder from the weapon's vicious recoil was nothing to the lash of failure.

'I'll spot for you.' Biniam snatched up his magnoculars.

Catmos shot a second bolt.

'Three marks off to the top-right,' Biniam advised. 'Wait! No shot!'

Through his scope's narrow view, Catmos saw Lieutenant Jepthad attacking the tyranid warrior.

The monster brandished its bony sword. The officer dodged the black blade, but was lashed by the living whip. He flung up his arms to defend his face. Merciless loops tightened round his chest, squeezing the life from him, dragging him towards the beast's glistening fangs.

Guardsmen racing forwards to his aid were forced back by a slavering wave of lesser tyranids. The lieutenant wasn't struggling in the whip's coils now. Arms hanging limp, he was dragged towards the massive creature's lethal talons.

Catmos steadied the long rifle. His whole universe was the view through the scope. One bolt would release Jepthad to a merciful death and still kill the monstrous warrior.

He frowned. He could see Jepthad's face. The officer's eyes were alert. The creature stooped, dagger-toothed mouth gaping, reptilian tongue tasting the air. Jepthad's hands were still free. Captain

Slaithe's power claw crackled with blue lightning. With a convulsive effort, Jepthad brought up his arm and drove the coruscating blades deep down the tyranid's throat.

The monster died with a screech of agony that sent a shiver of uncertainty through every single tyranid. Guardsmen still fighting in the compound seized their chance and took every shot they could.

But Catmos saw a new horror. The habitents covering the pits of the dead were heaving. Serpentine tyranids ripped through the fabric with twin pairs of rending claws. Scattering rotting limbs and heads, they undulated across the paving. As the Guardsmen ran to attack, the creatures reared up on a thick twist of their muscular tails or used the pincered end to murderous effect. One man lost a foot, his boot cut clean through.

Catmos spared a moment to wonder if that's what the lictor had learned, when it had devoured poor Talwhit's brain. This new way to get inside their defences, which it shared with the Hive Mind that spawned it.

The wriggling tyranids fanned out across the compound, some heading for the mortar crews now standing back to back, some attacking the Guardsmen still desperately trying to reach Lieutenant Jepthad, half-crushed beneath the fallen monster. Others writhed towards the steps that would take them down to the basement and the wounded lying there.

Catmos recognised a voice shouting defiance down below. A Guardsman planted himself solidly in the tyranids' path. It was Otharen, rallying as many men as he could, his lasgun firing steadily. As long as he was standing, the wounded would be defended.

Surely that was Nyal beside him? It was hard to tell, with every man in armour and helmet, but the tilt of his shoulders was familiar.

The young Guardsman ran forwards, dodging the slashing talons of a ravening tyranid. Firing his lasgun one-handed momentarily kept the foe at bay. He had a tube-charge in his other hand. Letting his lasgun hang loose on its sling for an instant, he twisted the tube's cap and threw the explosive hard into one of the pits. Corpses and tyranids alike were blown to pieces.

But Nyal didn't retreat. Cutting the tyranid still menacing him down with a final lasgun shot, he twisted the cap of a second tube-charge.

Catmos's heart pounded, his pulse counting off the seconds of the fuse. Then Nyal stooped and threw it, long and low, aimed right into the far end of the pit. This time the explosion was muffled, the compound paving buckling and then sagging as the tyranid tunnel was destroyed. Catmos allowed himself a breath of hope. Until he realised a second tyranid warrior stood in the ruined gateway.

Raising a massive weapon in its middle claws, it fired a metallic stream of crystals at a lascannon. The weapon exploded in a deluge of sparks. Its crew fell backwards screaming, shining acid stripping flesh from their hands and faces, eating away bone beneath.

Thirzat led a squad down the tower steps, his power sword levelled straight at the creature. The men charged towards the warrior. Otharen and the mortar crews followed, lasguns blazing. Lesser creatures invading the entrance died in droves.

No, Catmos decided. The tale of this day's heroics belonged to Jepthad, even if no one lived to tell it. He rested his rifle on the rail, focussed through the scope and carefully judged the breeze. This time his first shot sent a deuterium bolt through the warrior's eye.

He reached into his pocket for the deadly hypostick. 'Pruscyan. Enough for two.'

'Keep it for another day.' Biniam's magnoculars tilted upwards.

Down in the compound, the tyranid incursion had lost its deadly purpose. Commissar Thirzat was rallying the surviving Guardsmen to secure the gate. Bolter crews on the bastions were holding their own. The tower's lascannons angled downwards, blasting open the tyranid tunnels to reveal countless twisted corpses.

The breeze shifted and Catmos smelled the scorch of ozone. He looked up to see pinpricks of light piercing the cloudless blue as thrusters fired. Drop-pods screamed through the fragrant air. As the Guardsmen holding the compound began cheering, the Praetors of Orpheus landed on all sides beyond the walls. Tyranids scattered in every direction. None was fast enough to escape the righteous fury of the Space Marines and their murderously accurate fire.

PROMETHEUS REQUIEM
Nick Kyme

THE HANGAR GAPED like an open wound in the side of the ship, festering with rust and warp corrosion. It belonged to the *Glorion*, an ancient vessel from the long-dead KappFrontier Wars and was just one in a conglomeration of almost a hundred. Ruined cathedra mashed together in the violent act of joining, jutted alongside broken spires, shattered domes and the cleaved remains of many-tiered decks. The union of once-disparate vessels was as incongruous as the product of their fusion. Now a single drifting mass, such abominations were commonly referred to as 'hulks'.

The *Implacable* was an insect compared to this behemoth and its landing stanchions touched down on an area of deck plating capable of harbouring an entire fleet of gunships. Ten armoured figures stepped out from the embarkation ramp. They moved slowly. Not because of the massive Terminator suits they were wearing or because of the inertia of the zero-G, nor was it because their boots were mag-locked to the deck plating. They were wary. Hulks had ever been the province of alien creatures, hiding in the dark forgotten recesses, stirring from a deep-space slumber. But it was more than that. This amalgam, its many-hulled body ravaged by claw marks, colonised by strange bacterial growths and seared by solar wind, had been to the Eye. Spat from the warp like a birth mother expelling its nascent spawn, it had emerged back into the realm of real-space after almost a century's absence.

'I can smell the reek of the warp.' Praetor's voice came through the comm-feed in Tsu'gan's helmet. Though he couldn't see his face, Tsu'gan could tell his sergeant was scowling.

More than smell alone, the hangar walls bore visual evidence of the hulk's taint. In the glare from the halo-lamps spearing out of his armour, Tsu'gan picked out traceries of void-frozen veins and oddly shaped protuberances. Gaps in the bizarre growths resembled mouths, flash-frozen in distended hunger. The aberrations stained every vertical surface and ended in slurries of fossilised biomass that collected against the edges of the deck.

'Flamer.' Praetor's order was clipped, undercut by barely checked disgust.

Brother Kohlogh stepped out of formation and doused the wall in purifying fire. Like a match held to a stack of oiled timber, the flames raced across the tainted mass, devouring it to the eerie report of sibilant howling, just discernible above the heavy weapon's roar.

Tsu'gan watched Emek make the sign of Vulkan's hammer across his breast. None of the Firedrakes did it, but then the Apothecary was not one of them and more superstitious than most. He caught Tsu'gan's gaze briefly, held it, then looked away as Praetor drove them on. It was obvious he wanted to be off this ship as soon as possible. He had good reason.

The empyrean was a shadow realm, a world overlaid on reality like a dirty film of plastek. Fell creatures swam its tides, given form by fear, envy and a desire for power. They were parasites that preyed on the weaknesses of man. An old word gave them substance. *Daemons* they were called. No ship, hulk or otherwise, that had plied the warp could ever be wholly untouched by the experience. Daemons and their influence had a way of lingering...

'Makes your skin crawl, eh, little-wyrm?' asked Hrydor over a closed channel.

Tsu'gan's jaw clenched and he bit back his anger.

'Address me as Tsu'gan or brother,' he hissed.

Hrydor laughed loudly for everyone to hear. A giant, even amongst Terminators, he carried their squad's heavy weapon, a brutal assault cannon etched with kill-scars.

Praetor sent a crackle of energy up the haft of his thunder hammer to better survey the darkness. It also lit the green of his battle plate and deepened the shadows in the folds of his drakescale cloak.

'Keep it down, brother,' he said.

Hrydor nodded but wasn't done.

'Stay eager, little-wyrm. You and I shall fight together very soon.'

The magma lakes below Mount Deathfire on Nocturne were cooler than Tsu'gan's ire at that moment.

Aside from the tainted growths, the hangar was empty.

'How far to the *Proteus*?' asked Praetor.

'She's close. I can feel her.'

A flashing rune on Tsu'gan's retinal display identified the speaker.

Brother-sergeant Nu'mean. His impatience, uncharacteristic of a Salamander, was obvious even in his implacable Terminator suit.

Praetor turned, shifting his bulk.

'Are you a Librarian now, brother?'

'I am a Firedrake.' Nu'mean answered curtly. Not as deep-voiced as Praetor, but with an edge that could cut ceramite. 'And I know my own ship. She is near.' He stomped ahead as the already-freezing temperature dropped further.

'Emek,' Praetor ignored his fellow sergeant for now, 'how far?'

Unlike his predecessor who'd been all thin-faced cynicism, Emek was optimistic and curious.

After you've pulled a few more gene-seeds from your dead and dying brethren, your mood will change, brother, thought Tsu'gan, his voice bitter even inside his head.

Emek was consulting an auspex array built into the gauntlet of his smaller power armour. 'Based on ship schematics, approximately five hours through the *Glorion's* tertiary decks until we reach fusion-point and the *Protean's* aft section.' He looked up from his calculations. 'That's dependent on a straight route through the vessel – no encounters, clear terrain and re-establishing gravity.'

'Soon as we locate an active console you can set to work on that third condition, brother,' said Praetor. 'The other two we'll deal with as necessary.'

Every Terminator had a chainfist on his left hand, invaluable when exploring hulks where bulkheads and debris could make progress difficult. That was for condition two.

'Thermal scans from the *Implacable* suggest resistance will be light. The xenos are still largely dormant.'

Storm bolters, an assault cannon and the heavy flamer in Nu'mean's squad dealt with condition one.

'Then let us hope that remains the case.' Praetor's attention switched back to Nu'mean, who'd taken up an advanced position with his squad. For the moment Praetor was in command, but soon as they reached the *Protean* the other sergeant would take over. It had been agreed. Nu'mean had his atonement and would bear the responsibility of it alone. It was the Promethean way. 'You are certain he's here?'

'I know it in my blood.' There was a growl to Nu'mean's voice. 'He is here, still inside the ship.'

'A century drifting the warp tides, he might not have survived.' Praetor's normally booming voice softened. 'We may be searching for a corpse, brother... or something worse.'

Nu'mean let the words hang in the air then stared beyond Praetor, his gaze alighting on Emek.

'He is alive, held in cryo-stasis just as I left him.' He paused, about to add something. The hard veneer almost cracked when he turned away again.

Praetor gave a final glance to Emek, flanked by two green bulwarks of armoured ceramite – they were two of Nu'mean's squad, Mercurion and Gun'dar. Power armour was formidable protection on most battlefields, but this drifting space hulk was no ordinary battlefield.

'Keep him safe.' Praetor didn't bother to hide it in a closed channel. The Apothecary knew the risks. Praetor glared again at Nu'mean.

Subtlety was not a trait that Herculon Praetor held in any great regard. The mission was still his for the moment. His voice was thunderous and commanding as he took the lead, *'Firedrakes, advance on me.'*

THE MUZZLE FLARE from three storm bolters fired in unison lit the grimace on Praetor's face as he threw the xenos off his storm shield. Acidic vital fluids hissed against his armour as he crushed the creature against the wall.

The corridor was tight. Pipes and thick cabling hung from the ruptured ceiling where the genestealers had clawed through. Deck grating, half-corroded by xeno-blood, clanked underfoot. At least the warp taint was no longer present. At least… it was not *visible*. Hard gravity from the *Glorion's* malfunctioning systems kept the Firedrakes grounded. Recently revived air-scrubbers re-oxygenating the deck allowed Praetor to remove his battle-helm. Suspensor readings in retinal displays showed maximum lift capacity. Manoeuvring was tough. Tsu'gan tasted salt on his lips, his face covered in battle-sweat, secondary heart pumping to cope with the additional physical stresses.

The xenos showed no such difficulty.

Two bounded up the short corridor, jostling for position. Three Terminators faced them – Tsu'gan, his sergeant and Vo'kar – two more including the assault cannon were staggered behind them. Though Hrydor's heavy weapon was silent, Invictese's storm bolter barked between the front line's shoulder plates. Nu'mean's squad clustered behind them, guarding the rear.

Tsu'gan sent a burst into the creatures, rupturing the ribcage of the leader and ripping off a limb. The second got close enough to leap, its long muscled legs propelling it easily off the deck plate and into the air. The chainfist embedded in its torso cut its screeching to a strangled mewl and the genestealer's clawing lacked strength and purpose as it raked Tsu'gan's armour.

'Good little-wyrm!' said Hrydor. The flare from the storm bolters lit up the corridor like a tongue of fire. Tsu'gan felt their heat. Three xenos exploded against the fusillade. 'But look, there are more!'

Hrydor gestured with his chainfist. Roughly thirteen xenos corpses lay scattered around the Terminators for no losses or injuries. It was a vanguard, nothing more. The beasts were half slumbering, still not fully out of hibernation. Up ahead, a high-pitched keening presaged another wave.

The genestealers scurrying across the deck were easy kills. They bucked and jerked against the combined fire. Too late, the Firedrakes realised these were just sacrificial. Others – clinging to the ceiling and walls, bodies low to present a smaller target – reached them in force.

Tsu'gan staggered as he took a glancing blow to his battle-helm. The internal display crackled with static for a second then returned. The beasts were fast, much faster than the others. He swept his chainfist around, hoping to connect, but the genestealer had scurried over him and onto his back.

Pain sensors in his suit flared an angry red and Tsu'gan cried out. Flesh hooks from the 'stealer's maw punched against his armour joints, seeking a weakness. He couldn't reach to grab it, so thrust backwards instead. A satisfying crunch of bone resounded when he made contact with the wall. Barely recovered, his enhanced body pumping pain-regressing chemicals into his bloodstream, another sprang at him from its perch on the ceiling. In the darkness, despite his occulobe implant, he only just saw it.

Praetor's thunder hammer shattered it in mid-flight, the electrical discharge shocking the air and illuminating the xenomorph's death scream like a frozen pict-capture.

'Firedrakes, advance!' he boomed, mashing another with a punch of his storm shield.

Staccato bangs of bolter fire told Tsu'gan his brothers were with him as he raked the corridor ahead. Through combined effort, the Firedrakes had almost wiped out the second wave and used the brief respite to gain some ground. A wider corridor section loomed ahead, some kind of maintenance bay with old machinery strewn about like metal carcasses. The extra room allowed Nu'mean's squad to rank up alongside Praetor's.

Praetor raised his fist as they fanned out: three in front, sergeants to the centre with two behind, including heavies. 'Halt here.'

The dying echoes of gunfire faded until a tense silence, undercut by the dulcet movements of the *Glorion's* extant systems, resumed.

'We should proceed,' said Nu'mean, making his impatience obvious.

Praetor nudged one of the 'stealer corpses over. Feeder tendrils lolled from its mouth cavity like ribbed tongues. Before the sergeant went to his comm-feed he noticed a faint light dying in the creature's eyes. It could've just been an illusion, brought about by the intense conditions of the ship. Praetor activated the feed.

'Apothecary?'

'Still here, my lord.'

'The xenos are done,' Nu'mean persisted. 'Why delay?'

'He's been waiting for almost a century, brother – a few more hours won't make any difference,' Praetor countered. 'Besides, they are still here. Waiting.'

It was obvious the other sergeant didn't like it.

Tsu'gan remembered Nu'mean from before when he'd first teleported to Prometheus, the lunar space station and domain of the Firedrakes. The brother-sergeant had been the first to meet him. He had a weathered face with a long scar running down the right side that tugged at his lip and pulled it up into a permanent snarl. The right eye was slightly dimmed, and a small well of black infected the blazing red. A blade of red hair, shaved into an arc, fed across the right hemisphere of his skull. It put Tsu'gan in mind of a streak of flame. Despite the heat of the proving-forge and the gate of fire, the welcome had not been warm. Judging by Nu'mean's present demeanour, the years in-between had not softened him.

Praetor turned his halo-lamps to full glare and aimed them at the corridor section ahead. Ragged hoses hung down like vipers. Somewhere out of sight a steam valve vented. According to Emek, they were maybe an hour from the fusion-point and the *Protean*.

Like his battle-brothers, Tsu'gan followed his sergeant's example. At first, he saw nothing except ravaged metal, broken pipes and cables like spewed intestines rudely lit in harsh magnesium-white. Then something stirred at the edge of the cone of light, creeping slowly along the penumbra.

'In Vulkan's name!' Tsu'gan roared and his battle cry became a chorus with his brothers.

Like limpets attached to the hull of an ancient ship, the genestealers broke off from the walls and fell into a loping run. At the same time the grates in the ceiling crashed down and a steady stream of creatures poured out.

As Tsu'gan swung his storm bolter around, he was reminded of Nocturnean lava-ants mustering from their hive to repel an invader. Except here the lava-ants were larger than a man and their nest was a rotten hulk floating in the depths of space.

Every shell struck a xenos body. Limbs and gore exploded outwards in a series of ghastly blossoms, but the genestealers kept on coming.

'Something drives them!' Tsu'gan snarled, and went to take a back step when he felt a pauldron locked against his, stopping him.

Praetor was beside him, a ceramite rock in the face of the advancing alien tide.

'Only forwards, brother. Resist. Our will is greater.' Then he turned to another Firedrake. 'Hrydor, give us some breathing room.'

Moving from Praetor's right, Hrydor stepped forwards and triggered the assault cannon.

The air was instantly filled with the whine of its spinning barrel, spitting high-velocity shells at a phenomenal rate. Strafing left and right, Hrydor rejoiced loudly, singing litanies of the Promethean Creed as he eviscerated clusters of genestealers starting to clog the corridor.

'Seems we've stirred the nest, brother-sergeant,' he said.

Tsu'gan heard Praetor mutter. 'And I know of only one way to cleanse it... Nu'mean.'

The other sergeant nodded, gesturing to Brother Kohlogh.

'Burn it!' cried Nu'mean, and the Firedrake brought his heavy flamer to bear.

Liquid promethium ignited on contact with the weapon's burner, engulfing the corridor section ahead.

Despite the heat, some of the xenos were still determined to attack.

'Ve'kyt, Mercurion!'

Two more Firedrakes stepped to at Nu'mean's order, exploding the flame-wreathed bodies staggering from the conflagration with precise bolter rounds. In a few more moments, it was done.

The sounds of screaming persisted long after all the genestealers were dead, rendered to ash in the heat of the flamer's irresistible blaze. Smoke palled the air like a death shroud.

'What's that noise?' asked Emek. He'd moved up to the rear rank and no longer needed the comm-feed to be heard.

'Have you ever broiled crustacid or chitin?' asked Hrydor, allowing the barrel on his assault cannon to spin and cool before shutting it down.

The Apothecary shook his head.

'It's air, brother,' Tsu'gan snapped, a little impatient at Emek's apparent naivety, 'escaping from between the joins in the carapace.'

'Well, little-wyrm, it appears there is more to you than wrath and thunder.'

Tsu'gan wanted to smash the front of Hrydor's battle-helm into his face but resisted. Instead, he walked slowly to Praetor who pressed his hand against the wall while two of Nu'mean's squad checked the way ahead was actually now clear.

'Brother-sergeant?'

'Do you know what I feel when I touch the wall of this ship?'

Praetor's eyes were hard like granite. Since joining the Firedrakes, Tsu'gan had seen a different side to the sergeant. On Scoria, fighting against the orks he had been almost ebullient, bombastic. Now, he was dour and withdrawn. N'keln dying on the cusp of victory had changed him, just as Kadai's murder had changed Tsu'gan. Dead captains had a way of doing that to their fellow brothers-in-arms, even those not of the same company.

'I feel *sorrow*.' Praetor frowned. 'Something lives inside this ship, in its every fibre. It is neither Salamander nor genestealer, nor any physical thing I can touch or slay.' The sergeant kept his voice low. 'That bothers me, greatly. Place your hand against the wall, brother, and feel it,' he added, stepping aside.

Tsu'gan's reply was barely a whisper. 'I do not wish to, my lord.'

On their previous mission to the shrine world of Sepulchre IV the Firedrakes had faced an almost invulnerable foe. Fighting it had cost lives; brothers. The weight of that loss, futile as it had been, hung around Praetor's neck as tangibly as the gorget of his armour.

'Very well,' he said. His gaze lingered on Tsu'gan a moment longer before he lumbered away to convene with Nu'mean.

'Pain is everywhere, brother,' he added, his back turned. 'Embrace it in the fires of war or run and let it be your master. I can't make that choice for you.' Then he was gone, leaving Tsu'gan to ponder his wisdom.

THE FUSION-POINT WAS where an old enginarium deck had breached what sensors and ship schematics suggested was the *Protean's* medi-deck. That was good. It meant the cryo-stasis chamber would be close by upon entry. Not so good was the several thousand kilograms of debris preventing a direct burn, hull-to-hull, through to the next vessel.

Such a problem might prove an impasse to common explorators or even fellow Astartes. Terminators had no such issue.

'Heavies guard the rear,' said Praetor, 'Everyone else… cut her open.'

The sound of revving chainfists ground the air before the two squads went to work hewing and sawing.

'Apothecary, stand clear,' he added. 'Don't risk your cargo, brother.'

Emek nodded, checking the vial embedded in his gauntlet. The chemical solution sloshed benignly within.

'If we can locate a blast door or even a sealed bulkhead, I might be able to unlock it from here. It'll make our progress swifter.'

Praetor nodded to the Apothecary before wading in with his thunder hammer.

Emek looked again to the vial. A small injector needle on the end would guarantee delivery of the solution, which was red and faintly luminous. Emek knew little of its origin, but he knew it was potent. Scarcely fifty millilitres resided in a clear armourplas tube the size of the Apothecary's thumb.

So much, resting on so little a thing.

THEY FOUND THE door. It was a disused service hatch in the *Protean's* aft that led to a short maintenance conduit and the ship's medi-deck. Only wide enough for one Terminator at a time, entry was fairly slow. It did give Tsu'gan and the others first in the line a chance to reconnoitre their surroundings, though.

Unlike the *Glorion*, the old Salamander strike cruiser still maintained a flickering power grid. Lume-lamps cut up the dark in trembling flashes, revealing a gloomy interior. Gunmetal was scorched black in places from an old fire, long dead. Soot carpeted the deck underfoot and shifted like a torpid sea every time one of the Firedrakes moved. Ash clung to rafters and crossbeams like grey fungus.

They had emerged into a large, hexagonal room. Five of its sides branched off and terminated in a console, making the room some kind of hub. There were glyphs and icons crafted into the walls. Sigils of the Salamanders – the flame, the serpent and the drake's head – glittered wanly against the Terminators' halo-beams. The light above was hexagonal too and its design echoed outwards concentrically.

Emek was poring over a green-lit console as Tsu'gan approached him.

'Don't wander too far.'

'You worry too much, brother. I can look to my own protection.'

Tsu'gan snorted derisively. 'Did the *Ignean* breed that insolence into you?'

The Apothecary had once been one of Dak'ir's troopers, the one that Tsu'gan referred to as the Ignean. A snarl at the thought of the former sergeant sprang unbidden onto the Firedrake's face.

Emek declined to answer. Even now, engaged with new assignments, there was still acrimony between the battle-brothers from the old tactical squads.

'What are you doing?' Tsu'gan snapped when he realised the Apothecary wouldn't be baited.

'Checking emergency systems are online.'

'And?'

Emek turned. 'Even after a century, everything seems to be working. The cryo-stasis chamber is intact. Ships like the *Protean* were built to last.' He paused, looking Tsu'gan in the eye. 'Does it annoy you that I am privy to elements of this mission that you are not?'

Tsu'gan clenched a fist and the servos in his gauntlet seemed to growl.

'Your curiosity will get you killed one day, brother. Or perhaps worse… perhaps it will dent your optimistic spirit and break you.'

Tsu'gan was walking away when Emek spoke to his back.

'Is that before or after you've burned yourself to ash in the solitorium?'

'What do you know of it?' Tsu'gan stopped, and snapped at the darkness.

'When I took on Fugis's mantle, I took on his notes and data from the Apothecarion too. Your name is mentioned.'

Tsu'gan appeared to stiffen, but then Emek's voice softened. 'There's no shame in grief, but it's dangerous if channelled inwards.'

Tsu'gan didn't turn, though he wanted to. Finding out what Emek knew of his pain addiction would have to wait – something else had caught his attention. 'What do you know of grief?' he muttered instead, and walked over to an archway leading from the room into a wide gallery.

The long chamber was lined with doors on either side. It looked like some kind of isolation ward for patients receiving intensive treatment. The floor was partially tiled, some of the white smeared grey and cracked or chipped away. The doors too, plasteel with a single porthole window, were white. Some carried faded marks that in the half-light looked almost brown or black.

A smell, like ozone and burning meat, made Tsu'gan's nose wrinkle. The dull report of his footfalls thumped in time with his heart. A faint tapping became a chorus to these louder beats, like a finger on glass. Tsu'gan followed it. His auto-senses came back with no threats. Gravity and oxygen were at stable and acceptable levels. All was well on the *Protean*. And yet…

It was coming from one of the doors. An image flashed across the surface of Tsu'gan's memory but discerning it was like grasping mental smoke. His heart quickened. He approached the door, closer with every step. He realised he was reluctant, and chided himself for being a weakling. And yet…

Tsu'gan's retinal display was still reporting zero threats. No heat-traces, no kinetics, no gas or power surges. The long chamber was clean. And yet…

He reached the door, fingers to his chainfist outstretched and probing towards the glass. Tsu'gan was a few centimetres away when the lights flickered and he gazed upwards at the lume-lamps. When he looked back a face regarded him through the porthole. Partially dissolved flesh and sloughed muscle revealed more of a skull than any recognisable human visage. And yet, Tsu'gan knew exactly who it was.

'Ko'tan...' His dead captain glared at him through the glass. Tsu'gan was horrified when he saw bony fingers reaching up to match the position of his own, as if he were staring into some grotesque mirror and not glass at all.

Another smell quashed the stink of burning meat and melta discharge. There was heat and sulphur, the sound of cracking magma and the redolence of smoke. A hazy figure was reflected in the glass behind him.

Red armour the hue of blood, festooned with horns and scale...

Dragon Warrior...

Tsu'gan whirled around as fast as his cumbersome suit allowed, triggering his storm bolter as he let out a roar of anguish.

Praetor parried the gun aside, directing the explosive salvo harmlessly into the ground.

'Brother!' he urged.

Tsu'gan saw only foes. Heat shimmered off the Dragon Warrior's armour, hazing his outline. These were the renegades who had killed Ko'tan Kadai. How they came to be upon this ship mattered not. All that concerned Tsu'gan was the manner of their deaths at his hands – the bloodier the better. He gave up on the storm bolter and activated his chainfist instead. More were coming. He could hear them, pounding towards him across the deck. He had to finish this quickly.

Praetor braced the chainteeth against his shield. Sparks cascaded down onto his face as he deflected the blow upwards.

'Brother!' he repeated.

Spat through clenched teeth, it was a declaration of disbelief as much as it was anger.

Tsu'gan pressed the churning blades against the shield, his rage lending him the strength to overpower his enemy. The bastard was grinning – he could see fangs beneath the mouth grille of the Dragon Warrior's battle-helm.

I'll rip them out...

Then the red fog before his eyes faded and Praetor was revealed. A moment's distraction was all that the sergeant needed to land a blow from the thunder hammer's haft against Tsu'gan's chest. A jolt of energy shocked the Firedrake and put him on one knee.

The whine of the chainfist died and Praetor let his hammer fall to his side with it. But then he moved in close, ramming the cleaved edge of his storm shield under Tsu'gan's chin and bringing him to his feet.

'Are you with us?' Praetor asked.

Tsu'gan's tongue was paralysed. The world around him was only just making sense again. The others were looking on, weapons primed.

Praetor pressed the shield up harder, lifting Tsu'gan's head. 'Are you with us?'

'Yes…' It was a rasp, but the sergeant heard and believed it.

Nu'mean was not so quick to stand down. He levelled his storm bolter.

'It's finished,' Praetor told him, stepping into the other sergeant's firing line.

'The warp–'

'Infests this ship, this entire hulk, Nu'mean. It's done.' Praetor ushered Tsu'gan away to be cursorily examined by Emek. A side glance at Hrydor told the Firedrake to go with him and keep watch.

Nu'mean lowered his weapon.

'How can you be sure?' he asked, when Tsu'gan had moved away.

Praetor leaned in close.

'Because I saw things too,' he whispered. 'This floating wreck is alive with the sentience of the warp. Something is channelling it, into our minds. Tsu'gan was taken off guard, that's all.'

Nu'mean fashioned a snarl. 'He is weak, and not to be trusted.'

'He passed through the gate of fire and endured the proving-forge – he is one of us!' Praetor asserted. 'Can you say this mission, this ship, has not influenced your behaviour in some way? I have seen it plainly but will you admit it, Nu'mean?'

Nu'mean didn't answer him. He eyed Tsu'gan as their Apothecary conducted a bio-scan instead. By now the other Firedrakes were securing the chamber, checking each of the cells in turn and the hub annexe. 'You made a mistake with that one, brother.'

'There was no mistake. Guilt masters him for now. Know this: his destiny is with the Firedrakes. I won't abandon him–'

Nu'mean spat back with anger. 'As I abandoned others, is that what you are driving at, brother?'

Praetor moved in close. 'Get a hold of yourself, or I shall assume command of this mission. Are we clear on that, sergeant?'

Though he simmered with rage, Nu'mean conceded and gave the slightest nod before stalking away.

Praetor let him go, using the few seconds to gird his own emotions. He looked back at the portholes that lined the infirmary and his ire bled away, replaced by regret.

'I won't abandon him,' he repeated solemnly to himself.

There were faces staring at him from the portholes that only he could see. Gathimu and Ankar, slain on Sepulchre IV; Namor and Clyten, killed on Scoria, and a dozen others whose names blended into memory but were still his charges.

'We've already lost so many.'

'It is nothing, little-wyrm…' Hrydor was at Tsu'gan's shoulder as Emek examined him for injury. After releasing the pressure clasps, the Apothecary then carefully removed Tsu'gan's helmet. Immediately, the unfiltered atmosphere washed in. Despite the years, the air still stank of ammonia and counterseptic. The sanitised aroma made Tsu'gan's skin itch and he found himself yearning for the touch of fire. But there was no rod, no brander-priest's iron to slake his masochistic urge.

'What is "nothing"? Speak plainly, brother. You sound like a Dark Angel,' Tsu'gan shot back venomously.

'Hold still,' said Emek, seizing Tsu'gan's chin and shining a light in his eyes. They burned suddenly brighter. He reviewed the readings on his bio-scanner, logging the data for later analysis.

'I am myself.' Tsu'gan glared at the Apothecary, daring him to arrive at any other conclusion. The memory of Kadai's face still lingered like an old dream in his subconscious though, and he wondered what had triggered it.

'Physically, I can discern no adverse effects. Mentally, I cannot–'

'Then release me.' Tsu'gan jerked his chin away and took back his helmet.

Emek left with a parting remark. 'Your demeanour certainly remains as *amenable* as usual.'

'Are you sure you're a warrior, Emek?' Tsu'gan sneered, before ramming on his battle-helm. The pressure clamps cinched into place automatically as Tsu'gan went to Hrydor. 'Now, explain yourself.'

The other Firedrake didn't look intimidated. If anything, he was pensive. 'The bulk and the strain of the great armour you wear – they are difficult burdens, little-wyrm. It once belonged to Imaan. His aegis is woven into that of the suit.'

'I know that. I was at the ritual. I stood before the proving-forge and crossed the gate of fire. I carry Imaan's icon upon my flesh alongside many other honour scars, given unto me for the deeds I performed in battle. It's the reason I am beside you now. I am Zek Tsu'gan, former brother-sergeant of 3rd Company and now Firedrake. I am not your *little-wyrm*!'

Hrydor looked blankly at his battle-brother for a moment before laughing loudly.

'I can handle the suit and the mission,' Tsu'gan protested, earning a backwards glance from Praetor. It would be a few more minutes until they were done searching and securing the gallery. Then they could move on. Tsu'gan had that long to re-prepare himself. He lowered his tone in response to his sergeant's scowl. 'I saw… *something*. A relic of the past, nothing more. Old ship, old ghosts – that's all it is.'

Hrydor became suddenly serious. 'Perhaps you're right.' His voice took on a brooding tone. 'On Lykaar, before I became a Drake, I fought with the Wolves of Grìmhildr Skanefeld. It was a bitter campaign warred over winter-fall, and the ice upon Lykaar was thick. We Salamanders brought fire to counter the ice; the Wolves brought fury. It was a good match. Greenskins had invaded the planet, making slaves of its people and siphoning from its promethium wells like common pirates.'

Tsu'gan interrupted. 'What's the purpose of all this?' he hissed. 'If you must watch me, then do it in silence and spare us both this doggerel. Allow me to re-consecrate my arms and armour without your endless chatter.'

'Listen and you may just hear the purpose of it, brother.'

Yes, thought Tsu'gan, the Fenrisians have much to account for. They too are fond of overlong sagas.

'We were few,' Hrydor continued, 'but the orks and their stunted cousins had been fighting indentured men with picks and ice-nailers. They were ill prepared to face Astartes. But, there was something we did not know. A creature, a kraken, slumbered under the ice. Our warring disturbed it and brought it forth.' Hrydor's voice darkened. 'It took us by surprise. I was among the first. Before my bolter could speak, the beast seized me, swept me up in its tentacles. A lesser man would've been crushed, but my armour and Emperor-given fortitude saved me. Had Grìmhildr not intervened, casting his rune axe to sever the creature's hold, I doubt I'd have survived. Others on the field that day were not so lucky.'

'A stirring tale, I am sure,' said Tsu'gan, sarcastically, 'but we are ready to depart.'

'As always, you fail to see what is before you, Tsu'gan,' Hrydor replied. 'I see the kraken still. I will it to find me in my solitorium chamber, to face it and conquer it.'

Tsu'gan didn't move, still not understanding.

Hrydor rested a hand on his pauldron. 'Harbouring ghosts doesn't make you unique. All warriors have them, but it is the manner of how we deal with them that defines us as sons of Vulkan.'

Tsu'gan shrugged Hrydor's hand away and went to find Praetor. He was eager to move on. 'Whatever you say, brother.'

Having dispersed around the infirmary, the Firedrakes were forming back into squads and preparing to advance again. Hrydor was about to fall in when he caught a glimpse of something slithering away in his peripheral vision. His auto-senses came back with nothing and when he tried to follow it, the thing, whatever it was, had gone. Only the scent of the ocean, of ice and the deep reek of something ancient and long forgotten, remained.

'It's nothing,' Hrydor said to himself. The ship had begun to affect them all. 'Just an old ghost.'

ACCORDING TO THE ship schemata, following the medi-deck's south-east access conduit would lead them first to an emergency hangar and then to the cryo-stasis chamber. After reviewing the other options in the infirmary, this was determined the most expedient route and therefore sanctioned by Nu'mean as their best method of approach. Though it mattered little to the other sergeant, who'd become increasingly driven ever since they'd boarded the *Protean*, Praetor had concurred with this assessment. He led his squad separately to Nu'mean's, this time taking the rearmost position, whilst the other sergeant had the scent and the lead.

'Steady your pace, brother. The ship is badly damaged and may not stand up to such rigours.' Praetor said through the comm-feed.

Nu'mean replied on the same closed channel. 'It's not *your* conscience, though, is it, Praetor?'

'You'll make less ground if–' A flash of something in the shadows of the access conduit – which was long, narrow and badly lit – made Praetor stop. 'All squads, halt.'

A chorus of clunking feet gave way to the low murmurs of the ship as the Firedrakes stopped.

'What is it? 'Stealers?' Nu'mean sounded irritated.

Praetor's sensors came back empty. If the xenos were present, they were invisible to all mundane methods of perception.

'What's happening here...?' he whispered to himself. He noticed Hrydor eyeing the shadows keenly as well.

'Are we safe to proceed or not? I'm getting nothing on my scanners,' said Nu'mean.

Praetor looked at the Firedrake to his left. 'Tsu'gan?'

Tsu'gan had his eyes fixed forwards. He kept his voice low. 'I can smell burning flesh and ozone.'

Nor any physical thing I can touch or slay. Praetor's own words came back to him. 'Give me the status of the cryo-chamber.'

There was a pause as Emek checked his data.

'Fully functional, my lord.'

'Proceed or not?' Nu'mean didn't bother to mask his impatience.

Praetor hesitated. The sealed doors of the emergency hangar were less than a hundred metres away. Nothing but darkness ahead of them.

Something wasn't right, but what choice did they have?

'Lead on, Nu'mean.'

THE HANGAR WAS massive. Several bays, consisting of antechambers, refuelling stations and maintenance pads, comprised the vast space. The bulk of it, however, was taken up by the landing zone itself, which sat directly under a segmented adamantium-reinforced ceiling. There was evidence of force-shielding too, a last fail-safe to keep out the ravages of realspace when the roof to the chamber was open to the void. Six vessels were in dock, all Thunderhawk variants with stripped-down weapon systems, sacrificed for greater troop capacity. They were arrayed, one per docking pit, in two rows of three, noses angled inwards so the line of the ships crossed at diagonals and pointed towards the approaching Firedrakes.

Unlike the other doors in the *Protean*, Emek had been unable to open the one to the emergency hangar via its external console. They'd had to breach it. The air inside had escaped like a death rattle. Suit sensors revealed it was heavy in carbon dioxide and nitrogen.

The modified gunships were not alone. The dead kept them company.

'This is no gunship hangar, it's a morgue,' said Hrydor, panning his suit lamps into some of the darker recesses.

Skeletons in scraps of uniform – some in fatigues, others wearing what was left of their robes – were clustered against the dust-clogged landing stanchions of the vessels in dock. A few were strewn in the open, rigor mortis having curled their limbs grotesquely. Some carried lasguns and other small arms, or once had. There were other weapons, too, of non-Imperial design.

Nu'mean showed no respect for the dead, ploughing straight into the room, intent on crossing the four hundred metres of the hangar deck to the cryostasis chamber beyond as quickly as possible.

I've waited a century for this.

'Move out. We can do nothing for–' He stopped short when his boots brushed a corpse he had not expected to see.

'Xenos?' Tsu'gan saw it, too, noticed several alien bodies in fact. He recognised the lithe forms and segmented armour of the eldar. They were less badly decomposed than the humans, resembling desiccated corpses rather than fleshless skeletons. The eldar were grey and shrunken, their eyes dark hollows and their hair thin like gossamer. Some wore helmets of a conical design with angled eye slits to match their alien physiognomy.

Emek stooped by one of the bodies. Wiping away a veneer of dust, he found a strange sigil he didn't recognise. 'Some kind of advanced warrior caste? What were they doing here?'

Praetor appraised the scene. 'Fighting against us at first then fighting for their lives. There are claw marks here in this wall, too large and broad for any of these bodies.'

He shared an uneasy glance with Nu'mean.

'There is little time,' the other sergeant muttered in a small voice.

Swathes of diffuse light, scything through the dust-fogged air from above, flickered once and died. The power cut out, plunging the room into sudden and total darkness.

* * *

Tsu'gan felt his massively armoured body start to rise. Gravity, as well as the lights, had failed.

Lances of magnesium-white from their halo-lamps stabbed into the gloom, criss-crossing as the Terminators began to float around. Despite their bulk, they were lifting steadily. So too were the gunships. Untethered in their docking pits, the Thunderhawks rose as if in a slow-motion launch, like heavyweight dirigibles set loose on a skirling wind. Silently they pulled free of their landing stations, the slightest change in the air influencing their laboured trajectory.

Tsu'gan was trying to engage the mag-clamps on his boots but a *system failure* message scrolled across his retinal display in icon-code.

'Mag-locks are down,' he growled to his brothers. The lances of light issuing from his suit flickered intermittently. 'Halo-lamps failing too.' A final burst before the light died completely lit the broadside of a Thunderhawk, groaning towards him like a gunmetal berg.

'Vulkan's anv– *gnnrr!*' He crashed into the side of the vessel and rebounded. The impact was harder than expected, and his body railed against it painfully.

'Steer clear of the gunships. Use your proximity sensors.' Nu'mean's warning came too late for a rueful Tsu'gan.

'Expel gas from your pneumatics for guidance until locking cords are fixed,' he added.

Tsu'gan was already spiralling, waiting until he was more or less upright before evacuating a portion of the gas that fed some of the systems in his suit: oxygen, propulsion, motion – they were all vital to a lesser or greater degree but had a certain level of redundancy that made voiding a small amount of them non-critical.

In a matter of seconds, ghost-like plumes of gas were venting across the chamber as the Firedrakes fought to organise themselves. One of the drifting gunships collided with another of its fleet and the report was deafening. It didn't prevent Tsu'gan from hearing Hrydor cry out, though.

'The beast! I see it! Engaging!' A burst of assault cannon fire shredded the air, lighting up the dark with muzzle flare. It sent Hrydor surging backwards, where he spun and struck one of the chamber walls.

'In Vulkan's name,' he drawled, still groggy from the impact, and triggered the cannon again.

'Cease and desist. Power down – all weapons!' Praetor was floating towards him as fast as he could while staying out of Hrydor's deadly fire arc.

Tsu'gan was close by too and moved to assist. He could hear his sergeant muttering.

'Leave me, brothers. Leave me. You are at Vulkan's side, whose fire beats in my breast...'

He had no idea who Praetor was talking to. The rest of the Firedrakes were dispersed around the chamber. Some were trying to attach locking cords to anything stable. Others were acting... *strangely*. A rash of reports came over the comm-feed in rapid succession.

'...cannot move... my armour... like stone...'

'...systems failing... oxygen tainted...'

'...xenos! 'Stealers in the hold! Permission to engage...'

The last one Tsu'gan recognised as Nu'mean.

'All dead... abandon ship... all hands... dead... my brothers...'

Emek, who Tsu'gan caught a glimpse of in the corner of his eye, was disappearing below, heading for something on the deck but otherwise faring much better than the heavier Terminators. He was also one of the few unaffected by whatever was assailing them.

Then he saw him.

Face a patchwork of scar tissue; eyes crimson-lidded and burning with hate; armour of red and black with scales swathing the battle-plate; horned pauldrons and long vermilion claws upon his gauntlets. There was no mistaking it.

It was Nihilan.

The leader of the Dragon Warriors was here and his thrice-damned warp-craft was afflicting them all. Tsu'gan would cleanse the *Protean* of the renegades. He would end them all.

Nihilan's lips were moving. A voice like cracked parchment resonated inside Tsu'gan's head.

'I fear nothing! Nothing!' he spat back against the accusation only he could hear.

The renegade smiled, baring tiny fangs.

'I'll slay you now, sorcerer...' Tsu'gan sneered, aiming his storm bolter towards his hated enemy.

Tsu'gan stopped dead. His weapon, his gauntlet and vambrace, his entire arm...

'No...'

So wretched was his dismay that he could barely give it voice.

Armour of red and black covered Tsu'gan's body, usurping the familiar Salamander green. Small flecks of dust cascaded through the cracks in the joints as he felt his skin shedding like a serpent's beneath it. The reek of copper filled his nostrils, emanating from his own body. He knew that stink. It haunted his dreams with the promise of blood and prophesied treachery. Tsu'gan's battle-helm was no longer fashioned into the image of drake: it was bare and came to a stub-nosed snout rendered in bone. Skulls hung from bloody chains wrapped around his body.

'Arghh!' His anguish was louder this time as a Thunderhawk floated by, obscuring Nihilan from view for a moment. On its flank a face was impossibly reflected. Tsu'gan beheld his form and saw Gor'ghan there instead, the renegade that had slain his captain. It was he, he was it. Failure. Murderer.

The gunship passed. Nihilan was laughing, standing on the deck below.

Tsu'gan clawed his way to the sorcerer, grasping whatever he could to propel himself, using up the pneumatic pressure in his suit.

A pair of clashing gunships narrowly missed him, but Tsu'gan barely noticed in his determination to reach Nihilan. Around him, his brothers struggled against their own phantoms. Hrydor's belligerent wailing became as white noise. Tsu'gan ignored it all. They didn't matter. A glancing blow struck his pauldron, resonating agony through the suit that he bit down and endured. Only vengeance mattered.

A life for a life. Those were the words he'd used to justify murder.

Tsu'gan came close enough to reach his prey.

Locking hands around the renegade's neck, he squeezed.

'Laugh now, bastard! Laugh now!'

And Nihilan did. He laughed as blood spilled from his mouth, as the veins burst on his forehead, as his neck was slowly crushed.

Emek's voice broke through the veil that had fallen across the chamber and across the Firedrakes.

'Restoring power now. Brace yourselves.'

Gravity returned along with the lights.

The Terminators fell. So too did the gunships like asteroids from the sky.

A piece of Thunderhawk fuselage missed Tsu'gan by less than a metre. Chunks of debris broken off from the gunship's body during the impact rained against his armour, but he weathered it. In his hands, he was holding a corpse. Its neck was crushed and when he loosened his fevered grip, the head fell off.

Tsu'gan let the wretched body of a dead serf go. Disgust became relief as he saw the reassuring green of his battle-plate. The hallucination had passed. He was himself again, although the trauma of it still lingered as if waiting to be rekindled.

'What happened?'

Praetor was releasing his hold on Hrydor, who had also recovered but was shaken by his experiences, when he answered.

'There is something aboard this ship. Something kept quiescent by its systems,' he admitted. 'Like a healthy body rejects foreign invaders, so too does this vessel.'

'How is that possible, brother-sergeant? It's just a ship.'

Nu'mean came up alongside him. The Firedrakes were converging, finding strength in proximity and all wanting to know what the phenomenon was plaguing the corridors of the *Protean*. Mercifully, the Terminators had escaped being crushed to death by the plummeting Thunderhawks.

'A ship that has been to the warp.' He regarded Praetor. 'Its stench is redolent with every rotation of the life support systems. And that is not all.'

The moment was pregnant with anticipation, as if a terrible revelation was at hand. In the end, it was Praetor that broke the silence.

'Seeing will make an explanation easier.'

'Seeing what?' asked Hrydor, his composure returning. So powerful, so mentally invasive had their ordeals been that an ordinary man would be rendered a gibbering wreck. As it was, Space Marines were hewn of sterner material and found their faculties stressed but were otherwise not lastingly affected.

'In the cryo-stasis chamber,' said Nu'mean. 'We go there now. Come on.' He was leading them out across the bay, now trashed with the wreckage of the downed Thunderhawks and littered with small fires, when Emek spoke up.

'Something on the power fluctuation readings is wrong,' he said to no one in particular. The Apothecary was standing before the room's main operational console and had accessed a data stream concerning the recent power outage.

'It wasn't caused by a sporadic energy surge?' asked Praetor.

Emek turned.

'No, my lord. The power from the ship's systems was *diverted* to another section. It looks like it was used to open a previously sealed bulkhead door.'

'Genestealers don't do such things. They nest, confined to whatever area they've colonised. It's not in their nature to explore,' said Nu'mean.

Tsu'gan stepped forwards into the circle that had developed between the two sergeants and the Apothecary. His tone was mildly annoyed.

'Meaning what, exactly?'

Praetor answered without looking at him. His eyes were on the distant blast door and the way ahead to the cryo-stasis chamber.

'It means we are not alone on this ship. Someone else has boarded the *Protean*.'

THE REST OF the journey to the cryo-stasis chamber was conducted in silence. There was no way of knowing who or what else was aboard the *Protean* or their relative location to the Firedrakes. They exercised extreme caution now. Every junction, every alcove was checked and double-checked.

It took them several minutes, through several tracts of closely confined corridors, before they reached the area of the ship designated for cryo-stasis. A four-way junction led up to the chamber. The way behind them, they knew. Turning left and right were another two corridors. According to Emek, the right as the Firedrakes faced it went to a bank of saviour pods. The left went deeper into the *Protean* and a maintenance sub-deck. A short strip of corridor approximately a metre long continued ahead and brought them to the cryo-stasis chamber itself.

The room was heavily locked down. An almost impervious bulkhead door cordoned it off and kept it sealed from idle explorers. Formerly, the *Protean* had been Nu'mean's ship. The brother-sergeant possessed the access codes that would open up the chamber and reveal whatever it was they had ventured this far for, and with an Apothecary in tow.

The bulkhead retracted into the thick corridor walls on either side, slipping into previously unseen recesses that closed themselves off once the procedure was complete.

Cold air, charged with liquid nitrogen mist from inside the chamber, beckoned them closer. The room was not especially large or remarkable. It was square and held twenty banks of clear cylindrical, coffin-like receptacles capable of housing a Space Marine in full armour. This was where crewmembers could go during a long space journey. It was also a place to keep the badly wounded until a space station or dock could be reached which had superior medical facilities to those of the cruiser.

At that moment, as the Firedrakes entered and dispersed around the room, it had but one resident.

'We didn't bring you here to save anyone, Brother Emek,' said Praetor as he stood before the only occupied cryo-tank.

Within, a crystallised frost veneering the glass, was an alien figure. Peaceful, as if in death, its helmet had been removed. The eldar's almond-shaped eyes were closed. Its long angular face was androgynous and oddly symmetrical. It wore robes over segmented armour inscribed with peculiar, alien runes. Hands folded over its chest, it took on the semblance of a bizarre, sleeping child, disturbing and beguiling at the same time.

'No, not a saviour at all,' uttered Emek, regarding the serum within his gauntlet with fresh understanding. 'I am here as an executioner.'

'So now you know,' Nu'mean broke in, unwilling to wait a moment longer. Pipes fed down into the cryo-tank, pumping in the solutions and gases needed to keep the subject in suspended animation. It also had a console, as they all did, which controlled the tank's operation. A small port, ringed invitingly by brass, enabled *additions* to be made to the liquid nitrogen amalgam and the fluids that kept the occupant of the tank alive.

Praetor put his hand on Nu'mean's shoulder.

'Prepare him for what must be done. We will guard the entrance. If these interlopers are close...' He let the implication hang in the air for a moment, before ordering the other Firedrakes out, leaving Emek and Nu'mean alone with the frozen xenos.

Tsu'gan retired from the scene reluctantly, eager to know just why this one alien was so important and why they hadn't simply thrust chainfists through the glass and killed it without all the needless ceremony.

'Death to the alien,' he spat under his breath as he was leaving.

'The nerve agent will render the creature brain-dead,' Nu'mean explained. 'It is virulent and fast acting but must be applied through the brass receptor port.' He gestured to the ring on the console.

'I had thought my mission here was to revivify one of our lost brothers,' said Emek, unaware of his impropriety and eyeing the still alien body of the eldar. He knew a little of the race and recognised it as a farseer, some kind of eldar witch. 'Its psychic emanations have been affecting us since we boarded the *Protean*.'

'Yes,' Nu'mean answered calmly, rarely, now at peace with closure so close at hand. 'Warp exposure has bonded him to the ship, for it is a *he*. Praetor felt it, so too did I but didn't voice it. The cryo-process is the only thing keeping the wretch down. Without it, even the slightest breach, we would be exposed to his witchery. I lost over three thousand hands on this ship to capture this creature. Cruel fate threw us into a warpstorm just as his xenos kin fought to free him. I could do nothing for the men and women of this vessel. I lost battle-brothers, too. My order to curtail the evacuation condemned them all.'

Even with all the years now having passed, all those lives... all the ones the Salamanders had sworn to protect, were felt keenly by Nu'mean. A prisoner of war the farseer might no longer be, but he was still an enemy.

Emek's posture hardened noticeably. 'What must we do to kill it?'

Nu'mean began the procedure to open up the receptor port for the vial. He removed his battle-helm to do it, to better see and manipulate the controls.

'It will take only a moment. Prepare the vial,' he said.

Emek ejected it from his gauntlet and engaged the syringe at the end.

'Ready, my lord.'

'Almost there...' Nu'mean began before all power feeding the cryo-chamber cut out completely.

OUTSIDE, THE LIGHTS died.

Praetor was turning, heading back into the chamber when he saw the Apothecary recoil from the cryo-tank, a bolt of arc-lightning ripping him off his feet. It had come from the stasis tank. His cry echoed around the chamber as he spun and lay prone on the ground.

Another lashed out like a whip, ripples of psychic power coursing over the cryo-tank's surface in agitated waves. Nu'mean staggered as the bolt struck him but stayed standing, protected by his Crux Terminatus.

'Get back!' Nu'mean, not wishing to test the limits of his personal ward again, seized Emek by the ankle and proceeded to drag him bodily across the floor.

'Storm bolters!' yelled Praetor.

Tsu'gan stepped inside and unleashed a salvo. The explosive shells stopped a few centimetres from the frozen cryo-vessel, detonating harmlessly in mid-air. The impacts blossomed outwards, as if striking some kind of miniature void field, and dissipated into nothing.

It saved Nu'mean from another bolt of arc-lighting as he almost threw Emek through the doorway and then barrelled out of the chamber himself. The bulkhead slammed shut after him, Praetor on hand to seal it.

At least the doors were still working, evidently controlled by a different part of the vessel's internal power grid.

Even with the chamber sealed, with the power still out, Tsu'gan could feel the hallucinations returning. Though his logical mind told him they were not real, his senses railed against it. They told him he could smell copper, see shadows coalescing into foes in the long corridor ahead of them, taste the bitter tang of sulphur stinging his palate.

'Be strong of mind, brothers,' Praetor told them, even as Nu'mean was attending to Emek.

'He is badly wounded,' he said, all the old guilt and sense of impotence rushing back in a flood.

A large crack parted the Apothecary's plastron. Blood was welling within it. There were scorch marks too, a long gash of jagged black infecting the armour like a wound itself. Part of Emek's helmet was broken away. An eye awash with crimson blinked back tears of blood.

'I am wounded...' he rasped. He tried to look around but found he could not. Vital fluids bubbled in his throat and he could hear the slow rhythm of his secondary heart kicking as it attempted to cope with the trauma.

Tsu'gan looked on and found his anger towards the Apothecary had fled, to be replaced by concern. He was his brother and now, faced with seeing his potential death, realised he had acted ignobly towards the Apothecary. It was not behaviour worthy of a Salamander of Vulkan. Once tied to the Ignean Emek might have been, but he was not the one that Tsu'gan hated.

'He's dying,' he uttered.

Nu'mean ignored him. 'We must restore power to the cryo-chamber,' he told Praetor. 'I won't leave this unfinished.'

Praetor nodded. The Firedrakes were clustering the corridor. They'd set up a defensive perimeter, responding to their conditioned training routines. If there was one thing Salamanders knew how to do, and do well, it was hold ground.

'Stay here,' he said, 'and be ready to move in again on my signal. I have the schemata of the ship. I'll take my squad and find the central power room.' He glowered meaningfully. 'Then I'll find whoever shut it off and do the same to them. Bloodily.'

'In Vulkan's name, brother,' said Nu'mean as they departed.

'We'll need his will in this,' was Praetor's response as he clanked away down the corridor. A short distance, and a junction led them away from the medical deck and deeper into the *Protean's* cold heart.

TSU'GAN SCANNED THE shadows warily. This part of the *Protean* was largely untouched and possessed an eerie quality, as if all life in its empty corridors had simply ceased. No struggle, no damage, just *absence*.

'I'm detecting no signs of 'stealer habitation,' reported Brother Vo'kar. He partnered Tsu'gan as they advanced towards the central power room under Praetor's instruction.

'Keep a wary eye,' the sergeant advised. Behind them, Hrydor swept the darkness with his assault cannon. The last member of the squad, Brother Invictese, was a half-pace ahead of him. 'It's not the xenos we face here,' Praetor concluded.

Distance from the cryo-chamber helped. The mission chrono told the Firedrakes they had left Nu'mean's squad exactly thirty-three minutes ago. Tsu'gan estimated with some accuracy that they had travelled several hundred metres in that time. But despite the distance, he still felt the same old feelings from before tugging at his resolve.

A shadow darted ahead of them but before he had aimed his storm bolter it disappeared seemingly into smoke. Copper was heavy on the recycled air. Psychic fabrication or real, Tsu'gan had no way of telling. He saw Praetor eyeing the dark, too, finding apparitions in the deepest alcoves before deliberately looking away.

Hrydor's heart rate and respiratory functions relayed on Tsu'gan's tactical display were elevated.

Praetor had seen them too.

'Gird yourselves, brothers.' He didn't single any one of them out, but Tsu'gan knew to whom he was really speaking. 'Our minds are our enemies. Rely on your instincts. Use your mental conditioning routines to find balance. We were born in Vulkan's forge. We all crossed the gate of fire and were tested before the proving-forge. Our mettle is unbendable, as Firedrakes it must be so. Remember that.'

A series of solemn affirmations answered the brother-sergeant but all felt the uneasiness in the atmosphere, like a serpent crawling beneath the skin. Hrydor gave his last of all.

So far, they had encountered no resistance. According to the schemata, the central power room was not much further.

But, even as his halo-lamps strafed the dark, Tsu'gan couldn't assuage the uneasy feeling in his gut.

AT THE BULKHEAD door to the cryo-chamber, Nu'mean waited impatiently.

Emek was slumped against the back wall, still bleeding. He was conscious but not entirely lucid. He'd used whatever medical unguents and salves he had in his narthecium kit to do what he could. His brothers, under his faltering instruction, had done their best to aid him. He was in Vulkan's hands now. Either he would endure the anvil and emerge reforged or he would break against it. In any event, Nu'mean had taken the vial in its brass partial outer casing and mag-locked it to his vambrace. Though small, the device was not so delicate that he couldn't apply the serum himself. It would be difficult and better handled by an Apothecary but that option was no longer viable.

'Sergeant Nu'mean.' The comm-feed address came from further up the long corridor, where Brothers

Mercurion and Gun'dar guarded the junction Praetor and his squad had taken to reach the central power room.

'Report, brother.'

'Contacts on my scanners. Closing quickly.'

Nu'mean went to his own bio-scanner, one of the concomitant systems of his Terminator armour.

Several heat traces, distant but very real, were approaching. He deduced their origin from a section of the ship that had previously been sealed.

'Maintain defensive cordon,' he said to Brothers Kohlogh and Ve'kyt beside him.

'Hold position. Fall back only on my order,' he told the advance line.

Something is wrong, he thought. With the farseer active, he had expected to be assailed with visions and mental tortures by now. He had expected the screams of the dying, to witness the burning faces of the thousands he had condemned to death. But there was nothing, just the nagging sense of something out of kilter.

'Hold position,' he repeated and felt his unease growing.

HRYDOR WHISPERED SOMETHING, but not loud enough for Tsu'gan to hear. The Terminators moved in close formation through the final few corridors like the Romani legionnaire formations of old, some of Terra's battle teachings having permeated Nocturnean culture. Only Hrydor was lagging at the rear.

Several junctions went by, each leading off into another area of the ship, each a darkened recess that needed to be scanned and checked before they could proceed.

Tsu'gan was about to send Praetor a sub-vocal warning about his troubled battle-brother when a moment of revelation struck him. The nagging at the back of his skull, the itch he felt upon his neck and shoulders, the invisible tension that charged the air, he knew it. He'd felt it before. Watchers. Watchers in the shadows.

Something scuttled almost imperceptibly through the darkness. Tsu'gan got the impression that the shadows and it were one, blended as night on top of night.

The figures he'd dismissed earlier were not hallucinations – they were real. Nor had Praetor witnessed and refuted apparitions in the gloom but something very tangible and very dangerous; dangerous enough to foul the Salamanders' auto-senses.

Tsu'gan's warning came too late as something else set its influence against them and fell hardest on Hrydor.

'I see it!' he cried out, breaking squad coherency and clanking off back the way they'd come. 'Grimhildr...' he waved the imaginary Space Wolf over his shoulder in a bid to follow, 'the kraken... Bring your axe and bond-brothers. I have it in my sights!'

How long poor Hrydor had been quietly under the farseer's influence, they'd never know.

Praetor turned and saw him disappearing down one of the other junctions into an unknown part of the ship. 'Brother!' he called, but Hrydor was lost to his own version of reality.

Assault cannon fire echoed back to them loudly as he engaged the imaginary beast of the deeps.

Praetor was already moving. 'After him.'

'Where is he going?' asked Tsu'gan.

'To his death, if this continues. We are not alone here.'

Tsu'gan nodded and followed his sergeant.

The junction Hrydor had chosen led to a long corridor. He was still visible as the others reached it, firing bursts from his assault cannon before stomping ahead again.

'I can clip him, maybe take a piston out in his leg.' Tsu'gan was already taking aim. 'It will slow him'.

Praetor shook his head.

The scuttling sound returned. They all heard it this time, as well as a high-pitched keening as if issued by a flock of mechanised birds.

'Name of Vulkan…' The sergeant scowled, trying to track the source of the raucous noise as a bulkhead door slammed down to impede them. They lost sight of Hrydor, though Tsu'gan swore he noticed the shadows closing in on him just before they did, as if detaching from the very walls.

'Hold the junction,' Praetor told Invictese and Vo'kar. They assumed defensive firing positions at once. He turned to Tsu'gan. 'Get it down, now!'

Tsu'gan plunged his chainfist into the metal and cascading sparks lit the corridor.

It took several minutes to tear through the bulkhead.

Tsu'gan was the first to see to the other side.

'Gone,' he snarled, but then detected blood traces on the grated floor. The corridor had a vaulted ceiling, littered with pipes and narrow vertical ducts. Chains hanging down from the gloom jangled faintly. Praetor and Tsu'gan pulled at the gap in the bulkhead with their hands until it was wide enough to traverse. More precious seconds were lost.

Hurrying now, Praetor and Tsu'gan cleared the corridor in another two minutes. Leaving the others behind and rounding a tight corner, they found Hrydor's body.

THE XENOS WERE coming fast, dozens and dozens of them.

The long corridor afforded a decent fire point for Nu'mean's squad and the ceiling was solid enough that they didn't have to worry about ambuscade from above.

If the genestealers came from the *Protean's* aft they could hold them off.

A few metres from the cryo-chamber's door was the cross-junction bleeding left and right. Nu'mean had positioned himself, Emek and the other two Firedrakes in his squad here.

To the left was the chamber housing the bank of saviour pods. An incursion from that direction was unlikely. But if the xenos came from the right-hand corridor at the same time as the aft-facing one, the fight would likely be a lot shorter. Already, he could hear them: chittering, scuttling, loping. It would not be long.

Approximately fifty metres separated them and Brothers Mercurion and Gun'dar at the next junction. Another hundred or so and the long corridor terminated in a patch of darkness their halo-lamps were too far away to penetrate.

'Wait until you have a target then lay suppressing fire to slow their ranks.' Nu'mean ordered down the comm-feed. 'Let's see if we can clog the way ahead with xenos corpses, brothers.'

A belligerent 'affirmative' delivered in synch told him he'd been heard and that the Firedrakes were making their final oaths.

The door behind him, where his prey partially slumbered, felt hot against Nu'mean's back.

All of this for vengeance.

Nu'mean crushed his doubt in a clenched fist.

No price is too steep.

'Here they come!' The corridor ahead was suddenly lit by the muzzle flare of crashing storm bolters.

Fleetingly, through the press of bodies and gunfire, Nu'mean saw the rabid xenos exploding. They were relentless. Even at a distance, he noticed a fervent glow in their eyes. It gave the beasts aggression and awareness. Nu'mean realised then why they'd barely felt the farseer's psychic emanations. He was part of the ship and that extended to the denizens aboard. The eldar was channelling his power *through* the 'stealers, animating and guiding them like a substitute Hive Mind.

The bolter fire from Gun'dar and Mercurion lasted another few seconds before they began to fall back. They loosed in sporadic bursts after that, one then the other, overlapping their salvos.

Nu'mean could barely discern whole alien bodies such was the gore and dismemberment wrought by the guns.

'Running low,' said Mercurion.

'Aye, brother.' Gun'dar replied.

Nu'mean started forwards, but discipline took hold and he stopped. He went to the comm-feed instead.

'Fall back. Rejoin the line, brothers.' There was an urgency to the sergeant's tone that suggested he knew what was coming.

Genestealers were everywhere, clambering over the dead, clawing their way over wall, floor and ceiling. Such fury...

'Vulkan's fire beats–' Mercurion began. He was snapping a fresh load in his storm bolter, Gun'dar covering him, when a 'stealer got close enough to tear off half of his helmet and face. Brother Mercurion staggered, sputtering a few more rounds from his storm bolter, before another xenos punched a hole through his chest. A third leapt on his back. Then they engulfed him and a Firedrake was lost to the swarm.

'Rejoin the line! Rejoin the line!' But Nu'mean's imploring was for nothing.

Gun'dar fell moments later. Surrounded, he could not hope to hold out for long. His storm bolter lit up the corridor for another six seconds before it fell silent.

Nu'mean held on to his anger, prevented it from sending him crashing into the onrushing 'stealers to his doom and vainglory.

'Brother Kohlogh...'

The Firedrake took a step forwards to brandish his heavy flamer.

Nu'mean's voice was hollow. 'Burn it.'

HRYDOR HAD BEEN hacked apart. Chain-toothed weapons left scars across his armour. The cuts were heaviest at the weaker joints. His Terminator suit was badly rent and scorch marks suggested close-ranged plasma. Sections of partially dissolved ceramite, which left gaping crevices in Hrydor's sundered flesh, had been made by a melta gun. His assailants had set upon him from all sides and took him apart, piece by piece. Blood painted a grisly scene that glowed a deep, visceral red in the starkness of the halo-lamps.

A solitary figure stood mockingly at the end of the next corridor, poised at the junction. It was clad in archaic power armour, dark like twilight or deeper; it was hard to tell precisely. A battle-helm, morphed into the graven visage of some howling daemon, its crude mouth grille locked in a silent scream, looked stretched, almost avian, as did its clawed feet and gauntlets. Tilting its head on one side, the hideous thing clicked. The motion was strange, slightly syncopated, and its clawed foot grated the metal in time.

Tsu'gan's mouth curled into a snarl behind his helm. 'Raptor...'

Then he barrelled, headlong, down the corridor, storm bolter crashing.

Screeching in bird-like, mechanised monotone, the Raptor leapt into the air, the densely throated thrusters on its back coughing out plumes of smoke and fire to lift it.

Tsu'gan cursed. He missed.

Above them, the chains and pipes clanked noisily. Tsu'gan fired into the darkness of the vaulted ceiling where he thought he'd detected movement.

Cruel laughter, like a vulture's cawing and impossible to pinpoint, greeted his failure. Then came another blast of bird-like screeching, synthesised through a vox-grille mouth.

'Chaos Traitors!' he snarled to Praetor, scything chain links with another salvo and sending them cascading like iron rain onto his armour.

His sergeant's reply was cut off by the bulkhead door slamming down between them. He'd been caught. Tsu'gan spat another curse as several armoured figures, the first Raptor's kin, descended from above on bladed wings. Freefalling, they seemed to melt out of the shadows, and only engaged their jump packs to arrest their flight at the last moment.

Ozone from the melta stink and the reek of blood-laced, oiled chainteeth filled the air. The blades were buzzing already, growling for prey.

'You'll not kill me so easily, hellspawn,' he vowed, trying to shut off the other sensations pressing at the edge of conscious thought, the copper stink, the veil of sulphur...

These foes were real. Night Lords – terror-mongers and cowards, unworthy of the name Astartes, even when they'd been loyal to the Throne.

Raptors were pack-hunters and he had sprung their trap. The blades came in quick. Tsu'gan barely had time to see, let alone defend them.

IT TOOK PRAETOR three blows from his thunder hammer to batter the bulkhead door down and send it screeching from its moorings into the corridor at speed. Like most sons of Vulkan, his strength was prodigious, but even amongst the Fire-born Praetor had a reputation for incredible feats. Brought on by fury and determination, this one ranked amongst the toughest.

The closest Raptor didn't see it coming. Six thousand kilograms of half-metre-thick metal took the renegade down, slamming into its torso and nearly cutting it in two. A death rattle escaped from its skulled faceplate before it died.

Tsu'gan saw the improvised missile in time, twisting aside, but the flying bulkhead still grazed the front of his plastron and left a groove in the ceramite. The rents in his armour from the chainblades were light. The Firedrake took advantage of his assailants' shock, albeit a few seconds in duration, to gut one at close range with a burst of his storm bolter.

Crushing the Raptor's pauldron in his fist, he rammed the muzzle hard into its stomach and pulled the trigger. Tsu'gan was throwing the body aside as another tried to leap into the air to regroup. It got so far, arching its body to draw a bead with its plasma gun, when Tsu'gan reached out and seized its ankle. With barely a portion of his strength, he sent the Traitor smashing to the deck. It slid, claws scratching at the deck for purchase, in front of Praetor. The sergeant severed the creature's head with the edge of his storm shield.

'Feel Vulkan's wrath!' he bellowed, battering another Raptor aside that sprang over to engage him.

Tsu'gan was free of the flock and laid about him with controlled bursts. Warning icons blazed across his retinal display, intense thermal temperature spikes. The melta gunner weaved out of his initial salvo, firing small bursts of its jump pack to stay aloft, before Praetor blindsided it and slammed the Raptor into the wall.

By now, Vo'kar and Invictese had been summoned from the strongpoint and were placing careful blasts into the melee from the end of the corridor.

Like weird, metal dolls, the Raptors jerked and shuddered as they died.

Facing almost a full Terminator squad, they couldn't hope to win.

What had begun as a cynical ambush had turned into a bitter and desperate defeat before the might of the Firedrakes.

Barely four of the Traitors remained. The Salamanders were in the ascendancy. Two, blazing contrails from their jump packs, made for the vaulted roof. Combined storm bolter fire – so concentrated, so close – shredded their armour like tin.

A third lashed out at Praetor, but the chainblade it wielded ran afoul of the sergeant's sturdy armour. Broken metal teeth rattled the deck, followed swiftly by the Raptor's sundered corpse.

Tsu'gan came face-to-face with the lone survivor, their leader and the one who wore the daemon's distended face. It angled its head, fibre bundle cabling at its neck sparked as its body spasmed. Then the wretched, avian creature screeched at him. The goad forced Tsu'gan to swing – he wanted to feel its flesh and bone churning against his chainfist – but the Raptor leader had banked on this and avoided the blow, snatching up the fallen melta gun instead.

It looked like it was about to turn the weapon against the Firedrake before the creature boosted its jump jets and soared into the vaulted ceiling, burning through metal sheeting as it went, fashioning an escape route. Tsu'gan's bulk blocked a clear shot for the others and storm bolter rounds tore up the pipes above harmlessly before the Firedrakes were alone again.

'Night Lords,' spat Tsu'gan. 'Craven whelps and molesters. What are they doing aboard the *Protean*?'

Praetor couldn't answer. He was listening to the comm-feed.

'Nu'mean is in trouble,' he said when he was done. 'The Traitors will have to wait–'

Tsu'gan bristled. 'Hrydor's vengeance!'

'Will have to wait,' Praetor repeated firmly. 'Our brothers, those who yet live and breathe, need us to breach the central power room now.'

They were about to retrace their steps when an explosion, loud enough to resonate through Tsu'gan's armour, rocked the corridor. Metal debris fell in thick chunks. Dust and fire billowed out ahead of them in a blackened plume.

Praetor glared through the smoke and carnage, filtering out the interference from the explosion's aftermath. He muttered something. The rest of the squad had assumed battle positions, expecting another ambush. The sergeant consulted the scanner of his retinal display. He did this several times before he swore, an old Nocturnean curse.

'Brother-sergeant?' asked Vo'kar.

'Our way back is closed.'

'Lord?'

Praetor rounded on him, his fury affecting the burning embers in his eyes and setting them ablaze.

'We cannot proceed, brother! The Traitors have collapsed it. And unless we find another route to the central power chamber, Nu'mean and his squad are dead!'

THE RESPITE WOULD not last. The cleansing fire of Brother Kohlogh's heavy flamer had done its work well. Ashen genestealer bodies littered the corridor ahead, but more were coming, many more.

Nu'mean had his ear to the comm-feed, listening to Praetor's grim report. The conversation ran in several one-sided bursts.

'I understand, brother.'

'Do not attempt it. Cutting through will take too long.'

'Another route? There is none that will get you here fast enough.'

'You must. I can get Brother Emek off the hulk. His life is the only one you can save now.'

'In Vulkan's name,' he echoed the last transmission under his breath after he'd cut the feed.

He consulted the bio-scanner on his retinal display, looked at the lethal vial of toxin mag-locked to his armour. His enemy was within metres. He should be able to kill it. In any other circumstance, a sergeant of the Firedrakes should have been able to kill it.

The noises from the gloom ahead were getting louder.

It would be soon.

Act!

Nu'mean addressed Brother Ve'kyt. 'Get the Apothecary to the saviour pods. Ensure he is on his way and return here to the line. I will need you and Brother Kohlogh before the end.'

It was a risk. Putting Emek in one of the pods, which was not guaranteed to function, nor was his rescue once adrift in the void of space assured. And with his injuries… This was the only choice. Nu'mean knew what was expected.

Ve'kyt had gone, taking the groggy, half-comatose Apothecary with him.

Nu'mean rested his gauntlet on Kohlogh's shoulder plate.

'None shall pass, brother.'

Kohlogh nodded. The 'stealers sounded closer than ever. Vague shapes could be seen in the darkness ahead.

Nu'mean turned and approached the bulkhead door. The activation codes were on his lips.

'Seal it behind me,' he said quietly. 'Do not open it again. Whatever happens.'

'In Vulkan's name,' Kohlogh intoned.

'Aye for Vulkan...' Nu'mean answered, the chittering of the approaching beasts rising to a crescendo as he opened the door and entered the cryo-chamber.

HE WAS BARELY across the threshold, the door sealing shut behind him, when the arc-lightning struck. It was a dull pain at first, intensifying into something much more invasive and burning as Nu'mean took each agonising step.

His Crux Terminatus gave him some protection, but it was his Salamander tenacity that kept him moving across the fog-shrouded floor.

Like white-hot fingers running across his armour, the psychic lightning probed for flesh and for weakness. Slowly, the joints in Nu'mean's once-impervious suit were eased apart.

Above the crack of energy, he heard the battle outside. Bolter fire and flamer bursts mingled with the war cries of his brothers and the shrieking of the xenos. It was a fitting requiem to their last stand in this hellish place. This was not the ship of his memory. This abomination was the *Protean* no longer. Only wraiths lingered here, best forgotten. Nu'mean had learned that too late but now he would at least finish his mission.

Merely steps away from the cryo-tank, he saw the farseer slumbering, as serene as he had ever been. To look upon the alien, one would not know of the turmoil in his mind as he fought the invader that sought to kill him.

But kill you I will, Nu'mean vowed.

The horrors and cerebral tortures returned when the psychic lightning failed. Faces, rotten and withered by decay, glared at him with accusing eyes. Suddenly, there were hundreds, clogging the path to the cryo-tank, their zombified talons clawing at the Firedrake sergeant. Serfs and crewmen, brander-priests and even fellow Space Marines held Nu'mean at bay with their anger and his guilt.

Nu'mean gritted his teeth. The pain in his body was incredible, like his nerve-endings were being stripped and immolated, one by one. He couldn't see through the throng but felt the console. It was still primed for the lethal serum's delivery.

The farseer redoubled his efforts, sending wave after wave of arc-lighting cracking into the Salamander.

Nu'mean screamed with every blast, the flesh peeling from his bones. His gauntlets were on fire but he saw his purpose clear enough through the bloody haze.

'I am your death…' he rasped, and slammed the vial into the receptor ring. The toxin emptied quickly, feeding into the mechanism like an eager parasite. At once, the farseer convulsed. The tremors looked incongruous when matched against the calmness of his expression. In a few seconds he became still.

The battle beyond the door had fallen silent long ago. The genestealers couldn't get through, reduced to scratching the dense plating with their claws until they became bored and moved on.

Nu'mean was fading. Somewhere deep down he heard the clanging of the forge, of the anvil at the hammer's touch.

I will be there soon, he thought. I will be joining you all soon, my brothers.

Tsu'gan nursed bitter wounds, as he stood silently harnessed in the *Implacable's* Chamber Sanctuarine.

The mood was maudlin in the troop hold. No fewer than six Firedrakes had died trying to wreak century-old retribution. Somehow, the scales did not feel balanced.

He craved the burning of the solitorium, for the heat to purge the pain and impotent rage he harboured. The voice of Volkane, their pilot, interrupted his dark thoughts.

After escaping the wreckage of the *Protean* and returning to the *Glorion's* hangar deck via another route, they had attempted to re-establish communication with Nu'mean. It was to no avail. Apothecary Emek might yet have lived, however, and so they'd trawled the immediate area of space from where his saviour pod had been ejected.

Now, two hours later, they'd found him.

'Emergency ident-rune matches the *Protean's* signature.' Brother Volkane's voice was grainy through the comm-link.

Praetor spoke into the bulkhead's receiver unit.

'Conduct bio-scan and bring us in close.'

There was a pause of almost a minute before Volkane replied.

'Life readings affirmative.'

Tsu'gan saw Praetor shut his eyes briefly. It was as if a weight had lifted from his back.

'How long, brother?' he asked the gunship pilot.

'Approximately three minutes and seventeen seconds, my lord.'

'Bring our brother back to us, Volkane. Bring him back to the forge.'

'In Vulkan's name.'

'In Vulkan's name,' Praetor repeated, cutting the link. His eyes met with Tsu'gan's as he turned. A slight nod from the sergeant told the Firedrake all he needed to know.

Emek, at least, had lived. After being recovered from the saviour pod, he was laid prone in a medi-casket, strapped down to the hold floor like a piece of cargo. The Apothecary's face and much of his left side was badly damaged. Tsu'gan regretted his earlier remark to Emek about him one day being broken. He had not intended for it to be prophecy.

Praetor watched him keenly. The sergeant's eyes blazed without his helmet on. They matched the fury of Tsu'gan's own.

So much death in the name of something so futile and transient... Vengeance was not a filling meal; it left you cold and empty. Yet, Tsu'gan's desire for it still burned like an all-consuming flame. At that moment, it burned within them all.

They had given a name to their pain. Tsu'gan knew that name without the need for it to be spoken.
Night Lords.

MISTRESS BAEDA'S GIFT
Braden Campbell

LORD MALWRACK WAS rich, powerful and emotionally dead inside. Even though his was a race renowned for their passions and lust for life, time had tempered him. With every passing century he became all the more desiccated, both physically and spiritually, until all that remained was a perpetually scowling, slightly hunched old man who treated each new day with a dismal contempt. It therefore came as a great surprise when he suddenly found himself in love.

Malwrack and his daughter, Sawor, had been attending one of Commorragh's endless gladiatorial games and their box seat, perched high along the curving wall of the arena, offered them a spectacular view. Sawor watched with rapt interest as below her the combatants slashed each other with razorsnares, eviscerated each other with hydraknives and turned one another into large cubes of bloody meat with the aid of a shardnet. She was young and vigorous, and her senses were sharp. Even from so far above the killing floor, Sawor could smell its erotic mixture of sweat and blood, could taste the fear and adrenaline steaming from the participants, could see the detail of sinew, flesh and bone in every severed limb.

Malwrack, on the other hand, had long ago lost most of his senses. It happened with eldar his age when they let themselves go. Taste, touch and smell were greatly diminished now, as if coming to him from behind a thick blanket. Even his sight was cloudy and, grunting in dissatisfaction and submission, he reached into the folds of his robes and withdrew an ornate pair of opera glasses. For a time he too watched the ballet of carnage below, but it didn't bring him the same exhilaration as it did Sawor. Malwrack had seen such wych-work hundreds of times before on worlds throughout the galaxy. At first he felt only a deep malaise, but as his daughter began to cheer more loudly, he felt something else: envy.

He felt that quite a lot these days, truth be told. Well aware of his own infirmity, he hated nearly everyone around him; hated them for their youth. The one exception was Sawor. She was the only person in his kabal to whom he might extend forgiveness for an attempted assassination or coup. The mere thought of her made the wrinkled corners of his mouth twitch; the faintest echo of a smile. Of all the things he owned, of all the people who served under him, she was his most favoured. There was a word, a single word, used by the other, lesser inhabitants of the galaxy to describe this feeling, but it escaped his aged brain at the moment.

Malwrack's attention drifted from the fighting, and he began to look around the stadium. His wandering gaze eventually turned to the other box seats where the Dark City's social elite sat. One came to the theatre to be seen after all, and he idly wondered who was here today. Suddenly, he stopped and sat upright. Halfway across the arena sat a woman. She was alone, flanked on either side by a pair of stalwart incubi bodyguards. Her black hair, shot through with grey, was piled high atop her head and spilled around her neck and shoulders in thick waves. Her skin was flawlessly pallid, stretched smooth and tight like a drumhead. Her eyes were dark and luminous, her lips painted obsidian. As she reclined into her throne-like chair, Malwrack saw that she wore a form-fitting suit of armour with leg greaves shaped like spike-heeled stiletto boots, and an upper section that was more like a bustier than a protective chest plate. Black evening gloves ran from her tapered fingertips to her elbows, and the train of a charcoal dress with multiple layers flowed around her. A large pendant, obviously a shadow field generator, nestled between her pale breasts.

'Who is that?' he breathed.

Sawor's head snapped around, and she raised an eyebrow. It was a rare event to see her father actually interested in something. Quickly, she followed his line of sight until she too was looking at the statuesque woman across the way. With her younger eyes, Sawor could make out the intricate spider-web pattern etched onto the woman's dress with silver thread. She rifled through her memory, comparing faces to names. As her father's most trusted aide, his sole hierarch, it was her job to know every one of Malwrack's enemies. After a few seconds, she drew a blank. 'I don't know her,' she said.

'Find out,' he muttered as he continued to stare through his glasses. 'Now.'

Sawor nodded and immediately gathered up her weapons. Grasping a glowing halberd in one hand, she checked her sidearm with the other.

'Just discover her name, Sawor,' he said. 'Nothing more.'

Disappointed that she wouldn't be killing anyone this afternoon, Sawor shrugged and left.

Malwrack watched intently as the mysterious woman sipped from a goblet. Everything about her seemed to crystallise for him: the sensual, languid way she swallowed, the colour of her fingernails as she brushed a lock of hair from her face, the slight pulsing of the drug injector tube that ran into her jugular. It was as if the longer he observed her, the younger he became. His body stirred, pulse flaring, muscles tensing. He licked his lips, salivating for the first time in a decade. Something was washing over him in a sudden wave, a feeling that had been absent from his life for so long that he shook as if electrified. He knew then, without question, that he had to have this woman, had to impress and then utterly dominate her. His sole purpose in life now was to make her his cherished yet personal property. He was head over heels in... what was that word the *mon-keigh* used?

The woman furrowed her brow suddenly, cocked her head to one side, then looked directly at Malwrack. The old archon gasped and dropped his glasses. He awkwardly gathered up his belongings, and hurried out into the hallway. His own incubi, silent as ever, followed behind him. 'Been so long,' he muttered, chastising himself for his lack of obfuscation. Within minutes he was outside, seated aboard his modified Raider, waiting for Sawor. When she arrived, she had barely enough time to grasp onto the handrail before Malwrack signalled to the pilot. The machine bobbed slightly, then rocketed off into the air.

'You're in a hurry,' Sawor said teasingly. The wind whipped her hair and skirt out behind her in fluttering purple waves.

'What did you find out?' Malwrack demanded. He leaned in closer to hear her reply.

'I couldn't get very close to her,' Sawor prefaced.

'Because of her bodyguards?'

'Because of her entourage. She might have been sitting alone in that box, but the hallway beyond was filled with people. Not just her own servants either. There were representatives from half a dozen different kabals, all apparently waiting to see or speak with her.'

'I did discover a few things though. Her name is Baeda, and she's only just moved to Commorragh from one of the outlying web cities. Shaddom, I believe. She was apparently the consort of an archon there, and when he finally died, she inherited the entire kabal. Extensive resources at her disposal now, they say.'

Malwrack nodded and narrowed his eyes. That certainly explained why so many others were trying to gain access to her. A rich widow had come to town, and now the Dark City's most eligible bachelors were positioning themselves to claim her. He wondered just who his competition was.

As always, Sawor seemed to read his mind. 'I saw warriors there in several colours. The kabals of the All-seeing Eye, Poisoned Fang, and Rending Talon. That means Lord Ranisold, Lord Hoenlor and Lord Ziend.'

Malwrack knew them. Each one an up-and-comer who had managed to gain control of a kabal through exploitation and murder. They were as formidable as they were young and handsome.

'I need to get back into shape', he said.

It was some time later that Malwrack finally felt prepared enough to go and see the widow. He brought no bodyguards with him, no warriors. Only Sawor, who carried a large box and kept a respectable distance. To arrive at a woman's home with an army in tow not only betrayed fear and insecurity, he thought, but was quite rude. A deformed and mutilated servant answered the door, and ushered him through the cavernous house. As he passed an ornate mirror, Malwrack paused briefly to assess himself. His haemonculus surgeons had really outdone themselves, he thought. You could see the staples in the back of his skull that pulled his flaccid face tight. A half a dozen of his warriors had been scalped, and now his limp, greasy hair was replaced by a magnificent raven mane. A mixture of drugs and concoctions ran through his injection harness, toning his muscles and giving his eyes a healthy green glow. He curled his lips back, admiring his new stainless-steel teeth. He had dressed in his finest suit of combat armour, replete with a golden tabard, flowing purple cape and the largest shoulder pads that money could buy. This poor woman, he thought to himself, doesn't stand a chance.

He was brought into a grand sitting room filled with voluptuous, high-backed furniture. Arched windows looked out over the Commorragh cityscape. Baeda stood before them, drinking in the view. 'Lord Malwrack,' she muttered without so much as a turn of her proud head. Her voice was throaty and soft.

'Mistress Baeda,' he announced loudly. 'I welcome you to our fair city.'

At last she faced him, her eyes so black against her alabaster skin they looked like empty sockets. Her expression was that of an unreadable statue. Malwrack's pulse raced nonetheless, and his injector automatically compensated for the increased endorphin level.

'And?' she asked with some impatience.

Malwrack showed his new teeth. 'And, I come to proclaim my intentions.'

She did not swoon and fall on her knees before him as she had in Malwrack's fantasies, but instead blew out her cheeks, crossed the room and draped herself across a settee. 'Of course you do,' she said with a slight shake of her head.

Malwrack closed towards her and spread his arms wide. 'Lady, I am rich and powerful, and my kabal is composed not only of many fine warriors, but also of hireling wyches and Scourges. I command a fleet of war machines, and an armada of starships. Those who know me, fear me, and my combat prowess–'

'–is legend across the galaxy,' she finished. 'I've heard this speech.'

Malwrack was taken aback. 'You have?'

'From men more supple than you.' She looked past him then, towards Sawor and said coldly, 'At least you come with only one slave in attendance, though whether that speaks of respect or arrogance remains to be seen.'

Sawor's eyes flashed, incensed. 'I am no slave,' she hissed.

Malwrack raised a gloved hand to calm her. 'Sawor is my daughter,' he said calmly. 'She serves me willingly. Just as you must.'

Baeda's eyebrows arched. 'My, but the men in this city are bold! Do you suppose you are the first to come before me, making such overtures?'

'Not at all,' Malwrack replied. 'I know that Lord Ranisold, Lord Hoenlor and Lord Ziend covet you.'

'To name a few.'

'They pursue you no longer,' Malwrack said quietly. Sawor marched forwards, opening the box she carried. Inside, neatly arrayed, were a dozen faces, peeled away from the skulls of his competition. For the briefest of moments, an expression of shock crossed Baeda's face, but she instantly regained her composure. She stared at Malwrack.

'All that was theirs, is now mine,' he said. His gaze travelled hungrily up the length of her body. 'Just as you will be.'

With startling swiftness, Baeda was on her feet. Malwrack and Sawor were suddenly aware of incubi standing where there had been only shadows before. The tension in the air was palpable.

Baeda's voice was strained. 'You are... passionate, Lord Malwrack, but you do not impress.'

Sneering, Malwrack gave a curt nod, spun on his heel and walked towards the door. Sawor dropped the box. It clattered on the floor as she followed her father, spilling the remains of the archon's rivals like dried flowers across the parquet.

THE PLANET FRANCHI was cold, its days rainy and its nights foggy. It was covered in sweeping mountain ranges, dense forests and churning oceans of grey foam. In short, it was a world that any dark eldar could appreciate, and Malwrack was determined to present it to Baeda as a gift. In fact, Franchi had only one flaw: there were humans living on it. So, the old archon got to work.

First, his air force lanced and bombed their paltry fortifications and bastions. Then, once they had only ruins in which to hide, he unleashed his main forces upon the surviving defenders. His Raiders glided silently over the smashed cityscape, indiscriminately firing grenades into bunker and building alike. The corrupted wraithbone spheres exploded into a chalky powder so fine that even the Imperium's best filtration system couldn't completely block it out. It made its way into eyes, ears, and lungs, and once there, created such terrifying hallucinations that those affected could do nothing but scream and wail. As they rolled on the ground, clawing at their faces and gouging out their own eyes, Malwrack's warriors shot the good people of Franchi with hails of poisoned crystal shards or ran them through with bayonets. Those who weren't killed outright were hauled to their feet and bound with lengths of barbed chain. They would be spared a quick and painless death, lingering instead for years or even decades as slaves, playthings and foodstuffs when the dark eldar returned to Commorragh.

All in all, it was a thrilling, glorious time and Malwrack's followers delighted in it. Yet, he himself was strangely uninterested. He knew he should have been right there in the thick of it, revelling in the murder and mayhem. Instead, he stood alone in a city square filled with toppled monuments and heaps of dead humans, watching everyone else have all the fun. His thoughts remained focussed on Baeda.

He waded ankle-deep through spilled intestines, as fragrant to him as the flowers of spring, but all he could see was her face. Nearby, a commissar was struggling to free himself from where he lay pinned beneath the remains of his men. One of Malwrack's sybarite lieutenants ran up gleefully and shot him square in the face, detonating the man's head like an overripe melon. There were squeals of delight from the other warriors who watched the brain and bone fragments fly outwards like ruby-coloured fireworks.

All Malwrack felt was a burning desire to throw the widow to the floor and suffocate her body beneath his. To him, the slaughter on Franchi was work, not play. He committed genocide as one might polish silver, because his gift to her must be unblemished. It was irrational he knew, but he had to impress her. After all, he was in… he was in…. the *mon-keigh* word escaped him again.

His soldiers were now carving up the dead bodies with their knives, taking small trophies such as fingers, ears or teeth. He looked up at them from within his distracted thoughts and was about to say something, when there was an explosion. For a brief second, Malwrack saw his men engulfed in fire. Then, the ground beneath him heaved upwards and he was in freefall. Instincts taking over, he pulled his limbs in tight to his body and rode the shock wave. His personal force field flared to life, wrapping him tightly in a cocoon of black energy and utterly protecting him. Even when he hit the ground, the shadowy field absorbed the impact that would otherwise have shattered every bone in his willowy frame. Malwrack rolled up onto his feet, and sensing somehow that he was safe for the moment, the field became transparent.

Rumbling towards him out of the smoky haze was an Imperial tank, behind which he could make out several dozen human forms. He glanced behind him, but where his warriors had been a moment before, there was now only a smoking crater. Body parts were scattered everywhere, humans and dark eldar now indistinguishable from one another in death. Fury swept though Malwrack's mind; he had ordered all of Franchi's war machines to be neutralised before his main forces moved into the city, but obviously, something had been overlooked. As technologically underdeveloped as the *mon-keigh* were, he knew from painful experience that his forces stood little chance of survival unless this mechanical monstrosity was immediately destroyed.

The Guardsmen, who had been cowering behind the tank, were now fanning out around it. They were lightly armed, save for a trio who hastily began assembling a large cannon of some kind. Malwrack was alone, and out in the open. He snarled, disgusted with himself for letting this happen. He had not been focussed on the here and now, but had been distracted again by thoughts of how best to debase and titillate the widow Baeda. Then, as he often did, he redirected his loathing outwards, vomiting it upon the Guardsmen. There was a clunking sound from within the tank as it loaded another shell into place. Malwrack knew he had only one hope. He jerked his neck sharply, activating his drug injector, and charged.

The humans opened up with everything they had. They spat out a rain of lasgun fire and heavy bolter rounds. Autocannon shells flew wildly. The tank fired its main gun with a deafening roar, and the men who were huddled around its bulk winced and closed their eyes. The square exploded. For a moment, there was nothing to see but dust and smoke, but then a singular form leapt forwards, high into the air, and plunged down into their midst.

Malwrack's right hand was sheathed by an enormous glove with short swords in place of fingers. He flicked this now, activating its agony-inducing electrical properties, and killed three Guardsmen before the rest of the platoon could even blink. Their corpses twitched wildly and collapsed like discarded puppets. Then, they were all around him, punching, kicking, trying vainly to beat him with their rifles. Malwrack was calm and collected, his breathing controlled as he parried their blows. He found the humans almost comical in their ferocity; they did more frothing, cursing and grunting than they did actual damage. Still, they pressed in, refusing to break or flee. They pummelled away, hammering on his protective field as if trying to chisel rock with their bare hands.

It was mildly admirable, so Malwrack killed few, opting to maim instead. He swept another of them off his feet, removing the man's leg as he did so. Each time he slashed or stabbed, another Guardsman went down. They piled around his feet, wailing and screaming, whispering prayers to their God-Emperor or calling out for their mothers.

Suddenly, the telltales on Malwrack's forearm bracer lit up. His shadow field was a formidable piece of technology, but it was not infallible. There was only so much punishment it could take before it either overloaded or shut down to recharge itself. With a popping sound, it collapsed, and as it did, the butt of a lasgun slammed into his face. The old archon's head snapped around violently, and inky blood sprayed out from between his steel teeth.

Malwrack glared back at the man who had actually managed to hurt him, and drove the agoniser through his face. Arcs of electricity hissed and sparked. The man's eyes liquefied and ran down his cheeks, while he wailed like a thing possessed. The remaining Guardsmen recoiled at the sight and, while they were momentarily stunned, Malwrack finished them off in a whirling flourish. He killed four of them outright. The rest he left lying on the ground, fodder for his slave takers.

Beside him, the tank was trying to reposition itself so that it could once again bring its weapons to bear on him. Malwrack's eyes grew wide in horror. For a moment, caught up in the rush of the melee, he had forgotten all about the thing. Now, he realised that without his protective shield, any one of the machine's weapons would tear him in half. Certain that he was about to die, his last thought was of Sawor. She would lead the kabal in his stead, and she would do it well. His only regret was that he would no longer be around to see her come into her own.

Miraculously, the turret rotated away from him to face back into the square. Malwrack glanced over to see a Ravager coming to his rescue, firing as it came. Beams of black energy burrowed into the armoured side of the tank, and with a tortured sound, its turret exploded into twisted metal ribbons. Gouts of flame burst from every seam and joint, and its sponson weapons sagged. Malwrack recovered his composure and strode towards the waiting gunboat. Already, the gunnery crew was leaping down from the running boards and rushing to meet him.

'My lord,' one of them panted, 'are you all right?'

The archon pointed to the destroyed remains of the tank. 'Who is responsible for this?' he asked.

'An oversight,' another of his soldiers replied as bat-like aircraft raced across the sky. 'A military base outside of the city that escaped our orbital survey. It's being dealt with as we speak.'

Malwrack watched the jets pass, trailing sonic booms behind them. 'Well then,' he said, 'let's make certain it's properly taken care of.'

When at last he arrived, there was little left of the Imperial base save for wreckage. Buildings burned out of control. Dead Guardsmen and destroyed vehicles lay scattered about. A single bunker remained; its solitary door had been wrenched free.

Within it, his warriors reported, a handful of scared refugees had holed up in the hope that they might be spared. Lord Malwrack descended a narrow set of concrete steps into a damp, square room littered with blankets and pre-packaged food wrappers. The only light came from a few dim panels set into the walls. Four dead bodies lay splashed across the floor, the handiwork of his sybarites. The last two survivors had been reserved for him.

Malwrack assessed them quickly: a male and female, dressed in soiled, khaki uniforms accentuated only by identification tags around his neck, and a diamond ring on one of her fingers. They sat in a corner with their arms wrapped tightly around one another. The female buried her face in the man's chest, muting her sobs. He in turn rocked her gently and tried to whisper soothing words of comfort.

'Well,' Malwrack said joylessly. 'Best get this over with.'

At the sound of his voice, the man looked up, his eyes wide. 'Please,' he spat in his ineloquent tongue. 'We know what you are. Please, don't take us away with you.'

'Not to worry, *mon-keigh*,' he said in clipped Low Gothic. 'It's not you I'm after. Just your planet.'

In the name of expedience, he pulled his pistol from its holster, intending to shoot the female. Then, quite unexpectedly, there was an explosion of movement as the man launched himself forwards. He grabbed Malwrack's left wrist, bending it upwards, and a cloud of splinters tore into the ceiling. In a single motion Malwrack slammed his forehead down onto the human's nose, jerked his knee into the man's stomach, and drove an elbow into his back when he doubled over. Malwrack effortlessly shifted his weight, and kicked him square in the chest. The man's body collapsed against a computer display screen. Glass shattered and sparks flew. Malwrack leapt and drove his bladed glove through flesh, bone and concrete flooring. He snorted loudly as he inhaled the man's escaping life essence.

This, it seemed, was finally enough to snap the female out of her paralysis. She ran over to her partner's body, howling, and draped herself across it.

He chambered another round into his pistol, and looked down at the female. 'He doesn't deserve so touching a tribute as your tears and wails,' he said to her. 'Why do you weep for such an insignificant man?'

She glared at him with her cornered animal eyes. 'He was my husband,' she roared. 'I loved him!'

Malwrack suddenly brightened. He snapped the fingers of his gloved hand, and pointed at her with one of its talons. 'That's it!' he said with glee. 'That's the word I've been trying to remember. Thank you.'

Seeing her bewilderment, he knelt down to be at eye level. 'You know, it just so happens that I am in love myself. Tell me, did it take much for him to dominate you?'

'Dominate me?' she asked dumbly.

'Yes. We say *inyon lama-quanon*: to make another person one's prized property or subservient. But I like your barbaric term, "love". It's concise, powerful, like a killing blow.'

The woman stifled a hysterical laugh. 'I always thought the xenos profiles were exaggerated, but you really believe it, don't you? That there's nothing more to life than degrees of enslavement.'

'I'm afraid I don't follow,' Malwrack said.

'Love is about being together,' she continued. 'It's a sharing experience, an equal partnership. No ownership. No control. Love is about caring for someone so much that you can't bear to be apart.' She looked down at the blood-soaked remains of her husband and began to weep again.

Malwrack thought about the things he owned: his collection of hellmasks, his agonisers, his spire in Commorragh, his followers. Certainly he had his favourites among these, people and possessions held in high esteem. Yet, he was still confused.

Sharing? Partnership? Perhaps he had been trying to remember the wrong word.

'Now kill me,' the woman said with impertinence.

'Kill you,' the archon said slowly, 'so that you can be together again.'

The woman did not reply, and the warriors crowded in the doorway held their collective breath. Malwrack stood, his ancient knees popping, and holstered his gun. He glanced towards his lieutenants and with a curt nod, they filed up and out of the bunker. He turned to do likewise.

The woman gasped. 'What are you doing?'

'Leaving you to savour your agony, of course.'

He lingered in the doorway, waiting for her to say something courteous, but she simply stared at him, agape. Perhaps it was too much to expect proper manners from the *mon-keigh*. After a moment he sighed and said, 'You're welcome'. Then he left her to revel in her pain, if it were even possible. Poor, limited creature that she was, Malwrack doubted the woman could properly appreciate a decent bout of anguish.

However, it seemed ingratitude was a quality not limited to human females. Upon his return to the Dark City, Malwrack went to Baeda's home to present her with Franchi. Her servant informed him carefully that Baeda refused to see him. She relayed that she had no interest in the planet he had ransacked for her, for she had worlds and captives of her own. Frothing, Malwrack considered forcing his way inside, but thought better of it when confronted by a pair of Baeda's incubi. Attacking them would be an open declaration of war, and despite his growing frustration, he wanted to win the widow, not slay her.

Sawor was exercising when he returned home. Stripped down to the barest of coverings, skin glistening, she ducked and weaved her way around a half-dozen sparring partners wielding serrated knives. Shallow cuts adorned her arms, legs and abdomen, and her oily sweat made them sting gloriously. Part training, part foreplay, she loved these midday sessions almost as she did actual combat. All activity screeched to a halt however when Malwrack threw the doors wide.

'That woman!' he bellowed, spittle flying from his mouth. 'I'll make her choke on her arrogance.'

Sawor made a shooing motion with her hand and her companions backed away fearfully. She had seen her father angry many times, but this was something different. He reminded her of some caged monster that the wyches might fight in the arena, incoherent with frustration and rage.

'She defeated you in a fight?' she asked hopefully, thinking it to be the only logical explanation. 'Are our kabals now at war?'

'She wouldn't even see me,' he said breathlessly. 'I kill her suitors, but I do not impress. I go through all the effort of cleansing a planet for her, and she spurns it.'

Sawor bit her upper lip and said 'Father, you have my fear and respect, but you know nothing about women. Trophies? Planets? How could you expect her to be impressed by you when you gift her with such commonalities? She has standards, Father. If you want her, truly want her, you are going to have to give her something unique. Something that no one else has ever dared to.'

The old archon deflated a little. Had anyone else tried to quench his fury, he would have slain them in a stroke, but Sawor was different. As always, she was like a salve placed on a burn; thankfully the pain remained, but the ferocity of it was dimmed.

'You're right, of course,' he muttered. 'Something that takes her breath away. Makes her realise, instantly, that it's in her best interest to yield to me.'

He thought again of the married couple on Franchi. The woman had loved the man, but why? What had he given her in exchange for her submission? She had been the plainest creature in existence, practically rag-clad, except for–

Malwrack placed a hand on Sawor's shoulder. 'Gather the kabal,' he said. 'Our entire force. I know now what to give Mistress Baeda.'

CTHELMAX WAS A desert world. Outside a baleful sun beat down, but here, in the vast interior of the tomb complex, it was so cool that Malwrack could see his breath when he spoke. He and Sawor stood bathed in an eerie green glow. In all other directions stretched an inky blackness, stabbed by beams of light as the warriors set up a defensive perimeter and studied how best to abscond with their prize.

'Do you know what human males customarily use to buy the loyalty of their women?' Malwrack asked his daughter. 'Stones. Lumps of compressed carbon, especially.'

'I've never understood your fascination with *monkeigh* culture,' Sawor answered distractedly. There was something about this place, this city-sized mausoleum that genuinely frightened her. The sooner they left here, the better.

Malwrack was too enraptured to notice the slight. 'I have no idea what this thing is actually made of, but its size and rarity should finally stifle that damned widow.' He turned to Sawor and laughed.

The necrontyr power crystal towered above them. Its base fitted into some kind of circular pedestal from which arcane conduits ran off in all directions. It glowed from within, but dimly, like a lamp nearly out of oil. A sybarite approached and informed Malwrack that the men were ready to disconnect it. The archon nodded impatiently.

Sawor frowned. 'I think you misunderstood me. When I said you had to give her something no one else could, I didn't mean–'

The green light went out suddenly, as the crystal was separated from its base. It grew very dark, and very still.

Malwrack clapped his hands together. 'Right, let's get this back home.'

Sawor walked a few steps away. Her breath came in short spasms. There was something stirring here now, touching her latent senses. Then she heard it. Over the grunts of the men working, and of her father barking orders, there was a scraping sound from the blackness. Metal on stone. Tiny dots appeared in the distance, and for a moment Sawor thought that some kind of phosphorescent carpet was undulating towards them with fantastic speed.

Realisation splashed over her like cold water. 'Father!' she screamed.

Then the scarabs were on them, surging forwards like a wave. They swarmed around the disconnected crystal with hissing, chittering sounds. The warriors attempted to defend themselves with pistols and knives even as the tiny machines slashed at their leg armour.

Malwrack backed away and jerked his neck, feeling the drugs pour through him. He had time to see Sawor do likewise before his incubi formed a protective circle around him. From the darkness above, massive forms were descending with thick, pointed legs unfurling. Their faces were tightly packed clusters of camera lenses, glowing brightly. They made a churning noise, and from their abdomens more scarabs appeared, raining down. The archon's bodyguards began to slash out with their pole arms, their every motion fluid. Malwrack activated his shadow field, and shoved his way between two of his protectors. One of the tiny machines tried to amputate his foot. He impaled it on his bladed glove for its trouble.

He had an unobstructed view now. The power crystal, its base and everyone who had been standing on or around it were covered by hundreds of tiny insectoid robots. For each one his soldiers killed, the large spider-forms floating above made several more. Sawor was in full swing, surrounded by wyches and attacking anything that got too close to her. She was shouting something, but Malwrack couldn't make it out.

A moment later, there was a rush of hot wind and the sound of rocket engines. Sawor had called in reinforcements from their base camp outside, Malwrack surmised. More soldiers leapt from Raiders while behind them several slower-moving gunboats began to blow the scarabs apart with volleys from their energy cannons. The horde of machines began to thin. One of the large spiders crashed to the floor in a pool of slag. As if in response to the shifting tide of battle, twisting streams of green fire stabbed forth from out of the darkness. Humanoid shapes were slouching towards them, skeletal and hunched; cumbersome weapons hung heavy in their hands. Every soldier they hit flew apart into piles of burnt flesh and charred bones. The gunboats began to ignore the scarabs and turned their attention to this new threat.

There was a bright flash to Malwrack's left that cast twisted shadows across the broken floor. Another group of necrons, nearly two dozen in all, suddenly appeared. Above them floated a machine that looked like one of the scarab-making spiders with a skeletal torso fused to the top. In one hand, it raised a long stave. In the other was a glowing sphere. The ones on the ground immediately began firing their rifles. Two of the incubi were killed outright, but the armour of the others withstood the barrage. The archon's protective field turned opaque in several places, protecting his eyes from the blinding beams as it saved his body from vaporisation. Then it was his turn.

Malwrack leapt the distance and slashed out with his gauntleted hand. Five of the machines collapsed, heads severed and torsos ripped open. Wires spilled gut-like onto the ground. Behind him, his remaining retinue thrust forwards with their pole arms. Nine more of the things were destroyed. The floating machine brought its stave around in a sweeping arc, effortlessly decapitating two incubi, and the remaining necrons fell into the melee. There was a flurry of blows, all of which Malwrack easily parried. Then, responding to some command only they could hear, the machines began moving backwards, stunned perhaps at the ferocity of the dark eldar attack.

Malwrack let them retreat for the moment, and struggled to locate Sawor amidst the chaos. Despite the great strides he was making, the rest of his kabal was not faring half as well. Two of his gunboats were floating helplessly, abandoned by their crews and gutted by fire. The bodies of his soldiers were piling up everywhere, blackened and smoking. Amidst them, dead necrons were staggering back to their feet, reassembling themselves somehow until they again looked like gunmetal skeletons. Worse yet, two of the giant spiders were setting the crystal back into place. Newly minted scarabs swirled around them like a river of chrome. An archon came to power by knowing two things: when to fight, and when to run. For Malwrack, it was time to run.

'Back to the boats!' he yelled.

Those that could, began to fall back, weapons blazing and throats screaming. Malwrack and his remaining two guards ran to where Sawor stood alone again. Bodies, both flesh and bone and metallic, lay in pieces all around her. She herself was bleeding from a score of lacerations, none of which seemed to slow her down or lessen her fury. Malwrack grabbed her forearm, dragging her from atop the charnel pile, and together they sprinted towards a nearby Raider. Bolts of green energy flew around them. The last incubi staggered and fell, but Malwrack never so much as glanced back at his erstwhile defenders. If none but he and Sawor escaped this, he would consider the day a victory.

Underlings were clamouring around the transport. Malwrack shot one of them and impaled another, flinging the man into the encroaching necron phalanx. Sawor, following suit, lopped off the arm of one warrior who refused to give up his place for her. The machine lurched violently before it blasted up and out of the tomb. Dark walls sped past them as they raced towards the exit. Sawor held on tightly and craned her neck to look behind them. A squadron of necron vehicles was in pursuit, firing powerful beams at them, but their speed was no greater. The Raider would make it to surface first, where their base camp and a portal to Commorragh awaited. Despite all the carnage, it seemed that she and Malwrack would live to fight another day. Sawor looked over at her father. He met her gaze, and realising the same thing, he actually smiled.

They were almost to the exit when the Raider crashed. Without warning, serpentine enemies emerged from the walls and floor of the tomb. They lashed out with pointed tails and monstrously bladed hands, tearing through the hull and engine housing. The transport pitched downwards and cartwheeled through space with a terrible velocity. It careened through the exit, and impacted on the sand outside, crumpling and shearing. Malwrack's shadow field flared into protective mode, turning pitch-black as he was thrown free of the wreckage.

How long he lay there, Malwrack had no way of telling. His shadow field was clear, so any danger was apparently past. Slowly he sat up. While he waited for his vision to stop swimming, he registered a pile of flaming wreckage, a half-dozen bodies clad in purple armour and the silent entrance to the tomb. Presumably, the necrons within were under no instructions to pursue invaders out here into the desert. He looked around for Sawor, but didn't see her. He called her name, but there was no response from anyone. He called again, louder. Still no reply. With a twinge of panic, he limped to the bulk of the downed Raider.

He found her beneath one of the running boards, literally folded in half. Jagged pieces of the transport protruded from her in several places, the most gruesome of which exited through her gaping mouth. He made a mewling sound and dropped down to her side. He inhaled desperately, but there was nothing there. Her life essence, her soul, had dissipated. She was dead beyond any haemonculus's resuscitational skill.

'Get up,' he said.

He stood once more and looked down at her shattered form. 'Get up,' he repeated. 'I order you to get up.'

Malwrack realised with a start that he was powerless. No beating, no threat, no command would make her live again. This was not the way it was supposed to have happened, his kabal gutted, his successor gone. He activated the portal back to Commorragh, and strode purposefully through the gate, oblivious to the fact that as he did so, he was crying.

WHEN HER SERVANT refused him entry, he kicked down the door. When five of her incubi formed a wall across the foyer, he gutted two of them in a flash, and massacred the rest as they tried to fall back. On the grand staircase that led up to her personal chambers, an entire unit of warriors fired their weapons at him. He walked through the hail of splinters and, with shadow field blazing darkly, killed every last one of them. Then, he made his way upstairs. Throwing the doors wide, he found her in the room with arched windows where he and Sawor had first come to see her. She bolted off her settee, one hand flying up to her pendant, the other pulling an ornate handgun from the folds of her dress. Malwrack strode in, arms wide, eyes unblinking, head lowered. His tattered cape flowed behind him like a purple sea.

'What does a man have to do around here to get a little attention?' he roared.

Two more incubi, lying in ambush behind the door, lunged at his back. Malwrack spun low. His gauntleted hand tore out the throat of one assailant, then flashed back to impale the other before either one could even land a blow. When he rose and faced Baeda again, his forearm was dripping with gore.

She backed away, slowly, never taking her eyes off him. 'To what do I owe the pleasure?' she asked coldly.

'Don't you be coy,' he growled. 'Don't you even dare.'

'Is this about that planet you wanted to give me?'

He kicked a chair with such force that it sailed across the room. 'You know what this is about! It's about you. You've destroyed me.'

Baeda noticed then that something was terribly wrong with his face. Streams of water were gushing uncontrollably from his eyes. She'd never seen the like.

'I tried so hard to win you, and all you did was spurn me. I killed for you, and all you could say was that I did not impress. I should have stopped even then, just called the whole thing off and moved on, but I couldn't. It was like you'd infected me. You were all I could think about.

'I gave you a world, but you wouldn't even see me. Why wouldn't you see me? If you'd just let me in that day, she'd still be here, but no, you thought it would be more fun to refuse me. Was that your plan, mistress, to starve me? Like a dog? Deprive me of your presence until I just went rabid?'

He was babbling, Baeda saw, hyperventilating and lost in a dark train of thought. She could have shot him dead right then and there, he was so distracted, yet there was something about his behaviour that was fascinating.

'Who would still be here?' she asked him.

'Well, it worked,' he continued. 'I swore that I would have you, Baeda. *Inyon lama-quanon*. To the detriment of everything else. My followers, my armies, all gone.

My kabal is finished because of you; because I became so enraptured, and thought I'd finally found the perfect gift with which to win you.'

He still had not answered her question, and so she asked again. 'Malwrack, who would still be here?'

The old archon appeared to deflate, shoulders stooping, his chest caving in. He gave a heart-wrenching sigh and said, 'Sawor.'

Outside the room, Baeda could hear running footsteps. More of her soldiers and protectors were rushing to her defence. They would surely kill the old man, by weight of numbers if not by martial skill. Yet, she had to hear him out first. His tears, his ragged breathing, his palpable aura of loss were entrancing.

When he spoke again, his voice was almost inaudible. 'I took her to Cthelmax. There are ruins there. Very well preserved. I looked over at her. I was so certain that we would be all right. Then she was gone.'

Weapons clicked into readiness behind him as Baeda's forces piled into the room. At the slightest signal from her, they would open fire, and that would be the end of Lord Malwrack. He seemed to take no notice, however. Instead, his whole being shuddered, and he collapsed at the widow's feet.

'She's gone!' he cried from a place so dark, it made Baeda gasp. Malwrack could see now that Sawor had been no mere hierarch. She had been his sounding board, his strong-arm, his partner in all things. She had been his most prized possession, and he had loved her. He would never be complete again, and thus, there was no point in his life continuing.

Sobbing, he waited only for a volley of splinter fire or a killing blow from Baeda to end it all.

He felt her lift him up. Spent, he didn't resist. Baeda looked him square in the face, placed a hand on each of his cheeks, and clamped her mouth over his. Malwrack was certain she was giving him the kiss of death, but it just went on and on. Instead of stabbing or shooting him, he felt Baeda's body soften and press into his. Her tongue darted around his steel teeth. Her fingers dug into his cheeks. He kissed her back and wrapped his arms around her so tightly that her body armour creaked. When she finally pulled away, she had a dreamy expression on her face.

'*Lama-quanon*,' she said. 'I yield to you.'

'I don't understand,' Malwrack said. 'I have no kabal left to fight you with. You wouldn't take the planet, and I couldn't retrieve the crystal, so I have nothing with which to buy your obedience.'

'Of course you do,' she purred as her long fingers traced his wrinkled brow. 'You've given me the greatest gift imaginable: your suffering. There's a void in you now, a delicious emptiness that will never heal. Say you'll always give that to me, that you'll feed me with it the rest of our days, and all that I have will be yours.'

Malwrack looked over his shoulder at the horde of warriors behind him. Baeda began scratching at his armour as if she meant to undress him here, immediately, and in front of everyone, cement their new partnership in a torrent of public lovemaking.

A smirk slowly crept across Malwrack's face. He had squandered one kabal only to inherit another.

These soldiers would live and die at his command, and he was not, after all, defeated. Malwrack pointed to the doorway, and after a moment, the soldiers lowered their heads and shuffled out. He threw his bladed gauntlet to the floor, increased the flow to his drug injector, and grabbing a fistful of her hair, wrenched Baeda's head back. She smiled at him. Soon he and the widow would ride out across the galaxy together, inflicting anguish on any who could bear it. With his experience and Baeda's resources, there would be no stopping them. He could avenge his daughter's death a thousandfold upon the whole of creation.

'It's going to be glorious,' Baeda said cryptically. She kissed Malwrack again, deep and long. Through the window behind them, the spires and lights of the Dark City watched without comment.

IRON INFERNO
C. L. Werner

THE SKY WAS a livid bruise of ochre and mauve, what little daylight filtering through the murk turned a sickly yellow by the thick layers of dust polluting the atmosphere. Izanagi was a wounded world, maimed and mutilated by an assault from the stars. The shrieking winds that churned the dust clouds were like the pained wail of the planet, crying out in agony to an uncaring universe and an impotent Imperium.

Lord General Ro Nagashima wiped the grit of dust from his goggles and glared at the murky sky. The Prefect-Governor of Izanagi had assured him the astropaths had sent a psychic alarm into the aethyr. It was small consolation. Even if the psionic cry was heard, even if a relief fleet was mobilised, the vagaries of travel through the interstellar warp meant it could be years before help arrived. By that time, Izanagi might be far worse than wounded.

General Nagashima sighed into the rebreather mask that straddled his face, his breath echoing back into the comm-filters of his helmet as a harsh metallic wheeze. His gloved fingers brushed against the row of campaign medals sewn into the breast of his tunic. The tactile feel of old glories brought a bitter smile to his face. Annihilating the pirates of the Oni Cluster, bringing to heel the serf uprising on Tetso, defeating the renegade House Carcalla and their mercenaries, all of these had been wars he had fought in the further reaches of the Yamato System. There had been honour and grandeur in those battles. They had been a furnace that had forged him from a fragile man of flesh and fear into a warrior of steel and valour.

The general looked again at the ugly, dust-choked sky. This war was different. This was not some backwards corner of the system, some scraggly planetoid overrun by rebels or some pirate-infested asteroid. This was Izanagi, the jewel of the Yamato System. This was his planet. This was his home.

It had started without warning, a chunk of space rock vomited from the warp, hurtling directly towards Izanagi. Terror had gripped the world, every calculation of the observators of the Divisio Astrologicus came to the same result: Izanagi was doomed. The impact of such an immense meteor would kill the world and everything on it. There was no time to evacuate, only to kneel before the God-Emperor and make peace with Him before the end.

The impact of the immense meteor was felt across the planet, sending earth tremors that resonated across each continent. A great plume of dust billowed into the atmosphere, wrapping Izanagi in a mantle of darkness. Yet, it seemed, the Emperor had answered the prayers of His subjects. Impossibly, the immense space rock had reduced its velocity as it entered the gravity pull of Izanagi. True, it had struck with enough force to gouge a hundred-metre-deep crater in the lush forests of Kazi Basin, but even such a devastating impact was far from the planet-killing blow predicted by the arcane science of the tech-priests.

Even as the people of Izanagi celebrated their deliverance, the real danger began to make itself known. The thick layers of dust swirling in the atmosphere blinded the satellite surveillance systems of the prefecture and the agri-combines. Aircraft found it impossible to operate in the choking, gritty clouds, dust quickly clogging intakes and exhausts and reducing visibility to a few metres. Only by travelling directly overland was it possible for expeditions to reach the crater and investigate the strange space rock, a difficult journey of some hundreds of kilometres from the nearest settlements.

At first, the silence of the expeditions was blamed on the interference of the atmospheric dust on vox traffic. Then small settlements began to fall silent. Within a week of the meteor's impact, a chilling hypothesis was proposed by the observators. The meteor had not crashed into Izanagi. It had landed, been directed at their world by some manner of intelligence. Worse, the tech-priests of the Divisio Biologis were certain they knew what creatures had piloted the meteor into Izanagi. They called the object a *rok* and said that from its innards it had infected their world with the most persistent xenos threat in the universe.

General Nagashima shuddered as he thought about that moment when he had stood in a terracrete bunker and watched as the tech-priests dissected one of the specimens collected by their skitarii scouts from the Silent Zone. He had seen pict-casts of the aliens before, read of them in histories, but nothing prepared him for the shock of that moment.

Ro Nagashima staring into the dead eyes of an ork.

To call it man-like would have been sardonic and insulting to the grace of human physiology. It was a squat, four-limbed beast, its limbs swollen with grotesque masses of muscle, its ugly skull jutting out from its broad shoulders on the merest stump of a neck. Its skin was like old leather, green where it had not been blackened by the plasma guns of the skitarii. Huge fangs jutted from its lantern-jaw, beady red eyes glared from either side of its ape-like nose. There didn't seem to be room for a spoonful of brains in its thick, sloped skull, yet the ork had been carrying a bulky, ramshackle weapon that had the tech-priests scratching their shaven pates in confusion and muttering cantrips against the heresies of xenos technology.

This, then, was the enemy.

With orbital and aerial observation impossible, the human defenders of Izanagi could only monitor the advance of the orks by the expansion of the Silent

Zone. When settlements went quiet, they knew that the aliens were on the move.

General Nagashima clenched his fist as he remembered those long, frustrating weeks, watching the steady advance of the orks on his maps like a surgeon watching the spread of some malignant disease. Eventually, the officers of Izanagi's Planetary Defence Forces detected a pattern to the alien attacks. Knowing where the orks had been, they felt safe predicting where they would go. Studying his maps, Nagashima decided where they would cut out the disease threatening his world.

The general rubbed the fog of dust from his goggles and stared at the wind-swept hills all around him. The crop of boden-fruit was lost, the dead vines shivering in the breeze, but they would still serve Nagashima's plans. The boden-fruit required a careful mix of altitude and shade in which to flourish, and this had led to their cultivation on small, man-made hills. Vast plantations dedicated to the raising of boden-fruit peppered Izanagi, creating artificial landscapes of maze-like valleys.

This was where the ork rampage would end.

Nagashima was using those valleys now, hiding his PDF troops behind the hills. A paved service road cut through the hills, used by the serfs to gather the crops. It formed a direct route to Ko, one of Izanagi's hive-cities and the nearest processing plant for boden-fruit. The general smiled as he gazed down at the tempting stretch of road. Built wide and rugged to accommodate the hulks of the harvest machines, the road was ready-made for movements of armour.

Along its length for a distance of seventy kilometres, his engineers had set their minefields. At the mouth of the road, where it entered the valleys from the plain beyond, Nagashima had buried hundreds of aerial bombs, each of which could be detonated remotely when the ork column drove over them. The aliens would be caught between the buried bombs and the mines. It was then he would give the order for his troops to emerge from concealment in the hills and cut down the orks from either side.

He could almost find it in himself to pity the stupid brutes.

The general turned and stared out across the plain. Every trap needed bait, and Nagashima had provided the orks with a very good reason to cling to the apparently safe hills and valleys when they made their advance. Dominating the plain was a low mesa. He could see the imposing structure sprawled about its summit, the plasteel and ferrocrete immensity of the maintenance complex for the boden-fruit harvesters. It was an awesome structure, rising several hundred metres over the plain, dwarfing even the mesa it stood upon. Around this formidable complex, Nagashima's troops had dug a vast system of trenchworks, erected a jungle of chain-wire, constructed a nest of minefields and tank-traps. Behind these, a system of bunkers burrowed into the base of the mesa. Immense gun emplacements jutted from platforms in the sides and on the roof of the complex. Howitzers and siege mortars gaped from caves gouged into the face of the mesa, their steel mouths waiting to explode with fire and death.

General Nagashima could imagine the effect the mesa would have on the orks. Even their brute brains would recognise the horrible firepower arrayed against them. They would seek to bypass the fortifications and circle around it under cover of the hills.

The orks would not know that the entire complex was an illusion. Less than five per cent of the guns were real, just enough to give the impression of full batteries when they fired. The rest of the artillery was simply stretches of pipe welded together and painted to resemble the muzzles of cannon. Most of the bunkers were simply tarps riveted into the walls of the mesa. The minefields around the complex were really only a few metres deep, the chain-wire only active and lethal for a small stretch before giving way to normal stretches of chain strung between iron posts. Many of the tank-traps were simply wooden beams nailed together and painted to look like metal.

A token force manned the perimeter of the fortification, there to give the illusion that they were the vanguard of an entire army. If the orks sent scouts to investigate the defences, the custodian force was to punish them relentlessly, each platoon tasked to give the impression of a company, each company that of a battalion. At the same time, any scouts who entered the hills would find no trace of human occupation.

General Nagashima smiled beneath the mask of his rebreather.

Yes, he almost felt sorry for the filthy xenos scum.

THE BROWN SKIES of Izanagi smouldered into complete blackness with the onset of night. Neither moon nor star could penetrate the dust-filled murk of the atmosphere.

Kaptain Grimruk Badtoof pressed the magnoculars against his face, the human-built instrument looking like a tiny toy in the ork's immense hand. Grimruk scrunched his scarred face into a scowl and squinted through one of the lenses of the magnoculars. A thick finger pawed awkwardly at the modulator controls set into the side of the instrument. Guttural snarls rumbled through the ork's fanged mouth as he thumbed past the setting he wanted. It was with difficulty that he resisted the urge to dash the magnoculars to the ground and stomp them beneath his steel-shod boots.

Finally, the ork kaptain found the setting he wanted. The black world around him leapt into vibrant hues of green as the night-vision mechanisms became active. Grimruk always thought it was an appropriate thing, the way the human device made things green. It was almost as if the humans who made them had understood that the night belonged to the orks.

A low, bestial grunt trespassed into Grimruk's thoughts, asking him what he saw.

Grimruk didn't look to see which of his warriors had asked the question. With his free hand he simply struck out and swatted the speaker. There was a satisfying crunch of gristle and a truculent yelp of pain. The question wasn't repeated. He'd given his mob strict orders to keep their gobs shut. The last thing he needed was for one of them getting gabby and giving the humans warning.

Grimruk stared through the magnoculars, passing them across the bristling defences of the human position. He studied the lines of wire, the fortified bunkers and complex trench works. The ork grunted in appreciation as he passed his gaze over the artillery pieces poking out from the structure on top of the mesa. Those were some big guns, the kind of thing the mekboyz could really put to good use.

The ork's leathery features twisted in a brutish smile as he watched the figures of sentries moving through the wire. Grimruk paid careful attention to where they stepped, what they touched and what they didn't. When he wanted to, the ork could remember things with photographic detail. It was one of the benefits of having half his skull replaced by a painboy's experiment.

The kaptain watched the soldiers make their way back into the trenches, then followed them until they disappeared into one of the bunkers. With a satisfied grunt, Grimruk lowered the magnoculars, shoving them into the scrawny arms of Wizgrot. The thin, emaciated creature was much smaller than the hulking ork, though it shared the same leathery green hide. Where the ork's bulk was suggestive of awesome brute strength, that of Wizgrot was lean and sneaky.

The gretchin orderly took Grimruk's magnoculars and replaced them into the steel case he carried. Grimruk scowled at Wizgrot. Shivering, the gretchin sketched a salute and snapped his heels together. Grimruk cuffed him anyway, sending the orderly's spiked helm rolling through the dust. Wizgrot scrambled after the helmet, bringing barks of harsh laughter from the orks watching him.

Grimruk rounded on his troops, glaring at them with his good eye. The other, lost along with the better part of his skull, had been replaced by a crude electrical device, a scanner light that simply bounced from side to side in the pit of his empty eye socket. The rest of the ork's face on that side of his head was simply a mass of rusty steel plates bolted to his skull. Grimruk scratched at the line of scar tissue that marked the join between flesh and metal.

He reached a decision, one that brought a smile of sadistic amusement across his face. Grimruk settled his attention on Gobsnot, one of his lieutenants. Gobsnot was just stupid enough to make a good diversion. The ork kaptain grabbed hold of his underling's tunic, dragging him close so he could grumble new orders into the nob's ear.

Gobsnot turned away from Grimruk. Growling at the mob milling around listening to the exchange, he called out a few comrades. When the detail was mustered, the orks loped off into the darkness in the direction Grimruk had pointed.

Grimruk watched them vanish into the gloom, a cunning light in his eye. He reached to his belt and pulled a tattered mass of fabric and leather from where it had been tucked beneath it. His clumsy hands tugged and teased the worn, tortured material into a crude approximation of shape. Straightening himself to his full height of two and a half metres, the ork kaptain scrunched the battered hat onto his misshapen head. It was ludicrously small, barely covering the top of the brute's scalp. It wasn't the fit that concerned Grimruk, however. It was the message behind the hat. He'd torn it from the body of a boss human in the ruins of Vervunhive, one of the black-clad officers who kept their soldiers in line by shooting the ones that tried to weasel out of a fight. Grimruk smiled as he saw that his own troops understood that same message.

The kaptain studied his warriors, watching the eagerness building up inside them. He needed to squelch that right away. His hand closed about the heft of the immense chainaxe he carried. He thumbed the activation stud, grinning as the steel teeth of the weapon shuddered into life, whirring like lightning as they screeched along the edge of the axe.

Grimruk turned, his long coat whipping about him in the biting Izanagian wind. He didn't look back to see if his troops were following him. They were the best kommandos in the clan, the hardest fighters the Blood Axes could provide. They weren't afraid of anything. They'd follow him into Gork's mouth if he told them to.

Besides, if any of them did try to run out on him, they knew he wouldn't stop looking for them. He had a long memory for a kaptain. It was another side effect of having half his skull replaced by a painboy.

THEY MADE GOOD time even when they did reach the wire. Grimruk placed the credit for that on his foresight. He'd kitted his troops with red boots before setting out on their scouting mission. Even the lowest grot knew red ones were faster than others.

The massive ork kaptain crouched down beside the barbed fencing, his eye watching the terrain around him. He could just faintly see the flickering lights of the bunkers, sometimes the dim gleam of a soldier's lho-stick as he drew smoke into his lungs to fend off the cold of night. The sight gave Grimruk an idea. He snapped his fingers at Wizgrot. The weedy gretchin fumbled about among his many packs and belts until he found what his boss wanted. Grimruk stuffed the thick cigar into the corner of his fanged maw, clamping down on it with his heavy teeth.

Another snap of his fingers and Wizgrot was straining on tiptoe to light the ugly smelling rolls of dried squig-sinew. Grimruk drew a lungful of the filth into his chest and grunted. Now if any of the sentries did spot movement in the wire, they would see the gleam of his cigar and think it was just one of their patrols coming back. The size discrepancy between ork and human was a minor detail the kaptain chose to dismiss.

Besides, Grimruk considered as he took another drag, pretty soon the soldiers would have other things on their minds. The kaptain stared out at the darkness, wondering how far Gobsnot and his boyz had gone. They should be just about into the wire by now. Watching the way the human patrols had avoided that stretch of the perimeter, Grimruk was pretty certain there was something nasty waiting there for Gobsnot.

The deafening boom of explosives thundered through the night. Grimruk's grin broadened. It seemed Gobsnot's boyz had found some mines.

Instantly the trenchworks ahead of the orks burst into activity. Soldiers scrambled along the line, racing to positions closest to the disturbed minefield. The darkness evaporated as heavy floodlamps sparked into life, as the sizzling beams of lasguns slashed through the gloom. The barking chatter of a heavy bolter snarled into action while the dull crump of mortars and light artillery pounded the earth. More mines exploded as Gobsnot's embattled kommandos tried to retreat from the withering fire trained upon them.

Grimruk roared, slashing his chainaxe through the wire. Alarms wailed as the strands of barbed wire snapped beneath the chewing teeth of the axe. The kaptain just grunted in amusement. The humans had already deployed themselves to deal with Gobsnot's mob. It would take them time to train their guns in his direction. Time the soldiers didn't have.

Grimruk gestured with the churning edge of his axe at the trenchline, snarling at his warriors, inciting the maddened orks, fanning their eagerness for battle into bloodthirsty fury. Almost, the kaptain forgot to impress upon his warriors the strategy behind their mission. They weren't here just to kill things. The warboss wanted intelligence about the human strongpoint, intelligence the kommandos were to bring back to him.

The orks behind Grimruk lifted their weapons in the air, a chatter of boltguns, stubbers and combi-weapons barking into the night. Even the bark of their weapons was almost drowned out by the deep bellowing war cry of their owners.

'Waaaaaggggh!'

Like rabid beasts, the orks swept past Grimruk, dashing for the human defences. The kaptain saw the closest bunkers turn their weapons on the rushing kommandos. The first bursts of bolter fire were high, aimed at pre-selected targets at the edge of the wire. It took time to correct their aim, to swing the heavy weapons down and rake the oncoming rush of alien killers. By then, dozens of the orks were already pouring into the trenches. Those at the rear were ripped apart by the downturned bolters in the bunkers, their hulking shapes jerking and twisting as the explosive rounds shredded them, but it was too little to save the few soldiers detailed to remain at their posts during the slaughter of Gobsnot's mob.

Grimruk dropped down into the trench just as the heavy bolters began to find their range. A human soldier rushed at him, firing his rifle at the towering ork. Grimruk felt the las-bolt sizzle through his arm, the wound cauterising instantly behind the searing beam of light. Barely cognisant of the injury, Grimruk seized the soldier by the front of his tunic. The man screamed, trying to smash the ork's face with the plasteel stock of his weapon.

The lasgun smacked uselessly against the steel plates bolted to the ork's skull. Grimruk scowled at the panicked human, turning his head as the soldier tried to hit him again. Annoyed, the kaptain pulled the man into the whirring teeth of his axe. The soldier's body jumped and convulsed as the chainaxe chewed through him. Grimruk let the shredded mess tumble to the ground, then wiped some of the spattered gore from his coat.

Grimruk turned away from the mangled mess of his foe, his eye studying the battle unfolding around him. Wherever his kommandos had entered the trenches, they had seized control of them. The butchered remains of humans were strewn across the earthworks, a few battered survivors fleeing over open ground to reach the protection of their bunkers.

Further away, however, Grimruk could see a different story unfolding. Soldiers were pouring from the higher bunkers, others were racing back from the farther trenches and the fire line they had formed to deal with Gobsnot's mob. The kommandos controlled their section, but the kaptain knew they could not do so for long.

The ork kaptain gestured with his chainaxe at the bunker and roared. He could see a few of the closest orks acknowledge his order. They stopped attacking the escaping soldiers and took off at a lope for the closest bunker. Other orks, noticing the action of their comrades, gave off their own bloodthirsty pursuit and moved to support the bunker attack. The kaptain gave a satisfied grunt. That was what set his boyz apart from most of the horde. The kommandos understood the need to get a job done even if it meant pulling out of a scrap.

Grimruk snapped his fingers and pointed at the carcass of the soldier he had killed. Wizgrot leaned over the body and tore a ragged strip of cloth from the front of its tunic. The kaptain waited until his orderly stuffed the scrap of cloth into one of the bags the grot carried. Then he lunged at the wall of the trench. The ork's powerful arms had no trouble pulling his bulk up from the pit. Grimruk snapped a command over his shoulder to Wizgrot and hurried to join the rush on the bunker.

Wizgrot cursed and mumbled under his breath as he struggled to climb out of the trench and follow the lead of his kaptain. The short gretchin didn't try too hard, though. The possibility that the fighting would be over by the time he reached the bunker limited the enthusiasm of his efforts.

THE BUNKER WAS a big blockhouse of ferrocrete and plasteel. The humans inside were armed with at least two heavy bolters and had gutted three of Grimruk's kommandos in the first rush. The reminder that the soldiers had weapons more formidable than the lasguns of the trench defenders had curbed some of the enthusiasm for the attack. By the time Grimruk joined his troops, the orks were sheltered behind several tank-traps, leaning out from their cover to deliver ineffectual potshots at the fortified position.

Grimruk growled at the other orks as he joined them behind their scanty cover. He could hear the ferocity of the fighting down in the trenches. The humans were bringing up reinforcements to contain the incursion into their lines. Some of his kommandos might not appreciate it, but it wouldn't take too many humans to overwhelm them. Sure, they'd get a good scrap out of it, but the Blood Axe clan was built on the idea that there was more to winning than getting yourself killed in a big fight. If they were going to get what they needed and bring the information back to the warboss, then they had to move and move fast.

Grimruk bellowed at one of the kommandos near him. A huge-shouldered ork wearing a set of thick goggles over his eyes and lugging a giant metal barrel on his back turned and stared suspiciously at the kaptain.

The kaptain barked at the ork, a brute named Skorchslag. He motioned with his fist, ordering the commando to attack the bunker with his flame-spewing burner.

Skorchslag raised one of his singed fingers by way of reply.

Roaring back at him, Grimruk made a string of increasingly violent threats against Skorchslag if he didn't follow orders. The big ork still looked unimpressed, but when Grimruk drew the pistol from his holster, it seemed to convince Skorchslag he might do worse than follow orders. The kommando hefted his burner, the muzzle of the weapon dripping liquid fire. With a last look around, Skorchslag sprinted towards a tank-trap closer to the bunker. Instantly, both of the heavy bolters inside the bunker began to fire on the ork with the deadly flamethrower.

Grimruk slapped the shoulder of the kommando sheltering beside him, gesturing for him to rush the bunker from the other side while the soldiers were distracted by Skorchslag. The kommando seemed just as reluctant to break from cover. Snarling his annoyance, Grimruk pushed the other ork from cover, waited a moment to see if the soldiers in the bunker noticed him, then followed.

The two orks rushed across the killing zone in front of the bunker, diving against the thick wall of the fortification. They reached the safety of the wall an instant before the bolters tore through the tank lashed across Skorchslag's back. The kommando vanished in an explosion of liquid fire, transformed into a screaming, staggering torch. Another burst of fire from the bunker put the blazing ork down.

Grimruk ripped a wood-handle stikkbomb from his belt, nodding for the kommando with him to do the same. The two orks smacked the heads of the grenades against the wall of the bunker, then cast the activated explosives through the firing slits for the bolters.

The walls of the bunker failed to restrain the fury of the blast. In a shower of flame and debris, the bunker virtually collapsed in upon itself. The two orks who had attacked the fortification were thrown like rag dolls, smashing into the ground a dozen metres away.

Grimruk painfully lifted himself back onto his feet, one arm hanging limp and broken at his side. The kommando with him had fared even worse, the force of the explosion impaling his body on one of the tank-traps. The kaptain glowered at the mutilated ork, then scowled at the smoking wreckage of the bunker. He'd need to talk to the mekboyz about how much punch they packed into their stikkbombz.

Grimruk shook his head to clear the ringing from his ears. He stared at the ground, looking for the peaked cap that had been blown off by the explosion. He stopped looking when Wizgrot appeared beside him, timidly handing the battered hat to the ork. Grimruk snatched the hat from the gretchin and stomped towards the wrecked bunker. Now that the heavy bolters were quiet, other kommandos were breaking cover to close upon the destroyed objective. Grimruk pushed his way through the press of orks, determined to be the first to see whatever was left.

The bunker was a shambles, twisted supports protruding at crazy angles from shattered blocks of processed stone. Here and there the mangled wreck of a soldier jutted out from the jumbled mess. Grimruk snorted contemptuously as he looked at the walls. The stikkbombz had blasted them to bits, like they were nothing but paper. Maybe he'd suggest the mekboyz keep making the grenades the way they were. Provided of course that they let him know first.

The kaptain scratched at his scar and listened to the sounds of fighting elsewhere. The ground trembled as mortars began to shell the captured stretch of trench. Grimruk grunted in annoyance. It would be the height of satisfaction to climb up there and feed the humans their blasted mortars, but he knew he had bigger squigs to catch. He had to get information for the warboss, let him know how tough this human position was.

Grimruk glanced at the kommandos with him, then nodded at the rubble. The orks shouldered their weapons and began to dig, exhuming the torn bodies of the soldiers. Each time one of the corpses was exposed, the orks tore at the front of their uniforms, ripping apart the cloth. As they collected scraps of uniform, the kommandos cast aside the bodies of their enemies like so much refuse. Soon, even Grimruk was satisfied that they had exposed everything there was to find in the rubble.

Wailing sirens shrieked across the battlefield. In the distance, Grimruk could see some of his kommandos retreating through the wire. Howitzers shelled the ground as the orks fled. Squinting, Grimruk could see the reason for their withdrawal. A pair of big armoured vehicles had lumbered into view, their guns blazing as they mowed down orks. The appearance of tanks made it clear to even the most stubborn of the kommandos that they wouldn't be able to hold the trench.

Wizgrot pulled at Grimruk's coat. The orderly's scrawny arms were filled with the scraps of cloth the kommandos had collected. Grimruk took them from the gretchin and stared at the bloodied strips of uniform. It was a habit of humans to wear the colour of their mob on the collars of their uniforms. Grimruk had learned some time ago that the easiest way to tell how many humans were gathered in one spot was to see how many different glyphs they wore on their collars.

The other kommandos were under strict orders to collect collar tabs from every human they killed. Grimruk should have quite a collection when the survivors of his mission returned to the horde's encampment. Then the kaptain would be able to study them at leisure. The warboss would be pleased to know how strong the human presence was around the mesa, and it was always a good thing to be thick with the warboss.

Grimruk barked the order to withdraw to his troops. They had done what they had set out to do. They had tested the strength of the human positions and they had secured intelligence about how great their numbers were. That was what the warboss had demanded of them.

LORD GENERAL RO Nagashima smiled beneath the mask of his rebreather as he read the reports from the mesa. During the night, ork scouts had tried to infiltrate the lines. The defenders had allowed the aliens to penetrate deep enough to get a full taste of what the position had to offer, to see the fake bunkers and siege guns. They had allowed survivors to escape back through the defences, to take word of what they had seen back to their army.

There was one curious thing in the reports. The orks had torn the collar tabs from the soldiers they had killed. Nagashima was puzzled by this. Was it possible the brutes were trying to recognise which units were stationed on the mesa? Nagashima chuckled at the thought. If the aliens were that clever, then they would fall even more deeply into his trap. Elements from a dozen different regiments had been detached for duty in the custodian force. Should the orks understand the importance of insignia, then the xenos vermin would think there was an entire army group stationed up there!

Nagashima's PDF troops stood at the ready. If the orks were going to strike the hive-city of Ko, then they would come over the plain. To avoid the seemingly formidable mesa, they would need to move into the hills. Once they did that, the PDF would cut the orks to pieces.

The boom of artillery snapped General Nagashima from his thoughts. A furious barrage thundered from the plain. He turned his head as he heard excited vox-chatter erupt from the communications terminals arrayed about his command centre. Beneath his mask, he turned pale as the importance of the frantic voices shrieking from the vox-casters impressed him.

Orks, tens of thousands of them, an entire army. They had boiled down into the plain in a moving ocean of warbikes and battlewagons, of crudely cobbled-together tanks and lumbering, titanic Stompas. The aliens surged down onto the plain in a tidal wave of destruction. But they did not turn from the mesa. Their ramshackle guns and missile launchers sent barrage after barrage into the mesa, blasting apart the faux-defences erected by Nagashima's troops, obliterating the illusion of an impregnable bastion.

General Nagashima lifted his eyes, watching as a black pillar of smoke began to crawl into the dust-ridden sky above the mesa. Horror churned in his gut.

It was impossible! Everything had fallen into place! There was no way the orks could have guessed the mesa was a trick! Everything had been done to make the orks believe the mesa was a fortress manned by an army of Izanagi's PDF. The orks had taken the bait. Reason dictated that they would avoid the mesa, take the shelter of the hills and bypass the fortress as they made their way to the hive-city.

Instead, the orks had advanced directly upon the fortress, despite every appearance that it was here Nagashima had concentrated his forces.

Instead, or because? The sickening thought made Nagashima's knees turn to jelly. The horrified general sank into a campaign chair, his head sinking against his chest.

The orks were not human. It had been idiocy for him to expect the xenos to act like men. They had bought his deception. They did think the mesa was where he had concentrated his forces. But instead of scaring them off, the imagined strength of the position had drawn them in. The orks, spoiling for a real fight after weeks of ransacking isolated settlements, hadn't tried to avoid the fortress. They had come straight on, eager to slake their lust for battle.

General Nagashima listened to the panicked voices on the vox-casters. Gradually the chatter died away as the positions were overrun. The officers under Nagashima were already shouting commands to their staff, trying to remobilise their entrenched positions.

It would be too late to save the troops trapped on the mesa. And once the orks finished swatting aside Nagashima's mock defences there was nothing to stand between them and the billion inhabitants of Ko.

Nothing but the regret and shame of the general who had failed them.

SANCTIFIED
Mark Clapham

IT WAS A view that few would ever see, an uninterrupted line of sight from the interior of an Imperial battlecruiser in space to the surface of a planet, with only the slight shimmer of a protective energy field between the two. The world below filled the vision, the halo of the atmosphere glowing fiercely. Even the most jaded of humans would concede it a rare sight, one deserving of at least a moment's appreciation.

Kaspel tried to ignore it, and kept his back turned to the gaping hole in the ship's hull as much as possible. It was not that he suffered from vertigo – it was the presence of the world below that perturbed him.

As a tech-priest of the Adeptus Mechanicus, serving the glory of machines and the Emperor, Kaspel had never known the feel of alien soil beneath his boots, or faced one of the xenos in person. He had been raised on the brotherhood's home of Mars, and then had performed his sacred duties within the engineering decks of the Imperial Navy's starships. He had walked corridors of sanctified metal his entire life, and although he was proud to contribute to the fight against the enemies of man, Kaspel had no desire to have direct contact with either the aliens or their worlds.

He had his work. The tear in the hull of the Imperial battlecruiser *Divine Sanctity* was severe, the result of a damaged necron ship clipping the *Sanctity* in battle, demolishing part of the engineering deck and crippling one of the ship's engine units. The battle had raged a day, fire lighting the sky as the battlefleet had rallied to repel the enemy.

Humanity had prevailed, but while the rest of the battlefleet had continued to push back the necron forces, the damage to the engines of the *Sanctity* had left it stranded in orbit over the now-dead world. While the temporary energy shields maintained the atmosphere and gravity within the exposed sections, Captain Rilk was eager to rejoin the front as soon as possible, and had expressed this desire to Kaspel in no uncertain terms.

Kaspel had found these entreaties unnecessary and vaguely offensive – he was a tech-priest, and would restore all systems to full and blessed order with the correct repairs and rites, as efficiently as possible. What more or less would he do?

With the atmosphere restored, Kaspel and his servitors could work efficiently and swiftly. The most severe damage had been to one of the ship's engine units, each of which was a hexagonal tube of machinery as tall as a hab block that stretched down the full length of the vast chamber, terminating in a thruster cone at the rear of the ship. A plasteel wall separated the visible end of the engine unit from the thruster itself. The chamber was shaped around the engine unit, with crawl spaces above and below the unit, and an access walkway on either side.

From where Kaspel stood, staring down at the thruster end of the unit, the hull damage gaped to his left, while to his right teams of servitors were methodically repairing the damage to the engine unit. The hull tear stretched above and below, and to access the damaged engine the servitors had to negotiate a rig of temporary scaffolding, a flimsy mesh of wire and tubular girders that often opened out into a direct view of space.

The servitors did not have the sentience to be unnerved by the illusion of an endless drop below them. Kaspel only went on to the scaffolding when his attention was urgently required.

The work was going well today. Servitors could be unreliable, but with the correct monitoring and direct instructions, Kaspel found that their many hands – and other mechanical appendages – made light work of straightforward repairs. Unnerved by the sense of exposure from the tear in the hull, Kaspel was relieved to leave the engine chamber and returned to the darker sections of the engineering decks.

FOR THE NEXT hour, Kaspel roamed the dark corridors and access shafts which weaved around the mechanisms of the great engines, mostly on foot but occasionally using his three mechadendrites, mechanical arms connected to his spine, to climb to difficult areas. As he moved, he recorded progress and issued fresh instructions to the technomats, occasionally stopping to administer a necessary rite or prayer.

As he took a shortcut down an airshaft between two levels, his mechadendrites finding purchase where human fingers could not, Kaspel ran some diagnostic incantations, ritually working through the processes of the engine, and the ceremonies that would bring each repaired part back online.

There was something wrong. The work was progressing, but the systems were not responding as they should – whole areas which should have come back online were still dead. Curious.

Kaspel dropped out of the shaft, and landed on the deck, the floorplates clanking under his weight. The corridor he had dropped into was a functional tube plated with thick slabs of plasteel on the walls and floors. The more ornate decorations of the Imperial style were reserved for the other end of the ship, where the officers worked and lived. In the engineering decks, practicality ruled over aesthetics: pipes and cables threaded in and out of the walls, and unmarked doors led to small work areas filled with cogitator terminals and spare components.

Kaspel straightened the thick red robes which covered his utilitarian leather coveralls, and was about to proceed to the next point in his inspection when he noticed an arm extending from a recess further down the corridor. It was a fleshy arm, ending in a basic pincer attachment.

He approached to find one of the servitors slumped in the alcove, head to one side, mouth frothing and eyes wide. It was not uncommon for servitors to fail, to lose mental coherence and to be jettisoned into space, but there was something in the wild expression in those eyes which gave Kaspel pause.

He adjusted the vision in his augmented eye to thermal, and observed the heart of the servitor as a hastily pulsating mass within the servitor's chest, pumping hard. The lungs were also working overtime. It was as if… Kaspel dropped to one knee, and rolled the servitor over onto its front. He ran a gloved hand over the implants on the back of its neck, the mechanisms that turned a vat-grown humanoid into a robotic creature capable of basic tasks. Kaspel's fingers found what he had suspected: a neat cut had been made in one cable, and the wires within reversed.

The alteration was a simple one, but specific, reversing the neural dampener that prevented servitors from being distracted by physical pain. Someone had very precisely altered this unfeeling creature to make it experience intense agony. Kaspel tore out the cable, and then removed a couple of further connections, cutting off all power to the brain. The servitor shuddered briefly, and died.

Kaspel corrected himself as he stood up. The servitor had never been alive. However, such deliberate sabotage needed to be reported. Kaspel tried to vox through to the ship's head of security, but received nothing but static. He tried other officers, or an open channel, but found the same static.

No, not quite static. It sounded like random interference, but Kaspel could make out repeating patterns. This was a deliberate signal, blocking communications.

Someone was isolating the engineering decks.

Kaspel was an enginseer, not a warrior. While he had received basic weapons training, first on Mars and then on transfer to the Navy, that training had been to meet the basic commitments of any subject of the God-Emperor that, if caught up in battle, any human should be ready to pick up a fallen warrior's weapon and fight to the last. If the ship had been stormed, Kaspel was qualified to pick up a bolt pistol and loose a few rounds at the enemy.

This... Kaspel was not even sure what kind of situation he was in. He needed to exercise caution, and find out how deep the isolation went. He found a cogitator unit in an alcove, and ran some simple diagnostics. Not only was communication between the engineering deck and the rest of the ship blocked, but the bulkheads between the two had been sealed as well. Kaspel tried to override these obstructions, but found himself ejected from the relevant menus with a flicker of on-screen static.

That flicker of disruption meant one thing: scrapcode, chaotic data introduced into the ship's cogitation systems to cause disruption, in this instance invisibly blocking onboard communications.

Kaspel's breath quickened behind his mask: the creation and use of scrapcode was considered by the Adeptus Mechanicus to be heresy, a grave attack on the machine-spirit. Kaspel was an enginseer, engines and heavy mechanisms were his vocation. He knew some of the rituals and practices of maintaining cogitators, but nowhere near enough to circumvent and purge scrapcode. Kaspel would get nothing more from the cogitator.

The machine-spirit of the *Divine Sanctity* was under threat of corruption and it seemed, for now, that Kaspel was the only one who could try and save it.

KASPEL TROD LIGHTLY, and kept to the shadows as much as possible while following the curve of the corridor. There was nothing to see in the gloom, and little to hear except the ambient *glug glug* of thick coolant running through the pipes attached to the wall, pipes which ran all the way to the generatorium. The coolant absorbed the excess heat from the generatorium, the then-hot liquid flowing out to the extremities of the ship where proximity to the freezing void of space re-cooled the liquid.

Kaspel was approaching one of the areas where he had set servitors to work. He could hear the hissing of welding equipment, noise consistent with the work Kaspel had assigned, but nonetheless he was cautious, slowing his pace even further. This was a heavy work area, and various tools were leaning against the walls, organised by size so even the less efficient servitors could work out which was required. Kaspel carefully stepped around a stack of plasteel panels.

Then, for a brief moment, one of the welding torches around the corner flared spectacularly, the bright orange light consuming the corridor ahead, casting a deep black shadow on the wall. The silhouette was of two figures: the lumpen shape of a servitor, hanging crooked as if chained up by the wrists, and another taller, unnaturally thin figure, standing with its feet apart, one hand raised with hideously tapered fingers – were those blades? – spread out. In those short seconds of illumination, the tall figure's hand swung down, right into the guts of the other. Then the light source guttered out and the shadows disappeared, leaving only an echo of the noise of rended flesh.

Kaspel's breath caught in his throat, the rebreather in his mask briefly struggling to adjust. Thoughts raced through his mind. Whoever the second figure was, it wasn't a human or a servitor. Its proportions, the way it moved, were just *wrong*. Alien.

Kaspel made an involuntary step backwards, and there was a tinny crash from just behind him. He instinctively spun around, to see he had knocked over the stacked panels.

Any sense of relief was dispelled by the realisation of how loud that noise must have been. Kaspel barely had time to look back down the corridor, to see a lithe, shimmering figure seemingly carved out of shadows bounding towards him. Its movements were graceful, almost silent as its feet glanced off the metal deck, yet with a terrifying speed and power. The shadow-figure raised one hand as it descended on Kaspel, and he saw that it indeed wore some kind of bladed gauntlet.

Kaspel had little time to do anything but stumble backwards. His mechadendrites instinctively reached out behind him, cushioning his fall and pushing him over to land on his feet. Rather than try and stand up or break into a run, Kaspel rolled sideways again, towards the other side of the corridor.

The alien – and it was definitely alien – let out an unintelligible babble of frustration as Kaspel evaded its first blow, the blades on its hand tearing through the wall as its swipe went wide, cutting through plasteel as if it were paper. The shimmering shadow effect suddenly flickered, dissipating like interference on a cogitator screen, and Kaspel had his first proper glimpse of the enemy.

Standing before him was a figure in chitinous black body armour with elongated, deathly pale features. The long, cruel mouth was twisted in bitter frustration, well-deep eyes wide in hatred.

He had never seen one before, but Kaspel recognised the creature for what it was: an eldar. As the towering xenos moved towards him with terrifying speed, Kaspel used one of his mechadendrites to grasp the coolant pipe on the wall, pulling him to his feet. Then, a second later, Kaspel pushed himself sideways with all his strength, and once again the eldar's clawed hand tore down through the empty space where Kaspel had just been standing.

This time though, the eldar clawed into more than just the wall, the blades on his hand tearing into one of the coolant pipes. Where the five slashes gouged into the pipe, freezing liquid gel pumped at high pressure found release and sprayed into the corridor.

The eldar screamed discordantly, a terrible inhuman sound, as the freezing liquid hit it full-on. It reeled, consumed by a cloud of vapour as water droplets froze in the air around it.

A major freeze-burn like that would kill even the strongest human on contact, but Kaspel wasn't taking any risks. He picked up one of the wrenches leaning against the wall and, holding it with both hands, swung the tool around in a wide arc to make contact with the side of the eldar's head.

On contact, its head exploded in a shower of icy fragments, the pieces clattering off the floor and walls as they ricocheted in all directions. The blast of coolant had frozen its entire head solid on contact, rendering it brittle.

The eldar's headless body crashed heavily to the floor, its fluid grace all gone in death. The bladed gauntlet, and most of that forearm, also shattered into frozen pieces, blackened chunks spinning across the floor.

With a hiss, the fail-safes in the coolant pipe closed off the ruptured section, diverting the flow to backup pipes. The temperature in the corridor adjusted back to normal, the mist clearing.

Kaspel dropped to his knees, the wrench feeling heavier in his hands than it possibly could be. Too close. He had been unprepared, and his improvisation with the coolant had been statistically unlikely to work. A less practically minded person would have said that he 'got lucky'.

Leaning on the wrench, Kaspel pushed himself to his feet, and looked down at the eldar's headless corpse. So this was the enemy. Even dead, faceless and inert, it disgusted him, from the pallid exposed flesh to the unnatural sheen of its black armour.

Kaspel told himself that there was no point searching the body, that the armour was too tight to conceal any weapons beyond the shattered gauntlet, and that if the eldar carried any plans, Kaspel wouldn't be able to read the language. But he knew that these were just rationalisations – he couldn't bring himself to touch the body, to make direct contact with the alien.

Kaspel recognised the black armour, its shimmering shielding, from stories and briefings. These 'dark eldar' were tainted by Chaos, and combined the abilities and training of their warrior heritage with the unpredictable cruelty of the dark powers.

Kaspel, on the other hand, was a non-combatant, a worker of machines. Any attempt at direct confrontation between him and the eldar would end in failure, and the *Sanctity*, its mission, its crew and its machine-spirit would be doomed.

He needed other ways to kill them, to use methods of his own and the machinery he was an expert in. These eldar were an affront to the machine-spirit of the *Sanctity*, and that spirit would provide the means of their destruction.

If other eldar had been nearby, they would have attacked by now. Kaspel felt confident enough to walk around the corridor to where the gutted servitor hung from the ceiling. Kaspel ignored it, picked up its abandoned welding torch from where it was slowly melting a hole in the floor, switched it off and tossed it aside. Such a device had been useful in the eldar's torture games, but required too close proximity to be any use to Kaspel.

Kaspel couldn't risk using the coolant again, as there was only so much damage those pipes could incur before the system began to fail and threatened a terminal overheat. But there were other mechanisms that could be used.

Deep in thought, Kaspel reached for the welding torch he had just abandoned, and began to unscrew a panel on the side of the tool.

THE GENERATORIUM WAS the largest chamber on the engineering decks, dominated by the generator stacks, monolithic structures which lined one end of the room. Each generator stack was squat and metallic at the top and bottom, with transparent panels in the middle that showed the fierce currents of power flowing within, white-hot energy crackling around incandescent elements. In the open space before the stacks, freestanding cogitator terminals displayed the flow of power, while riveted columns stretched from floor to ceiling, bracing the entire room. Vast cables, heavily insulated, ran from the stacks and into the walls, floors and ceilings, feeding power all across the ship.

More functional workstations lined the walls at either side of the stacks, while directly opposite, the walls were peppered by half a dozen vast bladed fans set in wide air shafts, all of which were presently inert, but capable of draining the atmosphere from the room in seconds if required. Each fan was covered by a thin metal mesh, and set at head height from the floor.

The generatorium was not a quiet place: a relentless hum from the vast power within the generator stacks filled the air. Kaspel entered the room via a door in the shadow of the stacks and although he could hear raised voices over the din, he couldn't make out any words.

Edging around the stacks towards the voices, Kaspel began to make out the words. There were two of them, both male and neither human. They spoke in Imperial Gothic with no discernible accent, their words oddly stilted as if they had learned the language without ever hearing it.

'Let us try this again,' said one. 'How do we restore the power?' This voice was infinitely weary, as if talking to a child or pet.

'Tell us now,' said another, sharper voice. 'Then we will make it quick.'

There was a ragged, spluttering sound, and then a third, human voice spoke up weakly.

'I told you... I don't know.' There was a pause, another ragged breath. 'And if I did, you could–'

A laboured coughing fit cut off the insult. Kaspel recognised the human voice as Whallon, one of the captain's lieutenants who spent most of his days relaying orders around the *Sanctity*. He had doubtless been sent down to engineering to check on Kaspel's progress, only to get picked up by the eldar.

Kaspel didn't doubt Whallon was telling the truth – if Kaspel couldn't solve the power problem, a non-technical officer certainly wouldn't be able to.

When the eldar realised that, Whallon was dead. There was little time to spare. Kaspel checked the small pouch of liquid tied to his belt, and carefully untied it. The pouch was vacuum-sealed, but the contents were volatile. He held it gingerly in one gloved hand.

Prepared, he peered around the corner of the stack. There were only two eldar in the open space before the stacks, and they were standing over Whallon, who was tied to one of the pillars that braced the chamber. Whallon, slumped low with his arms wrenched back against the pillar, was staring up at the two eldar defiantly. His dress uniform had been torn open at the front, cuts and bruises dotting his face and chest.

Kaspel was fortunate again, as the eldar were standing with their backs to him as they repeated their questions with greater urgency. The more laconic eldar was leaning on an ornate stave, while the other held a viciously serrated blade. Both wore the same black armour as the creature that Kaspel had already destroyed.

He quickly surveyed the room, working out the distances. Technically minded, he easily calculated what was required. It was possible, narrowly.

'Tell us what we want to know!' hissed the blade-wielding eldar. He moved as if to stab Whallon with his blade, but it was just a feint – instead he pulled the blade away and brought his empty hand down, delivering a backhanded blow to Whallon's face. The studs on the eldar's glove left shallow cuts in Whallon's cheek.

Kaspel stepped out of the shadows, adjusting the volume controls in his mask vox for maximum effect.

'Ask me,' he said, his synthesised voice echoing around the room.

His words had the desired effect. The eldar snapped around, too well-trained to show surprise or dismay, or maybe just too alien to even feel such things. They did not reply, but reacted, starting towards Kaspel the moment they registered his presence.

But Kaspel had moved first, running not towards the eldar, but to the far wall of the chamber, where a pile of crates was stacked under the great extractor fans. That wall was slightly nearer to Kaspel than it was to the eldar, so he had a head start.

Not looking back, he kept running. They would want to capture him alive, to find out what he knew, or at least that was his hope. If he was wrong, a shot to the back would take him down soon enough.

When he reached the crates, Kaspel jumped onto the first one, which was only a third of his height. As he clambered on top of the next, the stave-bearing eldar threw his weapon. The stave tore through Kaspel's cloak and embedded itself in one of the storage boxes, narrowly missing his side.

The material tore as Kaspel climbed, and he cursed himself for not abandoning his cloak earlier. While his fingers scrabbled for purchase, he used his mechadendrites to tear the thin protective grille away from the fan. It came off in one go, rivets popping out and showering down.

The horizontal shaft was twice the height of a man, and three closely placed fans were between Kaspel and the next grille, after which the shaft dropped down to a further set of fans and, eventually, a discharge pipe that expelled fumes directly into space. Each of the three fans had sixteen blades, and Kaspel had to carefully manoeuvre to squeeze between them. As Kaspel pulled himself between the razor-sharp blades of the first fan, which was placed only slightly past the rim of the shaft, he dared to glimpse behind him. The blade-wielding eldar was below, about to strike. Kaspel pulled his booted feet away just before the sword came down, and rolled into the gap between the first two fans.

Kaspel scrambled to his feet in the narrow gap, and began to squeeze past the blades of the second fan. He slipped on the oiled, curved wall of the air shaft, and raised his arm defensively as he bumped into a fan blade. The blade cut straight through one sleeve of his leather coveralls, and grazed his left arm, drawing blood. He winced.

Kaspel shuffled quickly through. One fan to go. He looked back, to see the blade-wielder gracefully stepping between the inert blades of the first fan, angling its lithe limbs like a practised gymnast.

With little gap between each fan, Kaspel was at the final fan immediately after passing the second. Suppressing any dangerous haste, he pushed between the blades. One of his mechadendrites clanked against the blades, but he was through.

Kaspel turned his back to the thin wire mesh that was between him and a sheer drop, the pouch of liquid in his hand. The eldar were nearly upon him, the blade-wielder already stepping through the second fan, while his comrade was in turn a step behind him.

Kaspel threw the pouch between the blades of the fan, and it hit the vent wall just next to the second fan. The contents spilled wide, sloshing everywhere, and burst into flames.

Kaspel had carefully siphoned the liquid from the welding torch, knowing its volatility, especially when in an oxygenated environment. The eldar recoiled slightly at the fire, but were unconcerned. Why should they be? They were armoured, and it was only a little fire.

However, a little fire in the sensitive workings of a battlecruiser was a dangerous thing, and the systems were built to compensate. As the flame burst out in the vent, the fans came to life without warning, changing from completely static to a rapid spin in seconds.

Kaspel was blown back into the grille as the triple blades tore into the two eldar, cutting through their armour, flesh and bone without discrimination. The grille buckled under his weight but held as a blast of air and eldar remains was sucked down the air shaft, slipping through gaps in the mesh to slide down the shaft and be expelled into space.

The flames from Kaspel's amateur incendiary quickly went out, and the fans halted their movement as suddenly as they had started. Kaspel blinked, wiping gore from the lenses of his mask. Ignoring the alien remains smeared around the shaft, he began to carefully make his way back to the generatorium.

Whallon had a broken rib, and possibly a punctured lung. That didn't stop him from talking as Kaspel untied him.

'Came down here to find you,' he said, stretching his arms and wincing. 'Then this lot appeared out of nowhere. I think there's only a few more, including the leader. They tied me up and left me here to play with later. Then, when they had problems with their tech, they started asking questions.'

Whallon nodded towards a series of squat black devices spread around the base of the generator stacks. Kaspel hadn't noticed them before – there was something about their near-featureless blackness that made the eyes slide off them. As Whallon slowly pulled himself to his feet, Kaspel inspected one of the alien machines.

It was a black box with curved edges, seemingly made out of some kind of stone or crystal. Indentations in the top could be either controls or instructions. Translucent cables snaked from the box, some attaching to various points on the generator stacks, others to the nearby alien machines. Following the trail of cables, he could see that some led out into the corridors of the ship.

'I think,' said Whallon, 'these are for moving the *Sanctity*.'

'Yes,' replied Kaspel. 'I think you are right.'

The dark eldar had their own means of travel barely comprehended by other species. Could a device like this, provided with enough power, drag an entire battlecruiser through space? Kaspel had no way of telling. Whatever the device did, it was heretical technology outside the sacred machinery of the Imperium.

Kaspel decided against tampering with the eldar machine, as he had no idea what side effects that might cause. Best to leave it where it was for now, and deal with the immediate threat first. If the eldar managed to jump the *Sanctity* into the webway, the ship would be repurposed or cannibalised for parts while the crew would be converted into soulless, broken slaves. These were not fit fates for either the Emperor's machine or men.

'Where did they go?' Kaspel asked.

'Down into the engines,' replied Whallon, who had given up on standing, and slumped back against the pillar. 'I…' He coughed again, a splatter of blood at the corner of his mouth.

Kaspel nodded. 'Rest. Your injuries are not fatal, but may be if you strain them.' He put an arm around Whallon, and helped him stumble across the room to a chair in front of a cogitator terminal. 'The xenos have isolated communications with the rest of the ship. Eventually the bridge will realise and break through. When they do, they will need you alive to direct them.'

Whallon nodded. His skin was pallid and sheened in sweat, but he was still an officer. He would hold out.

'I will locate the xenos, and do what I can to stop them.'

Whallon nodded again, then pointed towards a dark corner of the room, near where he had been tied up.

'They had my bolt pistol before I could use it,' he said, pausing to take another painful breath. 'Threw it over there. Ceremonial, but it works.'

Kaspel nodded gratefully, and followed Whallon's gesture to find his holster belt, crudely cut in half where the eldar had torn it from the officer, but with bolt pistol still attached. The weapon was heavy, but well-polished and with ornate patterns engraved on the barrel. It was clearly decorative, a reward for some previous action, but it might prove useful.

Giving one last nod to Whallon, Kaspel checked the pistol's clip, and left the generatorium. Following the alien power lines, he headed back towards the engines.

WHILE ENGINEERS WERE more attuned to the workings of machines than of humans, Kaspel was nevertheless aware that he was in shock, and that his best hope for remaining efficient was to keep moving, to act without stopping to think. However, it did occur to him how fast his perceptions were being changed.

Since killing the two eldar with the fan blades, he had been covered in their drying blood. An hour ago, the thought of even a drop of alien blood touching him would have been horrific, a notion to be quickly suppressed. Kaspel's encounters with the eldar had changed him. Yes, the xenos were hateful abominations, but as repellent as they were, there was no need to fear them for their physical differences. It was not their blood, flesh or bone that was a threat, disgusting as it was.

No, what Kaspel knew was worth fearing, worth confronting, was the aliens' dark intent and capacity for inflicting their will on the human race. Their actions on the ship had demonstrated that. Only a small group had infiltrated the *Sanctity*, but they had violated everything in their path, torturing a loyal officer of the Imperial Navy, corrupting the cogitators with scrapcode and tainting the ship's precious power source with their vile machinery.

It was as Kaspel had always been taught, but never experienced – even the slightest touch of Chaos or the gentlest brush with alien thinking corrupted, and their every influence needed to be excised by force and fire. Kaspel had learned these abstract lessons long ago, but only now did he understand their basis in concrete fact.

One small area of corruption, untreated, could undermine the whole.

Kaspel stopped in his tracks, his thoughts racing ahead of him. Of course, that simple lesson... it was a principle that men of the Imperium lived and died by, yet it hadn't occurred to Kaspel that it could apply to the ship's predicament as well. It all made sense now; he could see where the problem was.

One of the *Divine Sanctity's* engine units had failed, not just in terms of its operation but in terms of diagnostics. The cogitative mechanisms which compensated for any error had misinterpreted the damage to the engine unit as a failure of the power supply, and tried to divert massive amounts of energy from the generatorium to rectify the imagined power failure. Thanks to this freak error, the other engine units could not build up enough power to move the ship. This was a problem, but one that had also prevented the eldar's parasitic technology from functioning properly.

Two problems, two sources of corruption in the machine. Purge both, save the whole. It was elegant simplicity, coming together like great cogs clicking into place. Kaspel instinctively, reverently, touched the golden cog of the Adeptus Mechanicus that hung on a chain around his neck. As ever, the machine provided a solution, and it was for the tech-priest to follow its lead.

Kaspel increased his pace. He knew where the eldar would be, and he knew how to deal with them.

KASPEL FOUND HIMSELF back where he had begun the day, in the chamber containing the damaged engine unit. The energy field that prevented the atmosphere from escaping through the tear in the hull still shimmered in place.

As he entered the chamber, walking under a bulkhead which would rapidly drop down and seal off the area in the case of an atmosphere breach, Kaspel heard raised eldar voices, and the clank of their armoured boots on scaffolding. The trail of alien cabling ran down the walkway, and disappeared to the right, into the gap in the side of the engine unit. The bodies of the servitors that Kaspel had left to work on the engine damage lay scattered across the walkway, swiftly dismantled by eldar blades.

As Kaspel had expected, the eldar were working on the core of the damaged engine unit, out of his line of sight.

To Kaspel's right, the vast hexagonal engine unit towered above him, as intimidating in its own way as the tear in the hull to his left, a looming structure that contained the power transformers and other machinery that converted raw energy into the thrust necessary to propel the battlecruiser through space.

Kaspel couldn't risk closing the bulkhead behind him, partially because it would close off his escape route, but mainly because it would alert the eldar to his presence, which would make his job far harder.

Battlecruisers were assembled in the space docks that orbited some of the Adeptus Mechanicus's forge worlds. Ships were built reverently, over many years, engineers and other adepts working tirelessly in the vacuum to build them. By necessity, the work was modular – components were forged on the world below, brought up in shuttles, and then installed into the frame of the growing ship. Beneath the hull, a ship was not just a single machine, but also many machines, brought into harmony as a single entity. Many parts, one whole.

Kaspel knew that what had once been brought together could be torn apart. The hull damage had taken out many of the supporting points which fixed the engine unit in place within the main structure of the battlecruiser. By Kaspel's reckoning there were five supports left that needed to be manually unbolted. The struts themselves were vast, but the levers for releasing them were easy enough to shift.

Once Kaspel had released the five struts, all he needed to do was breach one of the engine unit's many plasma capsules. The entire chamber would lock down and purge the atmosphere and, without the struts holding it in place, the engine unit itself would roll right out of the chamber into the vacuum.

Kaspel could take out one of the plasma capsules from the doorway with a single shot from Whallon's bolt pistol. He would then have a couple of seconds to step back into the corridor before the bulkheads came down.

Kaspel began to climb the side of the engine unit. Eventually, he reached a large strut which emerged from the wall and embedded deep into the unit itself. Kaspel found the red release lever on the side of the strut, and pulled it all the way back. There was a low metallic grinding, but thankfully this didn't attract the eldar's attention.

The collision with the necron vessel had demolished the other support strut on the outwards-facing side of the engine unit, whereas the other side had two struts intact. Using both his human arms and his mechadendrites, Kaspel climbed onto the top of the engine unit, crossed the top and lowered himself down the other side until he reached the parallel strut to the one he had already released. He repeated the process with the lever, and then lowered himself down to the walkway on that side. As quietly as he could, he ran to the thruster end of the chamber, then climbed up and pulled the release lever on the other strut on that side.

What remained were the two vertical struts which came down through the ceiling and into the top of the unit. Kaspel climbed back up the engine unit, and slowly made his way across the top of the machine. It was not a flat surface, and he needed his mechadendrites to maintain his balance.

He reached the first vertical strut, and pulled the release lever. All that remained was to release the last strut, return to the doorway and shoot out one of the plasma capsules.

His job nearly complete, Kaspel began the careful approach to the last strut, making his way back down the top of the machine, away from the thrusters. As he did, the voices of the eldar became louder. He was approaching the point where the hull damage had penetrated the engine unit deepest, where the eldar were doing their work.

Kaspel reached the last strut, and pulled the last lever. Nearly done.

He stayed atop the engine unit, moving quickly but carefully in the direction of the door. Where the engine had been damaged he had to shuffle around the temporary scaffolding rig that allowed access for repairs. He looked down into the web of scaffolding.

In the very heart of the engine unit, two eldar were at work, supervised by a third who was clearly their leader. Like Kaspel, the eldar had realised that the damaged engine unit was not just stalling the ship, but preventing them siphoning power from the generatorium to drag the *Sanctity* into the webway. They seemed to have found their own solution, and were rigging a complex mechanism into the heart of the damaged unit using white-hot, precision cutting tools.

Kaspel shuddered at this latest violation of the machine-spirit.

The leader, who had removed his helmet to reveal cruel features and deep black eyes, was obviously unhappy with the progress of his warrior technicians, and paced imperiously across the bars of the scaffold. He twitched to the left and right, and then, seemingly rolling his eyes back, he looked up.

The lead eldar's gaze caught Kaspel looking down. The alien barked a command to his men.

Caution abandoned, Kaspel ducked around the scaffolding and ran across the top of the machine as fast as he could, all the while trying not to lose his footing. Behind him he could hear the metallic clattering of someone climbing the scaffolding.

As he reached the edge of the machine on the hull side, only a short distance from the door to the rest of the ship, there was the harsh report of a weapon being fired, and then another. Something shattered against the ceiling near Kaspel's head, but the second shot was closer. A thin shard of crystal tore through Kaspel's shoulder, cutting right to the bone. He was overwhelmed with pain as he rolled off the top of the machine and fell the rest of the way, landing heavily on the walkway below.

Some part of his mind was warning him that the eldar used poison weaponry, but this was the least of Kaspel's worries. The fall had broken his leg, and his arm below the shoulder wound felt completely numb. He heard the screams of the eldar leader.

Kaspel rolled onto his back, and looked down the walkway. An eldar was running towards him, weapon raised.

He had seconds left to live. There was no more time, no escape.

Kaspel thrust his good hand into his robes, finding Whallon's bolt pistol. He looked around, locating the spherical, silver shape of a plasma capsule slightly further down the engine unit, its metallic bulge curving out of the machine's side. Kaspel raised the bolt pistol, and as he did so his mechadendrites reached sideways towards the engine unit, finding pipes and struts to hold on to.

Time seemed to slow, the eldar raising its weapon, as Kaspel took aim. He was not a warrior, but he was an enginseer, with a sharp eye and the mind to calculate trajectory. Kaspel squeezed the trigger.

The plasma breach was a ripple of fierce blue energy that consumed the nearest section of walkway, which tore apart, blasting the eldar out of the gap in the hull. The energy field fizzed as the eldar passed through it, out into the vacuum, but remained intact. Although Kaspel was just outside the range of the plasma breach, the walkway under him buckled, and he was left hanging limply from the side of the engine unit.

The lights in the chamber switched to deep red, and a klaxon sounded. Kaspel heard the bulkheads crash down, isolating the chamber from the rest of the ship.

Then it began, the entire engine unit detaching itself from the *Sanctity*, grinding free, rolling thrusters-first out of the ship. As it moved, the plasteel wall that separated the engine from the thruster itself ripped apart, and the atmosphere began to rush out of the chamber. Kaspel saw the eldar leader emerge from the damaged area of the engine, only to be sucked out into space. As the unit ground spacewards, the scaffolding covering the damage collapsed into a storm of splinters that scattered into space.

Kaspel didn't see the other eldar die, but he didn't need to. No one was leaving alive.

The solid grip of Kaspel's mechadendrites kept him from being sucked away as the engine unit slid free of the *Sanctity*. Then Kaspel was floating in the void, free of the ship's artificial gravity, clinging to the damaged machine.

The air was gone, the transmission of sound with it, and there was only the sound of Kaspel's own frantic breath echoing within his mask. His airtight facemask with its built-in rebreather would grant him a little more life in the vacuum than his enemies had.

The lenses in his mask were beginning to freeze up, but Kaspel looked back, and to his satisfaction saw that, with the damaged unit removed, the remaining thrusters were back online, firing in an automated test pattern. The *Sanctity* was alive once more, its machine-spirit safe, its crew free to rejoin the war on another front.

Kaspel's war, however, was over. While his augmentations allowed him to survive in the vacuum for a while, they did not add up to the protection of a spacesuit. He was frosting over. Subjected to the vacuum of space for much longer, the more vulnerable parts of his life support would crack.

Kaspel suspected that he wouldn't actually live long enough to see that happen. Propelled free of the *Sanctity's* grip, the engine block was beginning to feel the effects of the gravity of the planet below. Kaspel tightened his mechadendrites around the machinery behind him, and looked towards the planet below.

Soon enough, Kaspel would be burned away along with everything but the hardiest parts of the engine, incinerated as the engine unit entered the planet's atmosphere. But for a second, just before his vision was consumed by the glare of re-entry, Kaspel maximised the capabilities of his augmented senses, letting the rush of sensory data consume him.

For a moment, Kaspel took in the view of an alien world. The continents, vast and grey-brown, dappled with forests and streaks of mountain ranges. The seas and lakes, purplish blue. The wisps of cloud in the atmosphere. The irregular grey mass of once-great cities, long since deserted by whichever species had walked the soil.

As Kaspel fell towards his first and final contact with alien ground, he felt no fear, no fury, only awe at the scale and complexity of the world below, the endlessly intricate mechanisms of a universe that defied the knowledge and rituals of his science, that would be, to him, forever alien.

FACES
Matthew Farrer

IN THE END Jann couldn't stay away, and so here she came again creeping back into the tower's red-blurred shadow, hunched over with a rusted torque-stave in her hand. The shouting, drumming storm was two days gone now, and no matter how hard Jann listened all she could hear was the soft crackle of her footsteps in the sandflake drift and her own breathing, dry and frightened. At this hour, at this angle, the depot tower was a lightless block of black against the blood of the sky behind it. No movement, no voices. Even the great metal bulk of the pipeline was inert.

The storm's trailing winds had smoothed out the ground, and the only footprints in front of the south door were Jann's own. They staggered and lurched out from the little storm-hatch and disappeared behind one of the giant pipeline buttresses, the spot where she had crouched and shivered all through the night at the mercy of strange, taunting dreams. Now the slower, softer prints stalked back out of hiding and up behind her, padding steps, trying for a stealth that she knew would make no difference. She would have to go in there and find them, all of them. She would have to show her…

…face.

She took light steps towards the hatch, holding the stave this way and that, trying to think how she could best swing it if one of them were waiting just inside. It would be dark. The only parts of the tower that were ever properly lit were the control room at the top and the living deck. For a moment that thought almost soothed her. She thought of the dark rooms and halls, dark country she had never seen, riding high and quiet over it, and strange mountains kissed with silver light, but that image split and twisted her thoughts and her strength fled her for a moment. She moaned, softly, and craned up to the sky, but there was no white moon there to help her. There should have been a white moon. Jann had never seen a moon, not of any colour, but there should have been a white moon.

She dropped her eyes from the sky and stood swaying in the doorway for a moment. It seemed as though she were about to break through to some understanding of what was happening to her, but a blink and a breath and it was all gone like

(*moonlight*)

smoke through her fingers and she found herself stepping through the storm-hatch, breathing hard, trying to force her eyes to dilate, gripping the stave so hard that the corroded texture of its haft bit into her palms. She held it closer to her, like a walking-staff, and found a little comfort in that. No moon-gems, but it would do.

The engines embedded in the tower's thick foundations sent their rumbling beat through the walls. A deep beat, a walking-beat, for a slow promenade before the dance began. The implications of that thought gave her chills but her steps, already in time to the engines, began to quicken. The emergency lights shone in their little cages high on the rockcrete walls, red like blood that washed from the sky, yellow like the sparks flying up from an anvil. Jann didn't know whose thoughts these were any more.

Staring into the light, she thought she heard a movement somewhere in the dimness, but the accessway behind her was empty. Jann turned her

(*or was it really her*)

face inwards towards the red-lit corridors, and pressed on.

She found Gallardi in the machine-shrine, as she had expected to. He had broken the bright blue-white floodlamps that Tokuin had always kept bathing the hall, and now worked only in the same dim red emergency light that Jann had walked through. He had thrown open the maintenance shutters to the enginarium crypt below them and the machine-noise was louder here, a furnace roar. Conduits and energy sinks glowed cherry-red and added their light and heat. The air was clear, but Jann's senses brought her the faint touch of smoke.

'Brother?' she whispered. Gallardi was standing with his back to her, his slabs of shoulders working, his thick body swaying and folding where the fat overhung his belt. From the other side of him came the ring of metal on metal.

'Brother?'

In the racket of the shrine, the engines below and half a dozen of Tokuin's workshop machines running, there was no way the sound of her whisper could have reached him. But his body shivered at the murmur of her voice and he turned. Good Gallardi with his callused hands and soft voice, who'd liked to watch the sunset with her from the tower's roof. He'd sung songs with her (but what songs? Why couldn't she remember them?) and... and danced... under six white moons...

There was no white moon. Jann had never seen a moon. She sobbed and took a half-step forwards. She wanted her friend, so blessedly familiar. His thin legs, of which he was so self-conscious. His belly, with the old runnelled scar from the solder-splash accident years before they had met. His grizzled, shaven head and his, his...

...face.

There was a hammer in his hand, and he raised it.

'I can't greet you the way I want to, my beautiful little sister,' he said. Was his mouth moving? One moment Jann thought so, and then thought not. 'You're welcome and safe in my home, always, you know that. But I must work.' There was a shrieking hiss from behind him. The steelcutting press, left to run unsupervised, had overheated and was trying to shut itself down.

'We aren't safe, brother, either of us!' Now she found proper voice, although her words sounded strange to her own ears, high and singsong, almost not her own. 'It's happening again. I heard them fighting up on the operational deck.' Her memories seemed to float and split. The brawl between her crewmates splayed out and overlapped itself like a pict-screen trying to show half a dozen images at once. But every image horrified her. There was nothing she wanted to see. 'He knows! He...' She stumbled over the name. Crussman. He reared up through every one of her memories, stinking of lho-smoke and of the blood that slicked the front of his coveralls and dripped from his hand. The simple picture of him sent a killing scream through her thoughts, and still she stumbled over his name, because couldn't she also remember...

(Crussman twisted around the edge of the driver's seat in the high, cramped little cabin of the crane-rigger, looking down at them. 'Lifts like a dream!' he shouted over the engine and the winches. 'Easy to see how beat-up it got. Who knows how far the storm threw it to get to here?' There was a huge, cheerful grin on his face. This was the best bit of storm-scrap they'd ever...)

'Crussman,' she managed to say, although somehow she thought she had mangled the word again, made it something shorter, guttural. 'He knows about... about you. He knows you're here. He knows...'

Knows what you did. Knows where we are. Knows what he has to do. Knows what has to happen. None of the answers that sprang to her mind made any sense. From somewhere around them she thought she heard footsteps, light as rushing air, and faint laughter. If Gallardi heard it too, he didn't show it. The red light shone steady from the emergency lamps but seemed to flicker on the man's

(*that's not his real*)

face as he hefted his hammer again and turned away. Jann followed him around the machine-shrine, stepping over Tokuin's corpse without looking down at it.

'He was too strong for me,' Gallardi said in a voice gruff with sadness, and let one hand drop to point to his leg. 'Too strong. I forged my very breath into my steel, and what did it aid me? No, no. It's done now. I've given the last one to Sabila, but that path is not mine. Bloodletting is his. His soul is there. And mine is here. Bound here.' Jann looked where his hand pointed. Her vision swam and doubled. She saw Gallardi's bare, pale foot beneath the cuff of a standard-issue rust-brown crewman's legging, and she saw a leg thick like a pillar, muscle-packed, anvil-heavy, riven and bent under the scars of the terrible wounds that Crussman had dealt when he had dragged Gallardi back here, mutilated and bereft, and picked up his chains.

Crussman had never been down here. This place had been Tokuin's. It had been sacred to him. A place where he came to work as a supplicant, a priest, where Gallardi had come as a master. Jann understood why they had fought, but she couldn't understand what she was seeing now. The dark-skinned man with the big scarred belly was as true as all her memories, but yet she knew the limping master of the anvil as truly as she did the shining features of her own

(*but is this really my*)

face. She cradled her stave in one hand and reached the other out to him.

'I ran and hid,' she said. 'I... I think I slept. I think I dreamed. I dreamed about us. I don't know if I dreamed about you and... him...' she pointed back to the body behind her, unable to think of the name of the engineer with whom she'd lived and worked for two years, '...or if I remembered. I saw you fighting him...'

(*'Gallardi!' Tokuin had screamed. Augmetics covered the adept's eyes and nose but his mouth was flesh, not a vocoder, and there was ugly organic fear in his voice. 'Stop it! Stop what you're doing!' He had coughed and doubled over as a fist had found his belly, then arched the copper-inlaid utility-arm that sprouted from the base of his spine, arched it like a scorpion's tail to block the downwards swing of the pneumatic clamp that Gallardi had loaded his other fist with. The clamp bounced away with a clang and the arm shot forwards snake-fast into Gallardi's chin, but it was only a push, not a blow. Tokuin didn't really understand what was happening, he had not done the thing that the rest of them had done that Jann's memory couldn't quite piece together. Tokuin didn't understand the wrongness of this, didn't understand that Gallardi had to take mastery of the forge or everything was false, in a way even she struggled to understand. Tokuin pushed Gallardi and held him, and Gallardi thrashed for a moment in the eight-fingered mechanical grips as they held him by the jaw before he battered the slender end-joints of the arm with the clamp and shook it loose.*

'You're deranged, Gallardi!' Tokuin was a man of the machine-cloisters, no brawler, and he had staggered back through the workshop jerking with feedback as his battered arm malfunctioned. 'You're damaged! Jann! All of you! Where's Merelock? Make her take command again! You're all damaged!' He was retreating deeper into the forge and Jann wanted to call to him to stop, to explain how much more wrong he was making it, with his alien voice and his strange half-and-half face, but Gallardi was closing in again. 'It's those things, they've driven you mad! Gallardi! Jann, talk sense to him!' One of the mechanised pallet-jacks came to life and rolled forwards, Tokuin trying to manoeuvre its drive-block in front of Gallardi's body, its tines under his feet, but he spun and danced around it, lurched, caromed off the pipe-lathe and closed in. 'Take it off, Gallardi, it's wrecking your mind, Gallardi, listen–' And she had run away, then, because her friend was about to beat the enginseer to death and she had already watched Crussman snarling as he hacked at Crewman Heng's arm while Heng grinned and giggled and looked on, and she knew Sabila was going to try to make everything right and she already knew what would happen, even though beneath that she didn't know what was happening at all. She had covered her eyes with her hands and staggered away as behind her Gallardi began the murder.)

'There are two of us,' Jann said. She padded around Gallardi, walking a slow circle around him as he leaned against the welding cage, his head hanging. Jann could see the sweat and grime coating his skin, and the way his shoulders sagged. He must have been labouring all night, unsleeping. She couldn't imagine how exhausted he must be – but he couldn't be exhausted from working here, could he? This was his place, he and his forge were part of each other. How could he tire from this labour?

'We are at war within ourselves,' she went on. Gallardi didn't move. It had been a stupid thing to say. He knew they were at war. Had he not forged that war's weapons with his own hands here? But that didn't make sense either, she could remember that Gallardi had only taken possession of the forge a day, two days ago. Every answer was wrong, every question was wrong. She continued in her circle, her steps careful and rhythmic. It soothed her, seemed to move things towards familiarity again. 'Not between us but within us. Can you feel it? Two things in you? Have you dreamed it? Do you feel yourself to be... not your own?' She was three-quarters of the way around her circle, and movement seemed to be helping the words come, as her thoughts drifted into alignment like moons in the sky. She thought back to how Gallardi had spasmed and struggled as the half-forgotten other had put out a metal hand and seemed to push his

(but it didn't look like his)

face, push it almost loose from his skull. That meant something. She was sure of it. She let her eyes drift half-closed, started to turn in circles as she finished her orbit of Gallardi. Even as she was thinking how ludicrous the movements were, the circles within circles quieted her, helped her thoughts ride soft and quiet in courses that felt familiar.

She opened her eyes and saw clearly. Only for a moment, but enough. Gallardi was standing in the middle of an idiot chorus of rattling, over-revved workshop machines, all Tokuin's engines with their controls jammed into working positions with crudely glued or soldered fragments of metal or plastek trash. One had already overheated and failed, two more were rattling ominously. Tools and debris littered the floor. Panniers and slider shelves where Tokuin had reverently arrayed his tools and spare components were tipped and smashed, their contents piled up at their feet. And in the middle of it all, here stood Gallardi, half-naked, dull-eyed, animal-filthy, standing at a work plinth and crashing his hammer down as though he were an old smith from the hive-fringe shanties working an iron blade. But instead of a hammer he swung one of the heavy subsonic solid-reader wands they used to test the strength of pipeline segments, the gauge in the tip (which could look like a hammer to a blurred eye in dim light) already with its casing split and the smashed internal components visible, and on the plinth no glowing-hot metal bar but the shattered remains of a running-light assembly from the crane rig.

Gallardi brought his improvised smithy hammer down again, sending plastek chips scattering. He had always been too big, too heavy for grace but Jann had always admired the powerful, confident economy with which he moved. Now his movements were empty, jerky, like nothing living. She tried to read his expression in his eyes but when she cast her gaze up to his

(no please what's happened to his)

face she cried out, spun through a circle, looked again but couldn't unsee what she'd seen, and ran from the forge. If he had called after her, even her name, even just a wordless cry, perhaps she could have found the courage to stay, but here came that slippery, kaleidoscopic haze again, splitting and doubling her thoughts, and although she resisted it, somewhere in that haze came a knowledge that this was ordained, this was right. Gallardi was bound to his place. Her dreams would not change that.

('Can we winch it?' Gallardi asked in her memory as they stood looking at this thing they had found. It was hard not to stare. The thing's shape had a way of pleasing the eye, leading it softly along curves and through gentle turns. Jann thought of the strange, scalloped lines of the fungi that grew in the coolways under the hive-sprawls where they took their leave rotations, and then she thought of the lines of the muscled arms and shoulders of the boy she'd stepped out with when last she'd been there. That made her redden, but none of the others had noticed. Crussman and Heng were talking in quiet voices, Gallardi was simply looking at it. It was a made thing, but all the made things Jann had ever seen had the sledgehammer-heavy arrogance of Imperial design, all blocky angles and hard surfaces. Here Jann couldn't see a single straight line or flat plane. She didn't quite dare walk closer to it, none of them did until they'd told Merelock what they'd found, but she hunkered down and leaned forwards to stare at it. If those were control grips, then that had to be a seat, and if that were a seat then those things behind it were running-boards like their crane-buggy had, for them all to

hitch and ride on? And along the back, under a tangle of shimmering cloth whose colours seemed to ripple and shiver in the corner of her eye... an engine? A mechanism? Or a container? A saddle-pannier? Jann wondered if there were cargo in there, what this thing had been carrying, and how bitter it was to her now that they had not smashed the thing, burned it with their torches, driven the crane-buggy back and forth and back and forth over the cargo panniers, treading them to splinters without any of them ever opening them and looking inside.)

Her eyes blurred with tears as she ran up the stairs and she misjudged the width of the exit. The ends of the torque-stave clanged into the doorframe and it bent her over at the midriff, unhurt but groaning with shock. The stave fell from her hands and she folded and dropped through the doorway, crawling clumsily onward without thinking to pick it up.

When she remembered it, she pushed herself against a dry, slick wall, and clambered half-upright. This was the storage level, a maze of tiny paths winding between the dark stacks of bales and drums and pallets. She leaned against the heavy plastic wrap around a stack of filter-blocks and looked around.

High, clear laughter drifted up through the red-lit door down into the forge, and her stave was gone.

Jann's breath caught in her throat but she made herself move. Her hands grasped air. This place was cramped, smothering whatever marginal use the stave would have had as a weapon, but it still felt like too much of a loss. She told herself it was a rusted, useless torque-stave only fit for Tokuin's scrap-furnace, but the feeling that she had lost a part of herself clung to her as she shuffled away from the forge door. The stacked pallets and drums were all edges and angles, no soothing circles, and she could feel her chest hitching and jerking, wanting to echo the laughter she had heard.

'He must fight on his own,' Merelock's voice murmured at her shoulder, and although Jann made to jerk and scream with the shock, all that she gave was a gentle shudder and gasp. As Jann half-turned Merelock placed the torque-stave in her hands.

'A staff should no more be left in the grass than a spear, little cousin,' Merelock whispered. Her voice doubled on itself, acquired an echo. ''Twould be good to have you running at my flank, little one, if you'll stay with me. Green and white above the trees.' The sentence made no sense to Jann but the words had an odd power over her, and she tilted her head back as though she could look up through the thick walls and roof and see a night sky where the green and the white...

But Merelock was away, darting through the narrow spaces between the stacks. Jann smiled as she glided along behind, picturing Merelock as a night-hunting raptor, beak sharp as a spear, talons slitting the air, eyes as keen as its talons staring into the green-tinged darkness. But that laughter from the forge door would not leave her head now, and she found herself wanting to laugh, too, softly sing as she ran to and fro.

'On and ahead, cousin!' came the gruff hunter's whisper down the trail, and Jann quickened her pace even though she knew it was only Merelock's reedy voice from the other side of a pallet of hygiene packs. 'On and ahead to the Great Caern! We'll touch the stone for luck and turn about to hunt them!'

The geography of this place unfolded in Jann's mind with the quiet certainty of dream-knowledge, but as she ran up and down the aisles between the stores, her stave clanging awkwardly against crates and fittings, she was more and more aware that the place she was running through seemed phantom-like. Her mind kept dancing away through some great forest (she was sure that was the word; the last supervisor, Merelock's predecessor, had read books and had described forests to them), gliding between the boles of trees, up into the rich canopy, slipping along through the underbrush, airy as a moonbeam, following her fierce hawk.

All the places of the forest were known to her, their names talismanic weights in her mind. The Great Caern, the Tree of Hands, the Crying River, the Sky Hearth. Glorious places, wild places, and Jann cried out because *now* she was singing her dreams in the sky over the forest to a chorus of wind-chimes, and *now* she was tottering back and forth in a cramped and grubby storeroom, watching her portly little supervisor trotting ahead brandishing a splintered piece of pallet like some sort of spear, exulting at a mad beauty that she couldn't convince herself she was really seeing, laughing in the dark while her friend shuffled around in the forge with Tokuin's blood on his hands, crippled and beaten and... chained?

There was that strange ghost-certainty again.

Chained? She had seen no chains. Gallardi had killed Tokuin and taken the forge as his own. Why did her mind cling to the memory of him defeated and bound?

Pad-pad-pad came Merelock's feet around the end of the aisle. The supervisor had kicked off her workboots and was running barefoot, leaving bloody prints from where something had cut into her left heel. She had plastered engine grease across the rank swatches on her jacket and crude garlands of torn fabric flopped around her brow and her biceps. She shook the spear in one hand. Her other, Jann realised, was dangling at the end of a broken arm.

'This isn't the path,' said Jann, propping her stave across the aisle to block Merelock's way. 'Ma'am? Merelock, do you even know where you are? Do you recognise this place? Do you recognise me?'

The other woman stopped with her belly up against the pitted metal of Jann's torque-stave, then stepped back and hefted her spear. Jann suppressed a wince as Merelock's broken arm banged against a crate corner, but the supervisor didn't even seem to notice. In the dimness her

(how could I have ever thought that was her real)

face was impassive, perhaps a little watchful. The designs around her eyes and across her cheekbones curled like rich summer leaves, like falcon-wings.

'What strange questions you ask, little cousin! Have you been dreaming again? You should have asked me before you came down to sleep. There are places where it's not safe to sleep, and your dreams are too precious for any of us to risk. Enemies make their way into the wild places, cousin. Stay close to my side.'

'Merelock, listen to me! Where are you? Can you tell me where you are? Can you describe where you are? Do you know what happened to Gallardi and Tokuin?'

'I...' Merelock began, and then straightened. Her broken arm still hung but the other lifted her makeshift spear in a pose that brought back to Jann that maddening deja vu. 'I run the trail like the moon and the wind, little cousin. I am the sound of my horn and the flight of my spear. When the nights chill and the green moon walks silent and alone, so there do I walk under it.'

Other voices, other sounds. Something danced in Jann's vision like the ghost of a hololith display in the instant after it was shut down. Merelock seemed to stand in the centre of a larger form, something tall and mantled in beast-pelts, lifting a lean arm, her/his words wrapped around by the dim sounds of wild horns and quick breathing. Merelock's voice struggled for power and melody but Jann could feel the words coming from that other silhouette too. Their rhythm made her want to chorus along, dance in a circle with her stave lifted high before she could laugh and sing, leap and hang in the air, shine high and bright above...

The sensation was like jolting awake just before the final release into sleep: Jann broke the reverie, pulled back from the brink, immediately felt guilty at disbelieving that beautiful voice. Before the guilt could lull her and draw her under again she gritted her teeth, squeezed her eyes almost shut and hit Merelock's broken arm with a clumsy, looping blow.

The supervisor wailed in pain, but although she lurched she did not fall and the chunk of pallet stayed gripped in her fist the way the stave stayed gripped in Jann's. For a moment, behind the sound, something in the darkness that might have been a sigh or a chuckle, but when Jann cocked her head to listen it was gone.

'I am wounded, but not beyond fighting or mending,' said Merelock, bent halfway to one knee before Jann and cradling her arm. 'But see, Jann?' Jann shook her head, not understanding, and for a moment not recognising the name Merelock had used. Her name, she was sure, should be longer, softer, more like a breathy lullaby on the tongue.

'See, now?' Merelock went on. 'See how wrong it all is? My own domain, my hunting-paths. I climbed to spy and wait for my enemies and the bough cast me down. Wouldn't bear my weight.' Her head swimming, Jann got a hand under Merelock's good shoulder and helped her to her feet, craning over her shoulder to follow the woman's gaze. Her first thought was that of course it wouldn't have borne weight: she was looking at a ripped stretch of tarpaulin over stacked drums of distilled water, and who would ever think that Merelock's stout, stiff-limbed little frame would let her clamber up there without something going wrong? And yet it made perfect sense to her when Merelock talked of the stack as though it were a great tree, and one that had done her a personal wrong by breaking its branch and letting her fall. Falling. Falling and hurting. Jann breathed hard, shook her head, reminded herself of her purpose.

'Look at it again, Merelock. Please, ma'am. Is it what you think it is? Look at me, do you see your cousin? I think I almost have what it is that's happening to us, ma'am, almost in my mind, but will you help me to try and understand it?' She could hear herself cracking and begging, near tears, but she seemed to have broken the trail of Merelock's delusion. Hope bloomed warm in her. She met the other woman's gaze, held it. Let her be jarred by the pain, Jann thought. Let her think! Let her see it in my

(but it isn't even my)

face.

For a long moment there was no sound, and then Merelock began making a low noise in her throat. Jann leaned in, listening for words, but there was just a soft moan of breath. Jann kept her eyes on Merelock's, trying to ignore what her senses were telling her about the woman's features, trying to pull insight out of the air by simple concentration.

'Jann?' The doubling of Merelock's voice was gone. It was a simple voice now, the voice Jann was familiar with, but it was faint and confused. 'Jann, is that you? I can't recognise you. What happened to us? What happened? I hurt, Jann. I hurt. I can hear the forge engines. Where's Tokuin? Jann?'

'We're going up from the forge,' Jann told her. 'Up to the top level, where that thing is. I know we… weren't always like this. I dream how we were before we found it. I think if we all go and find it we might understand about those people in my dreams.'

'Up,' said Merelock, still in that small, childlike

voice. 'We'll go up.' She tried to hold out her broken arm but it wouldn't quite extend. 'You and I. Together.' Merelock wouldn't release her grip on her spear, so Jann held her as best she could under the broken arm and tried to help her along. 'We'll walk together. You and I. Together in the dark.' Grunting, Jann got Merelock to the end of the aisle and into a broader space where they could more comfortably walk abreast. 'You and I, walking in the dark,' Merelock said, 'and not our first such journey, no,' with an almost-chuckle that chilled Jann's blood. The sound seemed to be picked up and echoed in the gloom around them. Jann thought she heard soft, rapid footsteps counterpointing the echoes, but who could tell any more what was happening around her and what was the ghost-pantomime in her own head?

(*'Gallardi, Klaide, fetch a pair of piston-grips,' Merelock said. Her voice, never very powerful, was fighting against the stiff wind on the tower roof but there was still enough snap in it to cut through the arguments. 'Tokuin knows we've had a find, but he has some sort of ministration to attend to below before he'll come up and look at this thing. We'll make a start ourselves.'*

'Ma'am, Jann thinks there's definitely tech in there,' said Crussman, 'and I agree with her. Look, that long curve has the line of an engine cowl, and if you look under it you'll see, well, I'm sure it's machinery.'

'I'm sure you're right,' Merelock said as Klaide, Gallardi and Heng came past pushing the big piston-grip pedestals on their rumbling wheels. 'But the tech is the only thing I'm having him look at. If that stuff you think is machinery is part of the Mechanicus mysteries then we're best

served by keeping them sweet from the start, but whatever there is here that's not machinery is legal salvage of the Filiate Guilds. There's no lack of piety in doing things by the letter and sorting out what's ours.'

That was what Crussman had wanted to hear, and he and Sabila had actually clapped as the pedestals halted next to this thing they had found, the thing like a long iridescent arrowhead that looked so heavy and lifted so light, with its strange controls and its riding-rails. None of them had openly discussed the bright gemlike crystals embedded in its sleek curves: most of the deep-desert pipeline crews held the same half-formed superstitions about gloating over salvage before the bonus warrants had been signed. But Jann had found herself studying them, counting them, and wondering about the shapes she was sure now were cargo panniers. As Klaide shooed the others away and started working the controls, the arms extended with a piston-hiss and the three-fingered grips slowly positioned themselves over the pannier lids...)

Jann didn't want to think about it any more. Didn't want to dream, didn't want to remember. Wasn't it her dream that had begun all this strife? She had dreamed of uprising (although that didn't fit), she had dreamed of war between them all (but was that really what had happened?), she had dreamed of a bloodshed that the telling of her dreams had brought to pass, prophecy and fulfilment in one closed and shining circle like the edge of a full white moon. But she had never told anyone. She hadn't even been the one to see the thing wedged in under the pipeline by the winds. Who had seen it first? They had been out checking that the new fixtures at pylon 171 had survived the hypervelocity sandblasting of the previous day and Tokuin's drone had spotted something his image catalogues couldn't quite identify. They had gone to hunt it out. But Merelock hadn't gone with them. And wasn't Merelock the one who hunted?

The thought of her companion dragged Jann's consciousness back to the moment. Merelock was still muttering to herself.

'Oh, we ran together when the ghosts sang in the waterfalls, do you remember? And the quarrels, when I had rancour with my black-haired love, and you were always the quiet voice. You called to me when there was burning iron in the… the smoke… and you were the star by which my… my stave, my hunting, my friends…' That throaty, guttural note was creeping back into Merelock's voice like a hunting-cat slinking forwards through a thicket, but at the same time she was faltering, reaching for words as though each path of thought had run into darkness. That was wrong twice over. Merelock was the station supervisor, the order-giver, she should be the certain one. Merelock was one with her home, swift like running feet in the wild night, sure like the strike of a hunting spear or the lunge of the falcon. She should be the sure one, no indecision behind the features she wore.

Jann was still trying to work out what that thought meant when she looked up and saw the figure watching them. It held itself in the light from the stairwell up to the living deck, and where that light fell on it it seemed to fray into crisscrossing sparks and threads. The thing moved a dancing half-step towards them and its whole skin cracked, shivered and crawled with glowing colour. For a moment the display calmed, and then it bent an elegant leg, cocked its head just so and somersaulted lazily backwards into the gloom.

Jann stood and gasped, her mind thrumming like a plucked string but empty of thought. Her heart wanted to leap at the sight of the thing, but her bones wanted to chill. On her arm, Merelock was still sagging and murmuring, and up from the forge level came a burst of laughter and an echoing, grinding crash.

Jann moved. She forgot about supporting Merelock along, simply dragged the other woman into a shambling half-run through the twisting, giggling shadows. Merelock stumbled at the foot of the stairs but pushed herself up with her spear and managed to keep pace. Climbing, Jann shot a look over her shoulder to see the supervisor panting hard two steps behind her, leaning forwards to run so she was bent almost double. Merelock's cap was long gone and her braid had disintegrated, her black curls hanging in her face, and Jann jerked around to face up the stairs again, glad that she hadn't seen Merelock's

(I can't even remember her real)

face in the brighter lights of the stairwell. None of the minds rioting in her head seemed able to predict what they'd see without the merciful blurring of the shadowy lower floors.

The light grew brighter as they rounded the hairpin and clambered up the second flight. The glow-loop over the door to the living deck was defective, Merelock never quite having managed to bully Tokuin into making time to fix it, and so they came into the ransacked dormitory and into flickering light and weeping.

The weeping voice was Klaide's, and peering past the clinking and winking of the light just above her Jann could make him out. He was slumped across a twisted nest of bedclothes and curtains, torn from the sleeping-booth partitions and now choking the dormitory aisle. In the middle of it all Klaide knelt tilted against one of the stripped curtain frames with one hand cupped against his face. It was a pose of grief so classic as to look contrived, as though Klaide was the centre of one of the bright-lit tableaux that enactors performed in front of the temples on holy nights.

At that thought Jann's scattered thoughts seemed to interlock and move in unison. Insight was as brief as a bright moonbeam spearing down through clouds, but as powerful. She shook her arm free from Merelock and ran down the aisle, so fleetfooted she almost seemed to glide over the debris and litter, and knelt at Klaide's feet.

'Klaide? It's me, Klaide,' although if he had asked her who 'me' was she'd have struggled to answer. 'Klaide, it's okay. You don't need to grieve. We're not... like this. We're not...' It had seemed so clear in that brilliant moonlit moment but now she was grasping for the words. 'We're not who we are, Klaide. I think I understand. I've dreamed us as...' and her voice choked in her throat because she wanted to say *ourselves* and she wanted to say *others*, and both of those and neither were true.

'You don't understand,' Klaide told her, his voice a travesty: rumbling and chesty as Jann had known it in the years they had been crewmates, not the clear contralto she knew it should really be. 'He's gone, he's...' and Klaide's body began to shudder, not with weeping now but with some more profound convulsion. He began shouting, spitting out words in a half-shriek.

'Dying-dead-he's-dead-he-will-yet-die-he-dies!' and while Jann tried to hold the man's hands down and murmur soft moon-songs to soothe him, still she understood. He had gone away to die. Who had? Jann couldn't fix on a name, two separate sounds slid into and out of her mind, but she knew he was Klaide's (champion-child-student-subject-follower), and she knew that whoever he was he had gone to die. He had gone to fight. He was already dead and they mourned. He lay dying, his wound mortal and his blood bright red as a moon whose light waxed upon his death and drenched the green and white moons and drowned their beauty.

He was all these things, all these states, always walking out to his doom, always lying stricken, lying dead. In all these states he was timeless as the tableau they made up now: Klaide grieving, Merelock poised over them with her spear high, Jann kneeling and placating, speaking of dreams. Even as she fought back tears of grief and fear, the form the three of them made felt so right, felt like she was falling into the steps of a dance she had been singled out for while even her own mother was yet waiting to be born.

She thought she heard a soft sigh of recognition from somewhere around them, but could see nobody but the three of them.

She looked at Klaide again. He had wrapped himself in a green curtain-cloth, and torn the front of his tunic so that the edges now echoed the crude garlands of torn fabric Merelock had adorned herself with. He had yanked off his metal collar of rank, and the electoo that ringed his bull-like neck, the badge of a Mechanicus-ordained lay artisan, stood out in the brightness. Its hard geometry made a cruel counterpoint to the tapering lines of Klaide's own features, elegant even in the depths of grief. It was not Klaide's own

(any more than this is my real)

face, but finally, finally Jann was coming to understand how that could be.

She found herself talking then, not even sure if Klaide or Merelock had mind enough left behind their

(I can almost remember their)

faces to understand, but letting the words pour out of her like moonlight. She talked about Gallardi taking the machine-shrine from Tokuin because of the steps and the songs that called him to the forge. She talked about her moonlit dreams flowered into prophecies as she spoke them, as her fingers traced the delicate intersecting circles worked into her strange, brittle skin. She talked about the memories she had dreamed and the dreams she couldn't quite remember, the strange, clumsy creatures they had all once been, with their brutish names (Gallardi, Klaide, Merelock, Jann, surely just the grunts and honks of beasts?) and the reeking, lumpen tower they called home. She talked about the temple tableaux and the passion-plays and the mythic dances, the pageant of Alicia Dominica where the Saint stood before a king with a face like the sun, sometimes to draw her sword on a traitor or sometimes to plead for her doomed children; the *Life of Macharius*, that her brothers had learned word for word, the general waging war across the heavens, the lay of the ninety-nine swords, the great strife of an aeon past when a murderous hand crushed the martyr-hero and spread his blood, so scarlet-red, the tales of the six magnificent warriors who had walked alive from the end of that great tribulation, ready to hand on the light of their learning.

They were good stories, powerful stories, and they sang in her blood, danced the way she thought she remembered dancing in moonlight to the drum and the cymbal, even as she remembered them all crying and howling and jerkily trying to dance on the roof of the tower when they had found the

(I don't want to think about the)

faces, broken the locks and found them and...

Now it was Jann sobbing, oblivious to the surprised looks from the other two – this was not her part, these were not her steps. But she staggered to her feet, cast the torque-stave away from her. She had no staff, she had no moonstone necklace, barely had a self. As the stories and the dances solidified in her mind she could feel Jann fragmenting and slipping away. She wanted to tell them, wanted to shout it at them, but the weight of understanding was too great and all she could do was cry for what was happening to them. She struggled to her feet and leapt over Klaide, a broken leap for the broken thing that she had become, and ran for the next stairwell, still sobbing. Behind her, Klaide and Merelock took each other in a clumsy embrace, but Jann didn't see or care. She understood now. There was no hope.

The lights were out on the operations deck, and only the glows of the instrument and monitor banks shone back at her. She felt the scraps of her mind twist and reach in two different directions to try and make sense of them, and for a moment she paused in her stumbling run to stare at the clear plastek desk where she had pored over the meteorological charts and dune maps. The edges of memories brushed at her again. Sitting at that table hot-eyed and yawning when Merelock had insisted on having the route for a maintenance round ready by the morning shift. Sitting on the table at Quarter Relief, a cup of rough alcohol in her hand, helpless with laughter as Gallardi and Crussman did one of their little songs mocking the guild controllers. Looking at the weather auguries and telling Merelock that yes, they could head out now, it was safe to move, and plotting a route to where the alerts showed that something had been carried up against the pipeline by the storm.

She couldn't bear that thought, that any action of hers might have helped along what had happened. Jann slumped against the doorframe, lifting her hands to her eyes to blot out the table and its memories, and when she lowered them it was on the table watching her. The shock of terror rhymed and meshed with the shock of familiarity so that she couldn't tell them apart. She gulped and found herself stepping forwards, reaching out a placating hand that her fear then made into a fist. The tall thing on the table, fringed and crested in colours that swirled and mixed with the air around it, posed and mocked her movements, and then it went from wearing all colours to no colours, fading from her eyes as it stepped back off the table, leaving her just the ghost of laughter.

It wasn't a mirage, she thought dully to herself, and it wasn't a memory. Something really had been in here with her, perhaps was in here still. Something that had– but she found herself pushing that idea away before it had managed to get any traction in her thoughts. They were being watched, nothing more. Nobody had done this to them. They had done it themselves.

(They were hushed as they came in procession down from the roof deck, each carrying one of their strange new trophies. Their chatter had broken off after Crussman's shout, but now their silence was reverent instead of startled. Jann thought of the weighted silences that came over the throngs watching the grey and white banners unfurl from the sides of the hive spires the day after Tithing Day. Thinking of grey and white and silence, she felt empty eyes watching her from the thing she carried, which she knew was stupid. Crussman's words – 'It's full of faces!' must have unnerved her more than she'd

realised.

And yes, once broken open the panniers had been full of faces. They had been mounted like artworks on the pannier's inner wall, each one veiled in a cloth of shifting, rippling colours the like of which Jann had never seen before. Some of the cloths had fallen away with the jolting of the craft and the cracking of the panniers, exposing the piece beneath it. Without realising it Jann had taken a pace towards one of them, a mask made to slip tightly over a head longer and slenderer than hers. Its features were odd and stylised, tilted so that the mask's wearer would always seem to have their face tilted slightly skywards. Stylised silvery-grey curls lined the porcelain-white face, and the alien features still carried a sweet and wise serenity that made Jann want to sigh.

She had caught herself and pulled herself back, and then looked around her and realised they had all reacted similarly.

'All right then, salvage divides equally,' said Merelock from behind them, trying to be brisk. 'We all know the rules.' And because it was the rules, Merelock took first pick. She reached out and unhooked a dark green mask, stern and masculine, with designs that might have been leaves curling about the cheekbones and the edge flaring with a design that seemed to evoke a tousled mane. Klaide pushed past her as she stepped away. One of these toys would be all right for his brother's little one, he muttered as though needing an excuse, and paused for a moment before he plucked up a mask that was as pale and delicate a green as Merelock's was dark, one that dusted to gold around the edges and on which a single deep-blue crystal tear glittered below one eye. Jann, equal in rank to Klaide, had darted in next for the face in white and silver-grey. It didn't seem to be warming from her hands, and in spite of how light it was she couldn't force it to bend or flex. Gallardi had picked a mask in a stunning orange-red which seemed to glow with its own light and pulse with yellow sparks when he turned it this way and that. The colour faded to an iron-black around the border, and Gallardi pronounced himself well pleased. 'I might even wear this back down there,' he had beamed, 'and see what Tokuin makes of it.'

Heng had complained about being left to last so Crussman had laughed and clapped him on the shoulder and sent him in next. Heng came away looking unhappy with a mask pinched in his fingers, a fierce and glowering one whose features struck Jann as somehow still feminine. Sabila, thoughtful, was carrying a golden mask, the set to its eyes and thin mouth speaking to Jann of youth and determination.

Crussman had been the daring one. There had been three compartments at the back of the pannier, three that were sealed tighter than the grips could easily break loose. Crussman had peered this way and that through the crumpled hull over them and seen a way to draw out what was inside. It was a mask the colour of old, rusted pig-iron, worked with rough designs that could have been streaks of corrosion or dried blood, worked into a snarl of such savage malevolence that when Crussman had held it up the very air around it seemed to darken and the rest of them had flinched back as though struck. Whatever little joke he'd been about to make died and slid back down his throat.

The expression on that mask had haunted them all, and

when the wind had picked up and Merelock had suggested they go below they had all unconsciously given Crussman a wide berth. He was still smiling and waggling the thing in front of him, but Jann could tell he was forcing it. She had gone to sit beside Sabila in the control deck as they worked to raise a link to the depot, sitting beside the vox terminal turning the white mask over and over in her hands.

When the screaming started, Jann never had a moment's doubt what had begun it. Crussman had succumbed. He had put on his mask.)

And Jann was running again, pushing herself up the stairs to the roof-deck where the craft still sat in the holding gantry, lashed down against the wind. Both of the splintered lines of thought racing in her head were now revolving around that memory. The thing they had found, the crashed craft and the two containers they hadn't opened. Sunlight, kingship, a golden sword. Surely there was help there?

She had forgotten about her last three crewmates, but not for long. On the roof of the tower, on the landing pad under the cranes and gantries, Crussman and Sabila were at war.

Jann found herself empty of surprise. This was just another piece of mad whimsy, even while it had the inevitability of night falling. Jann nodded to herself as she slunk into hiding beneath a crane gantry. It was all so obvious. Everything had led to this.

Crussman's right hand gripped a cable-cutter from which he had stripped the safety cage. Whether by purpose or chance (*purpose*, Jann's mind whispered, *it's all on purpose*) he had cut his left hand with it:

the palm glistened red and a steady stream of blood dripped from it as he moved. She gasped at the sight, couldn't take her eyes off the bleeding hand as the skinny pilot brandished it, thrust it forwards like a threat, held it theatrically high to counterbalance the roundhouse swings of his cutter. She had known she was going to see it, should have been prepared: every time she had thought about Crussman now it felt like that bleeding hand was gripping her heart. But surely the hand was bleeding for Sabila, and surely Sabila was still alive?

And so he was, alive and fighting although he must have known as soon as he left Klaide crying below that he was good as dead. Creeping from cover to cover, Jann watched the cycles of their battle, circling back and forth across the wide circle of the landing pad, Crussman's cutter arcing and smashing against the length of ceramite rod Sabila had taken from Gallardi's machine forge, and which he swung at Crussman like a sword. The cutter rang off the rod, and though the impact sounded light Sabila was driven down on one knee. Crussman flung back his head and screamed, holding the cutter two-handed over his head, and the sound of it wrenched Jann down to her very core.

She crawled between the tanks of ornithopter fuel and then darted behind a crane stanchion, peering around it. Sabila was on his feet, squaring off against Crussman, holding his makeshift sword high in challenge as Crussman held out his bloody hand and howled. The challenge, the defeat, the one sword, the bleeding hand, timeless and ever-renewing, a cycle as unbreakable as summer's decay into winter.

They closed and battled again as Jann ran around the lip of the landing pad, Sabila's movements swooping and elegant even as his slender arms shook with exhaustion, Crussman fighting back with a wild predator's savage purity of motion. And now Jann could see another form creeping and stooping behind Crussman as he roared and fought. Heng was shadowing Crussman in a bouncing stoop, clutching at the air and jabbing his fist and stump back and forth in manic counterpoint to the clash of weapons. Each time Sabila was knocked sprawling Heng would give a shrill, reedy cackle that made Jann flinch down deeper into cover. She knew what would happen if Heng turned his

(but now I know who really owns that)

face towards her and set eyes on her. He would know her name, he would recognise her, cackle and call, and from then on every path she walked would lead downwards and every day the shadows would lean a little closer to her, and night would come slithering on velvet-soft scales. In the last moments before she managed to tear her gaze away and start crawling again, Jann saw that Heng too had wounded himself. His thick bare forearms were mottled with bruises and gouges from where he had clawed at his own skin, and bitten at the flesh of his wrist beneath the stump where Crussman had hacked away his hand. That struck a chord of familiarity with her, a ripple of understanding like silver wind-chimes in her mind, but some of the wounds were bleeding and that was wrong, as wrong as the endlessly-renewed battle between Crussman and Sabila was right. Shuddering, Jann crawled towards the crane.

It was in there. A face they hadn't seen yet. She was sure it was the answer. The half-memory of it was in her mind now, like warm sunlight and her grandfather's voice, soft, meaningless comforting words to the tearful little girl who'd scraped her shin. She knew it had to be there. She could feel it.

Crussman howled again behind her, and mixed with it were two other cries: genuine pain from Sabila, and angry dismay from Heng. All Crussman wanted was to end Sabila, because all Crussman's nature understood was the ending, but somehow all three of them knew that ending it was wrong, something that would cast them adrift. Jann knew the reason, but she could barely have told them even if they had had mind enough left to listen. The wisdom was hers, not theirs, and that was part of the cycle too. The gritty bars of the gantry were under her hands now, and she grunted as she hauled herself up. Her reflexes seemed to belong to someone older than her but yet lighter, moon-beam-light.

She groaned as she closed on the craft and put her hands on it. Seeing it brought low like this grieved her, like seeing a beautiful dawn-bird cowering on the earth with a crippled wing, and she mourned for it with her heart even as the strange feel of its hull repulsed her skin. She stroked her fingers down the high spinal ledge, along the compartments ripped by the ugly metal arms, and found the final two, the ones they hadn't been able to breach.

Her fingers touched it and her thoughts seemed to touch it as well. She couldn't tell if she were remembering opening it, or thinking of opening it, or imagining opening it, or dreaming she had opened it. Behind her on the landing pad Sabila gave another cry, a choking, dying cry. Crussman's voice was ragged, his vocal cords worn to tatters; Heng's voice was the yowl of a cat in the dark. Jann barely heard them. This was salvation. Her senses were already reaching out for the voice she needed to hear. The sun-voice. The father-voice. The king-voice.

The compartment opened under her fingers. Jann retched, screamed, knew she was not dead but damned, poisoned, eaten, violated. Everything that was left of herself rotted in an instant. Her body seemed to go strengthless, boneless. She sagged, and would have fallen but for her torso wedging itself between two crossed struts.

Jann felt infinite desire and infinite contempt. She was paralysed, body and mind, except for the all-drenching cascade of fear. The face at the bottom of the compartment held her, ran her through as though she were a damsel-fly run through with a sleek stinger. She could not even sense an effort in it, or a will: it was something in herself that made her helpless to it, held her fast. Tears stung her eyes and her vision doubled and blurred. That didn't help. That face's grip on her mind remained, iron-cold and silk-strong. Only when her balance finally gave way and she sagged and fell to the metal decking at the gantry base did the extra distance stretch and lessen the hold.

Still in a half-sprawl, Jann reached for a strut to try and pull herself up. She didn't know what to do, couldn't think of words or a plan. The thought of that wonderful voice and the touch of the sun on her shoulders, that was gone, dropped without a trace into the abyss that had opened under her mind. Trying to increase the distance between herself and the terrible, devouring silence that seemed to be welling out from under the open lid, she forced herself onto her knees and began to shuffle back towards the landing pad. Whatever Crussman did to her, she would almost welcome it now. Anything to dislodge the memory of that face.

She stopped dead when she saw them come out of the shadows.

Six of them made a half-circle that closed smoothly on Crussman. As fatigue took the pilot and he started to sway and then stagger a step this way and then a step that, the six moved with sinuous ease, step and counter-step, the formation never breaking. Crussman's murder-scream was now not much more than a rasping moan, but still he had enough fury to drive his muscles: he lifted up the cutter, ready to drive it through the dying Sabila's skull at his feet. Maybe he hadn't seen the figures, maybe he didn't care.

Either way, there was nothing he could have done. The semi-circle parted, three scintillating figures darting one way and three darting the other in graceful unison, and through the centre of the gap they opened up came another figure, leaping and turning in the air, wrapped in shades of red and flashing gold that sparkled and dripped in the early evening gloaming. It landed on the balls of its feet and pirouetted, wheeling and spinning around Crussman's sagging, grubby form. The tails of a long coat whirled around it, now a rich blue, purple, silver, green, scattering shards and coins of light. A high crest of silver – hair or feathers, it was hard to know – ran up its hood and down between its shoulder blades, and Jann could hear the soft *shh-shh* as it whipped from side to side.

The bright shape froze in a deep fencer's pose over Sabila, and after a moment the dazzling sparks that had swirled around it coalesced onto it. Jann could see its lithe limbs, the crested hood, the outline of its coat and mask. One slender arm was up, staying the cutter's death-stroke. Dimly, she became aware that the six other strangers were echoing its stance in perfect, precise unison.

The newest stranger held its pose for a moment, and then suddenly its face and then its whole body flashed golden, pouring out a deep and beautiful light like sunlight that set Jann's heart leaping for a moment with a hope she couldn't quite understand or describe. But then its colours sank into black, shot through with coiling veins of red like cracks in the crust of a lava flow, and its upraised arm flicked through three curt, precise motions. For the first time since the faces had broken them all Crussman seemed to be speaking, or trying to, but now with his throat so delicately open he could not make the words. He crumpled, his legs folding and his arms falling into segments where the shining figure had cut them apart.

Heng, groaning and crooning, tried to scrabble away from Crussman's killer, and the figure straightened to its full, frightening height and watched him go. Its companions closed in, now moving in low crouches that put them almost on all fours, keeping their colours muted so that lined up on each side of their master they looked almost like shadowy wings. As Jann watched, their colours shifted from smoke-grey to the dirty white of old bones, and their faces blurred and arranged themselves into screaming harridan masks bursting from shocks of scarlet hair. Wailing, they scrabbled forwards hard on Heng's heels, caught his ankles and pinned them, caught his wrists and pinned them, held him writhing and gasping until the master stranger, still a shape of coal-black and smoulder-red, shot an arm out again. This time, instead of sparks of light, the arm was surrounded by dancing specks of blackness, swarming like cinders borne up from a great fire, and with each twitch of the arm Heng's body shuddered, bled, died, bled more and finally came apart.

The masks, the grief, the madness, the deaths: Jann had little left to her now, but somewhere in the ruins there was still the survival urge, and the capacity for fear. She found her feet, turned, made to flee and hide before they could turn their attention to her.

It was standing behind her. Staring up, her gaze met the darkness of its hood.

This was not the horror that the simple mask had been. The darkness beneath the deep fold of cloth was a space. A neutrality. Her eye and mind could find no purchase in it.

Jann stood perfectly still. Her muscles seemed to relax, as though they understood that all this was finally ending.

The hooded figure's cloak whispered as it took a step towards her. Its arms were held demurely in front of it, the hands folded below the cloak-folds of its chest. The hands were five-fingered, slender, longer than a human's, and now they rose up to push back the hood.

'No', Jann wanted to say. Nothing more than 'no'. It was all she could think of. But the hood fell back.

It was Jann's own face she was looking at, and it made her weep. The beautiful maiden-face, upturned to watch the white moon, the sacred circles shining on its skin. One of Jann's own hands crept up and wonderingly traced the lines of her own features.

Then the face opposite her began to change. It stretched, deformed. It became a caricature of itself, an exaggerated travesty of grotesque eyes, canted cheekbones, a tapered chin and high forehead that mocked the lines of Jann's own... her own...

...face.

Her hands pressed in on the side of her head. The figure opposite her did not move, except that now its features changed again. Now it became a bestial face, a vermin face. Crude and gawping, the features lumpy, meaty, the eyes muddy, the mouth slack. A repulsive face. An alien face. The face she had carried all her life.

Jann's fingers began to work. She dug them into herself, drawing blood with her broken and dirty nails. She found sweaty, gritty skin on which her fingers skidded, and smooth and cool skin with a firmness that her touch did not recognise. She dug and gouged and a bright bolt of madness sheared through her. Her fingers seemed to slide into her very flesh and she could feel her skull soundlessly parting. Her thoughts whirled and swarmed out of her into the cooling air like moths. She felt herself split and part. There was a sensation of bone cracking, tissue tearing, but no sound, no blood, no physical pain.

The white mask landed softly at her feet.

And now there was no kinship left with any of these strangers, no familiarity. There was the stink of blood and offal where poor sweet slow-talking Heng lay dead, and the butchered body of twinkle-eyed Crussman, and here she stood, and what was her name now? What was her name?

She jerked and fell backwards, rolled, got her feet under her by nothing more than blind chance, and ran, shrieking and wailing, not a scrap of mind left in her any more. She ran with nothing more than a merciful roaring void inside her, a perfect hollow, and her course took her away from the strangers, away from the gantry, towards the edge of the roof-deck. The rail was not high, and she hit it at a flat run.

Jann was still thrashing her limbs as she fell, trying to flee, but it was only a moment before the packed earth at the tower's foot ended it.

Quietly, without haste, they assembled on the roof. They made their way up through the stunted, squalid spaces where the animals had lived. They moved in soft procession, angular and high-stepping like bright wading birds, moving through precise sequences of poses both careful and utterly relaxed. Their colours and masks flickered gently in the dusk. None of them spoke.

They made a circle around the roof, then the circle became a spiral, leading them inwards, until they broke the spiral and spread into a pattern that made the fire-rune, the rune of lost glory and the dream of rekindling, with Ehallech at its crux.

Ehallech carried a bright mask in his hands, the Fire Mask, the visage of Vaul. Ehallech was learning the craft of the weaponwright and the myths of the crippled god of the forge had great meaning for him. It was only right that he be the one to take the mask from Gallardi, whose corpse now lay next to Tokuin's amid silenced machines below them.

The troupe broke after a moment and then silently formed around Lhusael, who carried the dark-green mask she had taken after her blades had killed Merelock. Lhusael was a devotee of her people's most primal, heartfelt stories, the stories of their parents and progenitors. Already she had mastered the spirit of Isha, danced that role, sang the grieving-songs, learned the intricate blade katas that represented the harvest-mother's tears. Now she was completing her grasp of those story-cycles by learning the role of Isha's husband, silent Kurnous, the god of the hunt, whose face was in the Hunter's Mask that had driven Merelock to prowl the dark paths with a spear in her hand. Behind her, moving in beautiful synchronicity, came Melechu, who had spent so long behind a bone mask dancing in the retinue of Nysshea the troupe's death-jester. Now was the time to balance the role of death with the role of a life-giver: Melechu's bridge into that role was Isha's sacred grief, and so she had taken the Mourning Mask from Klaide, the visage of Isha of the harvest, weeping for her dead champion and her lost children.

When Nysshea had danced in the jester's train, her brother Edreach had danced with her. Before that, when she had danced the role of the fire-ghosts in Vaul's train, he had mirrored her by dancing a water-sprite in the footsteps of Isha. Now that they had both been chosen for greater roles, he was balancing her again: as she took on the role of Isha, he became Eldanesh, the greatest hero of the mortal eldar, the champion upon whom Isha smiled, who went forth to do battle with bloody-handed Khaine and met his fated death. Deftly, elegantly, never falling out of the overarching rhythm, Edreach dipped low and plucked the Hero Mask from Sabila's corpse, holding it high and proud. Others before him had interpreted Eldanesh as a doomed victim, even a fool, but Edreach revered him as one whose courage was exalted by the manner of his death.

Sheagoresh kept his vigil over the two mon-keigh corpses as the others broke the circle and reformed around him, coalescing around those in the troupe who held the ceremonial masks aloft, each Harlequin selecting a mask and shifting the colours of their *dathedi* to match it. In moments the Fire Mask was surrounded by flickering orange; the Mourning

Mask by the gentle golden-green of sunrise over an orchard; the Hunter's Mask by the dusk-dark shades of the green moon that was Kurnous's totem; the Hero Mask by bright silver and gold.

And still more came, running swift-footed up the stairs or alighting from the shrouded air-sleds that took silent position at the building's edges. When Dheresh'mel walked down the curved prow of her airsled and stepped smoothly onto the roof, Sheagoresh rose and stepped back, muting his colours to yield to her. For many journeys Dheresh'mel had danced in the footsteps of Eldanesh, finding ways in every pageant they played, every war they fought, to interpret another telling of his story. But she had learned Eldanesh's sagas from Ytheommel, the Great Harlequin of her old troupe whom the green beasts had laid low under the forest-spires of Toiryll, and whose name-element she had taken to carry his story on. Since that war her spirit had darkened. Her performances had become rougher, tinctured with anger. It had only been at their last resting that she had come to Sheagoresh and formally relinquished the Hero's Mask. Now it was time to step into a new role, and cast her life-story through a new perspective.

Sheagoresh bowed as she walked forwards, silently, already moving as though she were in armour, and reached down to Crussman's corpse. She straightened again holding the Blood Mask, the snarling face of Kaela Mensha Khaine, the Bloody-Handed God, lord of murder, whose wars had raged across heaven, slaying Eldanesh and binding the crippled and beaten Vaul to his anvil. There was silence and stillness as she carried the mask away. The mythic roles would pass around the troupe at every performance, but always there was one to lead and define them, and a new heart in the portrayal of Khaine would mean changes.

Sheagoresh looked over to the gantry base, to where Jann had been standing, at the one who was closer to him than any lover or sister could be. Ythoelle did not pick up the mask for herself: as the troupe's Shadow Seer she wore the Mirror Mask, and would until her dying moments. But as he walked to her and past her he saw that she had taken up the Moon Mask from where the last of the thieving vermin had dropped it, the face of Lileath, the maiden-goddess, dreamer and prophetess, whose symbols were the white moon, the staff, the closed circle, the wind-chime. Her hood was forwards again; as he walked past he could see the Mirror Mask fading into and out of many faces. At least one of them, he knew, would be his own.

There was no one to wear the Moon Mask, not yet. Abhoraan, who had danced the part since she had first joined the troupe so many years ago on the dragon-steppes, had been one of the ones who had died when their air-sled could not outrun the storm.

Soon they would perform the elegy for Abhoraan and her companions, and it would fall to Sheagoresh to decide what form that would take, what performance, what elements of the great myths they would draw on to take this tragedy and weave into the fabric of their living stories, to give it meaning and closure. It was a task he did not expect to enjoy, but every tale had its songs of mourning as well as its dances of triumph, and the tale that was his life was no exception.

Shapes moved around him. His Harlequins bounded and swung up through the scaffold to the wreck of the air-sled, ready to free it so it could be carried with them when he gave the signal. Their colours and faces danced, each reflecting a role that the Harlequin felt it right to play at this task and at this stage in their own life narratives. He lifted his arm for silence and their forms stilled, their colours muted.

The last sealed compartment flowered open at his touch and he gave voice to a low, resonant song, a single sustained note from deep in his chest. Those around him took up the song and flared their colours in salute as he took out the Sun Mask, the face of Asuryan, the Phoenix King, Monarch of Heaven, the teacher of the six great Phoenix Lords. Sheagoresh took it, held it in both hands, stepped slowly back off the gantry. His flip belt engaged with a thought and he felt the shift as his weight all but vanished: he stretched out and turned as he fell, always keeping the mask above him, and touched down feather-light on the rockcrete pad, one knee bent, head bowed but shoulders square and proud, both paying fealty to the mask and claiming ownership of it.

He stayed there, muted his colours down and made his own face blank. There was only one mask left to collect.

All around him, the others knelt. Colours shut off into black and greys and faces became featureless. A jetbike, the bare off-grey of wraithbone given form but no colour, adorned only with a black swathe wrapping its tail vane, coasted to a silent halt in the middle of the landing pad and Sheyl'emmen stepped down from it.

Her face was in shadow, like Ythoelle's, but unlike Ythoelle she made no move to shift her stiff, flaring hood. Hair cascaded from it, void-black and marble-white, and white silver chains twined around her hands and hung jingling from each fingertip. Vanes of wraithbone jutting from her shoulders caught the wind; at the sound of that moaning whistle every Harlequin shuddered and closed their eyes.

Sheyl'emmen did not look at any of them. Her step was steady and her sombre expression did not change. She walked with the careful stillness of a prisoner walking towards the scaffold. At the gantry she lengthened her step into a bound, and with her belt taking her weight away she sailed smoothly to stand on a crossbar before the ripped-open pannier. The other Harlequins turned in place to present their backs to her as she reached in and plucked out the mask that the last mon'keigh had glimpsed.

The mask did not glower or snarl, it had no artful changes to its scale or features. It was the face of an eldar, classic, genderless. There was no expression in the eyes, no set to the mouth. It was a blank face, blanker than the featureless grey hoods the Harlequins had taken on around it. It was a face that could place itself over any nightmare the beholding eye could imagine.

Sheyl'emmen the Solitaire picked up the Hell Mask and, like Sheagoresh before her, leapt off the platform, spreading her cloak out to cast its dread shadow into the heart of every eldar on the platform. She landed opposite the Great Harlequin and the two of them stepped and danced and spun together, neither visibly acknowledging the other. When a half-circle was complete and each stood where the other had a moment ago, they raised their masks in precise unison and donned them. Sun Mask, Hell Mask, Asuryan and Slaanesh, the two faces that the grubbing vermin had not soiled with their touch.

Then, shadow-fleet, Sheyl'emmen was gone: astride her jetbike with a single leap, then arrowing across the platform and away through the night, the vanes on her back shrieking in the slipstream. Sheagoresh leapt into the air then, head back, throwing his arms wide. Light came, a beautiful blaze from the Sun Mask driving back the night, bringing the Harlequins' colours to joyous life as they capered and danced.

In that moment, each feature-shifting holographic face became the mask they all wore beneath every other, the Harlequin Mask, Cegorach the Laughing God, trickster and knower of secrets. Every face was different, as every Harlequin's imagining of the leader of their great dance was different, but as Cegorach's features burst onto each of their faces every Harlequin burst into laughter. Some gave the coarse guffaws of an oaf who has seen a clumsy joke, some the elegant trill of a princess admiring the tumbling of her jester. There was the joyous laughter of tragedy from which a traveller has returned, and the wrenching laughter that casts a cloak of merriment over direst grief. Air-sleds and jetbikes left their holding positions and made interweaving circles, bright and laughing figures leaping up to catch hold and ride them, their colours leaving bright and shimmering mosaic-trails.

The laughter pealed out from the top of the tower like bells, and hung in the air behind the line of jet-bikes and air-sleds like the wake of a boat. Deep in the wasteland beyond where the mon-keigh travelled they would slip into the webway, and soon they would be breathing the fragrant air of a maiden world, rich with spices and flower-perfumes, dancing in warm water across delicate coral sand while the waves chuckled in amongst the roots of the mangrove towers and the moons danced and pinwheeled overhead.

They would mourn their dead, and re-enact the greatest of their myths: the Dream of Lileath, the Veil of Isha, the War in Heaven, the Doom of Eldanesh, the Fall. With the tale-telling they would reconsecrate their precious ritual masks, the heart of the troupe, and then they would roam again, roam up from the coral oceans to the great sighing seas of grass. They would find the camps of their cousins and steal in amongst their tents and tethered dragons, dazzling and bemusing them with shadow and laughter, and then they would make themselves known, step into the light, and dance for them. Perhaps they would tell one of the great stories, perhaps they would tell one of the lesser, perhaps one of the younger stories of the Devourer or the bestial wars about the great Gate.

Or perhaps they would dance a newer story still. A story of strays and travellers, forced by the decay of their old paths to leave the safety of their webway and make quick and secret passage across a world of crackling dunes and bloody, moonless skies. A story of a monstrous storm that not even these swift travellers could outrun. A story of the search for what the storm had taken from them, something more precious to them than the features of their own faces. A story of ugly, upstart animals who had meddled with something they should never have seen, a story of insolence punished, thievery justly rewarded, desecration turned back on itself. A story of how the great tales would try to play themselves out even through such lumpen mockeries of minds.

That was the power of the tales. That was the power of the masks. It was a story Sheagoresh had never imagined when he left his old troupe and wrought a new cast of great masks to form the core of a new one, but now they had lived it, the story was part of theirs, to tell and reinterpret and dance for themselves and for others all down the coming years.

The wind picked up, dust-cloud and nightfall drew curtains across the desert. Dull emergency lights glowed in the tower corridors, control telltales sparkled on the operations deck, a vox-alarm squawked unanswered. Nothing moved, and Pipeline Maintenance Depot 347-South-East was swallowed by the desert night.

UNITY
James Gilmer

The black bird perched easily on the corpse's chin. The thing pecked again and opened a fresh wound in the Imperial Guardsman's face, just below the left eye, and Tam felt Gesar's hand close around his wrist and force his pistol downwards.

'No noise.'

'We can't let a Guardsman lie like that. It's not right.'

The Astartes squared off in front of Tam and stared him down. Gesar's helmet had been lost in the fighting. Blood caked up around the cut along his chin and cracked open as he talked.

'It doesn't matter what he was when he was alive. He's dead now and we're not. We will push on for Emperor and Throne. Your job is to live and kill the xenos scum that did this. You will do your duty, not shoot a bird because it offends you for following its nature.'

The Raven Guard Astartes was harsh, but right. They'd been on the run for hours now, and had to be behind the advance of the fire warriors if not the human infantry and kroot shock troopers. Tam's regiment had broken at the battle of the communications hub, and the Astartes had been retreating when Tam had climbed down from his sniper's nest and met up with him.

'Sorry, my lord, it won't happen again. We're coming up on the farms. Maybe the farmers will give us shelter, or we can just take it.'

Tam knew he just had to stay close to the Space Marine. If there was one thing beyond the Emperor that he had faith in, it was of the holy vengeance that was the Adeptus Astartes. The Space Marines, living instruments of the Emperor of Humanity, would always see them through. Gesar would get him out alive. There was simply no other being that could stand against the Emperor's angels of death.

'Farmers can sell out, corporal, or be forced to reveal our location. There were human soldiers with the tau forces this time, do not forget that.'

The Tau Empire was a collective of races, ruled over by the caste-based tau, who sent their own fire caste into battle alongside other races, including mercenary human traitors. This had been Tam's first engagement with them and their member races. It was actually Tam's first battle against any xenos, and he counted himself lucky that he had survived to find the Raven Guard already on the move and plotting to escape or strike back at the invading horde.

Gesar hooked a thumb and pointed beyond the dead Guardsman propped up against the tree.

'At least he did his duty at the end of things. A blood trail leads away. The colour and scent is not human.'

Gesar stepped over the corpse and the black bird flew off as he swung the boxy bolter at it. Tam knew it'd be back, but it was a nice gesture anyway. The Guardsman had been dead some time, as the deep furrows in his chest weren't steaming in the brisk air, and his face had long gone purple in the cold.

'Kroot hound. One of the kroot's creatures, they set these things on us at the front of the comm station. I saw four of your regiment go down to one of these before I put a bolt through the thing's head.'

Gesar kicked at the corpse that he'd found. It was lightly dusted with snow, but Tam could see thick grey fur on the creature's back. Dried blood covered the muzzle and the claws. It was a huge thing, easily bigger than a man, although the Astartes was larger still, and from the blood trail that Tam could make out it had crawled off to die after having a few rounds put through it by the Guardsman.

'We still haven't come across any bodies from your regiment.' Gesar nodded back at the man's body. They hadn't found any of the other survivors who had broken and run when the line had collapsed at the uplink station. This was the first Imperial Guard corpse they had come across.

The Imperial Guardsman's unit badge was Coruna Imperial Guard, and showed crossed rifles behind a lupine skull. Tam's own badge showed a winged chainsword denoting the 3rd Tantulas Regiment.

'My lord, we've seen lots of skirmish sites, and everything from dead tau to dead kroot to dead traitors. Where the hell are our men?'

Gesar shook his head at the question and ran a hand through closely cropped white hair. The Astartes had the same albino skin and dark pebbles for eyes that all of the Raven Guard Tam had seen in paintings or on the pict-viewer possessed. At each battle site Gesar had done the same thing: surveyed the area, cursed under his breath and then exploded into motion again.

It was a struggle to keep up with the Astartes. Tam had even considered dropping his sniper rifle after the first hour of running, but he'd held on to it. It was a thing of beauty. Prayers to the Golden Throne and dirty poems inscribed in the stock, a telescopic sight he prayed over every night that he'd been chosen to carry in his role as a sniper, with a lovely bayonet for close-quarters work that his father had forged himself back on Tantulas.

'We need to move. If we make the farms we might find answers. The tau do not exterminate but turn those they can. If not willingly then they may use other methods to turn the population. We will either protect this world or cleanse it of traitors and xenos even if we must do it one at a time.'

Tam knew better than to question the Space Marine. The Astartes was not only his best bet of surviving this world, but he would also kill Tam himself if he thought the Guardsman faltered in his duty.

What little Tam did know about this Raven Guard and his Chapter had been the company gossip that had filtered down through the ranks after the Astartes had appeared at their camp. Gesar had been cut off from his battle-brothers and diverted to help hold the uplink station. Then it had been a bloody morning battle between tau energy weapons and the rush of human infantry, and the time for questions and rumours had given way to pulse blasts and bolter rounds shattering the crisp air.

The humans serving with the tau had worn blue and gold, not very different from the colours the tau fire warriors had their armour kitted out in. Ges'vesa was what Tam had heard them called over the vox-casts the tau's turncoat humans had made before landing. 'Human Helpers' in the Tau language, and traitors who would find only death at the hands of those loyal to humanity and the Emperor's Divine Grace.

The pulse rifles the fire warriors carried had better range than most of the Guardsman weapons. They had held off taking shots at the comm station from the depth of the forest. The Ges'vesa had come in first. Two waves that broke against the combined defence of the Imperial Guard and Gesar holding the line. Tam had heard Gesar's voice, vox-casting at full strength, right up until the kroot shock troopers hit.

Taller even than Gesar, kitted out in animal pelts and hefting rifles they swung like clubs, the bipedal kroot were nasty close-quarter fighters. Tam had taken a few out, and not one had looked the same through his scope. The most he could say was that they were tall, lanky and fast.

The hounds had rushed in first. The howling that they raised sounded like wolves, and the things had crossed the clearing before Tam could sight in on any of them. Deadly-quick with long muzzles and nasty teeth, they were in among the squads before anyone could clear pistols or fix bayonets.

Tam knew Gesar had lost his helmet sometime around then. One moment Gesar had been at the head of the line, the next Tam had heard a chainsword rev and a cry to Corax, primarch of the Raven Guard, carry over the fighting.

Gesar had taken the time to clean the hound's blood off his chainsword after the fight, but his white and black armour was still spotted with blood and scarred by claw marks.

The kroot themselves, bipedal and vicious, had come next. A hail of high-calibre rifle rounds broke the ranks, and the hounds that were among them spread them out even further, and then the kroot hit the line.

The things had muscles like whipcord, and they twirled their rifles like clubs, smashing aside any Guardsman in their way. Tam hadn't been able to get clear shots once they got in close. He'd earned a few kills, but often after a Guardsman had gone down from a rifle butt cracking open his helmet or a curved knife punching through a flak jacket.

Most of the kroot had looked somewhat avian. They had sharp, elongated features to their skulls, and while Tam had heard stories of xenos and what they looked like, the kroot unnerved him. A quick glace could confuse one for human. Right up until you saw the faces. Some of them were avian, some almost ape-like, and no two looked the same.

Tam had sworn most of them had black pools for eyes, but he knew he'd seen one look right towards his perch with the slit-eyes of a cat. Green flecks set against tan skin and black pupils.

He'd had to dive off the rock mound he'd been using as a position when the thing sent a volley of rifle fire his way. In this way he'd started his own, private retreat, from the battle of the comm station.

It wasn't a thing he was proud of, but he could hear the lines below him falling apart. A commissar had been screaming for discipline and shouting that he'd shoot any man or woman who ran right up until his voice had cut off with a scream and a hound's howl.

The only thing Tam focussed on was the distinctive sound of Gesar's bolter. It was unmistakable amongst the other sounds of the fight. He'd made his way down the ridge and past a few others running for cover. The kroot were circling the uplink building and the whole of the defence was breaking up and falling back.

He'd seen a kroot sweep a Guardsman's legs out from under him and almost ran on. The man's scream brought him back, and Tam drew his pistol and dropped into a firing stance he'd had drilled into him a hundred times during training. The double-tap dropped the first kroot, but two more were too close and he swore he felt the bullets pass by him in the chill air.

Bolter rounds had taken both of them from behind, and like that he and Gesar were in tactical retreat. There hadn't been much tactical to it in Tam's mind, but he wasn't going to argue with an armoured-up and pissed-off Space Marine. The ranks had broken too badly to rally anyone, and before Tam knew it there were just the two of them crashing through the trees down the mountain's slope.

They had held up as long as they could in a culvert at the base of the mountain. Rifle cracks and the hiss of energy weapons vaporising air carried on the wind, but they only found the scenes of fighting, and the only bodies were in tau colours.

Gesar was getting edgier as they moved through the forest. It didn't help that night was coming on, and the forest was starting to thin. They'd be out of cover and into the first of the farmlands that covered Coruna. With the frost on, there wasn't a lot of crop cover, and that meant a hike across open terrain with an enemy that had much better auspex devices than a helmetless Space Marine and an Imperial Guard sniper.

'My scope is kitted out for NV, if it comes to that.'

Gesar nodded and was moving with long strides again. Tam could tell the man was thinking hard on the scenes they'd found, and the distinct lack of Imperial bodies.

'My lord, excuse the question, but you don't think our people made it out, do you? You think they're prisoners or surrendered, is that it?' Tam was having nine hells' worth of trouble keeping up with the Space Marine, and he had no idea how the man, with that much armour on, could move so fast or quiet. It wasn't a natural thing, any more than the Astartes not stopping once for food or water. Tam had caught a drink from his canteen and a ration bar eaten between stops at battle sites. Gesar seemed to keep moving on pure spite.

'Blood all over the place. Human blood, even where there's not bodies, and too much for a normal man to walk away from. Your regiment is good, for Imperial Guard, but no one is that good. No blood trails from wounded either.'

It was the truth of the matter. Tam had thought that maybe the Imperials had carried their wounded off with them after the first couple of skirmish sites they found. There was just no way they could or would have been able to carry every wounded man off the field while under retreat from an enemy that was fielding things like the kroot hounds though.

'Your regiment was broken up on the opposite ridge and at the uplink station. The Coruna Regiment was supposed to be down in the farm land. If we got cut off we should have run into more tau by now. I need to find out where they went.'

Gesar was slowing down as they broke into more open ground. There was less and less cover with every step. They'd be hitting the edge of the forest in moments, and the sun was only just starting to go down.

'Hold up here.' Gesar stopped almost faster than Tam could register. One moment the man was in motion, a mass of armour plates and determination, and the next he was still as death and twice as ugly.

'We can't cross open fields during dusk. We'll wait an hour or two and you can employ the night scope to see if we're clear.'

'My lord, despite the strength of spirit that blesses this rifle, I'm afraid it's not as powerful as the auspex devices of your lost helmet or of the tau forces. If they have thermal viewers or anything fancy they'll pick us out immediately.'

Slate-black eyes caught him and Tam thought the Space Marine was death itself. The only colour on the man was the cut along his jaw that broke open in a thin red line, much smaller now than the open wound had been, against the white alabaster of his skin as he ground his teeth in frustration.

'You will follow your orders, Guardsman, and you will not make me repeat myself.'

Tam nodded quickly. The last thing he needed was an enraged Astartes on his hands. It was a rare thing to find one so willing to talk to a lesser soldier such as Tam, but for the Astartes to let Tam keep pace, to let him talk to the Space Marine as he had... Tam intended on staying either behind or beside the Astartes until they hooked up with wherever his regiment was or until they could find a way off this planet. He would also do his best to stay on the good side of the man's humour.

'Yes, lord. Do you think there are still Imperial forces in this sector?'

'Our only way to find out is to find a farm and see if they have any communication with the larger world. This is a farm planet: there isn't much but animal shit and crops most of the year. The cold season only lasts a few weeks standard. Most of the farmers will be sitting it out and waiting for the next planting cycle. The tau absorb their enemies into their empire, they will not simply kill but will find those who are willing to turn traitor and anyone who doesn't join willingly will be made to join their cause, their crusade for their Greater Good.'

'They were broadcasting that before they landed. Is it a religion?'

Gesar had set himself down on a log and was checking his spare bolter clip, lips moving in silent litany, and making sure the action on the weapon was still smooth. His jaw muscles rolled in the way that Tam had come to recognise as the man grinding his teeth in suppressed anger.

'It seems to be their belief system. The blue-skinned xenos always vox-cast. They swear that they mean no harm, and they preach a kind of tolerance. They poison minds with xenos lies and try to turn those who are weak in their faith to the alien cause. Sometimes cowards and traitors do throw their lot in, and then my brothers and I simply have more targets to shoot.'

Gesar had a rag out and was wiping the bolter down. The man moved in a prayer for a steady hand and he absently clicked the magazine in and out a few times and cleared a round through the chamber.

Tam had to admit that he didn't quite have Gesar's fire for the Imperium, but then any selected for the Adeptus Astartes gave themselves to the Emperor gladly. Body, soul and everything in between was transfigured to create humanity's angels of death. The look Gesar gave him seemed to see right through Tam's every thought.

'The Raven Guard hollows you out; they hollow you out and fill you with the Emperor's Will. They gave me certainty. These things speak our tongue, they field humans from dozens of worlds, and they hire xenos mercenaries to do their fighting.'

Tam started as the Space Marine snapped a round into the chamber and holstered his bolter. In the thin light the Space Marine bled into the background and was just another shadow among the trees.

'Stars are almost out, lord. Once the sun finishes going down I'll be able to move up to the border and take a look.'

Tam might as well have been talking to a granite statue. The Space Marine was a study in patience and potential violence. He was looking past Tam, and whatever he saw in the dark places was not the sort of thing Tam wanted to be meeting.

'You have shown yourself to be a loyal servant of the Emperor. Gather your strength and honour about you. Do not allow the xenos to take you. If it should come to that, it is better we both die than to let ourselves fall into their hands.'

Tam would put up a fight if it came to it, but the tau had said anyone who laid down arms would be welcomed as soldiers in a greater fight.

'I can see you thinking. Even with hardly any light, I can see almost as good as that scope. Had I my helm I could see better than that scope. I know what's in your head, and you do not want to throw down arms.'

'I'm not a coward, lord.'

Gesar's teeth stood out in the low light. A waxy moon was rising over the mountains, and the yellow light only added to the death's head ghost image of the pale Astartes.

'I'm not talking about courage; you have steel in your back, but you don't know what these xenos do. The tau spread their lies, but I've heard what they pay the kroot off with. The humans among them are traitors, and the tau are vile as any alien, but the kroot are another thing.'

'With respect, they die like anything else. I don't care if it's their dogs they want to send after us or if they come their own ugly selves. I'll shoot anything without Imperial colours on.'

'You still haven't caught on, have you? It is not from fear that I spoke of self-destruction. There is no greater sin that I could think of, except for allowing yourself to fall to these creatures. You have no conception of what alien means. There is a reason we do not suffer them to live. They are not even remotely like us, they do not think like us, and for all the traitors that march with them they care not for anything human.'

Gesar kept his voice down as much as he could, but Tam had no trouble hearing the menace in his words. Gesar shook his head and sighed. The cold was creeping in even worse, and Tam wondered if the Space Marine's armour was heated, or how well it protected him from the elements.

The Space Marines probably pumped coolant into Gesar's veins when he joined up. Tam had heard plenty of stories of what went into the making of an

Adeptus Astartes. They were the Emperor's Will made manifest, and whatever the Apothecaries of their Chapters did to their bodies to make them into the protectors of mankind, it raised them to something greater than normal humanity.

The Space Marines held Chaos back from the Imperium. They faced down xenos and mutants and any traitor or madman who was stupid enough to defy the High Lords and the Emperor's Will. Tam allowed that the Astartes probably didn't think much of ground-pounding Imperial Guard snipers, but this Raven Guard didn't really have a choice of companions on this armpit of a planet.

Tam set his back against a tree and slid down to the ground. He had his rifle up and was checking the NV mode when Gesar spoke again.

'It's the traitors that turn my guts. These traitors are just toy soldiers those blue scum march out. Their talk of unity is nothing but lies; they would sacrifice every human they found if it meant something to their Greater Good.'

'They say they want to kill mutants and the damned too. Is there any quarter to be had with them?'

'He who is enticed by aliens will face the Emperor's vengeance.' Gesar's reply was automatic, the reply of rote and training, and Tam wondered if he had pushed the man too far.

'Do not suffer any alien to live, corporal. If you had seen a fraction of what I have among the stars, perhaps you would understand the truth of that.'

He was on dangerous enough ground simply talking to one of the Astartes, but it was another thing altogether to let your mouth run off in front of them. He could feel a cold fury in the flint-black eyes of the Astartes and thought it best to try to calm him.

'I'm not enticed by any damned xenos or fool. I just hear what the tau broadcast as sure as anyone. I'm not saying we shake hands with them and call it a day, but why are we pouring blood out over empty fields?'

'They were invited in.'

It took Tam a moment to understand what Gesar had said. The Tau Empire had been invited. Humans had offered up the whole planet as a welcome present for them, and the tau had given thanks and sent in a force to take it.

'Your regiment was deployed to make sure that the Coruna Regulars stayed loyal to the Emperor and humanity. There's every chance some of your brothers in the Coruna Guard turned traitor, and if that's the case it's a long walk to a spaceport occupied by xenos and traitors.'

There was no accusation in Gesar's tone. The Space Marines had their own heretics and warp-twisted Chapters, and Tam wondered if the Raven Guard had fought his former brothers in the past, although Tam would have been insane to raise the subject with the Astartes. However, the idea of Imperial Guard throwing down arms or taking up arms against their own was still a bitter pill.

The night turned from pale yellow to flecked green through Tam's scope, and he had enough ambient light to really kick the range up on it. If they were moving out, they could do it at any time.

'I've got my night eyes up, lord. I can make my way to the clearing and take a look around, but maybe you should hang back. Any auspex devices might pick you up before it would spot me.'

Tam had thought twice about using the scope to look back at the Space Marine. There was no sense pointing a gun anywhere in the man's general direction. Not when the Astartes was obviously working on a head of hate and ready to do some serious violence.

'Very well, you move up into the clearing and see if you can see down the fields. There should be some farms not far off the edge of the forest. I can see you against the moonlight. Signal if everything is clear.'

Tam nodded and moved off. Working his way through even the thinner woods with just an NV scope to guide him was not easy work, but it wasn't long until he broke into clear ground and saw bare fields stretching out in front of him.

Dimly, he heard a slight noise that could have been an animal, but Tam knew it was Gesar coming up to the edge of the forest. There were some sounds that you couldn't fully disguise, and an armoured boot on underbrush was one of them.

Tam panned back and forth a few times with the scope. The only thing that was showing was a light source down-range about half a kilometre. It was visible through the scope as a rough intrusion of white into the green static that filled his vision.

A farmhouse? It was the only thing that Tam could think would be out this far. There was something farther distant to the south that could have been a silo.

There was no telling for sure in these conditions. Tam had been born on the undeveloped side of Tantulas, and this sort of dark was second nature to him, with or without the night vision.

He waved Gesar up and the sounds of boots meeting frosted ground came closer and closer until he felt him standing off to his left. He couldn't even hear Gesar breathing, but he could feel the man towering over him.

Tantulas was a higher-gravity world than Coruna, and Tam could feel it with every step he took. He also knew that his shorter stature compared to the Coruna Imperial Guard and especially the Space Marine had been the topic of a helmetful of jokes and a half-dozen fights since the short Tantulasians had disembarked on Coruna a standard month ago.

'We will be exposed making that barn.'

'It's a barn?'

'Use your brain as well as that scope. It's not the main house. There are dozens of barns like that all over the edge of the fields for storage and animal pens.'

'Yes, lord, I wouldn't mind having some thermal imagers so we could get a look for body heat, but I don't see anything on the NV. Should we cross the field?'

'There is nothing to be gained by standing here, and should we encounter enemies you will have to use your NV to spot targets for me. My helm had thermal viewing, but the ruins of it lie back at the uplink station. I've only two clips left for the bolter, and then it's sharp instruments and small arms against Emperor only knows what.'

'Okay, moving on my mark. One, two, three... mark; moving up!'

Tam felt his boots snag on a few twisted plants clinging to the frosted ground, and there was no way to cover the sound of Gesar moving across the field, but the soft crunch of armoured boots wasn't as loud as he feared. He kept his head on a swivel and panned the field as he moved directly for the barn.

As they closed in on it, the fact that it was just a barn became even more obvious. And from somewhere Tam heard the soft hum of refrigeration machinery.

'They have the coolers running in the middle of the frost?'

'Focus your mind, corporal. Some of these farms had livestock, so they might have freezer units to keep the meat fresh when they begin butchering them at the start of frost.'

It made sense, and so the two Imperials moved up slowly towards the main door. A single flight of steps led to a small door next to the larger main door that looked like it could readily accommodate vehicles.

Tam gently reached out and tested the door handle. To his surprise, it turned easily in his hand.

'Should we enter, lord?'

'It bears investigation, corporal, and it appears that there are lights on. You may want to switch to your pistol if the fighting gets close-in.'

Tam swung the sniper rifle back over his shoulder and drew his pistol carefully. Then he slowly pushed the door open and even the low light left green explosions in front of his eyes.

'That's my night vision gone for a few minutes,' he muttered under his breath, and from the sharp intake of breath he thought Gesar was reacting to the same thing.

Then his vision cleared and he saw the bodies.

It was a refrigeration unit, and hanging on hooks from the ceiling that would normally hold skinned animal torsos were at least a hundred Imperial Guard troopers.

Even in the chill of the refrigeration unit, Tam could see where pulse bolts, bullets and blunt force had killed many of them. Puckered wounds stood out in sharp contrast to the darker skin of the Tantulas Imperial Guard's bodies.

He flicked his eyes around but most of the bodies, the ones still dressed, were all clothed in the colours of his regiment. Some had already been stripped naked, but the shorter stature, larger muscles and darker skin marked them out as his brothers and sisters, and not the Coruna Regiment.

'What is this, lord? What the hell are they doing?'

'I've heard stories about the kroot. It's not just their hounds that have a bit of a snack on fallen prey. It's them. They have some deal with the tau. Those xenos pay them off in bodies and blood. This is what I suspected, corporal.'

The two Imperials slowly made their way into the abattoir. Tam could see the drain funnels cut into the floor where the blood could flow. There was surprising little given the number of bodies, and what was there had formed pink slurry in the frost.

'This is their Greater Good? They give over the bodies of good men to those things? What the hell for?'

'Remember your place, corporal, and harden your heart. This is hardly the worst I've seen from xenos scum, although the thought of the traitors that must have helped them do this sickens me.'

Tam's eye caught sight of something further on: a series of tables lining the far wall, and on them were slabs of meat. His eyes registered the general shape, but something about it wouldn't let his brain believe what he was seeing.

'They skinned them... they cut their clothes off and they skinned them. The thing over there, that thing on the trolley, it's–'

Tam turned away and gagged towards a funnel notch in the floor. It tore his stomach up to retch, and in the end he only brought up some bile and a few chunks of his ration bar. It didn't help him feel any better.

'We can't do anything for these men, corporal, we have to move on. It appears the Planetary Governor has made a deal with the tau, and from the looks of things their PDF units probably got the drop on your men as they pulled back towards the farms. I can see Imperial weapon marks on these bodies, not kroot or pulse rifle burns from fire warriors.'

It was unthinkable. Coruna Imperial Guard soldiers ambushing the Tantulas Regiment as they fled the comm station, and they would have helped the kroot take them. Anyone that resisted would have been killed like that Coruna soldier they had found in the woods. Or maybe that had just been a bit of blue-on-blue contact and the hound hadn't known any better.

There wasn't much comfort to be had in any case. There was a barn full of corpses and Tam was desperately trying to find some way to save them. The least he could do was make sure that the kroot didn't get them.

'Can we blow the building? A final mercy for them, my lord? Is there anything I can lodge these grenades in that would take out the whole damn thing?'

Gesar shook his head and gestured back towards the door with his bolter.

'We have what I needed to know. The only thing we can do is get this information into the right hands. If Coruna has fallen, there may yet be loyalists out there, and my battle-brothers are still out there. The Raven Guard was born for this. Corax guide me; we can find those remaining and tell them of this abomination, and we will cleanse the xenos from this planet even if I must do it all myself!'

'Wait, lord, we can't just leave these bodies. It's not right. What the hell do the kroot want with bodies? If they want meat they can just grab a farm animal, why do they need to skin and fillet an entire regiment?'

'Gravity.'

The two Imperials swung at once towards the voice. It was coming from deeper in the building, and Tam noticed that some of the bodies were swaying slightly, as if something had brushed past them.

'Identify yourself! I am a representative of the Imperium and the Throne, and I order you to identify yourself!'

Something like a laugh came from above them, and suddenly half the lights in the building switched off. It wasn't dark enough for Tam's NV sight to be of much use, but it did cast long shadows through the building.

'The Tantulas Regiment... their bodies are adjusted to higher-gravity worlds, and they all have excellent eyesight. It's why so many of them serve as snipers.'

The rest of the lights suddenly went out and Tam swung his rifle up with practiced ease, his thumb flicking the NV switch.

'Watch your eyes! Chem-glows out!' Gesar was moving as he spoke and Tam saw half a dozen green sticks fly from the man's hand to land in a semi-circle in front of him. The light was dim enough to not foul Tam's NV, but he also suspected that it gave Gesar enough light to see by. Behind them the red emergency light of the building's exit was also casting a pale glow.

'Conserve your ammo and work for the door!' Tam was already moving as slowly as he could, letting the rifle drift from right to left, but all he could see in the darkness were the bodies that hung from the ceiling.

'The tau would educate you, if only you embraced the ideals of the Greater Good and of unity! What you see are those who died from wounds or wouldn't surrender!'

Tam was trying to track the voice, which sounded human, and he thought he heard another voice out there as well, but it wasn't speaking in a human tongue. Gesar must have either seen or heard something because he fired a short burst which was followed by a shriek and a small mewling sound that trailed off in a final whimper.

'Very, very well done, Space Marine. You're going to be quite the prize yourself. So many of those lovely organs stuffed in you. So many genetic marvels handed down from your Emperor. Your blood holds many prizes. I want you to know that only the best warriors will take your flesh. Your body will be a singular honour for all who fight.'

'Corporal, prepare your explosives. I can hear them moving around us. They're going to try to rush us any second... *For the Emperor and Throne!*'

A second burst from the bolter, and this time Tam caught a glimpse of the kroot that Gesar hit. Explosive shells shredded a hanging body but through the green tint of the night vision Tam watched the head of the kroot turn to a smear as the body fell.

Then the kroot began their rush. Tam heard Gesar's bolter sound again and then the clack of the clip hitting empty.

'Changing mags! Cover me! Take! Take! Take!'

Gesar had moved in front of Tam and was now down on one knee. The empty clip clanged as it hit the metal floor, and as Gesar was slapping his last clip in Tam was firing over him.

There were at least a half-dozen kroot in the first wave, and Gesar had accounted for two with his last burst. Three more went down as Tam swept his rifle from side to side. Their alien faces filled the NV sight and the green tint made them all the more nightmarish.

Tam was pointing more than shooting, and suddenly there was a kroot above Gesar, about to swing its rifle down on him like a club. The kroot crumbled like flash paper under a burst from the bolter.

'Back! Back to the door! Keep moving!'

Tam was partly turned as Gesar gave the order, and saw the door swing open and a pulse rifle suddenly appear in the opening.

The face that filled his scope was human, and Tam's finger pulled the rifle's trigger again and again, and the only thing his scope showed was a dark stain on the wall as his rifle clicked on empty.

'Enemy at the door! Lord! We have Ges'vesa at the door!'

Tam was turning back as the bullet took Gesar in the neck. The Space Marine had been rising to his feet, another burst echoing from his bolter when his head jerked oddly and Tam felt a warm spray across his face.

Tam screamed the Space Marine's name, but he was making gurgling noises and had one hand up to his neck while the muzzle flash of the bolter left afterimages across Tam's line of sight.

If they could make the door they still had a chance. Tam tore one of his frags from his webbing and threw it into the open doorway. If there were more traitors outside they'd be in for a nasty surprise.

Even as he heard the grenade bounce through the door he moved forwards and tried to hook an arm around Gesar's elbow, trying to drag him back towards the door. A final burst from the bolter sounded and it clacked on empty.

There was an explosion and screams from outside the door, and Tam was still trying to find some way to lever the Raven Guard up, to get him at least stumbling towards the door. They could still try to fight their way out. Anything was better than being stripped and hung like a side of meat.

Gesar was making angry gurgling noises and Tam looked up just in time to see the kroot about to make a swing with a nasty hooked boning knife.

Tam thrust his rifle forwards and caught the alien, strangely lupine compared to the others Tam had seen, under the jaw and the blade slid in easily. Before he could pull back, the kroot had grabbed the barrel and dragged the rifle out of his hands.

Gesar had given up on pushing himself up, and drew his chainsword, determined to fight from his kneeling position. Tam drew his own pistol and fired off a few rounds at the shapes moving beyond the glow of the chemical lights. He heard the dull smack of rounds hitting dead flesh, but was rewarded by one grunt and what he supposed was a xenos curse from the darkness.

Then his world exploded in a flash as the indoor lights came on once more. He was too dazzled to pick targets but Gesar managed to lunge at one kroot who had taken the moment to charge in. The chainsword caught at the perfect angle just above the sternum and bit deep, the Space Marine's weight and strength carrying the toothed blade right down through the splintering clavicle and into the vessels of the kroot's heart.

Gesar was still trying to pull the blade free when another kroot came whirling in from the right. Tam didn't have time to bring his pistol around before the kroot's rifle butt connected with Gesar's skull above his ear. The wooden stock of the rifle cracked and blood washed down Gesar's face.

Tam emptied his pistol into the kroot's ape-like face and flicked the magazine ejector as he patted his webbing for another clip. He knew there was no way they would make it to the door, just as he knew there would be more soldiers waiting for them even if they did.

There was one way out now. The last fragmentation grenade. Tam didn't know how much it'd take out, but he was pretty sure at close-quarters the thing would turn him into bloody chunks and do for Gesar well enough.

'Lord, Emperor forgive me, I'm sorry, but they won't get you. I promise they won't get you!'

It was the most he could do for the Astartes who had at least kept him alive this long. Tam hoped that if the Emperor did take them to a better place that his last act of courage would be well received.

Just as he felt his hand touch the grenade, a bullet shattered the head of his humerus. His entire left arm went numb and flopped uselessly to his side.

Gesar landed on top of Tam's legs as he fell backwards. Tam could tell the Space Marine was badly concussed. If he wasn't dead yet the amount of blood pouring out of him meant that he didn't have much time. Which was a small mercy, but Gesar would never have wanted the kroot to have his body.

Tam flipped his pistol away from his working right hand and reached for the frag. There was suddenly a shadow above him and his hand exploded in pain as a rifle butt smacked it away from the grenade and fingers broke under the violent strike.

He screamed despite himself and looked up into a cat-eyed kroot. Green slits for eyes. The same eyes that had looked right up at him at the comm station.

The kroot spoke a harsh language that Tam couldn't understand. It was all hard explosions of words, strange pauses and rolling sounds deep in the thing's throat. Then a human voice joined the kroot's, and above him a man in the livery of the blue and gold worn by the human traitors stepped into view. His gaze on the kroot was almost beatific.

'You fight well. The tau like their little human helpers, but the ones here are too weak. You have strong meat, good bones and very good eyes.'

It was the voice they had heard earlier in the building. It seemed that this was the kroot's translator, and he listened carefully and repeated what his master said as the kroot stamped around Tam and examined him.

'Traitor... you betray our Emperor and your people. You are worse than the mutants who scuttle from the warp. A daemon is an abomination, a mutant a twisted thing, but you have damned yourself... for what?'

The traitor was obviously from Coruna, and Tam wondered if he had worn the garb of the Coruna Imperial Guard before he had taken to the kroot's side. There was no telling how far and how deep the treachery went.

'You have not seen the magnificence that is unity. You do not... cannot understand the glory of a Greater Good beyond our corpse Emperor. The tau have shown us truths you lack, the kroot have shown us the glory of unity.'

Gesar was gurgling and his arm rose weakly up as if searching for a weapon. Tam thought he heard a curse trembling on the Astartes' lips. Then he saw another kroot walk up and calmly thrust a blade under his chin, and Gesar's arm fell and was still.

'Why? Why the bodies?'

The kroot seemed to study him, and Tam looked around and saw the differences in colour, in height, in everything about the kroot. They were a melting pot of different physical attributes even more diverse than the multitude of humans scattered across the stars.

'Blood will tell. The kroot seek only unity, and your meat tells the kroot how to be. They give the gift of unity, and they become stronger. They will take your flesh in unity and become better fighters in low gravity. They will see better. They need fresh meat. Their only constant is change.'

'We're soldiers, we're not something churned out of the fabritoriums!'

The traitor continued to translate for the kroot leader as the xenos studied Tam through those alien cat-eyes.

'This is the way of all flesh. The tau don't care what happens to the dead, and they never check to see if humans could survive wounds, so we get as many bodies as we need, and it makes us stronger.

They don't care because it serves their Greater Good.'

The kroot leaned in closer, and drew a thin knife from an arm sheath. He slid the tip carefully up Tam's face until the point rested under Tam's right eye.

'Your Emperor and priests fill their giant warriors with machines and organs to make them strong. Their meat is powerful, but the kroot need all kinds. Otherwise they would break down. You're saving their race. You should be proud. Instead of being flung away in the name of a dead Emperor you'll become one with the kroot, and in your unity you will bring them strength and help them survive to spread deliverance.'

'Don't... please, don't do this to me!'

The traitor was directly translating the kroot's words again, and Tam noticed that the man had backed up, away from the xenos who were gathering around him. Tam could hear a catch in the man's voice, and the traitor's eyes cast downwards.

'You will live on, human, isn't that what your kind like? Isn't that why they spread out among the stars? Isn't that why your Emperor puts his organs and blood in his Space Marines? You will live forever as part of the kroot, and someday a human will look at one of us and see your eyes... such good eyes.'

Tam screamed until the moment the rifle butt connected with his forehead, and dimly he felt rough hands and claws pulling at his clothing and lifting him up.

He thought he saw a light for one moment, and felt someone tugging at his eyelids, and he thought of the black bird, pecking at the nameless Guardsman in the woods, and then everything went black as the knives came down.

THE CORE
Aaron Dembski-Bowden

'Look out at my father's Imperium.
Do not unroll a parchment map or analyse a hololithic starchart.
Merely raise your head to the night sky and open your eyes.

Stare into the blackness between worlds – that dark ocean, the silent sea.
Stare into the million eyes of firelight – each a sun to be subjugated in the Emperor's grip.

The age of the alien, the era of the inhuman, is over.
Mankind is in its ascendancy, and with ten thousand claws we will lay claim to the stars themselves.'

– Primarch Konrad Curze
Addressing the VIII Legion during
the Great Crusade

I

It knew itself only as the Eldest.

More than its name, this was its place in creation. It was the oldest, the strongest, the fiercest, and it had tasted the most blood. Before it had become the Eldest, it had been one of the lesser breed. These weakling creatures were the Eldest's kin, though it remained distant from them now, seeking to quieten a hunger that would never fade.

The Eldest twitched in its repose, not quite asleep, not quite in hibernation, but a state of stillness that haunted between the two. Its thoughts were sluggish, a slow crawl of instinct and vague sensation behind its closed eyes. The consciousnesses of its kin whispered in the back of the Eldest's mind.

They spoke of weakness, of a lack of prey, and that made such whispers ignorable.

Nor was the Eldest a creature capable of dreaming. Instead of sleeping, instead of dreaming as a human would, it remained motionless in the deepest dark, ignoring the thought-pulses of its weakling kin and allowing its somnolent thoughts to linger on the hateful hunger that pained it to its core.

Prey, its sluggish mind ached, burning with need.
Blood. Flesh. Hunger.

II

The demigods moved through the darkness, and Septimus followed.

He was still unsure why the master had demanded he accompany them, but his duty was to obey, not to question. He'd buckled himself into his ragged atmosphere suit – a poor comparison to the demigods' all-enclosing Astartes war plate – and he'd followed them down the gunship's ramp, into the blackness beyond.

'Why are you going with them?' a female voice had crackled over his suit's vox. To reply, Septimus had needed to switch channels manually, tuning a frequency dial built into the small suit control vambrace on his left arm. By the time he'd patched into the right channel, the female voice had repeated the question in a tone both more worried and more irritated.

'I said, why are you going with them?'

'I don't know,' the servant replied. He was already falling behind the Astartes, and was practically jogging to keep pace. For all the use it was, the luminator mounted on the side of his helm cast its weak lance of light wherever he looked. A beam of dull amber light speared ahead, cutting the darkness with illumination so thin and dim it was almost worthless.

The spotlight brushed over arched walls of unpolished metal, gantry floor decking and – after only a few minutes – the first body.

The master and his brothers had already passed, but Septimus slowed in his stride, kneeling by the corpse.

'Keep up, slave,' one of them voxed back to him as they descended deeper into the dark tunnels. 'Ignore the bodies.'

Septimus allowed himself a last look at the body – human, male, frozen stiff in the heatless dark. He could have been dead a week, or a hundred years. All sense of decay was halted with the vessel powered down and open to the void.

A rime of frost coated everything with a crystalline second skin, from the walls to the decking to the dead man's tortured face.

'Keep *up*, slave,' the voice called back again, snarling and low.

Septimus raised his gaze, and the weak beam trailed out into the darkness. He couldn't see the master, or the master's brothers. They'd moved too far ahead. What met his questing stare instead was altogether more gruesome, yet not entirely unexpected.

Three more corpses, each as frost-rimed and death-tensed as the first, each one frozen tight to the metal floor of their corridor tomb. Septimus touched the closest ice-hardened wound with his gloved fingertips, making a face as he touched torn bones and red meat as unyielding as stone.

He felt the decking shiver under thudding footfalls. With the ship open to the void, the approaching demigod's steps were soundless, sending tremors through the floor. Septimus raised his head again, and the lamp beam illuminated a suit of armour the troubled, turgid blue of flawed sapphire.

'Septimus,' the towering suit of armour voxed. In its dark fists was a heavy bolter of bulky, archaic design, much too large for a human to carry, adorned with bleached skulls hanging from chains of polished bronze. The cannon's muzzle had been forged into a wide-jawed skull, the barrel thrusting from the skeleton's screaming mouth.

Septimus knew the weapon well, for he was the one who maintained it, repaired it and honoured the machine-spirit within. He rose to his feet.

'Forgive me, Lord Mercutian.'

The warrior's slanted eye lenses scanned him with unblinking scrutiny. 'Is something amiss?'

Mercutian's voice, even over the vox, had a quality most of the others lacked. Nestled among the inhuman depth and resonance was a hint of altered vowels, born of his accent. The refined edge to Mercutian's speech hinted at a youth of expensive education, and it coloured his Nostraman.

'No, lord. Nothing is amiss. Curiosity overtook me, that's all.'

The warrior inclined his head back down the corridor. 'Come, Septimus. Stay close. Does the additional weight trouble you?'

'No, lord.'

That was a lie, but not much of one. He carried a heavy ammunition canister over his shoulder, in addition to the oxygen tanks on his back. The canister was densely packed with folded belts of ammunition for the massive bolter cannon clutched in Mercutian's gauntlets. The warrior carried two similar containers himself, locked to his belt.

Another voice crackled over the vox – also speaking in Nostraman, but with a bladed end to each syllable. Septimus knew the hive ganger accent well enough. He'd learned to speak it himself, as a natural inflection when his master had taught him the language. Most of the demigods spoke in the same way.

'Hurry up, both of you,' the voice barked.

'We're coming, Xarl,' replied Mercutian.

The warrior led the way, immense gun lowered, boots thumping noiselessly on the decking. He stepped over the dead bodies, paying them no heed.

Septimus moved around them, marking how each one had been disembowelled with gruesome totality. He'd seen wounds like these before, but only on hololithic biological displays.

As he followed Mercutian, the slave adjusted the tuning dial on his wrist.

'Genestealers,' he whispered into the private channel.

The woman on the other end was named Octavia, for she was the eighth slave, just as Septimus was the seventh.

'Be careful,' she said, and she meant it.

Septimus didn't reply at first. Octavia's tone showed she knew just how insane her own words were, given the existence they shared as pawns of the Night Lords.

'Have they told you why we're here? I'm not buying the salvage story.'

'Not a word,' she said. 'They've been silent with me since we left the Sea of Souls.'

'We used to salvage hulks all the time back on the *Covenant of Blood*. At least, when we weren't cut to pieces by Imperial guns. But this feels different.'

'Different how?'

'Worse. For a start, this one is bigger.' Septimus checked his wrist chronometer again. He'd been on board the hulk for three hours now.

* * *

III

THREE HOURS BEFORE, a wicked blade of a vessel had translated in-system, leaving the warp's grip in a burst of plasma mist and engine fire.

The ship was the dark of a winter's midnight sky, its edges embossed in the kind of beaten, shining bronze that covered the armoured torsos of Terra's ancient heroes in those ignorant, impious generations before mankind had first reached out into the stars.

A thing of militaristic beauty – armoured ridges and gothic spinal architecture, presented in sleek viciousness. It was a barbed spear, blackened-blue and golden bronze, surging through the void.

There were no active vessels nearby, Imperial, xenos or otherwise, but had any been present – and had they possessed the capacity to break the auspex encryption haze projected by the dark ship – they would have known the ship by the name it bore in the Horus Heresy ten thousand years before.

In that foulest of ages, this ship had hung in the skies above Holy Terra as the world's atmosphere burned. A million ships painted the void with flame as they raged at each other, while the planet below, the cradle of humanity, caught fire.

This ship had been there, and it had slain vessels loyal to the Golden Throne, casting them from orbit to tear through Terra's cloud cover and hammer into the Emperor's cities.

Its name was *Ashallius S'Veyval*, in a dead language, from a dead world. In Imperial Gothic, it translated loosely as *Echo of Damnation*.

* * *

The Echo of Damnation ghosted forwards on low-burning engines, cutting space in silent repose. On its bridge, humans worked in unison with beings that hadn't been human for generations.

In the centre of the ornate chamber, a figure sat on a throne of black iron and burnished bronze. The Astartes wore ancient armour, the pieces cannibalised from a dozen and more dead warriors over the years and repainted with great reverence. Jawless skulls hung on chains from his shoulder guards, rattling with each of the warrior's movements and every shiver of the ship he commanded. The face he presented to the world was a skulled faceplate, with a single rune drawn from a dead language branded into its forehead.

A hive of activity pulsed around the seated figure. Officers in outdated Imperial Navy uniforms bereft of insignia worked at various consoles, tables and cogitator screens. An ageing human at the broad helm console pushed a heavy steel lever into its locked position, and consulted the display screens before him, reading the scrolling runic text that spilled out in merciless reams. Such a flow of lore would be meaningless to inexpert eyes.

'Translation complete, my lord,' he called over his shoulder. 'All decks, all systems, all stable.'

The masked figure upon the throne inclined its head in a slow nod. It was still waiting for something.

A voice – female, young, but stained by exhaustion – spoke out across the bridge, emerging from speakers in the mouths of daemon-faced gargoyles sculpted into the metal walls.

'We made it,' the voiced breathed. 'We're here. As close as I could get.'

At last, the enthroned figure rose to its feet and spoke for the first time in several hours.

'Perfect.' Its voice was deep, inhumanly low, yet possessed of a curiously soft edge. 'Octavia?'

'Yes?' the female voice asked again, breezing over the bridge. 'I... I need to rest, master.'

'Then rest, Navigator. You have done well.'

Several of the human bridge crew shared uncomfortable glances. This new commander was unlike the last. Acclimatisation was slow in coming, as most of them had served under the Exalted – or even worse masters – for many long years. None were used to hearing praise spoken in their presences, and it aroused suspicion before anything else.

From an alcove in the bridge chamber's western wall, the scrymaster called out his report. Although he was human, his voice was mechanical, with half of his face, throat and torso replaced by inexpensive, crude bionics. The augmetics that served in place of his human flesh had been earned for his actions in the Fall of Vilamus, five months before.

'Auspex is alive again, master,' he called.

'Illuminate me,' said the armoured commander. He was staring at the occulus, but the great screen at the front of the bridge chamber remained half-dead, blinded by ferocious interference. He was unconcerned, well used to such static annoyance after a journey through the warp. The occulus always took a while to realign and revive.

Sometimes, he saw faces in the greyish storm of confused signals that blasted across the crackling viewscreen – faces of the fallen, the lost, the forgotten and the damned.

These always made him smile, even as they screamed at him in voices of tortured white noise.

The scrymaster spoke while staring down at his auspex displays, spread over four flickering screens, each one detailing a spread of numerical lore about the ship's surroundings.

'At three-quarters velocity, we're fifteen minutes and thirty-eight seconds from boarding pod range from intended target.'

The commander smiled behind his faceplate. Blood of the father, Octavia. All praise to your skills for this, he thought. To break from the Sea of Souls this close to a moving target. For such a young Navigator, she was skilled – or lucky – beyond all expectation, adapting to racing through the secret pathways of the empyrean with tenacity and instinct.

'Any contacts from nearby vessels?'

'None, master.'

All good so far. The commander nodded to the left side of the bridge, where the defensive stations were manned by ragged-uniformed officers and servitors capable of focussing on nothing but their appointed duties.

'Maintain the Shriek,' he ordered.

'Yes, master,' one of the officers called. The man, an acolyte of the broken Mechanicum, possessed an additional pair of multi-jointed arms extending from his back-mounted power pack. These worked on a separate console beside the one he manipulated with his biological fingers.

'Plasma bleed is significant,' the acolyte intoned. 'The Shriek can be maintained for another two point one-five hours before aura-scrye inhibitors must be powered down.'

That would be long enough. The commander would cease the Shriek as soon as the region was absolutely secure. Until then, he was content to let the *Echo of Damnation* fill nearspace with a thousand frequencies of howling noise and wordless machine-screams. Any other vessels in range to trace the *Echo* on their scanners would find their auspex readers unable to detect definitive targets in the jamming field, and their vox channels conquered by the endless static-laden screams.

The Shriek had been Tech-priest Deltrian's most recent invention. Invisibility to Imperial scanning had its uses, but it also fed with greedy abandon on power that other areas of the ship needed to function. When the Shriek was live, the void shields were thin, and the prow lances were completely powered down.

'All remaining power to the engines.' The commander still watched the distorted occulus. 'Bring us closer to the target.'

'Lord,' the scrymaster swallowed. 'The target is… it's vast.'

'It is a Mechanicus vessel. The fact it's huge is no surprise to me, nor should it be to you.'

'No, master. It reads as significantly larger than vessels of approximate design and specification.'

'Define "vast",' said the commander.

'Auspex reports indicate a mass in approximation of Jathis Secondus, master.'

There was a pause, during which the bridge fell almost silent. The loudest sound was the commander's breathing, which rasped in and out of his helm's vox-speaker. The crew were still unfamiliar with their new master, but they could all too easily recognise the harsh breathing of an Astartes on the edge of losing his temper.

'We have dropped from the warp,' the commander hissed through closed teeth, 'to seek a ship fused within a space hulk. And you are telling me the scryers indicate this hulk is the size of a small moon?'

'Yes, my lord,' the scrymaster cringed.

'Do not flinch when addressing me. I will not slay you for delivering irritating information.'

'Yes, master. Thank you, master.'

The commander's next reply was interrupted by the occulus, at last, resolving into focus. The static cleared, the distortion bled away.

The screen showed, with treacherous clarity, a distant mesh of conjoined, ruined spaceships, fused together as if by the will of some capricious, mad god.

And it was, as the commander had cursed, the size of a small moon.

One of the other Astartes by the commander's throne stepped forwards, his own dark helm inclined towards the occulus.

'Blood of Horus… There must be two hundred ships in that.'

The commander nodded, unable to look away. It was the largest drifting hulk he'd ever seen. It was, he was almost certain, the largest any human or Astartes had ever seen.

'Scan that insane mess for the remnants of the Mechanicus exploratory vessel,' he growled. 'Hopefully it will be one of the ships merged at the outer layers. Acolyte, cease the Shriek. Helm, bring us in closer.'

A muted 'Compliance, master,' came from the primary helmsman.

'Make ready First Claw for boarding operations,' the commander said to the other Astartes. As he re-seated himself on the metallic throne, he stared at the growing superstructure filling the occulus. Details, warped contours, mangled spires, were beginning to become visible.

'And inform Lucoryphus of the Bleeding Eyes that I wish to speak with him immediately.'

WHEN ITS CLAWS were not in use, they closed into awkward talons, curling in upon themselves and betraying a creature no longer suited to walking along the ground. Its movements had a jagged hesitance as it entered the chamber, punctuated by twitches in its limbs and flaw-born tics in its enhanced musculature. This spasming posture had nothing to do with cowardice, and everything to do with the fact that the beast was caged – forced to act as one of its former brethren – forced to walk and speak.

Such things had been alien to the creature, if not completely anathema, for some time now. It walked on all fours, hunched over in a cautious stalk, hand-talons and foot-claws clanking on the deck. The cylindrical turbine engines on its back swayed with the creature's awkward gait.

The being's helmed face showed little evidence of the ties to its bloodline, now changed by war and the warp into something altogether more hateful. Gone were the runic markings and a painted skull over blessed ceramite. In place of traditional Legion signifiers, a sleek faceplate offered a howling daemon's visage to the world beyond, with a mouth grille set in a scream that had lasted since its god-father died.

The twisted face flicked to watch each of the other Astartes in turn, snapping left and right like a falcon choosing prey. The servos and fibre bundle cabling making up its armour's neck joints no longer purred with easy locomotion, they barked with each accusing twitch of its face.

'Why summon?' the creature demanded in a voice that wouldn't have been out of place creaking from the gnarled maw of a desert vulture. 'Why summon? Why?'

Talos rose from the command throne. First Claw moved as he moved, five other Astartes approaching the hunched creature, their weapons within easy reach.

'Lucoryphus,' Talos said, and inclined his head in respect before saluting, fist over both hearts, his gauntlet and forearm covering the ritually mutilated Imperial eagle emblazoned across his chest.

'Soul Hunter.' It snarled a chuckle from lungs that sounded much too dry. 'Speak, prophet. I listen.'

* * *

Soon after, the *Echo of Damnation* drifted in close, dwarfed by the immense hulk and utterly eclipsed in the shadow it cast from the light of a distant sun.

Two pods blasted from housings in the ship's belly, twisting like drills through the void until they pounded into the softer metal of the hulk's skin.

On the *Echo's* bridge, two signals pulsed back to the communications array. The first was soft-voiced and coloured by vox crackle. The second was delivered in short, sharp hisses.

'This is Talos of First Claw. We're in.'

'Lucoryphus. Ninth Claw. Inside.'

IV

Ten hours in, and seven hours since he'd last spoken to Octavia. The ship through which they travelled had gravity and air cyclers active, which was a small mercy.

Septimus knew better than to confess his hunger to the Astartes. They were above such things, and had no mind to be concerned with mortal needs. He had dehydrated ration tablets in his webbing, but they did little more than take the edge off his hunger. First Claw moved through the dark corridors with a relentlessness made sinister by their silence. An hour before, Septimus had risked stopping to take a piss against a bulkhead, and had needed to sprint to catch back up to them.

His return had been greeted with nothing more than a growl from one of the squad. Clad in ancient armour, a bloodied palm-print smeared across the faceplate, Uzas had snarled at the returning human.

As greetings went, by Uzas's standards it was almost cordial.

They'd travelled through fourteen vessels, though it was a nightmare to decide just where one finished and another started, or if they were moving through the aborted remnants of a malformed ship they'd already crossed in another section.

Most of the time was spent waiting for the servitors to cut – cutting through sealed bulkheads; cutting through warped walls of fuselage; cutting through mangled metal to reach a traversable area beyond.

THE TWO SERVITORS laboured with mindless diligence, their actions slaved to the signum control tablet held in Deltrian's skeletal hands. Drills, saws, laser cutters and plasma burners heated the air around the two bionic slaves as they carved their way through another blockage of twisted wall.

The tech-priest watched this through eyes of emerald, the gems sculpted into layered lenses and fixed into the sockets of his restructured face.

Deltrian had fashioned his own body to exacting standards. The schematics he had designed in the construction of his physique were, by the standards of human intellect, closer to art than engineering. Such was the effort necessary to survive the centuries alongside the Astartes, when one lacked the immortality allowed by their gene-forged physiology.

He knew he made the human uneasy. He was familiar with the effect his appearance had on unaugmented mortals. The equations in his mind that mimicked biological thought patterns reached no answer to rectify this adverse effect, and he was not certain it was – technically speaking – an error to be corrected. Fear had its uses, when harvested from others. This was a lesson he had learned from his association with the Night Lords.

The tech-priest acknowledged the human now with an inclination of his head. The serf was one of the chosen, and deserved a modicum of respect due to his position as artificer for First Claw's armour and weapons.

'Septimus,' he said. The human started, while the servitors worked on.

'Honoured adept,' the slave nodded back. The corridor they occupied was low and claustrophobic. First Claw were busying themselves elsewhere, patrolling nearby chambers.

'Do you know why you are here, Septimus?'

SEPTIMUS DIDN'T HAVE an answer.

Deltrian was an ugly thing of darkened metal, fluid-filled wires and polished chrome – a metallic skeleton complete with its circulatory system, and wreathed in an old robe of thick weave, the colour of blood in the moonlight.

It must have taken a perverse sense of humour to reforge your own body over the decades into something that looked like a bionic replica of some pre-Imperial Terran death god. Septimus didn't share the joke, if indeed it was one.

For the moment, Deltrian's eye lenses were deep green, likely cut from emeralds. This was by no means a permanent feature. Often, they were red, blue or transparent, showing the wire-works behind, linking to a brain that was at least partly still human.

'I do not know, honoured adept. The masters have not told me.'

'I believe I am able to make an approximate analysis.' Deltrian laughed, buzzing like a vox slipping from the right frequency.

There was a threat buried in that. Irritation made Septimus bold, but he kept his hands from resting on the two holstered laspistols at his hips. Deltrian might be favoured as an ally from the Mechanicus, but he was just as shackled in service to the VIII Legion as Septimus was.

'Feel free to enlighten me, honoured adept.'

'You are human.' The skinless creature turned its death's-head grin away to regard its servitors once more. 'Human, and unarmoured in enclosing ceramite. Your blood, your heartbeat, your sweat and breath – all of these biological details will be detected by the predatory xenos species aboard this hulk.'

'With all respect, Deltrian,' Septimus turned, looking back at the long corridor they'd walked down, 'you're deluded.'

'I see you and I hear you all too well, and my engineered stimulus array is comparable to the senses of the genestealer genus. My aural receptors register your breathing like a world's winds, and your beating heart like the primal drums of a primitive culture. If I sense this, Septimus – and I assure you that I do – then you should know that the many living beings sheltering on this derelict sense it as well.'

Septimus snorted. The idea of the Night Lords using him – one of their more valuable slaves – as bait, was...

'Contact,' voxed Talos.

In the distance, bolters began to bark.

V

THE ELDEST STIRRED from the cold, cold darkness of the nothingness that was as close to sleep as its species could know.

A faint pain echoed, faded but troubling, in the base of its curved skull. This weak pain soon spread with gentle insistence, beating through its blood vessels and twinning with the creature's pulse. The pain cobwebbed down the Eldest's spine and through its facial structure, emanating from its sluggish mind.

This was not the pain of a wound, of defeat, of a hunter denied. It did not eclipse the hunger-need, but it was even less welcome. Its taste and resonance were so very different, and the Eldest had not felt such a thing for... for some time.

Its kin were dying. The Eldest felt each puncturing hole, each ravaged limb, each bleeding socket, in this echoing ghost-pain.

In the darkness, it uncoiled its limbs. Joints clicked and cracked as they tensed and flexed once more.

Its killing claws shivered, opening and closing in the cool air. Digestive acid stung its tongue as its saliva ducts tingled back into life. The Eldest drew a shaking breath through rows of shark's teeth, and the cold air was a catalyst to its senses. Its featureless eyes opened, thick ropes of drool slivering down its chin, dangling from its maw to fall in hissing spittle-droplets on the decking.

After dragging itself from the confines of its hiding place, the Eldest set out through the ship in search of the creatures killing its children.

It smelled blood in the air, heard the rhythm of a prey's heart, and scented salty sweat on soft skin. More than this, it sensed the buzzing hum of living sentience, the brain's fleshy electricity of emotion and thought.

Life.

Human.

Near.

The Eldest clicked to itself with bladed mouth-parts, and leaned forwards into a hungry run, bolting through the black passageways with its claws hammering on the metal.

Kin, it sent silently, *I come.*

VI

LUCORYPHUS AND HIS team were not slowed down by the presence of a human or a tech-priest. Nor did they rely on lobotomised servitors to breach obstructions. Instead, several of Lucoryphus's Raptors were armed with melta guns, breathing out searing surges of gaseous heat intense enough to liquidate the metal it blasted.

As a pack, the Bleeding Eyes – still growing used to their new designation of Ninth Claw – moved at far greater speed through the amalgamation of twisted ships. Unlike Talos and First Claw, Lucoryphus and his brothers had no specific target. They scouted, they stalked, they sought whatever of worth they could find.

And so far, that had been nothing at all.

The boredom was made bitter by the fact that had they been heading deeper in search of the conjoined Mechanicus vessel at the hulk's core, Lucoryphus was sure the Bleeding Eyes would have been there by now, and on their way back out.

Vox was increasingly erratic as Ninth Claw pressed ahead of their brothers, and Lucoryphus was fast losing patience with First Claw's progress. The initial hesitations had come from their human slave holding them back. Then their tech-adept had forced them to lag behind while he – while *it* – bled information from various databanks and memory tablets in the ships First Claw was cutting through.

'Vaporiser weapons,' Lucoryphus's hissing voice carried over the vox, 'Melta-class weapons. No cutting. No cutting servitors. Much faster.'

Talos's reply was punctuated by the dull juddering of bolters. 'Noted. Be aware, we've encountered an insignificant genestealer threat. Minimal numbers, at least in this section. What is your location?'

Lucoryphus led his pack onwards, through spacious corridors, each of the Raptors hunched and loping beast-like on all fours. The construction of these passageways was utterly familiar.

'Astartes ship, Standard Template Construct. Not ours. Throne slaves.'

'Understood. Any xenos presence?'

'Some. Few. All dead now.' The cylindrical engine housings on his back idled in disuse, occasionally coughing black smoke from vent slits. 'Moving to enginarium. Vessel still has partial power. Some lights bright. Some doors open. Ship not ancient like others. This is close to hulk's edge.'

'Understood.' More bolter fire, and the dim sounds of other Astartes cursing as Talos replied, 'These things are stunted and weak. They seem almost decrepit.'

'Genestealer xenos present for many decades. No prey, no strength. Beasts grow old, grow frail. Still deadly.'

'It's no struggle, yet.' The chatter of bolters began to die down. 'Report status every ten minutes.'

'Yes, prophet. I obey.'

On four claws, the once-human stalked on, his slanted eye lenses following the contours of the walls.

The corridor at last opened up into a large room, blissful in its dark silence, populated by towering generators and a wall-mounted plasma chamber that still – against all expectations – emitted a faint orange glow from the volatile cocktail of liquids and gases roiling in the glass chamber's depths.

Without needing orders, the Raptors spread across the engine deck, moving to consoles and gantries, taking up firing positions to cover the room's exits. Several of the pack let their thrusters whine into life, boosting their way up to the higher platforms.

With difficulty, Lucoryphus fought down the urge to soar with them. Even in the confines of the ship's interior, he ached to leave the trudging discomfort of the ground behind.

Indulging a little, he cycled his turbines live with an effort as simple and natural as drawing breath. The kick of thrust carried him across the enginarium, to land in a neat crouch before the main power console. Eight dead servitors lay scattered around the controls, reduced to figures of bone and bionics.

One of Lucoryphus's best, Vorasha, was already at the console, his curving finger-talons clicking at the controls.

'Plasma chamber depleted,' Vorasha's voice slithered from his helm's snarling speaker-grille. 'The power has bled from the chamber over decades, yes-yes.'

'Restore it.' The Raptor leader emphasised the order with a short, sharp sound somewhere between a shriek and a whisper. 'Do this now.'

Vorasha's talons clicked on keys and worked levers. 'I am not able to do this. Most of the vessel is lifeless. Can send power from section to section, yes-yes. With ease. Open bulkheads too dense to burn through fast. Cannot restore all power to all sections.'

Lucoryphus's reply came in a keening, aggrieved tone. 'Many redundant sections. Kill power in them. Then we move.'

'It will be done,' said Vorasha, and began to divert what little power remained in the ship's blood vessels, forcing it into the sections that the Bleeding Eyes Raptors had to cross. At his estimate, Vorasha was going to be able to save them almost an hour of burning through locked bulkhead doors on their way through the ship.

'What is this ship?' Lucoryphus asked, his faceplate turned to the ceiling, seeking any indication of allegiance or identity.

The answer came from one of the others. Zon La found a body no more than ten seconds after his leader had asked the question. Armoured in green, it lay on the raised gantry deck above the enginarium floor; cut into pieces by the violence of alien claws, it displayed its brotherhood all too clearly in the bronze dragon emblem across its breastplate.

'XVIII Legion,' the Raptor hissed, recoiling in disgust. Zon La's tongue ached with the sudden need to spit his corrosive saliva onto the skeletal corpse.

Vorasha, linked to the ship's faded power core, turned to Lucoryphus. 'Power killed in redundant decks. Ship name is *Protean*, yes-yes, XVIII Legion.'

Lucoryphus chuckled behind his faceplate. The red eye lenses stared out, with scarlet and silver tears painted in twin trails down his cheeks. It was a visage shared by all his bothers in the Bleeding Eyes. Each of them watched the world through helms with slanted eyes and cried tears of quicksilver and crimson.

'Salamanders. We killed so many in the Old War. Amazed any still draw breath.'

'Wait-wait.' Vorasha never really talked – he hissed and clicked in place of true speech, but the other Raptors could make out the meaning in his broken language with ease. 'I sense others. I hear others nearby.'

Lucoryphus was as tense as his brothers, head tilted.

He had heard it, too. Weapon fire.

'Salamanders,' Zon La rasped. 'Still alive on ship.'

Lucoryphus was already making his ungainly way to the double doors that led deeper into the ship's decks.

'Not for long. Nine of you, remain with Vorasha. Nine more, with me.'

XARL AND UZAS, both warriors of First Claw, sprayed the hallway with suppressive fire, bolters kicking in clenched fists. Uzas's field of fire was random, chewing down whichever alien beast drew his attention each particular second. Xarl was all controlled aggression, bolts punching home into the skulls of the closest aliens and crippling those that sought to rise again.

Both of them picked up the crackling declaration from Talos, and both were equally infuriated. The Bleeding Eyes, several hours deeper into the amalgamated hulk, had encountered loyalist Astartes.

Salamanders.

Too far away – far too far – for First Claw to reach them. Talos ordered his brothers to maintain the guardianship of Deltrian and purge the corridors of alien threats.

Xarl concentrated his anger into a killing urge, drawing his chainsword and tearing left and right, weaving wounds among the genestealers that reached the embattled warriors. Uzas, never one for subtlety or self-discipline, howled his bitterness through the uncaring hallways and tore into the aliens with his bolter, his chainblade and even his bare hands.

* * *

'Lucoryphus, this is Talos.'

'No words now. Hunting.'

'Assess the enemy threat first. Do not engage without assured victory.'

'*Coward!*'

'We have the *Echo of Damnation* in the void nearby, fool. We can cripple their ship in space and deploy boarding pods at our leisure. Do not engage without assured victory. We do not have the strength here to face down Terminators.'

No reply came, except for the rabid charging of hand-claws and foot-talons on metal decking.

Talos exhaled slowly. It left his helm's vox-speakers as a daemonic rasp. This was not going to plan.

His standing orders for the strike cruiser had been to power down and activate the Shriek if any Imperial vessels came into the system. There was little chance the Salamanders' ship had detected and destroyed the *Echo*, but Talos was far from sanguine. Deltrian was taking too long, and Lucoryphus, as always, was an uncontrollable element.

'First Claw to *Echo of Damnation*.'

'…cr… s… aw…'

The vox was still worthless. They'd have to get back to the hulk's outer layers to restore contact.

'Deltrian,' Talos voxed. 'Status report.'

VII

The Eldest rounded a corner, clinging to the walls with claws that crunched purchase in the arched, ancient steel. It didn't slow down, not even for a fraction of a heartbeat. Burning saliva stung its jaws as it drooled down its chin.

Prey.

Two. Ahead.

The Eldest leaped over the bodies of fallen kin, moving its headlong dash to the ceiling as it tore forwards, still not slowing in its stride. Claws ripped handholds in the corridor's roof with vicious speed. Bodily, it shoved its lesser kin aside, bashing through those tall enough to obstruct its passage. In better times, their links to the Eldest's mind would have sent them scurrying aside respectfully, sensing their lord's approach.

'Reloading.' Mercutian dropped to one knee and ejected a spent ammunition belt from the massive heavy bolter.

At his side, Cyrion took aim with his own weapon, and the corridor echoed with the familiar crashing of a bolter letting loose on full auto.

'Reload faster.'

'Keep shooting,' Mercutian snarled.

'It's on the damn ceiling…'

'*Keep shooting.*'

Beneath and around, the hard bodies of its kin were shattering and bursting under the prey's defences. The prey ahead – two of them – unleashed a sickening stream of burning anger that blasted the Eldest's kin apart.

The heated projectiles began to crash against the Eldest's skin.

It suddenly remembered what pain felt like.

* * *

Mercutian buckled the ammo feed into place and lifted his heavy bolter again. It took three awful seconds to power up again, then its internal mechanisms clunked into life.

An instant's glance saw Cyrion's bolter fire laying waste to the weaker creatures, but the huge beast was shrieking its way through a volley of bolter fire, still sprinting across the ceiling, eating up the metres between them.

He didn't rise to his feet. Remaining where he was, he pulled the trigger handle and felt his armour's stabilisers kick in to compensate for the cannon's recoil.

The heavy bolter shook as it disgorged a stream of high-velocity explosive bolts, each one pounding chunks of chitinous meat from the creature's exoskeletal flesh.

As the twelfth bolt struck home, the beast fell from the ceiling, plunging into the seething mass of lesser creatures below. Mercutian lowered his aim, and let his cannon chew into them next.

The Eldest smelled its own blood, and this was somehow more shocking than the pain of its burst-open, bleeding wounds. The scent overpowered the wounds of its kin, eclipsing them in richness and potency.

The lord-creature drew in its damaged limbs, curling them close to its body. It had misjudged the prey. The prey was fierce. The prey could not be battled as equals, but must be stalked as meat to be hunted.

This was the Way. The Eldest's hunger had blinded it to the Way, but the pain of its mistake served as the most forceful of reminders.

Hunched and defeated but utterly devoid of shame, the Eldest tore its way back down the passageway, slaying its own kin in its need to retreat from the prey.

Minutes later, in the silent darkness again, it uncurled its wounded limbs, waiting for the blood to stop flowing.

A single thought-pulse screamed noiselessly through the decks above and below. More of its kin spread across the hive, weakened by hunger themselves, uncoiled and rose from their own states of near-slumber.

The Eldest moved away, seeking to come at the prey alone next time, and with greater patience.

Mercutian lowered the heavy bolter and sank back against the wall. Cyrion locked his bolter to his thigh, and drew a pistol and chainblade.

At last, the corridor was mercifully quiet. Occasionally, a dead alien would twitch.

'Talos, this is Cyrion.'

'Speak,' the prophet's voice crackled back over the vox.

'Area secure for now. Be warned, one of these genestealers is huge. Mercutian hit it dead-on with enough bolts to burst a daemon and it just howled and ran away. I swear by our father's name, it sounded like the bastard thing was laughing as it went. We're falling back to the irritating tech-priest now.'

'Understood. Deltrian insists this is the right ship. He has breached the starboard data storage pod. At last.'

'So it's a Titan-carrier?'

'It was. It looks like more of a xenos hive now. A nest of genestealers on the edge of starvation.'

'It would be pleasant to know we hadn't wasted a great deal of time in coming here.'

'That,' Talos laughed, 'would mean that something went right for once.' The link went silent.

A dead genestealer shivered no more than seven metres away from where Cyrion was standing. Cyrion blew its head apart with a single shot from his bolt pistol.

Mercutian hauled himself to his feet with a grunt. 'I can see why the Throne sends Terminators into these places.'

THE ELDEST LOPED through the dark tunnels, its crouched run taking it along walls and ceilings without a thought. Deeper into the hive it ran, ever deeper, moving around the prey that reeked of strange metal and powdery fire. They were strong, and the Eldest was weaker than it had ever been before. It needed to feed on easier prey to regain its strength.

And there *was* other prey. The Eldest could still smell it, even over the reek of its own wounds.

The other prey-scent was salt-blooded and strong, and it was this meal that the Eldest sought with patient intent.

The armoured prey were defending it, though. They encircled it, blocking off passageways and lying in wait, ready to inflict more pain. The Eldest had to avoid them, clawing and crawling through the tightest spaces and ripping new tunnels in the hive's steel walls.

As it ran and tore and leaped and ripped, it could sense-hear more of its kin rising from their slumbers.

It came, at last, to an expansive section of the territory claimed by its kin, where few of its cousin creatures dwelled. The human prey was here, hiding in this immense chamber.

The Eldest unfolded its wounded limbs again. The blood no longer flowed. True regeneration might come in time. For now, a cessation of leakage and pain was enough.

In the darkness, the Eldest drooled and moved forwards once more. Something primal and instinctive opened within its mind, and an unheard shriek tremored out through the ship.

Its kin must be summoned.

SEPTIMUS WATCHED THE servitors working in the chamber. Occasionally, his breath would mist the visor of his atmosphere suit, but when it cleared the scene was much the same: the bionic slaves were loading up with heavy cogitator memory pods and strapping them to their backs. Deltrian, the robed tech-adept, monitored their activity from beside the main console in a room full of stilled monitors and data processors.

Thousands of years before, this had been the heart of a Mechanicus warship, carrying Titans and enhanced soldiers across the stars. In this very room, tech-priests had worked their esoteric trade, storing the information of countless crusades, the gun camera footage of hundreds of battlefields, the countless vox transmissions from generations of Titan commanders and infantry officers, and most vital of all, the code-keys, voice imprints and encryption ciphers of the Titan Legion to whom this ship had once belonged.

All of it added up to what the skeletal tech-adept had come for: the chance to lay claim to a million secrets of the Cult Mechanicus. Such lore was worth any risk. Its potential uses were infinite in the Old War against the false Emperor and the dregs of the True Mechanicum that still lingered, gasping and ignorant, on the surface of Great Mars.

Yet it had been difficult to persuade the Night Lords of the necessity, of the possibilities on offer. They had been lured in with the temptation of potential scavenging. It was a crude compromise by the tech-priest's reasoning. Insofar as Deltrian was able to emulate human emotion any more, he had a degree of regard for the warriors of the VIII Legion, but he mourned their lack of vision in regards to the lore he sought here.

Still, they were always reliably earnest in pursuit of piracy. He'd played to that predilection.

'Did you hear that?' Septimus asked, his breath audible over the vox. 'First Claw has engaged some kind of huge creature.'

Deltrian diverted an insignificant portion of his attention to replying.

'Corporaptor primus.'

'What?'

The human's voice patterns indicated the confusion of misunderstanding, rather than not hearing correctly. Deltrian emitted an irritated spurt of static from his vocabulator – the closest he could come to a sigh.

'Corporaptor primus. The patriarch of a genestealer brood. The alpha, apex predator.'

'How do you kill something like that?'

'We do not. If it finds us, we die. Now cease vocalisation. I am engaged in focussed activity.'

Deltrian enjoyed another three minutes of relative silence, then the muffled clanking of distant footsteps, far too fast to be human, far too soft to be Astartes, echoed through the console as the adept worked. The distant tread vibrated the panels – the tremors imperceptible to a mortal, but registering on the sensitive pads of the tech-adept's metal fingers.

He spared a moment of his concentration to send a short burst of digital code to display written Gothic text across First Claw's visor displays:

**Genestealer threat
has breached perimeter.
My work
is at a sensitive stage.**

With this task completed in less than the time it would take a human heart to beat, Deltrian continued working, entering numerical crack-keys to pierce the cogitator console's encoded information locks. He was close now, close to being able to bleed the console's memory banks, and loathed the fact a distraction would soon arrive.

VIII

THE BLEEDING EYES crouched, gargoyles of ceramite with twisted faces rendered into silent howls. The tunnels here were wider, freer, with ceilings sporting secondary decking and mazes of overhead cables. It was on these decks, and among these dense cables serving the low-power ship as veins, that the Bleeding Eyes waited.

Beneath them, their prey had taken the bait. The green-armoured warrior in bulky Terminator plate stomped without a hint of grace, pounding his way through the corridors, firing at shadows with his underslung rotator cannon. Something was wrong. From their perches, the Night Lords listened to the Throne-loyal Astartes admonishing enemies that did not exist, evidently fighting a battle that had naught to do with the present. Burning holes streaked the walls where the cannon's stream of fire pitted the metal in long bursts of anger.

The Bleeding Eyes shared muted vox-chuckles and stared down at the deluded warrior. He was clearly afflicted by a most amusing madness.

And yet... he *had* taken the bait. Shar Gan still led the Terminator on, appearing at junctions and corners, offering the flash of dark armour and screeching through his helm's vox-speakers. Whatever the Salamander believed he was seeing, he still gave relentless chase to Shar Gan, paying no heed to the Raptors crawling several metres above him, making their way on all fours across decking and power cables.

Only when Lucoryphus had deemed they'd come far enough, did they spring the trap.

'Seal the doors,' their leader hissed. Both bulkheads slammed closed, cutting the corridor off from the rest of the ship. At a distant control console elsewhere on the ship, Vorasha and the second team of Bleeding Eyes were laughing.

In the corridor below, the Terminator halted, retaining enough sense to realise he was trapped. The warrior looked up at last, as ten chainblades revved into snarling life.

The Bleeding Eyes held to the decking, the overhead cabling, even the walls and ceiling. Lucoryphus whispered into the vox, a moment before his Raptors pounced.

'Kill him.'

TALOS ENTERED THE data storage chamber. Gravity had been restored in this area of the Mechanicus ship, and with the recommencement of gravity came the reintroduction of an artificial atmosphere. The ship automatically sealed off the voided sections with bulkheads.

The restoration of air also brought a new aspect to this curious hunt. Sound had returned. It was unwelcome – the inner workings of the storage modules rattled and clanked like the engine of some struggling vehicle. Pistons hammered within the cogitators' innards. Talos had no desire to know why the archaic storage machinery required such moving parts, and the sound – in the six minutes since air had been restored by Deltrian's servitors – was growing steadily more irritating.

Variel had reached the chamber a few minutes before the prophet. As Talos entered, the newest member of First Claw nodded in greeting, but said nothing.

Variel's armour showed his newfound allegiance, but lacked much of the ornamentation worn by his brothers. On his pauldrons, instead of the VIII Legion's fanged skull flanked by daemon wings, Variel's insignia displayed a clawed fist, rendered in black ceramite, broken by ritual hammering.

On Variel's left arm, his vambrace was a converted narthecium unit, containing liquid nitrogen storage pods, flesh drills, bone saws and surgical lasers. While his faceplate no longer bore the white paint of an Apothecary, he still carried the tools of his specialised craft. Instead of human skulls hanging from chains on his armour, Variel's war plate was decorated by the shattered helms of Red Corsair Astartes. It was these differences, subtle but significant, that set him apart from the others of First Claw.

Both Talos and Variel clutched their bolters, barely watching Deltrian work, instead focussing their attentions around the spacious chamber and the rows of blank cogitator screens.

Septimus hadn't removed his helmet, even with breathable air restored. He walked closer to Talos, casting a sidelong glance at the busy tech-priest.

'Master,' he voxed to the towering Astartes.

Talos spared Septimus a momentary look. The slave's long hair, lank with sweat, was tied into a scruffy ponytail. The bionic portions of his face were glinting with reflection from the overhead lights – well maintained and clean.

'Septimus. Be ready. The xenos are near.'

The Legion serf didn't ask how everyone but him seemed to know what was coming. He was long-used to his human senses rendering him disadvantaged in the company of the warriors he still instinctively referred to as demigods.

'Master, why did you bring me here?'

Talos appeared to be watching a distant, shadowed wall. He didn't answer.

'Master?'

'Why do you ask?' the warrior said, still paying little attention. 'You have never questioned your duty before.'

'I seek only to understand my place and role.'

Talos moved away, bolter at the ready. The Night Lord's mouth grille emitted a vox-distorted snarl. Septimus tensed, and didn't follow.

'I sense your fear. You are not here as bait. Remain sanguine. We will keep you alive.'

'Deltrian suggested otherwise.'

'We might be here for days, Septimus. If our armour needed repairing, I wanted you at hand to do your duty.'

Days…? *Days?*

'That long, master?'

There was a series of clicks as Talos changed to a limited vox channel, between himself and his slave.

'In respect for our honoured tech-adept, I will not say that Deltrian works slowly. I will alter the description, citing instead that he works meticulously. But you are not dense, Septimus. You know what he is like.'

Yes, but still… 'Master, could this really take days?'

'I sincerely hope not. It has already taken long enough. If the–'

'*Soul Hunter.*'

Talos swore softly, and in Nostraman the curse came out like gentle poetry. The voice coming over the vox was harsh, almost screeching. Lucoryphus's blood was up, and it filtered into his voice with astonishing clarity.

'Acknowledged, Lucoryphus.'

'Too many of them.'

'Confirm xenos sightings in–'

'Not the aliens! Bastard sons of Vulkan! Two full teams. They kill and kill. Nine Bleeding Eyes are dead. Nine to never rise again. Nine of twenty!'

'Be calm, brother.' Talos bit back the urge to rail at the Raptor leader for his accursed vainglory. Such idiocy had cost nine lives in a battle that could never have been won without patience and caution..

Letting them slip the leash had been a mistake.

'I go now to Vorasha,' Lucoryphus hissed. 'We slaughter them all this time.'

'Enough. Will you fall back now? Will you wait until we regroup on the ship and strike from the void?'

'But the—'

'*Enough.* Fall back to your second team and abandon the *Protean*. Return to First Claw and we will make ready to leave. Let the Throne's slaves scurry around for their own salvage.'

'Understood.'

'Lucoryphus. Confirm your intentions.'

'Will fall back. Find Vorasha. Return to First Claw.'

'Good.' Talos terminated the vox-link, swallowing a mouthful of bitter, acidic saliva. Not for the first time, and not for the last, he reflected that he loathed the duties of command.

LUCORYPHUS CAST THE melta gun aside, letting it clatter to the deck. He wouldn't be needing it again. The thrusters on his back still streamed thin smoke from coolant vents, powering down after the sudden boost necessary to send him up into the ceiling in order to escape the chattering storm bolters of the Salamanders' elite warriors.

With the melta gun – a weapon stolen from the twitching corpse of Shar Gan – he had seared a whole in the ceiling and escaped up to the next deck.

He'd been hit himself. With a cracked breastplate, Lucoryphus could feel his armour's strength depleted, some vital power feeds cut by explosive bolter fire.

Bipedal walking was an awkward trial even when uninjured, so Lucoryphus crawled as he'd become accustomed, all four claws finding tight purchase on the gantry floor.

He moved with unnerving speed, though it hurt to do so.

'Vorasha...' his lips were wet with blood. The pain of his wounds was an irritant, but no more than that.

'Yes-yes.' The vox distortion was savage now. Lucoryphus's war plate was in worse shape than he'd first thought. His visor kept fuzzing with static at inconvenient moments.

'Orders are to return to First Claw.'

'I heard this,' Vorasha replied. 'I will obey.'

'Wait.'

'Wait?'

'More Salamanders than we first saw. Many more. Find xenos nests. Awaken aliens. Lead aliens to Salamanders. Both enemies fight, both enemies die. Vengeance for Bleeding Eyes.'

Vorasha's reply was a serpentine snigger, *Ss-ss-ss*.

'*Go now!*' Lucoryphus screeched. '*Lead xenos to Salamanders!*'

IX

WITH A MOIST *snick*, the membranes covering the Eldest's sensitive eyes peeled back. It looked down the long chamber, seeing telltale suggestions of flickering movement. The human-scent was stronger now. So much stronger.

The Eldest stalked forwards, claws scraping on the metal floor. Two of the more dangerous prey-breed, those with the hammering weapons of punching fire, had entered the chamber. Though the Eldest's bestial intelligence did not count them capable of slaying the creature, it had learned its lesson well. This was not a hunt to make alone.

From its place of hiding in the shadows, The Eldest had been screaming in silence for some time. Its kin were coming, dozens upon dozens of them, coming through the tunnels and chambers nearby.

It would be enough to overwhelm even the most dangerous prey.

'I SEE IT,' Talos voxed.

He stared into the darkness, looking away into the six hundred metres of shadowed chamber to the north. 'It emerged from the wall a moment ago.'

'I see it, too.' This, from Variel. He approached Talos and hefted his bolter, his thermal sight easily piercing the gloom. 'Blood of the Emperor, Mercutian wasn't lying.'

'A broodlord,' the prophet murmured, watching the hideous alien – all chitinous limbs, clawed appendages and bulbous skull – creep closer. 'An immense one. Fire when it reaches optimal range. Avoid damage to the wall cogitators.'

'Compliance,' Variel said, and Talos could still hear the edge of reluctance in the newcomer's tone. His induction into the VIII Legion was still fresh, and he wasn't used to taking orders.

Talos raised his bolter, sighting through the targeter and drawing breath to summon the others. The vox chose that moment to erupt in sounds of gunfire and Nostraman curses. All of First Claw were engaged, flooded by waves of the weakened beasts.

The others evidently had their own problems.

On Talos's red-tinted visor, a proximity rune turned white. In the very same moment, Talos and Variel opened fire.

DELTRIAN'S FINGERS BLURRED as they tapped keys, pushed levers and adjusted dials. The locking code obscuring the information he desired was remarkably complex, and forced a degree of instrument adjustment even as his personally designed crack-keys did their work in the cogitator's programming. This was not an unexpected development, but it necessitated a division of attention that the tech-adept found galling. Added to the annoyance, the firefight fifty metres to his left was a raucous irritation, for bolters were hardly quiet weapons, and the corporaptor primus – a breed of xenos Deltrian had never witnessed firsthand – howled endlessly as it endured the process of being blown apart by explosive rounds.

The *crack-crack, crack-crack* of Septimus's laspistols joined the throaty chatter of boltgun fire, forming a curious percussion.

Almost… *Almost…*.

Deltrian emitted a bleat of machine code from his vocabulator, the sound emerging as a tinny and flat pulse to anyone untrained in comprehending such a unique language. It was as close to a cheer as he had come in many years.

Sixteen separate memory tablets slid from the main cogitator's data sockets. Each one was the approximate size and shape of a human palm. Each contained a century of recorded lore, right back to the ship's founding decades.

And each was priceless – an artefact of unrivalled possibility.

'It is done,' the tech-adept said, and began to gather the data-slates, apparently unaware that no one was paying him any heed at all.

He turned to the melee in time to see the alien beast, its body a mess of burst wounds and both ovoid eyes left as ragged, fluid-weeping craters, cleave Variel's leg at the knee with one of its few remaining limbs. A scythe of blackened bone, its bladed edge cracked and bleeding, chopped down in a lethal arc.

Ceramite armour shattered. The Astartes went down, his leg severed, and still he fired up at the horror drawing closer to slay him.

The death blow came from Talos. His armour a broken mess of claw-chopped metal plating, the prophet took another flailing limb strike to the side of the head in order to risk coming close enough to use his power sword. Lightning trembled along the golden blade as it sparked into life, even as the genestealer patriarch clashed a half-amputated sword-limb against the Night Lord's helm. White-painted shards of his faceplate tore free, scattering across the metal decking like hailstones.

Talos was close enough now. With half of his face laid bare and bleeding from the creature's last blow, he rammed the relic sword into the beast's spine, plunging it two-handed through exoskeletal armour, toughened subdermal muscle flesh, and finally into vulnerable meat and severable bone.

A twist, a wrench, a curse and a pull. He sawed the sword left and right, foul-smelling blood welling up from the widening wound.

The alien shrieked again, acidic ichor spraying from its damaged teeth to rain upon Variel's armour in hissing droplets. Talos gave his golden blade a final wrenching pull, and the beast's head came free.

The creature collapsed. It twitched once or twice, the savage wounds across its body leaking sour fluids as well as dark blood. The smell, Septimus would later tell other slaves back aboard the ship, was somewhere between a charnel house and a butcher's shop left open to the sun for a month. It broke through all air filters, clinging right to the sinuses.

Variel's armour was pockmarked gunmetal-grey where the corrosive juices from the beast's maw scored away his war plate's paint. His severed leg wasn't bleeding – the coagulants in Astartes blood were already working to seal the wound and scab it over. Any pain was dulled by his armour's narcotic injectors dispensing stimulants and pain suppressors into his bloodstream.

Yet he growled a curse as he dragged himself away from the stilled beast, and swore in a language only he understood. Deltrian analysed the linguistic pattern. It was most likely a dialect of Badab – a tongue from Variel's home world. The details were irrelevant.

Talos's suit of armour was almost entirely stripped of colour, the acids and burning blood having blistered the ceramite and scorched the dark paint away. He regarded the creature's steaming body, with half of his face visible due to the damage he'd taken to his helm.

The tech-adept saw the prophet scowl, and fire another bolter shell into the dead alien's severed head. What remained of the genestealer's skull vanished in an explosion of wet fragments that clacked off the walls, the floor and Talos's own armour.

Septimus looked on, catching his breath. He knew repairing and repainting both of these ancient suits of battle plate was going to be a time-consuming process. He felt it was to his credit that he didn't say so here, and busied himself holstering his Guard-issue laspistols, before leaning against the wall.

'To hell with that,' he breathed.

Deltrian watched this scene for exactly four point two seconds.

'I said, "It is done".' He couldn't keep the rising impatience from his tone. 'May we leave now?'

X

WHEN THE ECHO *of Damnation* pulled away from the hulk, the Shriek fell silent as plasma contrails misted the void behind the ship. Engines running, breathing the mist into space, the *Echo* tore away from the vast amalgamation of forgotten ships.

On the command throne, his armour still a grey and cracked ruin, Talos watched the occulus. It showed a slice of deep space – no more, no less.

'How long ago did they leave the system?' he asked. These were the first words he had uttered since returning and taking the throne. The answer came from one of the ageing human officers, still in his Imperial Navy uniform, albeit stripped of the Emperor's insignia.

'Just over two hours, my lord. The Salamander vessel was running dangerously hot. We think the Shriek unnerved them – they broke orbit and ran, rather than seek the signal's source.'

'They did not find the ship?'

'They barely even looked, my lord. They withdrew their boarding teams and fled.'

Talos shook his head. 'The sons of Vulkan are placid and slow, but they are Astartes and know no fear. Whatever sent them crawling from the system was a matter of grave import.'

'As you say, my lord. What are your orders?'

Talos snorted. 'Two hours is not an insurmountable head-start. Follow them. Make ready all Claws. Once we catch them, we will tear them from the warp and pick apart the bones of their ship.'

'Compliance, master.'

The prophet allowed his eyes to drift closed as the ship rumbled into activity around him.

THE HALL OF Reflection housed what few relics remained to the warriors of Talos's warband. In more glorious eras, such a chamber would have been a haven for prayer, for purification through meditation, and to witness the Legion's history through the weapons and armour once borne and worn by its heroes.

Now, it served as something not quite a workshop, and not quite a graveyard. Deltrian was lord of the chamber, a haven where his will and word were law. Servitors worked at various stations, repairing pieces of armour, replacing the teeth-tracks of fouled chainswords, forging new bolter shells and creating the explosive innards.

And here, in ritually preserved stasis fields, the ornate sarcophagi of fallen warriors were mounted on marble pedestals, awaiting the moment they would be mounted in the bodies of dreadnoughts and sent to war once more. Several fluid-filled suspension tanks bubbled away, most empty – in need of flushing and scrubbing – and a few occupied by naked figures rendered indistinct by the milky, oxygen-rich amniotic fluids.

Deltrian had returned to his sanctum several minutes before, and was already inserting the data tablets into the sockets of his own cogitators, to drain the lore into his own memory banks. The doors to the Hall of Reflection remained open. Deltrian allowed the data transfer to occur unwatched, and instead waited for the guests he was expecting.

At last, they arrived. Twelve warriors, in a ragged line. Each of the dozen Astartes showed signs of recent and grievous battle. Each of them had survived a harrowing six further hours on board the hulk, fending off genestealers and hunting the accursed creatures back to their nests.

The Salamanders had done an admirable job in their purging, but had still lost a total of six warriors on board the *Protean*, thanks to the efforts of Vorasha and the Bleeding Eyes diverting wave after wave of xenos beasts into their section of the ship.

Six souls lost, six warriors fallen. It did not seem

many, on the surface of things. The Night Lords had lost nine – all of them from the Bleeding Eyes. Lucoryphus seemed untroubled.

'The weak fall, the strong rise,' he'd said as they boarded the *Echo of Damnation*. Deltrian observed that this was as close to philosophy as the degenerate warrior had ever come. The Bleeding Eyes leader had no reply to that.

Deltrian watched the twelve Astartes enter the Hall of Reflection now. Each pair carried a great weight between them: the broken bodies of armoured Salamander warriors. One of the butchered warriors was carved with both surgical precision and gleeful brutality, slain by the Bleeding Eyes and earning the ignoble honour of being the first to fall. The others showed a vicious spread of genestealer wounds: punctured breastplates, sundered limb guards, crushed helms.

But nothing, Deltrian mused, that would be irreparable.

The Night Lords arranged the bodies on the mosaic-inlaid floor. Six dead Salamanders. Six dead Salamanders in Terminator war plate, complete with storm bolters, power weapons and a rare assault rotator cannon – practically unseen amongst the Traitor Legions, who were forced to wage war with scavenged equipment and ancient weaponry.

This haul, this sacred bounty in the blessed Machine-God's name, was worth infinitely more than the lives of fourteen Night Lords. Deltrian caressed the draconic emblem of the Salamanders Chapter, embossed in black stone on one dead warrior's pauldron. Such markings could be stripped, the armour itself modified and refashioned… the machine-spirits turned bitter and of more use to the VIII Legion.

Let the Night Lords spit and curse for now. He could see it in their black eyes: each one of them recognised the value of this haul, and each one hoped to be one of the elite few ordained to wear this holy armour once it was profaned and made ready.

Nine lives in exchange for the secrets of a Titan Legion and six suits of the most powerful armour created by mankind.

Deltrian always smiled, for that was how his skullish face was formed. Now, however, as he regarded his newfound riches, the expression was sincere.

AMBITION KNOWS NO BOUNDS
Andy Hoare

'Give me a reading, Joachim,' Brielle Gerrit shouted against the raging wind. 'I can't see a damn thing!'

'Augur says two-fifty, ma'am,' Brielle's companion and advisor called back, his voice barely cutting through the howling cacophony of the storm. 'We should have visual any–'

'There,' Brielle called, and halted, craning her neck to look upwards. Against the churning, dark, purple clouds there was revealed an even darker form. She attempted to gauge its height, but her senses were confounded and unable to decipher its alien geometry. The rearing, slab-sided structure could have been standing scant metres in front of Brielle, or it could lie many kilometres distant.

'Two-fifty.' Brielle repeated her advisor's estimate of the range to their destination. Even as she looked upon the structure's form, its cliff-like planes appeared to shift, as if new surfaces and angles were revealed by the slightest change in perspective. 'If you're sure. Is everyone ready?'

Brielle turned to inspect her small party, its members appearing from the all-enveloping shroud of the storm. She lifted the visor of her armoured survival suit, the cold air rushing in to sting her exposed cheeks. Squinting against the wind, she noted with satisfaction the deployment of the dozen armsmen that accompanied her from her vessel, the *Fairlight*, which waited in high orbit above this dead world to which she had come in search of riches for her rogue trader clan. Each was heavily armed, and appointed in rugged armour, their faces obscured by heavy rebreather units. Their leader, the taciturn Santos Quin, stepped forwards, shadowed by the far smaller form of Adept Seth, her senior astropath.

'All is ready, my lady,' Quin answered, his tattooed face just visible through his own suit's visor. 'But the storm rises,' he added, casting a glance upwards at the churning skies.

'Understood,' Brielle replied, nodding, before looking to the astropath. 'And you, adept, have you anything to report?'

The astropath stepped forwards, bowing his helmeted head to his mistress. Through his visor, the adept's face was visible as a gruesome mass of scar tissue; his eyes were hollow pits and his nose and mouth were barely discernible. The soul binding, the ritual by which the astropath had been exposed to, and sanctified by, the Emperor's Grace, had blasted his body such that the man was in constant pain. Yet, although the normal range of human senses was denied to him, Adept Seth was possessed of far greater perception than any ordinary man.

++*This place is dead to me, mistress,*++ the astropath replied. His voice was little more than a guttural rasp, so ravaged was his throat, yet Brielle heard the man's words clearly for he spoke with his mind, directly into her own. ++*Dead, yet I hear echoes, reverberations of ancient thoughts, or the hint of a sleeper's dreams. I cannot tell which.*++

Brielle caught the sneer that crossed the face of Santos Quin at the astropath's words, and knew that the man's feral world origins made him distrustful of Seth and his powers. Yet, she knew what the astropath referred to, for she imagined that she too had discerned the very faintest of echoes, distant thoughts carried on the unquiet winds. She knew not what alien mind might have given rise to such thoughts, but she believed, hoped, relied upon the fact that they were mere echoes of some ancient and long-dead power.

'Well enough,' Brielle said, lowering her visor. 'We continue, with caution.'

BRIELLE STOOD BEFORE the pitted, black wall of the vast alien structure. Although the surface was but an arm's length in front of her, she felt compelled to reach out and lay a palm upon it, just to be certain. Even through the tough glove of her survival suit, Brielle felt the cold radiating from the stone-like material, a cold that touched not only her skin, but her soul too.

'Mistress.' Brielle withdrew her hand at the sound of the astropath's voice. 'Please, try not to–'

'I know, Seth,' Brielle replied. 'I know.' She looked around, and addressed Quin. 'We need to find a way in. Have your men spread out.'

The warrior nodded silently, and moved away to speak to the armsmen. In a moment, they, as well as Brielle's advisor Joachim Hep, had departed, all bar Quin himself having moved out in search of a means of entering the vast structure. Brielle saw Quin test the mechanism on his boltgun, before lowering his sensor goggles to scan the depths of the storm. He would stand vigil over his mistress, no matter what.

Brielle resumed her study of the alien form. She craned her neck upwards, noting that either the storm clouds had lowered or the ever-shifting planes of the structure had elongated, for now the top appeared to be lost to the storm above. She pondered, not for the first time, the risk inherent in this expedition, but knew that vast riches were to be claimed on such worlds as this. As next in line to sovereignty of the mighty Clan Arcadius, it fell to Brielle to carve her name across the galaxy, to pierce the darkness in the name of the Emperor, to face whatever might lurk in the depths of the void and to overcome it, for the sake of humanity. And, she mused, smiling coyly behind her visor, to amass untold wealth and undreamed-of glory along the way.

It was Brielle's hope, and that of her clan, that this unnamed world, far out in the void between spiral arms, might yield such riches. The galaxy was strewn with the ruins of civilisations far older than the Imperium of Man, and planets such as this were home to dusty tombs sealed before mankind even looked to the skies above ancient Terra. Such tombs, when discovered, had been known to contain relics of long-dead alien races, artefacts of wonder for which the pampered nobility of the Imperium's ruling classes would pay a staggering price just to possess. The vast majority of these items were considered curiosities or art, having no discernible function. Others could be studied, their functions and exotic abilities unlocked. Brielle knew that dilettante collectors and self-proclaimed experts in the proscribed field of xenology would give their all for such items.

Yet, Brielle was struck with a cold sense of dread, an unutterable feeling that something was terribly amiss with this dead planet.

'Something stirs, my lady,' Adept Seth warned, as if giving voice to an unnamed fear gnawing at the periphery of Brielle's consciousness.

'What do you sense, Seth?' Brielle answered, casting around her for any sign of danger. Quin hefted his boltgun across his broad chest, and took a step closer to his mistress.

'I sense... a guttering flame... the flame is the soul, all but extinguished, yet it refuses to die...'

'I need a little more than that, Seth,' Brielle responded, biting back a less politic remark. 'Are we in danger?'

'Something knows we are–'

Before the astropath could complete his sentence, the vox-channel burst into life. Howling static assaulted Brielle's ears, before the voice of Joachim Hep cut in. '…a way in. Repeat, we have found a way in.'

'Stay where you are,' Brielle answered, not entirely sure whether or not Hep had heard her through the raging atmospheric interference. 'Quin, lead the way.'

'Recent damage, Joachim?' Brielle asked of her advisor. Though aged, the man stood almost as tall and broad as a Space Marine. She waited as he studied the vast rent in the cliff-like side of the alien structure, his eyes taking in every detail with practiced skill.

'I would say so, ma'am,' Joachim replied, without turning his gaze from the sight before him. 'Millennia of storm damage brought this about, but the damage itself has only recently occurred.'

Brielle's gaze moved from her advisor to the great fracture in the alien tomb. Though only a metre or so wide, the crack ran upwards what must have been many hundreds of metres, or would have been, if it weren't for the damnable geometry of the place. Brielle moved closer, aware of Quin keeping pace behind. She leaned in to examine the ragged edge of the crack, to glean some idea of the material and what might have damaged it.

++*Time, my lady,*++ Adept Seth spoke into Brielle's mind. *'The only force which could damage such a place as this, is time itself.*++

Brielle raised an eyebrow and cast a wry glance at her astropath, aware that he had read her surface thoughts. She turned back, leaning in yet closer to the damaged surface. She fancied she could see signs of repair, if only at a minuscule scale. Perhaps this place could heal itself, she mused. Perhaps that explained how it could have withstood the ravages of this storm-wracked world for so many long, lonely aeons.

'Let's go,' Brielle said, stepping into the fracture before Quin could take the lead.

SCANT METRES INTO the fracture, Brielle was plunged into utter darkness. She paused, allowing senses other than sight to come to the fore. She extended her awareness as far as she was able, attempting to gain some idea of her surroundings. She strained her hearing. The storm still raged outside, but now its howl was muffled and distant. She heard too the action of the rebreathers worn by her companions, and discerned the sure, heavy tread of Santos Quin as he sought to overtake her, to take the lead lest the party encounter danger and his mistress be threatened.

Savouring the darkness for but a moment longer, Brielle reached her hand to the mechanism at the side of her helmet, lowering a set of goggles over her visor. The headset buzzed as lenses whirred to focus on what Brielle's own eyes could not register. The goggles were capable of registering many different wavelengths, overlaying what they perceived over Brielle's own vision.

The blackness was replaced by a kaleidoscopic riot of colours, shot through with grainy static. Brielle adjusted a control at the side of her helmet, and the image resolved into something she could make sense of. Before Brielle, there stretched a circular tunnel into which she and her party had stepped. She looked behind, confirming that the tunnel stretched off in both directions, evidently running perpendicular to the outside wall through which, via the fracture, they had entered.

Satisfied that no immediate danger presented itself, Brielle used the control to cycle through a range of settings, the sight before her changing from one of vivid green hues to another of black with violet highlights, to yet another of purest white with shadows of turquoise. She paused on a vista of deep greens, seeing on the curved wall nearby an intricately carved icon. She stepped closer, aware that Quin did likewise. The icon was revealed to be a series of circles and lines, joined together into what must surely have been some long dead alien script.

'Joachim.' She turned to address her advisor, and he stepped forwards, past Santos Quin, who grunted as he stepped aside. 'Set your readers to sigma-twelve, and look at this.'

Joachim, his goggles already lowered, reached to his helmet and adjusted the controls. A moment later, his head scanned the walls of the corridor.

'I've never seen its like, ma'am,' Joachim Hep replied after a long pause. 'Though it puts me in mind of…'

'Of what?' Brielle replied, uncertain she wanted to hear her advisor's answer.

'Of the machine scripts of the servants of the Omnissiah, ma'am.'

'But this place is ancient,' Brielle answered, as much to assuage her own uncertainties as to answer her advisor. 'It predates the Mechanicus by countless millennia. There can be no connection.'

'Quite, ma'am,' Hep replied, nodding gravely to Brielle.

'Then let's continue,' Brielle ordered, 'this way.' She made to set off, but this time allowed Santos Quin to take the lead. The feral-worlder raised his boltgun as he advanced into the darkness, using his own set of goggles to pierce the gloom. The warrior used silent hand signals to direct his armsmen to the proper order of march, ensuring Brielle, Hep and Adept Seth were well protected in the centre of the line. Brielle allowed Quin to do so, grudgingly reminding herself that she would, after all, inherit the Warrant of Trade of her rogue trader house, and Quin was only doing the duty her father had bestowed upon the warrior.

Before making off along the tubular corridor, Brielle paused briefly, imagining she heard, at the very edge of perception, an out-of-place sound. She imagined she heard a metallic chitter. She listened intently, but heard no more. With a glance back beyond the rearmost armsmen, she set off.

'NOT A SOUND,' Brielle whispered over the vox-net, edging forwards to peer over Quin's shoulder. She knew she need hardly have given the order, for the armsmen of the party followed the feral-worlder's lead, and he himself stood motionless and silent against the curved wall at the end of the corridor.

Brielle found herself gazing into a vast blackness.

She was about to lower her goggles to scan the space in a different wavelength when she caught a glimpse of a dim, green glow amidst the darkness. Focussing, her eyes adapted, and after a few minutes she could make out a hint of the space before the party. What she saw made Brielle gasp.

The passageway in which her party waited opened out into some manner of chamber so vast that Brielle was struck by a nigh-crushing sense of insignificance as she tried in vain to comprehend its benighted dimensions. Brielle imagined herself an insect crawling across the worn flagstones of the mightiest of cathedrals, the vaults above lost in darkness. A cold shiver ran through her body as she realised the notion was not entirely her own imagining.

So vast was the space that its surface appeared to rise and fall with the curvature of the planet on which it stood. Brielle dismissed the notion; a structure so large would have been detectable from orbit, and the tomb had not measured so vast on their approach. Nonetheless, the geometry of the place played all manner of tricks upon Brielle's senses. Just as she had been unable to gauge the true size of the structure from outside, she now found herself unable to estimate its internal dimensions, and the sensation was deeply unsettling.

As Brielle's eyes adjusted further to the gloom, she saw that across the dark floor of the chamber there lay a gently undulating sea of what must surely have been dust. How long had this place stood, she pondered, that its floor should have accumulated such a layer of sediment? Looking closer, she saw low dunes, their crests gently aglow with the ever-present green illumination.

'Joachim,' Brielle addressed her advisor, who stood at her back. 'Do you see a source for the back light?'

Brielle waited while Hep scanned the vast space before them, then turned her head to look to his face as he answered. 'I do not, ma'am,' he replied. 'It may be the result of some background effect, an energy source not detectable by the augurs.'

'My lady,' Quin growled low. Brielle turned her gaze from her advisor to the warrior, instantly alert in response to his tone. 'Ahead, a hundred paces.'

Brielle squinted as she sought out the point Quin was indicating. After a moment, she found it.

'Tracks?' Brielle whispered.

'Aye, my lady,' Quin replied. 'Something small.'

'Vermin?' Brielle asked.

'Possibly,' Quin growled back. 'Though I see little for such a creature to hunt.'

Brielle nodded. 'When?' she asked.

The feral-worlder glanced back at his mistress. 'Hours, or decades, my lady. Such is the stillness of this place I can scarcely tell.'

Brielle made to answer, but Adept Seth spoke first. ++*An aeon... and a day, mistress,*++ he whispered, the sound of his voice whispered directly into her mind. ++*An epoch past, yet still to occur.*++

Growing uneasy with the astropath's manner, Brielle replied curtly, 'Speak plainly, Seth, please.'

The astropath turned his monstrous face towards Brielle. She knew that even though the man lacked conventional sight he was looking straight at her. 'My apologies, mistress,' he whispered. 'I know such things make little sense. But just as your eyes have difficulty perceiving the true dimensions of this place, so too do my own senses. This place is weighted, mistress, weighted with ages impossible for such as us to comprehend. Perhaps the gods themselves—'

'Enough!' growled Quin. Brielle's gaze lingered on the face of Adept Seth for a moment, before she turned back towards the warrior. 'Such words gain us nothing.'

Brielle took a deep breath, steeling herself to go on, before taking a step forwards into the vast chamber. She glanced back to her party, the dust of impossible ages rising around her boots. Looking back at them, she felt a moment of giddy recklessness, knowing her father would disapprove were he here to witness her actions. An instant later, the feeling passed, to be replaced with the crushing deadness of the tomb. 'Enough indeed,' she breathed, and set out across the ocean of dust.

SOON AFTER SETTING forth across the chamber, the party had come upon the tracks that Quin had spotted from the passageway. The feral-worlder's hunting senses had told him that some form of insect perhaps a metre in length had made the tracks, and that the fine layer of dust overlaying them told him the trail was not recent. Despite this news, Brielle's feeling of unease had not been assuaged, but had instead increased the further into the dust sea the party had advanced.

At first, Quin had advised that the explorers should proceed with caution, treading softly lest great plumes of the thick dust carpeting the ground be thrown up with their passing. Brielle was soon forced to countermand this order however, for otherwise they would never have made any progress at all. And besides, she had mused, who might be watching? She had no answer to that question.

As she walked, Brielle attempted once more to gain some idea of the nature of her surroundings. She craned her neck to look upwards, and was immediately greeted with a wave of nausea as the distant planes high above shifted. She looked back to the ground, and a second wave of sickness came over her, causing her to stumble and come to a halt.

'Ma'am?' Joachim Hep was at Brielle's side in an instant, his firm hold grasping the shoulder of her armoured survival suit. A moment later, the rest of the party halted, the armsmen taking guard positions while their taciturn leader worked his way back down the line towards Brielle.

'I'm fine, Joachim,' Brielle answered. 'I'm fine. It's this place. It plays havoc with the senses.'

'That it does, ma'am,' replied Brielle's advisor, stepping back having satisfied himself that his mistress was able to continue. 'I cannot read it either.'

At this, Quin interjected. 'My lady, how much time do you perceive to have passed since we set out across this chamber?'

Brielle looked to the warrior, distracted, beguiled even, for a brief moment by the swirling patterns of his facial tattoos. 'How much time?' she repeated, turning her head to look back the way the party had travelled. 'I would say... Emperor's mercy...'

'How long, my lady?' Quin pressed.

Brielle looked back to the feral-worlder, her throat suddenly dry. 'Three, three and half...'

'Minutes?' Quin asked.

'Hours,' Brielle said, the sight of the passageway mouth, a hundred metres behind, still fresh in her mind.

'...aeons,' Adept Seth whispered.

'Behind us,' Brielle whispered into her vox-link, having subtly disengaged the external amplivox. She made an effort not to change her stance or the pattern of march as the party continued on its way across the dusty chamber.

'Yes, my lady,' Quin answered, having followed her lead and adjusted his own communications in the same manner.

'How long?' Brielle asked.

'For me?' Quin turned his head as he walked, raising an eyebrow sardonically.

'Fair point,' Brielle conceded. 'How long?' she repeated.

'No more than thirty minutes,' Quin said.

'Can you tell where?' Brielle asked. Brielle herself had been aware of movement to the party's rear for several minutes.

'In this half-light,' Quin answered, 'it's hard to be sure. But, I would say that we are being tracked by one observer, using the folds of the dust as cover, to our rear and left.'

It took a supreme effort of will for Brielle not to turn and look in the direction Quin had described. She could not help but imagine a crosshair aimed at the centre of the back of her head, making her skin suddenly itch beneath her armoured helmet. She felt an irresistible, inexplicable urge to pull the helmet free and shake out her plaited locks, which felt as if they were pasted to her scalp. She shook the notion off, adjusting her step, treading softly through the dust, focussing her every sense behind her for any sign of pursuit.

Brielle imagined she heard a distant voice, so quiet it was little more than a thought. She glanced towards the astropath, and noted that his head was cocked at an odd angle, as if he too were intently listening to something. She focussed upon that distant whisper, half-hearing the forming of alien words, yet not quite able to discern them fully.

++*There are more, mistress*++ the astropath's thought-message touched her mind, his withered, scarred mouth not moving at all.

++*Where?*++ She formed the reply in her mind, unsure whether the astropath would hear her. Evidently, he did hear, for the thought came back immediately, ++*Everywhere, mistress. All around us. They slumber… yet they stir.*++

With a conscious effort, Brielle closed her mind. She had felt the touch of madness in the astropath's thoughts, a cold dread verging on the insane. Her eyes met briefly with those of Quin, who nodded to the fore. Whilst Brielle's attentions had been otherwise engaged, the party had come upon the opposite side of the vast chamber. She looked back, seeing that they had somehow crossed the impossible distance in what felt to her like the course of barely five or six hours.

Brielle stood at the very brink of a wide chasm, cut with unreal precision into the black rock of the alien tomb's dusty floor. Far below, there emanated a lurid green glow, the same glow, she mused, as had suffused the chamber they had just crossed, yet here it was direct to the point of blinding intensity. Far above, the vaults were lost to blackness, and Brielle saw no other way forwards than to cross the vast chasm.

'Deploy the line,' she ordered.

Santos Quin motioned to one of the armsmen, who stepped forwards and unlimbered a heavy grapnel launcher. The man braced his feet wide, and aimed the launcher at a point on the ground across the chasm, some forty metres distant.

'Fire!' Quin ordered.

The launcher's report was deafening, the explosive crack filling the stillness of the tomb. Brielle experienced an instant of profound dread, as if their intrusion must surely be noted, as if the sound would bring attackers down upon them in an instant. She glanced all around, half-expecting the shadows on the black stone walls to resolve themselves into the dreadful forms of long-dead guardians. She shook off the notion, but guessed that the other members of her party shared it. Even Quin was casting cautious looks all about.

Ambition Knows No Bounds

Brielle was brought back to the present by the impact of the grapnel as it struck the ground on the far side of the chasm. She watched as the module at the end of the line activated, power hooks springing forth to bite into the stone, before the energy was shut off an instant later, leaving the blades embedded in the ground. The armsman activated the mechanism on the launcher, and the line tightened. Using a similar system of power hooks mounted at the launcher's base, the armsman secured the device to the ground on the party's side of the chasm, and stepped back.

Brielle made for the line, before both Quin and Hep stepped forwards to block her path.

'With respect, ma'am,' Hep said, bowing as he did so lest he give undue offence. 'Please, Brielle,' he continued, his voice low. 'I cannot allow you to cross first. Your father would have me flayed by the bilge-rippers.'

Brielle suppressed a smile, despite her mild annoyance, for she was ever ill at ease with others taking risks on her behalf. Yet, she knew her advisor, one of her father's oldest friends, was correct. She smiled gracefully as she returned his bow and stepped aside.

'And I,' interjected Santos Quin, 'cannot allow you, Joachim, to cross first.' The warrior held up a hand to wave away any objection Hep might voice. 'I too have duties to observe.'

Brielle watched, amused, as Joachim Hep considered Quin's words, before he too stepped aside, allowing the feral-worlder to approach the secured grapnel launcher. With a gesture, the warrior deployed his armsmen so as to cover the far side as he prepared to cross. Unravelling a cord from his belt, Quin attached himself to the grapnel line, and lowered himself over the edge of the chasm.

Brielle watched as Quin progressed, slowly at first, but with increasing speed, across the wide chasm. She imagined for an instant that the green light blazing from below flickered for a moment, as if in recognition of the intrusion, but cast off the idea as imagination born of tension. A sound caught her attention, and she looked towards Adept Seth, noting that the astropath was mumbling under his breath, his ruined mouth working, the incoherent words muffled by the helmet of his survival suit.

'Seth,' Brielle called softly, mindful of disturbing the stygian silence of the tomb. The astropath appeared not to have noted his mistress's call. 'Seth!' she hissed, her teeth gritted.

'Mistress?' Seth replied, finally comprehending that he was being addressed.

'What is it, Seth?' Brielle asked, once more forcing down concern at the astropath's manner.

'I…' Adept Seth stammered. 'I think we should leave now, mistress.'

'Leave? What are you talking about, Seth? What's wrong?'

'It's the sleepers, mistress… it's their dreams… I can't…'

Brielle weighed the situation in her head. Her astropath appeared to be losing his grip on reality, but she needed him here, to communicate with her vessel in orbit, and for the edge his prodigious powers could provide in a dangerous situation. Yet, it appeared now that those same powers were proving his undoing, for it seemed to Brielle that the echoes of the dreams of the long-dead builders of this vast tomb were somehow afflicting him. If it came to it, she knew she could order one of the armsmen to incapacitate the astropath, to bind and drug him until the expedition was completed, but in so doing she would handicap their efforts significantly. She could not afford to lose the astropath, not yet, at least.

'My lady?' Brielle heard Quin address her over the vox channel. She turned, to see that the feral-worlder had made it safely across the chasm. 'My lady, I will have one of the armsmen attend to the adept, have no fear. Now please, it is safe for you to cross.'

'Thank you, Santos,' Brielle answered, noting that one of the armsmen had moved closer to the astropath, evidently responding to a surreptitious order from Quin. She approached the lip of the chasm, and stood at its very edge for a moment, gazing past her feet into the lambent depths far below. She experienced again a wave of disorientation, having little to do with any fear of heights and more to do with the subtly wrong geometry of the tomb. She could not quite place it. It appeared sometimes that no two planes intersected exactly how they should, as if perspective were somehow out of kilter. Taking a deep breath, she pushed such concerns to the back of her mind and withdrew a cord from her belt. She seated herself at the edge of the chasm, and clipped the cord to the grapnel line.

In a single motion, Brielle swung out beneath the line, suspending herself below it. She tested the cord attaching her belt to the line, and, satisfied that it was properly attached, began to winch herself across. Above her, Brielle could see little more than darkness, the vaults far overhead twinkling with what she took to be stray reflections from the actinic energies raging below her. Pulling herself along, one hand over the other, she concentrated not on the hundreds, perhaps thousands of metres below her, but on those minuscule points of green light twinkling in the darkness overhead. She judged herself halfway across the mighty gap before she noted that the lights above appeared to be growing in brightness.

'...dreams... the guttering flame... stirring...' Brielle heard Adept Seth over the vox-channel, and craned her neck to look towards Quin. Doing so, she saw that the feral-worlder's gaze was turned upwards, transfixed upon those same green lights that had held her own attention as she had crossed the gap.

She looked back upwards, to see that those same lights were now twice as bright, and were swooping down towards her!

'My lady!' Quin shouted. 'Beware!' The warrior raised his boltgun in both hands, bracing its butt against his shoulder. The weapon's staccato bark was deafening, and its discharge illuminated the darkness with blinding orange fire.

Hanging precariously halfway across the depthless chasm, Brielle felt suddenly painfully aware of how exposed her position was. She had no time to seek out the targets Quin was firing at, or to engage them herself. Instead, she gritted her teeth and hauled on the line, dragging her body into motion, hand over hand.

Even as she concentrated upon crossing the chasm, the air all around Brielle was filled with flashing light, the discharge of the armsmen's heavy-gauge shotguns as they blasted at the foe Brielle could not see.

'My lady!' Brielle heard, surprised by how close Quin's voice sounded. She looked around, to see that, somehow, she had traversed the chasm, and Quin was reaching out a hand to help her climb up over the lip. She looked to his outstretched glove, before something behind him caught her eye.

'Quin!'

The warrior followed his mistress's gaze, turning on the spot and bringing his boltgun up, one-handed.

The weapon barked, its report shockingly loud at such close quarters, even through Brielle's survival suit helmet. Something exploded, peppering Brielle and Quin with small metallic shards. With relief, Brielle saw that her suit was intact, its armour having protected her from the potentially lethal shrapnel.

'Are you hurt?' Brielle asked the warrior, aware that he had been closer to the detonation than she.

'Not badly, my lady,' Quin replied, before shouting a warning to one of the armsmen across the chasm.

Brielle looked across the gap, towards the remainder of the party. She was greeted by the sight of the armsmen arrayed in a semicircle, their backs to the edge of the chasm, with Joachim Hep and Adept Seth at the centre of their formation. While the fighters blasted into the darkness above, Hep was attempting to get Seth to cross the chasm.

From the darkness above the group flashed silvered, insect-like attackers, each little more than a metre in length. From what Brielle took to be the head of each creature, there shone a green light, clearly akin to that which blazed so brightly in the depths of the chasm she had just crossed. One of the metallic creatures swooped down upon an armsman, the green at its front increasing in brightness until the attacker was surrounded by a nimbus of pulsating energy. The armsman racked the slide on his shotgun and unleashed a blast at near point-blank range, but the creature swerved aside as it dived towards its target.

As the attacker fell upon the armsman, the green field surrounding it increased in intensity still further. At the last, his attacker closing, the armsman rotated his shotgun and drove its solid stock upwards, ramming it hard into his attacker's head. The green light exploded as the shotgun crunched into the attacker's fore section. The armsman was driven backwards, falling to land at the very edge of the chasm. His attacker plummeted, out of control, right above his supine form, and was lost in the pulsating depths far below.

'Everyone across, come on!' Brielle yelled, reaching for the bolt pistol holstered at her hip. Bracing the weapon in both hands, she drew a bead on the nearest of the insectoid attackers as it circled overhead.

'Hep!' she called. 'Get Seth over here, now!'

Not waiting for an acknowledgement, she squeezed the trigger. Brielle's pistol barked, and the shot struck home, burying itself in the outer shell of the creature's body. The impact caused the creature to swerve abruptly, but before it could correct its course, it exploded into a thousand metallic shards, the miniature explosive warhead of the bolt round having detonated itself with lethal effect after penetrating the target's armour.

As Hep forced the astropath onto the grapnel line and helped him cross, Brielle and Quin kept up their fusillade, the bolt rounds accounting for another three of the creatures. Then suddenly, the attackers broke off as one, as if in answer to some unheard order.

'Is anyone hurt?' Brielle asked Quin.

'Not seriously, my lady,' the warrior answered. 'I do not think these creatures were made for fighting.'

Brielle looked to Quin. 'Explain.'

'My lady, these creatures appeared to me to be testing our defences and our capabilities. I believe they were little more than sentinels.'

'Sentinels?' Brielle repeated. 'Sentinels guarding what?'

'This place, my lady,' Quin answered. 'They guard this tomb against intruders. Against desecration.'

'Against thieves,' Brielle finished, allowing herself a wry smile.

'THEY ARE CLOSE now, mistress... can't you hear them?' Brielle heard Seth mumble from her side as the party made its way through a maze of narrow passageways. Despite herself, she was beginning to lose her patience with the astropath, but knew there was little she could do about it now.

'What is it you hear?' Brielle replied. 'Please, Seth, speak plainly.'

'I hear these...' Brielle turned as she walked, and saw that Seth was trailing his outstretched hand along wall, his unfeeling, gloved fingers following the intricate engravings that covered its every surface.

'What do you mean?' Brielle asked, knowing that she was unlikely to receive a coherent answer, but preferring to keep the astropath from descending into total madness.

'It is all connected, mistress... all of it. They barely dream at all, mistress, not like we do...'

Brielle shook her head and turned her gaze back to the path ahead. The passages through which the group moved were narrow and dark, the only illumination provided by a green light emanating from the endless streams of alien script running along the walls. She tried not to look too closely at the script. To her, the interconnected circles and lines formed nodes and links, described hierarchies and progressions, told of alien domination and processes in which the human race had no part.

She shook her head once more, this time to clear it of the odd notions that crept into her consciousness whenever she looked too closely at the patterns on the walls.

'Seth,' she said. 'Do not lay hands upon the walls...'

'We must leave,' the astropath announced, halting in his tracks. 'We must turn back, mistress, now.'

Brielle stopped and turned on the astropath, ready to admonish him or order him sedated. And then, she caught an echo, a sound from the direction in which the party had come.

'It's the chasm, my lady,' Quin said as she looked to him for his assessment. 'The sentinel creatures.'

'It's them!' Seth shrieked, and turned as if to flee.

'Restrain him,' Brielle ordered. Quin motioned to a nearby armsman, who moved in behind the astropath and gripped both of his arms at the elbows.

'Why would the sentinels be active once more?' Brielle asked, not expecting any of her servants to answer. She shared a glance with Santos Quin as he raised his boltgun and made to continue along the passageway. She lingered a moment, listening intently to the last of the sounds from behind as they echoed and faded to silence. She imagined for a moment that the sentinels might be attacking once more, before rejecting the notion, and following after Quin.

LEAVING THE DARK, sigil-lined passageway behind, Brielle stepped out into a vast, circular chamber. The space was dominated by hundreds of tiered galleries, each one stacked upon that below, the highest lost in darkness far above. Each tier was lined with alcoves, in each of which a dully gleaming, humanoid statue stood.

'Joachim?' Brielle asked, as her advisor stepped up beside her. 'What do you think?'

Hep's gaze took in the vastness of the chamber, scanning the galleries with an expert eye. 'I have never before seen the like, ma'am,' he replied. 'But I can think of half a dozen cartels that would pay a fortune for just one.'

'My thoughts exactly,' Brielle replied with a broad grin that was quite inappropriate on the lips of the daughter of a bearer of a Warrant of Trade. She crossed to the nearest of the statues. She stood before the metallic form, seeing that it had evidently been crafted to resemble some form of skeletal warrior, its face an impassive, skull-like death mask. Across its broad, ribbed chest, it held what was unmistakably a weapon.

'The Catacombs of Skard were attended by metal grave guards,' Brielle mused aloud, recalling gleefully an expedition into the subterranean vaults of that doomed world two years earlier. 'They bought the clan an entire world...'

'They did, ma'am,' Hep replied, standing beside his mistress. 'But they were cast of solid rhodium. These appear...'

'Mechanical?' Brielle interjected. Her eyes followed the many cables and pipes that led from sockets in the alcoves to points on the statue's body. Was one of those cables twitching? 'These are not mere gravegoods. Some manner of xenos technology is at work here...'

'They slumber...' Brielle heard Adept Seth sob from behind. The astropath had been restrained by two of the armsmen, but he continued to mumble an incoherent stream of nonsense. 'We must leave!' Seth bellowed, his voice echoing for long moments in the galleries high above.

'Sedate him, now!' Brielle ordered the armsmen restraining the astropath. She would save the apologies for later, when the party was back on the ship and its hold was full with xenos-tech.

Then, a voice filled the chamber.

'You would do well to heed his words.'

Instantly, Santos Quin was at his mistress's side, his boltgun raised as he scanned for the source of the voice. With a single gesture, he motioned for the armsmen to form a protective ring, with Brielle, Seth and Hep at its centre.

Raising the visor on her helmet, Brielle called into the darkness, 'Who addresses me?' As she spoke, she turned slowly around, seeking any sign of the individual who had spoken.

'I address you,' the answer came back. The voice was strangely lyrical in tone, not human, but not wholly alien either. Brielle followed the sound to its source, and saw a tall figure step from a dark portal on the other side of the chamber.

'We claim this place, by right of conquest,' Brielle called out, advancing towards the chamber's centre as she spoke, her servants aiming their weapons at the intruder. 'Be gone, or face the consequences.'

'Consequences?' the reply came back, the figure stepping forwards from the shadowed archway. A suspicion began to form in Brielle's mind. 'Pitiful idiots,' the speaker replied, scorn dripping from every word. 'You truly have no conception of your folly. Even as the galaxy crumbles to ash all around you, you flounder in your own filth, dragging yourselves and all of creation down with you.'

'Such arrogance I've only ever heard from the lips of the eldar,' Brielle replied, now certain of the intruder's species. She came to a halt near the centre of the chamber and placed her hands at her hips, surreptitiously loosening the catch on the holster of her bolt pistol and the scabbard of her chainblade.

The figure approached, and came to a halt opposite Brielle. Her intuition had been correct. Before Brielle stood a tall, lithe humanoid figure, dressed in a long cloak of shifting, chameleonic fabric. Across his back, the eldar carried a long rifle, confirmation, if Brielle needed it, of his caste.

'Pathfinder?' Brielle asked, seeking to wrong-foot the alien with her knowledge of his kind. As she spoke, she counted another three aliens waiting in the shadows not far behind.

'Indeed,' the eldar demurred, nodding his head a slight degree. 'If you have knowledge of my kin, then you know the folly of disregarding my warning. Leave this place. Do as your seer begs you. He has the truth of it, while you are blinded by avarice.'

Anger welling in her breast, Brielle raised a pointed finger as she advanced on the eldar. Her armoured boot thudded into an object on the dusty ground before her. 'I know that you speak in riddles. I know that you lie. I know that you can't be trusted,' she spat, jabbing her finger at the eldar. 'I know that you'd slaughter a million humans if your witches foretold it would save a single one of you from breaking a nail!'

'And what of it, child?' the eldar replied bitterly, ignoring the jibe but understanding Brielle's meaning all too well. 'My people have beheld the birth and the death of gods, while yours have barely crawled from the mud that begat you. What use reason, what use wisdom, when you seek nothing more than your own destruction, and care not if the galaxy burns along with you?'

'More lies,' Brielle retorted. She glanced down at the object at her feet. Half-submerged in the dust of aeons, there laid an ornate stave, a faint green glow shining at its bladed tip. 'More words to cover your own arrogant selfishness.'

'I say again,' the eldar said, his glance following Brielle's to the stave on the ground before her. 'Disturb nothing, and you may yet live. We all may yet–'

'You dare threaten me?' Brielle returned. 'You dare order me to do anything?' She reached down and lifted the stave. It was heavy, and cold. 'I'll disturb whatsoever I choose, xenos.'

'No!' the eldar shouted, his former arrogance wavering. The alien looked around, as if searching for something amongst the galleries, his slanted eyes wide with fear. He reached for the long rifle slung across his back.

Before Brielle could react, the air around her erupted as a dozen weapons discharged as one. The eldar staggered, his body hammered as round after round slammed into it. An instant later, the remaining aliens returned fire, their own weapons unleashing a hail of silent, yet deadly precision projectiles.

Bringing her right arm upwards in a sharp movement, Brielle unleashed the deadly payload of one of the miniaturised weapons she wore as ornate, yet lethal rings. A jet of chemical liquid arched forth, erupting into flame as it arrowed towards the nearest of the eldar's companions. The target saw his peril and rolled aside, the now-blazing liquid fire splashing down nearby. For an instant, Brielle cursed her misfortune, for the ring bore only a single charge. Then, a single gobbet of the fiery liquid splashed out, catching the eldar's flowing, chameleonic cloak. Before he even realised his peril, the eldar had been engulfed in the hungry fire.

With a cold outer ruthlessness that belied the disgust within, Brielle drew her bolt pistol, levelled it calmly at the living torch before her and put a bolt shell through the unfortunate's skull, ending his suffering for good.

Even as the dull crump of the bolt-round detonating inside the eldar's skull echoed away, a burst of alien fire scythed through the air around her. Brielle dived aside, the stave still in her hands. She hit the dusty ground and rolled, coming up into a ready stance, to see that the firefight was already over. The aliens who had fired upon her lay dead, or grievously wounded, while the one she had killed with her concealed flamer guttered. Several of her servants were writhing on the ground, suppressing screams of pain from wounds that appeared no more than pin pricks, but had, she knew, probably wreaked havoc upon internal organs.

'The xenos!' Hep called out. 'He lives still, ma'am, beware!'

Brielle looked across to the centre of the chamber, seeing that the eldar lay in a rapidly expanding pool of his own blood. His head was raised upon his straining neck as he looked straight at her. Seeing that the dying alien presented little danger, Brielle stood, pulling herself up on the alien stave as she did so.

'Listen to me, human,' the eldar coughed, blood flecking his lips as he spoke. 'If you leave this place now, you may still avert a disaster you cannot possibly comprehend.'

Reaching the place where the alien lay, Brielle looked down upon his broken form. The hiss of venting gases sounded from one of the galleries high above. She knelt at the eldar's side, and leaned forwards to bear witness to his last words.

'There are forces in this universe you know nothing of,' the eldar whispered, his fading gaze sweeping the highest of the chamber's galleries. 'Minds that have slumbered for aeons turn their attentions upon us once more…'

A sharp, cackling laugh sounded from behind Brielle, and she was struck by the terrible realisation that Adept Seth's ravings might have contained something of the truth.

'What forces?' Brielle said. 'What minds?' She turned her head sharply as she thought she caught sight of movement in one of the alcoves nearby.

'My lady…' Quin said.

'Wait!' Brielle answered, aware that the eldar's life was fading before her very eyes, but knowing that she must bear witness to what he had to say to her. 'Tell me,' she demanded.

'Your race will discover, in time,' the eldar responded, coughing. He vomited blood across his chest. A loud hiss sounded from very nearby, causing Brielle to look to the nearest of the alcoves and the skeletal statue within. 'But you...' The alien smiled grimly through bloody lips, fixing his gaze upon Brielle as she turned back to him. 'You shall find out all too soon...'

Before the eldar could complete his sentence, the dusty ground on which he lay appeared to subside beneath him. Brielle looked on in frozen horror as the eldar sank into the dust. The alien's eyes widened in terror as realisation of his fate hit home. A moment later, an area of dust three metres across was sinking, and then, a wide, circular hole opened up. The eldar tumbled downwards, dust cascading after him, and was gone.

'My lady!' Quin shouted. Brielle stared down into the dark hole that had opened up directly before her, and then turned to face Quin. 'What?'

The feral-worlder's only answer was to look towards the nearest of the alcoves. Within it, a pair of green lights shone. Looking closer, Brielle saw that the eyes of the metallic statue had come alive. She looked upwards, turning as she did so to take in the row upon row of galleries lining the chamber all the way up into the darkness far above. Dimly glowing within every single one of the thousands of alcoves was a pair of lights.

Brielle brought up her bolt pistol, as a sub-sonic drone sounded from somewhere very far beneath the ground on which she stood. Before her, a lurid green glow appeared in the dark hole in the centre of the chamber. She took a step backwards as her servants appeared at her side, their weapons raised.

'Ma'am I strongly suggest we–' Hep started.

'I know,' Brielle interrupted. Anger filled her, along with cold dread. In an instant, her dreams of the riches this place might yield evaporated, to be replaced by the raw instinct to simply survive. She realised with a start that the stave she still held in one hand was now glowing fiercely at its bladed tip, its haft feeling suddenly cold even through the glove of her survival suit.

And then, a column of blinding green light appeared, lancing upwards from the hole before her. Motes of drifting dust glittered as if trapped by the shaft, and the low rumble rose in volume, the ground now visibly trembling.

'Fall back!' Brielle called.

A scream cut the air, almost deafening even over the steadily increasingly sound emanating from the trembling ground. Brielle turned, to see Adept Seth bent double, both hands clamped across his helmet as if the astropath tried in vain to cover his ears. At the sound of the roar of Quin's boltgun, she turned back towards the column of green light.

Within the shaft, a figure was rising. At first, all Brielle could make out was a humanoid form wreathed in a pulsating nimbus of light. As the figure rose upwards, she saw that it was floating, as if held aloft by the light itself. It was huge, easily three metres tall, its body a metal skeleton swathed in rags that appeared to writhe as if stirred by some unseen current.

'We leave,' Brielle ordered as the figure rose to a height of ten metres above the hole. 'Now!'

Before her servants could react, the figure's eyes came suddenly alive, aglow with the same green light that illuminated those of the statues, yet a hundred times brighter. Its death-mask head turned, as if it awakened, and regarded the sight before it.

That terrible gaze settled first upon the cowering form of Adept Seth. The astropath shrieked once more, and vomited inside his helmet, his face obscured by the dripping fluids. The skeletal figure's eyes blazed still brighter, and a wet crump sounded from within the astropath's helmet, the inside of the visor turning in an instant to the vivid red of fresh blood flecked with the grey of brain matter. Brielle watched in mute horror as Seth's body toppled lifelessly to the ground, a great cloud of dust billowing up from the ground around it.

Casting off the unadulterated shock, Brielle levelled her bolt pistol and drew a shaky bead on the figure's head. Breathing a silent prayer to the Emperor to guide her hand, she squeezed the trigger. Her shot struck the figure square across its metal brow, but the bolt exploded, leaving little more than a black smear to mark where it had landed. The creature appeared not even to register her attack.

A moment later, Quin bellowed a savage curse born of the barbaric world of his birth. The warrior raised his boltgun and in scant seconds emptied an entire magazine at his foe. Several dozen bolt-rounds, each sufficient to reduce a normal body to a bloody ruin, glanced harmlessly from the metal form above.

'Quin!' Brielle bellowed over the deafening roar of the armsmen's shotguns joining in the fusillade. 'It's no use! We're leaving!'

But the feral-worlder appeared not to hear his mistress's words, or was perhaps held in the grip of some barbaric death-frenzy. Brielle reached for his shoulder, but he shrugged her off as he reloaded his boltgun. 'Go!' Quin shouted.

Brielle made to repeat her order, but the savage fury in Quin's eyes told her that she would be wasting her breath.

'I made a pledge,' the warrior said, his eyes alight in his tattooed face. 'I promised your father... Please, my lady, allow me to keep my word.'

Looking around her, Brielle saw the metal statues in the ground-floor alcoves had come to life and were even now advancing towards the centre of the chamber. She saw too that Quin hoped to buy her time to escape, with his very life. For an instant she considered ordering him to leave, begging him to leave, but she knew that neither course would work. Unable to speak, she nodded silent thanks to the warrior, hefting her bolt pistol in one hand and the glowing stave in the other. A small part of her mind prayed the warrior's sacrifice was worth it, and his death would be a noble one.

'With me!' Brielle called out as she retreated towards the passageway. Joachim Hep appeared at her side, a laspistol raised before him, followed a moment later by a dozen armsmen. At the sound of Quin's boltgun opening up once more, she turned to run for the passageway.

A metallic warrior barred her path. Instinctively, she brought her bolt pistol to bear, opening fire from a distance of scant metres. At the same moment, her companions did likewise, and the foe was rocked backwards as its skeletal body was hammered by round after round of precision fire.

For a moment, Brielle feared that this enemy's metal form would prove as impervious to attack as that of the larger figure that floated above in the shaft of green light. She gave heartfelt thanks as she saw angry sparks erupt from within its chest, followed an instant later by a small explosion.

'Again!' She ordered, firing three more bolt-rounds into the enemy's chest. The armsmen pumped shell after shell at the foe, forcing it backwards still further.

And then, the metal skeleton blew apart, ripped asunder by an explosion deep within its armoured ribcage. Jagged metal shrapnel lanced outwards, one piece shattering the armoured visor of Brielle's helmet, and slashing a deep cut across her forehead.

Even as blood from her wound ran freely into Brielle's eyes, she rushed onwards, almost gaining the passageway before turning to take one last look at the scene.

Quin had stopped firing once more, evidently having emptied another two-dozen bolt rounds into the floating figure. Even as he ejected the spent, sickle-shaped magazine, the figure turned its gaze upon him, as if noticing his presence for the first time.

Quin slammed home a fresh magazine and looked up into the blazing eyes of his enemy. The figure reached out a metallic skeletal arm, ragged swathes of cloth flapping as if in some aetheric breeze around it. As Quin raised his boltgun once more, his tattooed face a mask of savagery, the figure's palm blazed with pulsating green light.

The feral-worlder convulsed, his boltgun slamming to the ground at his feet. Brielle screamed his name, but it was too late. Before her eyes, Quin's survival suit appeared to melt away. First the armoured plates dissolved, as if the metal were being peeled away, one layer of atoms at a time. Then the fabric too disappeared, to reveal the warrior's tattooed flesh beneath. For a moment, Quin stood naked before the metal daemon above him, and then the tattoos that covered his body faded, followed an instant later by his skin.

Quin's bloodcurdling death-scream split the dusty air of the tomb chamber as his skin dissolved and the raw musculature beneath was revealed. Layer by layer, the flesh was peeled away, atomised to nothing by the awful power of the green radiation. At the last, only Quin's skeleton stood, silhouetted against the blazing shaft of green light, and in an instant, that too was gone, the last of his marrow reduced to dust evaporating on the unnatural wind.

Before Brielle could react, the floating horror came fully to life, stepping from the column of green light before descending to the dusty ground with an earth-shaking impact. With a single motion, several thousand of its skeletal minions took a pace forwards, those on the ground level forming a circle around Brielle and her companions. Resigned now to the inevitable, but unwilling to go meekly, Brielle took a deep breath and raised her bolt pistol for one final act of defiance.

Before she knew it, the metal horror had strode across the chamber, and stood, towering over Brielle. Even as her finger tightened on the bolt pistol's trigger, it regarded her through blazing green eyes. It extended its hand. Brielle steeled herself for the same fate that had befallen Quin, her skin burning with dreadful anticipation of such a grisly end.

But instead of that metal hand erupting in green, pulsating light, it appeared to make a gesture. The breath stuck in her throat, and Brielle relaxed her finger, for but an instant. Her mind raced as she sought to decipher the figure's gesture.

Then it came to her. The metal daemon was demanding she surrender the stave she still held in her left hand.

'You want this?' She growled, girding her muscles and bracing her feet on the ground.

'Then have it!' With titanic effort, Brielle hurled the stave at her foe. The blade flared green as it crossed the space between them, almost blinding her. With unerring accuracy, the tip struck the skeletal figure in the centre of its ribcage, piercing armour that had proven impenetrable to dozens of boltgun rounds. A shaft of green light shot outwards, accompanied by a piercing machine howl, and the stave continued its course, burying itself up to the haft in the figure's chest.

The skeletal horror stood transfixed by its own weapon, blinding green light now splaying in all directions from its wound. It stood, unable to move, its hellish death-mask face staring at Brielle as it writhed as if in agony. For an instant, Brielle felt some unutterable hatred of truly cosmic scale turned upon her, and knew total, soul-rending insignificance before that impossibly ancient malice. And then, the moment passed, and she tore her eyes away from the dazzling sight before her.

Seeing that the skeletal warriors around the chamber appeared to have faltered in their advance, as if they shared something of the pain Brielle had inflicted upon their lord, she saw the chance to escape, and grasped it for all she was worth.

'Hep!' she shouted above the infernal metallic howl emanating from the transfixed metal giant. 'Gather the men. I've had just about enough of this place!'

BRIELLE STOOD UPON the bridge of the *Fairlight*, Joachim Hep at her side. The wound at her brow was dressed, while Hep's right arm was set in a sling.

'A close call, ma'am,' Hep said flatly.

Raising an eyebrow at the understatement, Brielle turned to face her advisor. 'Aye, Joachim,' she replied. 'And costly. Santos will be missed. But,' she continued, 'it may not have been in vain.'

Hep rounded upon his mistress, unease writ large across his craggy features. 'Ma'am...' he started.

'Easy, Joachim.' Brielle smiled as she raised a hand to forestall her advisor's inevitable objection to what she was about to say. 'If what the pathfinder said is true, there must be more of these places, these tombs, out there,' she nodded towards the void through the viewing port. 'Just think, Joachim. Just think. We gained entrance to that tomb, and we had no idea what waited for us.'

'Ma'am...'

'That place makes Skard look like a downhive scavmart,' she grinned. 'Just think what the Mechanicus would give to get their hands on that tech. They'd give anything to study just one of those machine warriors... what if we could broker contracts with each of the forges, one sample to each, exclusive rights...'

'Brielle!' Hep interjected. 'Your father would march me from the torpedo tubes if I allowed you to...'

'Next time,' Brielle pressed on, a mischievous light entering her eyes, 'we'll know what awaits us.' Feeling suddenly breathless at the thought of the riches she might bring to her house, she pressed on. 'Next time, Joachim, no conceited eldar will interfere with our efforts. Next time, we'll take it all...'

ABOUT THE AUTHORS

DAN ABNETT

Dan Abnett is a novelist and award-winning comic book writer. He has written many novels for the Black Library, including the acclaimed Gaunt's Ghosts series and the Eisenhorn and Ravenor trilogies, and, with Mike Lee, the Darkblade cycle. His Horus Heresy novels *Horus Rising* and *Legion* are both bestsellers. He lives and works in Maidstone, Kent.

Dan's website can be found at *www.DanAbnett.com*

JULIET E. McKENNA

Juliet E McKenna has been interested in fantasy stories since childhood, from *Winnie the Pooh* to *The Iliad*. An abiding fascination with other worlds and their peoples played its part in her subsequently reading Classics at St. Hilda's College, Oxford. After combining bookselling and motherhood for a couple of years, she now fits in her writing around her family and vice versa. She lives with her husband and children in West Oxfordshire, England.

NICK KYME

Nick Kyme hails from Grimsby, a small town on the east coast of England. Nick moved to Nottingham in 2003 to work on *White Dwarf* magazine as a Layout Designer. Since then, he has made the switch to the Black Library's hallowed halls as an editor and has been involved in a multitude of diverse projects. His writing credits include several published short stories, background books and novels.

You can catch up with Nick and read about all of his other published works at his website: *www.nickkyme.com*

BRADEN CAMPBELL

Braden Campbell is a classical actor and playwright, currently living in Milton, Ontario. His theatrical work has seen him perform across not only across Canada, but in England and New York City. For the past five years he has also worked as a freelance writer, particularly in the field of role playing games. Braden has enjoyed Warhammer 40,000 for nearly a decade, and remains fiercely dedicated to his dark eldar.

C.L. WERNER

C. L. Werner was a diseased servant of the Horned Rat long before his first story in *Inferno!* magazine. His Black Library credits include the Chaos Wastes books *Palace of the Plague Lord* and *Blood for the Blood God*. He is also the author of *Mathias Thulmann: Witch Hunter*, *Runefang* and the *Brunner the Bounty Hunter* trilogy. Currently living in the American

South-West, he continues to write stories of mayhem and madness set in the Warhammer World.

Visit the author's website at
www.vermintime.com

MARK CLAPHAM

Mark Clapham was born and raised in Yorkshire, studied and worked in London for over a decade, and is now an itinerant writer and editor based in Exeter, Devon.

Mark has written prose and scripts for characters including Doctor Who, Bernice Summerfield and Iris Wildthyme, as well as comic scripts for acclaimed indie publisher Accent UK. Mark is Content Editor for the Shiny Shelf review site and blogs at the modestly named *www.markclapham.com*

MATTHEW FARRER

Matthew Farrer lives in Australia, and is a member of the Canberra Speculative Fiction Guild. He has been writing since his teens, and has a number of novels and short stories to his name, including the popular Shira Calpurnia novels for the Black Library.

JAMES GILMER

James Gilmer is a graduate of the Clarion Writers Workshop as well as a former newspaper stringer, graduate of Michigan State University with an English B.A. He currently lives in San Francisco with his wife, works full-time as a surgical and trauma radiographer, and is working on more projects for everyone's favourite grim future where there is only war.

AARON DEMBSKI-BOWDEN

Aaron Dembski-Bowden is a British author with his beginnings in the videogame and RPG industries. He's been a deeply entrenched fan of Warhammer 40,000 ever since he first ruined his copy of Space Crusade by painting the models with all the skill expected of an overexcited nine-year-old.

His previous novels for the Black Library are *Cadian Blood* and *Soul Hunter*.

ANDY HOARE

Andy Hoare worked for eight years in Games Workshop's design studio, producing and developing new game rules and background material. Now working freelance writing novels, roleplaying game material and gaming-related magazine articles, Andy lives in Nottingham with his partner Sarah.